W9-AGZ-428

SINA GRACE · SIOBHAN KEENAN · CATHY LE

Ghosted in L.A.

VOL. 1

BOOM! BOX

Ross Richie..CEO & Founder
Joy Huffman...CFO
Matt Gagnon..Editor-in-Chief
Filip Sablik.................................President, Publishing & Marketing
Stephen Christy...President, Development
Lance Kreiter.....................Vice President, Licensing & Merchandising
Arune Singh...Vice President, Marketing
Bryce Carlson.................Vice President, Editorial & Creative Strategy
Scott Newman.......................................Manager, Production Design
Kate Henning...Manager, Operations
Spencer Simpson...Manager, Sales
Elyse Strandberg..Manager, Finance
Sierra Hahn...Executive Editor
Jeanine Schaefer...Executive Editor
Dafna Pleban..Senior Editor
Shannon Watters..Senior Editor
Eric Harburn..Senior Editor
Matthew Levine...Editor
Sophie Philips-Roberts..Associate Editor
Amanda LaFranco..Associate Editor
Jonathan Manning..Associate Editor
Gavin Gronenthal...Assistant Editor
Gwen Waller..Assistant Editor
Allyson Gronowitz..Assistant Editor
Jillian Crab..Design Coordinator
Michelle Ankley...Design Coordinator
Marie Krupina..Production Designer
Grace Park...Production Designer
Chelsea Roberts...Production Design Assistant
Samantha Knapp.......................................Production Design Assistant
José Meza...Live Events Lead
Stephanie Hocutt...Digital Marketing Lead
Esther Kim...Marketing Coordinator
Cat O'Grady..Digital Marketing Coordinator
Amanda Lawson..Marketing Assistant
Holly Aitchison...Digital Sales Coordinator
Morgan Perry..Retail Sales Coordinator
Megan Christopher.......................................Operations Coordinator
Rodrigo Hernandez...Mailroom Assistant
Zipporah Smith...Accounting Assistant
Sabrina Lesin...Operations Assistant
Breanna Sarpy...Executive Assistant

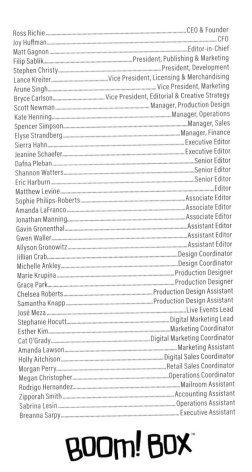

BOOM! BOX™

GHOSTED IN L.A. Volume One, April 2020. Published by BOOM! Box, a division of Boom Entertainment, Inc. Ghosted in L.A. is ™ & © 2020 Sina Grace. Originally published in single magazine form as GHOSTED IN L.A. No. 1-4. ™ & © 2019 Sina Grace. All rights reserved. BOOM! Box™ and the BOOM! Box logo are trademarks of Boom Entertainment, Inc., registered in various countries and categories. All characters, events, and institutions depicted herein are fictional. Any similarity between any of the names, characters, persons, events, and/or institutions in this publication to actual names, characters, and persons, whether living or dead, events, and/or institutions is unintended and purely coincidental. BOOM! Box does not read or accept unsolicited submissions of ideas, stories, or artwork. "Spinster Cycle" is © of Rosie Tucker, The Sunshine Sound ASCAP. All Rights Reserved. Used with Permission.

BOOM! Studios, 5670 Wilshire Boulevard, Suite 400, Los Angeles, CA 90036-5679. Printed in China. First Printing.

ISBN: 978-1-68415-505-7, eISBN: 978-1-64144-663-1

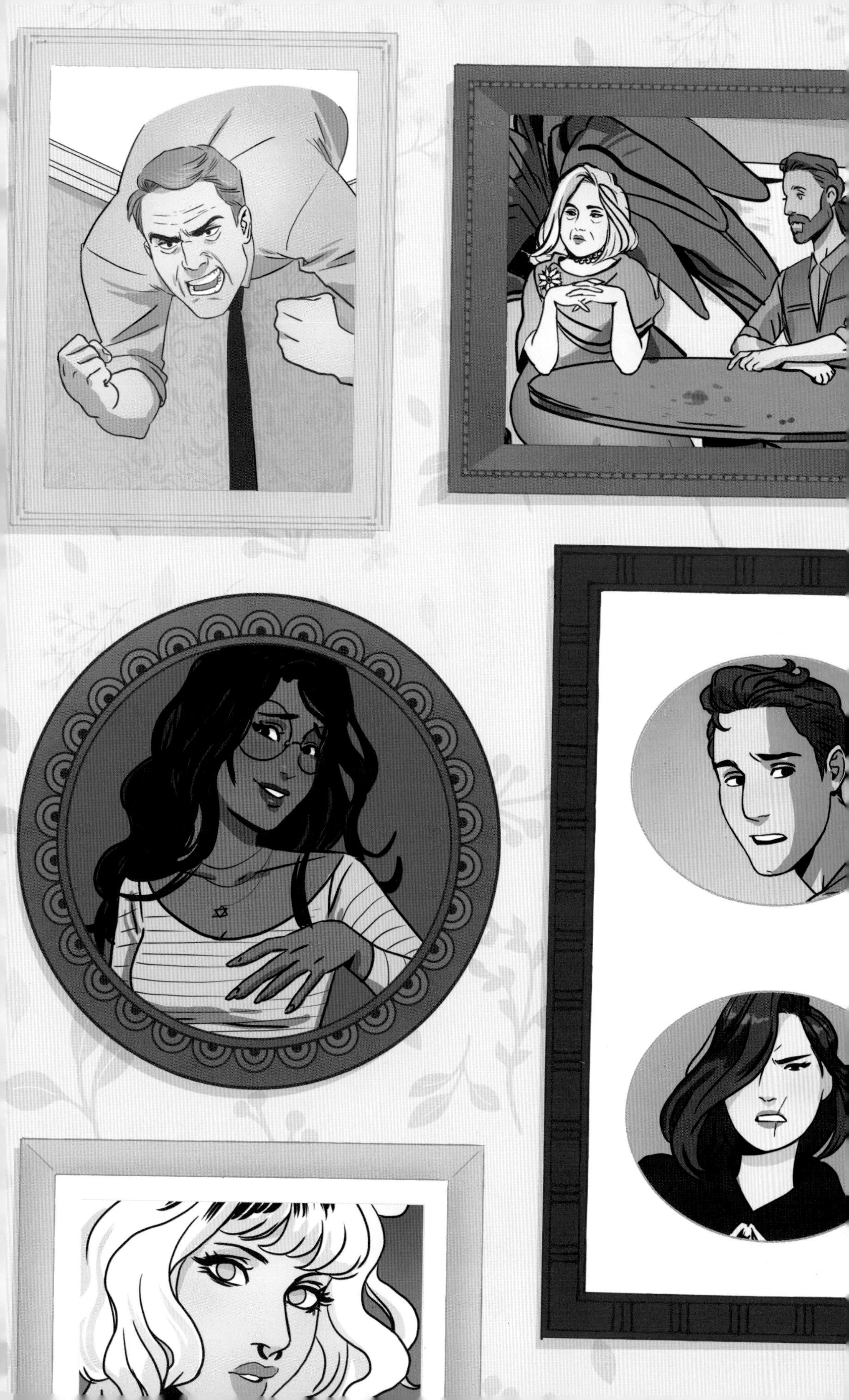

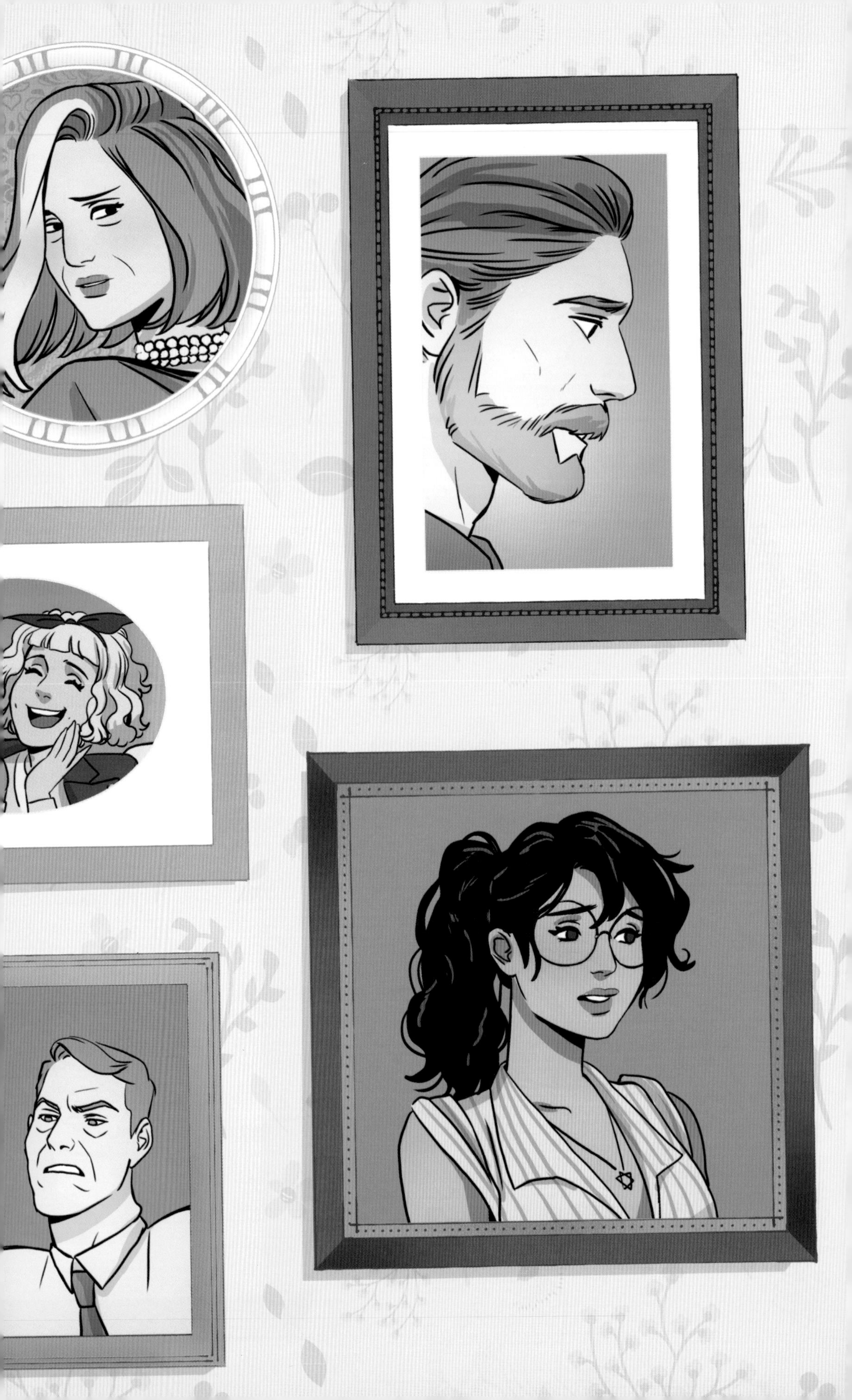

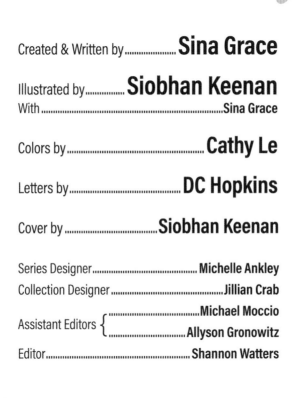

Created & Written by......................**Sina Grace**

Illustrated by.................**Siobhan Keenan**
With...Sina Grace

Colors by....................................... **Cathy Le**

Letters by... **DC Hopkins**

Cover by ....**Siobhan Keenan**

Series Designer... **Michelle Ankley**
Collection Designer ....**Jillian Crab**
Assistant Editors {.......................................**Michael Moccio**
.................................**Allyson Gronowitz**
Editor.. **Shannon Watters**

Chapter One

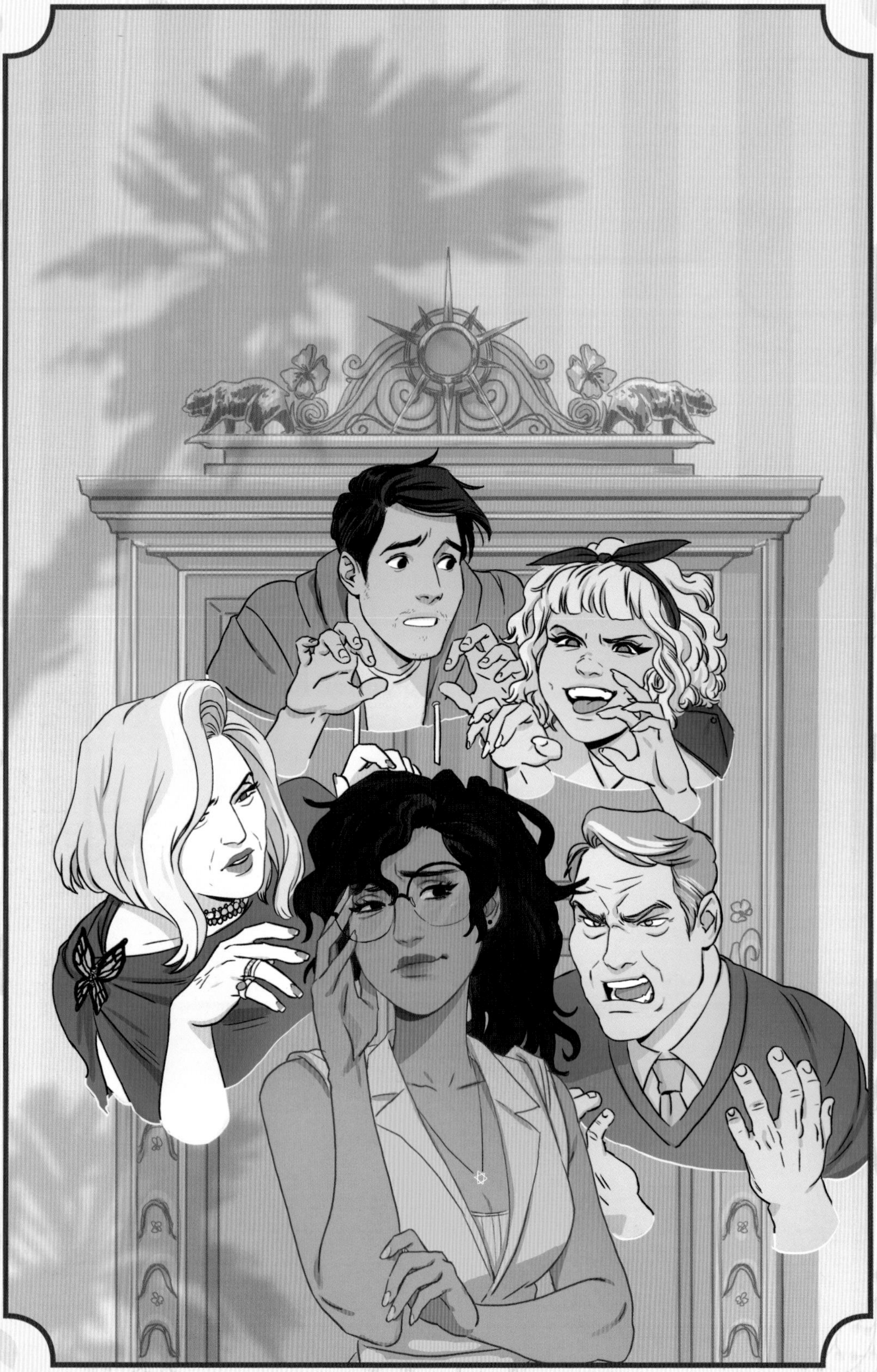

Issue One Cover by **Siobhan Keenan**

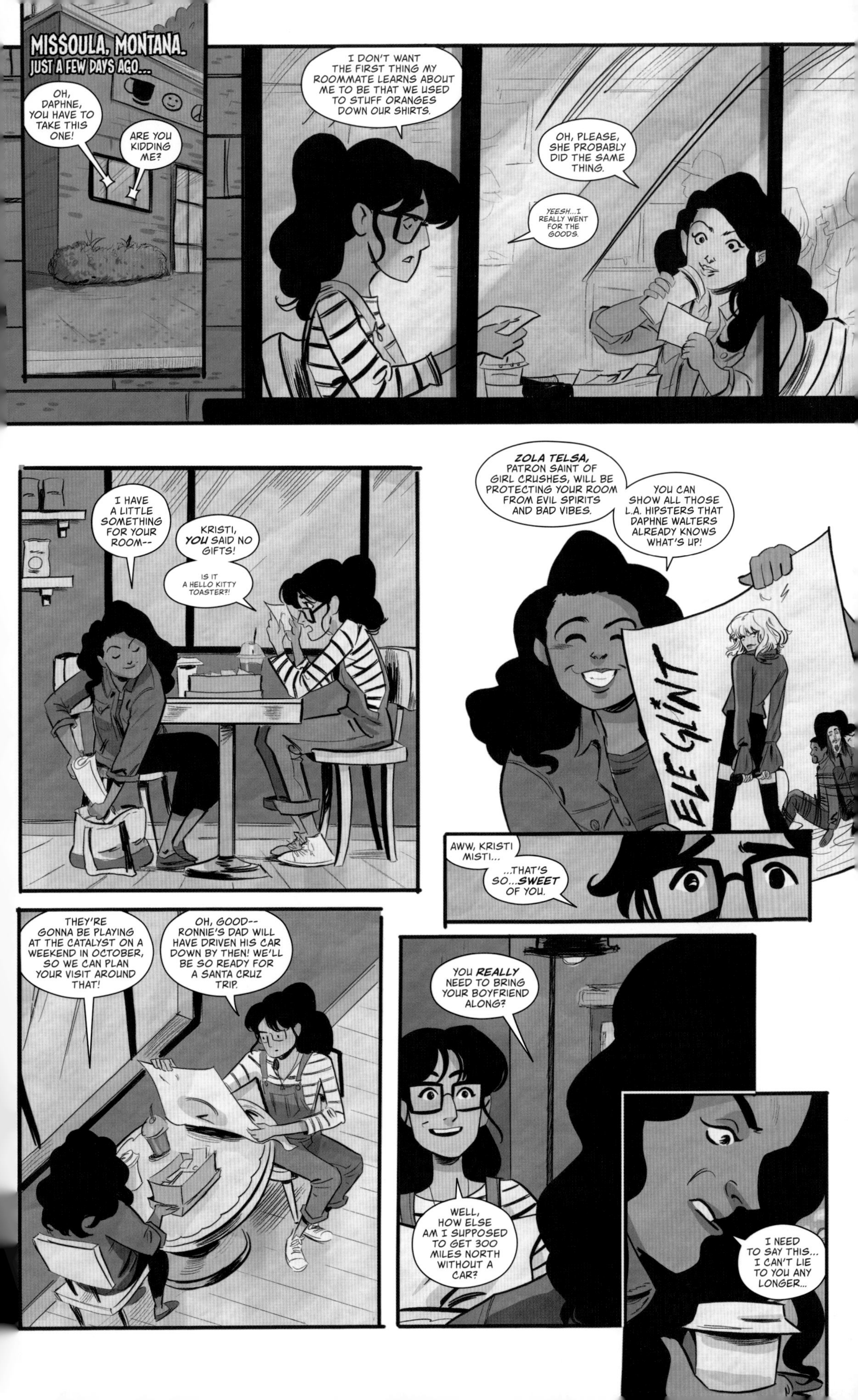
MISSOULA, MONTANA. JUST A FEW DAYS AGO...
OH, DAPHNE, YOU HAVE TO TAKE THIS ONE!
ARE YOU KIDDING ME?
I DON'T WANT THE FIRST THING MY ROOMMATE LEARNS ABOUT ME TO BE THAT WE USED TO STUFF ORANGES DOWN OUR SHIRTS.
OH, PLEASE, SHE PROBABLY DID THE SAME THING.
YEESH...I REALLY WENT FOR THE GOODS.
I HAVE A LITTLE SOMETHING FOR YOUR ROOM--
KRISTI, YOU SAID NO GIFTS!
IS IT A HELLO KITTY TOASTER?!
ZOLA TELSA, PATRON SAINT OF GIRL CRUSHES, WILL BE PROTECTING YOUR ROOM FROM EVIL SPIRITS AND BAD VIBES.
YOU CAN SHOW ALL THOSE L.A. HIPSTERS THAT DAPHNE WALTERS ALREADY KNOWS WHAT'S UP!
ELEGÏNT
AWW, KRISTI MISTI...
...THAT'S SO...SWEET OF YOU.
THEY'RE GONNA BE PLAYING AT THE CATALYST ON A WEEKEND IN OCTOBER, SO WE CAN PLAN YOUR VISIT AROUND THAT!
OH, GOOD-- RONNIE'S DAD WILL HAVE DRIVEN HIS CAR DOWN BY THEN! WE'LL BE SO READY FOR A SANTA CRUZ TRIP.
YOU REALLY NEED TO BRING YOUR BOYFRIEND ALONG?
WELL, HOW ELSE AM I SUPPOSED TO GET 300 MILES NORTH WITHOUT A CAR?
I NEED TO SAY THIS... I CAN'T LIE TO YOU ANY LONGER...

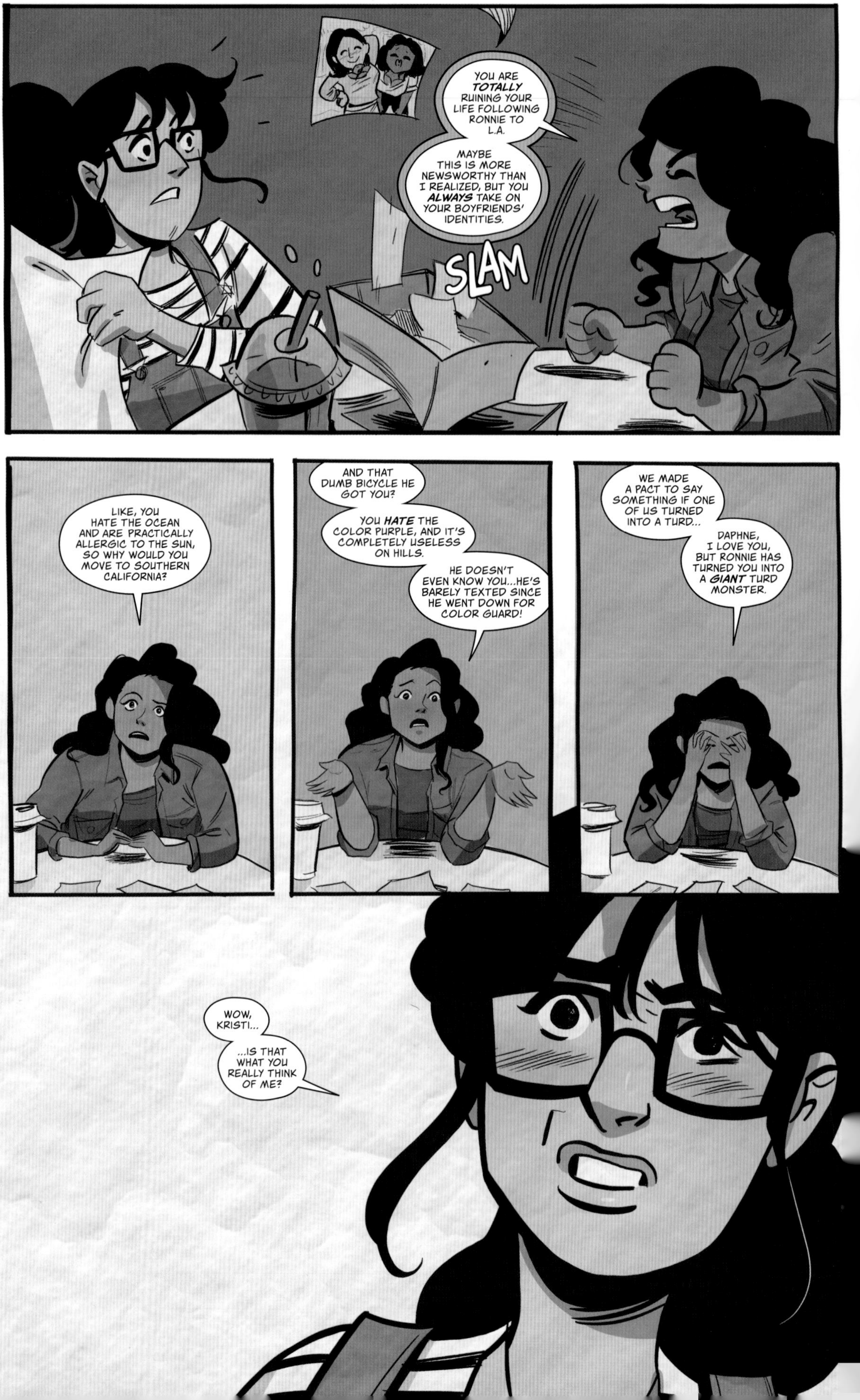
YOU ARE **TOTALLY** RUINING YOUR LIFE FOLLOWING RONNIE TO L.A.
MAYBE THIS IS MORE NEWSWORTHY THAN I REALIZED, BUT YOU **ALWAYS** TAKE ON YOUR BOYFRIENDS' IDENTITIES.
SLAM
LIKE, YOU HATE THE OCEAN AND ARE PRACTICALLY ALLERGIC TO THE SUN, SO WHY WOULD YOU MOVE TO SOUTHERN CALIFORNIA?
AND THAT DUMB BICYCLE HE GOT YOU?
YOU **HATE** THE COLOR PURPLE, AND IT'S COMPLETELY USELESS ON HILLS.
HE DOESN'T EVEN KNOW YOU...HE'S BARELY TEXTED SINCE HE WENT DOWN FOR COLOR GUARD!
WE MADE A PACT TO SAY SOMETHING IF ONE OF US TURNED INTO A TURD...
DAPHNE, I LOVE YOU, BUT RONNIE HAS TURNED YOU INTO A **GIANT** TURD MONSTER.
WOW, KRISTI...
...IS THAT WHAT YOU REALLY THINK OF ME?

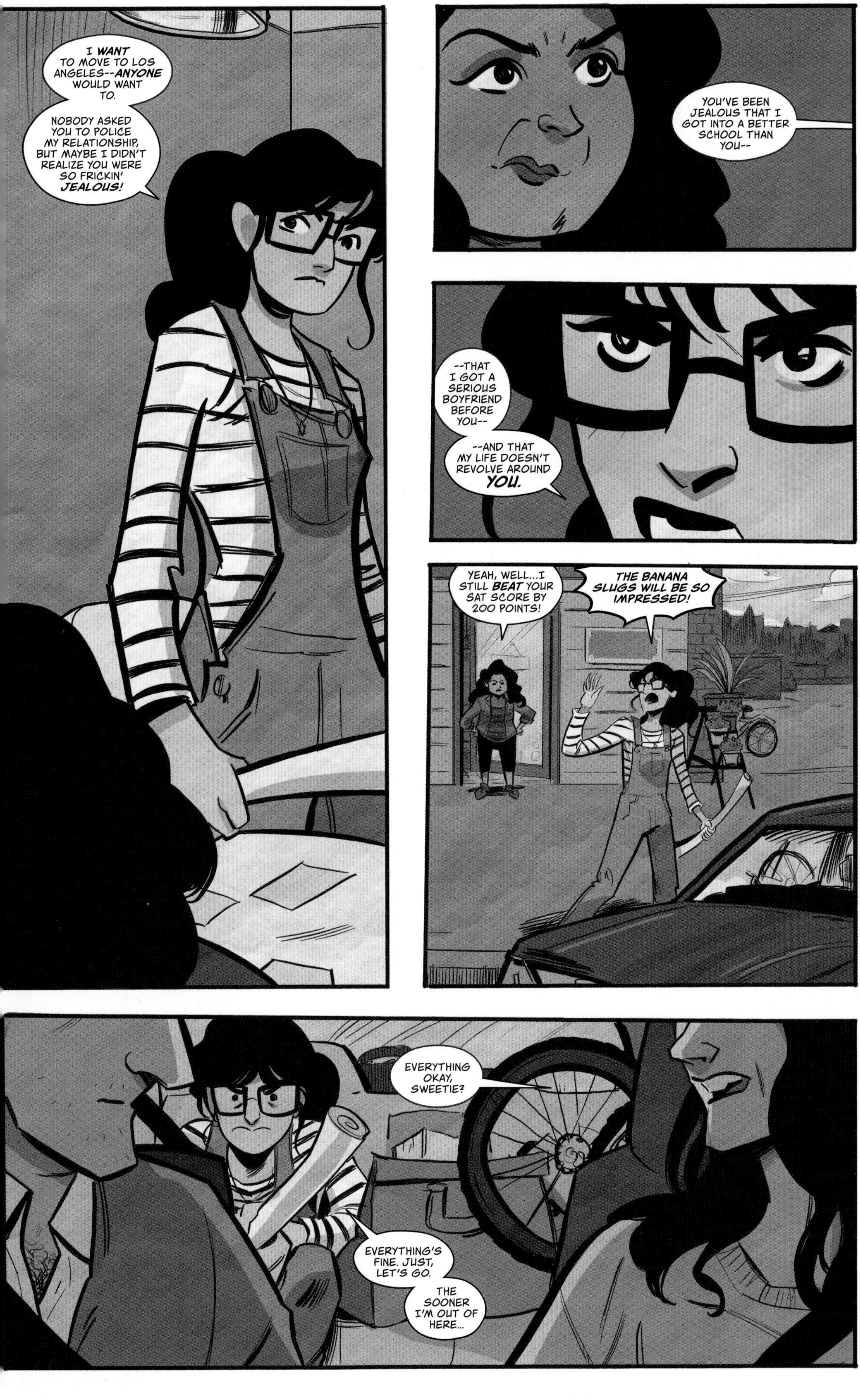

I WANT TO MOVE TO LOS ANGELES--ANYONE WOULD WANT TO.
NOBODY ASKED YOU TO POLICE MY RELATIONSHIP, BUT MAYBE I DIDN'T REALIZE YOU WERE SO FRICKIN' JEALOUS!
YOU'VE BEEN JEALOUS THAT I GOT INTO A BETTER SCHOOL THAN YOU--
--THAT I GOT A SERIOUS BOYFRIEND BEFORE YOU--
--AND THAT MY LIFE DOESN'T REVOLVE AROUND YOU.
YEAH, WELL...I STILL BEAT YOUR SAT SCORE BY 200 POINTS!
THE BANANA SLUGS WILL BE SO IMPRESSED!
EVERYTHING OKAY, SWEETIE?
EVERYTHING'S FINE. JUST, LET'S GO.
THE SOONER I'M OUT OF HERE...

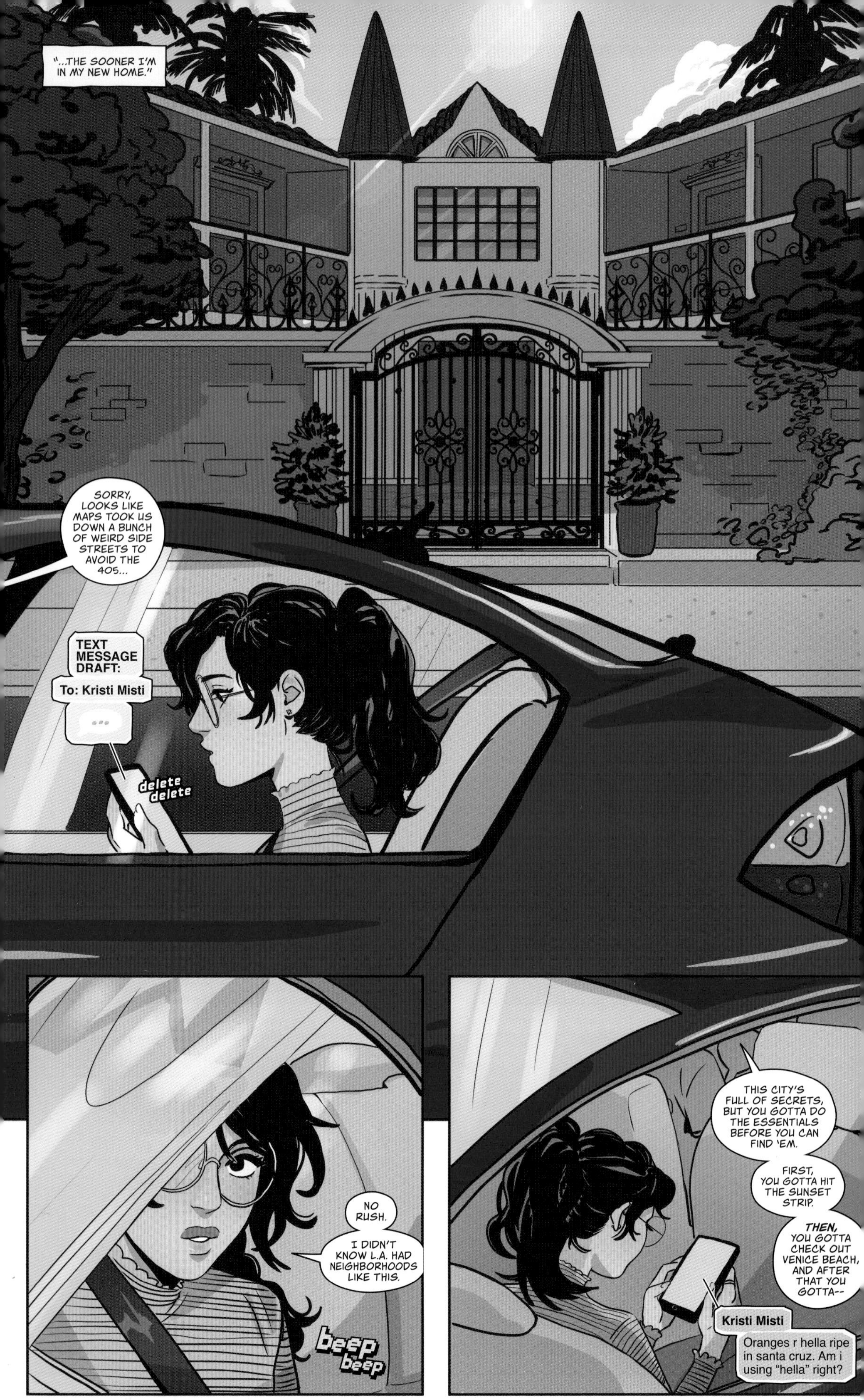
"...THE SOONER I'M IN MY NEW HOME."
SORRY, LOOKS LIKE MAPS TOOK US DOWN A BUNCH OF WEIRD SIDE STREETS TO AVOID THE 405...
TEXT MESSAGE DRAFT:
To: Kristi Misti
...
delete delete
NO RUSH.
I DIDN'T KNOW L.A. HAD NEIGHBORHOODS LIKE THIS.
beep beep
THIS CITY'S FULL OF SECRETS, BUT YOU GOTTA DO THE ESSENTIALS BEFORE YOU CAN FIND 'EM.
FIRST, YOU GOTTA HIT THE SUNSET STRIP.
THEN, YOU GOTTA CHECK OUT VENICE BEACH, AND AFTER THAT YOU GOTTA--
Kristi Misti
Oranges r hella ripe in santa cruz. Am i using "hella" right?

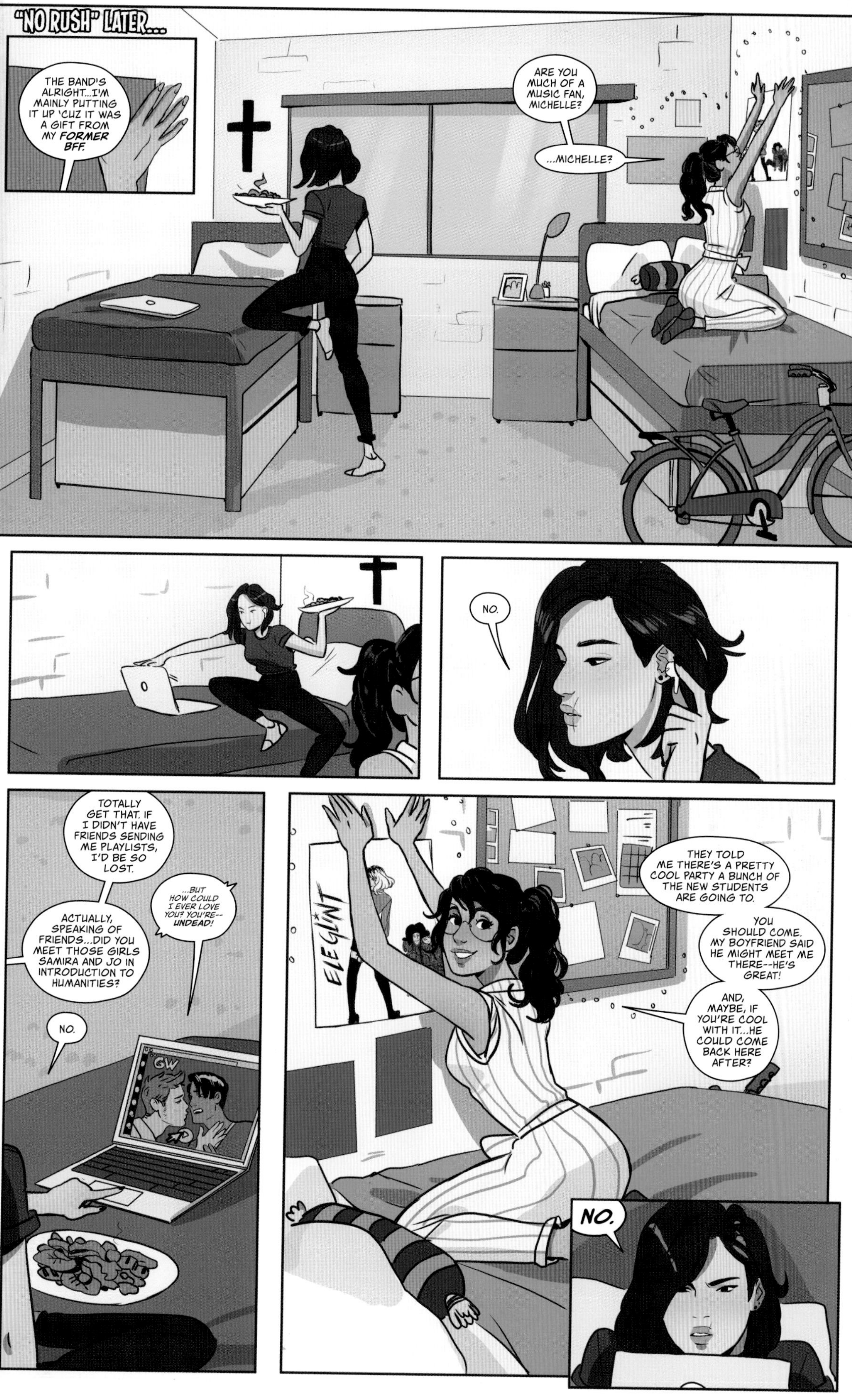

"NO RUSH" LATER...
THE BAND'S ALRIGHT...I'M MAINLY PUTTING IT UP 'CUZ IT WAS A GIFT FROM MY FORMER BFF.
ARE YOU MUCH OF A MUSIC FAN, MICHELLE?
...MICHELLE?
NO.
TOTALLY GET THAT. IF I DIDN'T HAVE FRIENDS SENDING ME PLAYLISTS, I'D BE SO LOST.
ACTUALLY, SPEAKING OF FRIENDS...DID YOU MEET THOSE GIRLS SAMIRA AND JO IN INTRODUCTION TO HUMANITIES?
...BUT HOW COULD I EVER LOVE YOU? YOU'RE-- UNDEAD!
NO.
GW
ELEGINT
THEY TOLD ME THERE'S A PRETTY COOL PARTY A BUNCH OF THE NEW STUDENTS ARE GOING TO.
YOU SHOULD COME. MY BOYFRIEND SAID HE MIGHT MEET ME THERE--HE'S GREAT!
AND, MAYBE, IF YOU'RE COOL WITH IT...HE COULD COME BACK HERE AFTER?
NO.

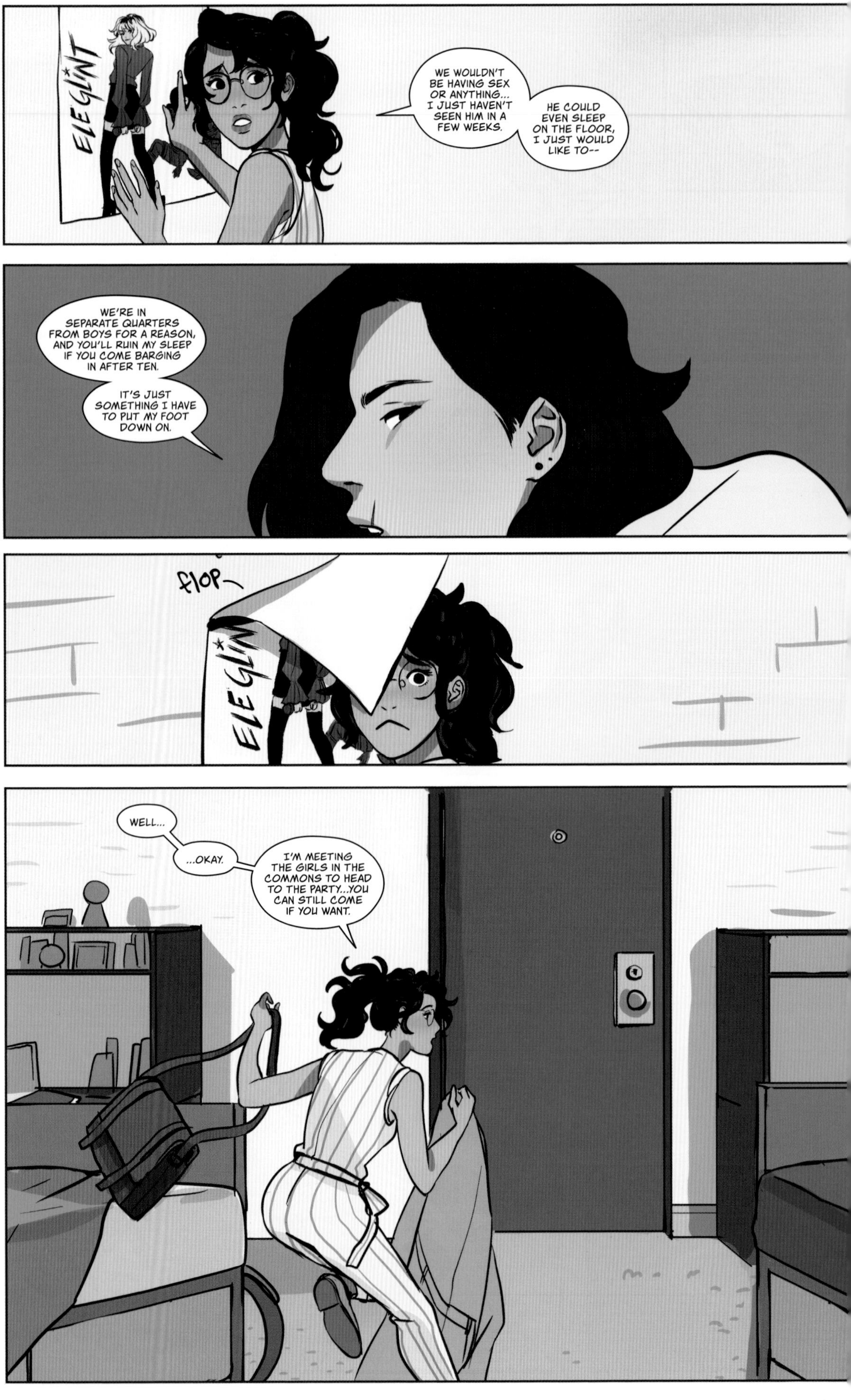
ELEGLINT
WE WOULDN'T BE HAVING SEX OR ANYTHING... I JUST HAVEN'T SEEN HIM IN A FEW WEEKS.
HE COULD EVEN SLEEP ON THE FLOOR, I JUST WOULD LIKE TO--
WE'RE IN SEPARATE QUARTERS FROM BOYS FOR A REASON, AND YOU'LL RUIN MY SLEEP IF YOU COME BARGING IN AFTER TEN.
IT'S JUST SOMETHING I HAVE TO PUT MY FOOT DOWN ON.
flop
ELEGLINT
WELL...
...OKAY.
I'M MEETING THE GIRLS IN THE COMMONS TO HEAD TO THE PARTY...YOU CAN STILL COME IF YOU WANT.

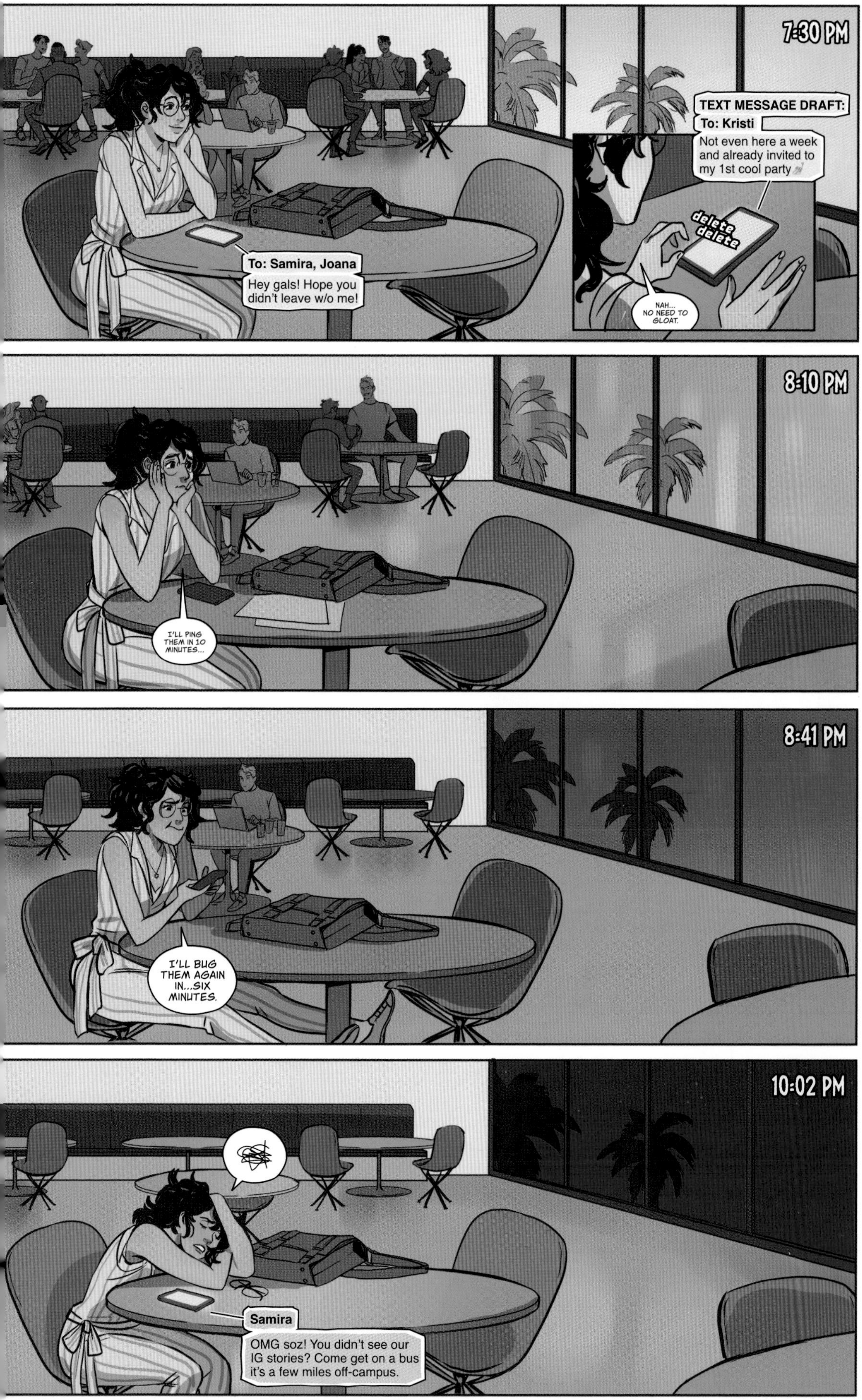

7:30 PM
To: Samira, Joana
Hey gals! Hope you didn't leave w/o me!
TEXT MESSAGE DRAFT:
To: Kristi
Not even here a week and already invited to my 1st cool party
delete delete
NAH... NO NEED TO GLOAT.
8:10 PM
I'LL PING THEM IN 10 MINUTES...
8:41 PM
I'LL BUG THEM AGAIN IN...SIX MINUTES.
10:02 PM
Samira
OMG soz! You didn't see our IG stories? Come get on a bus it's a few miles off-campus.

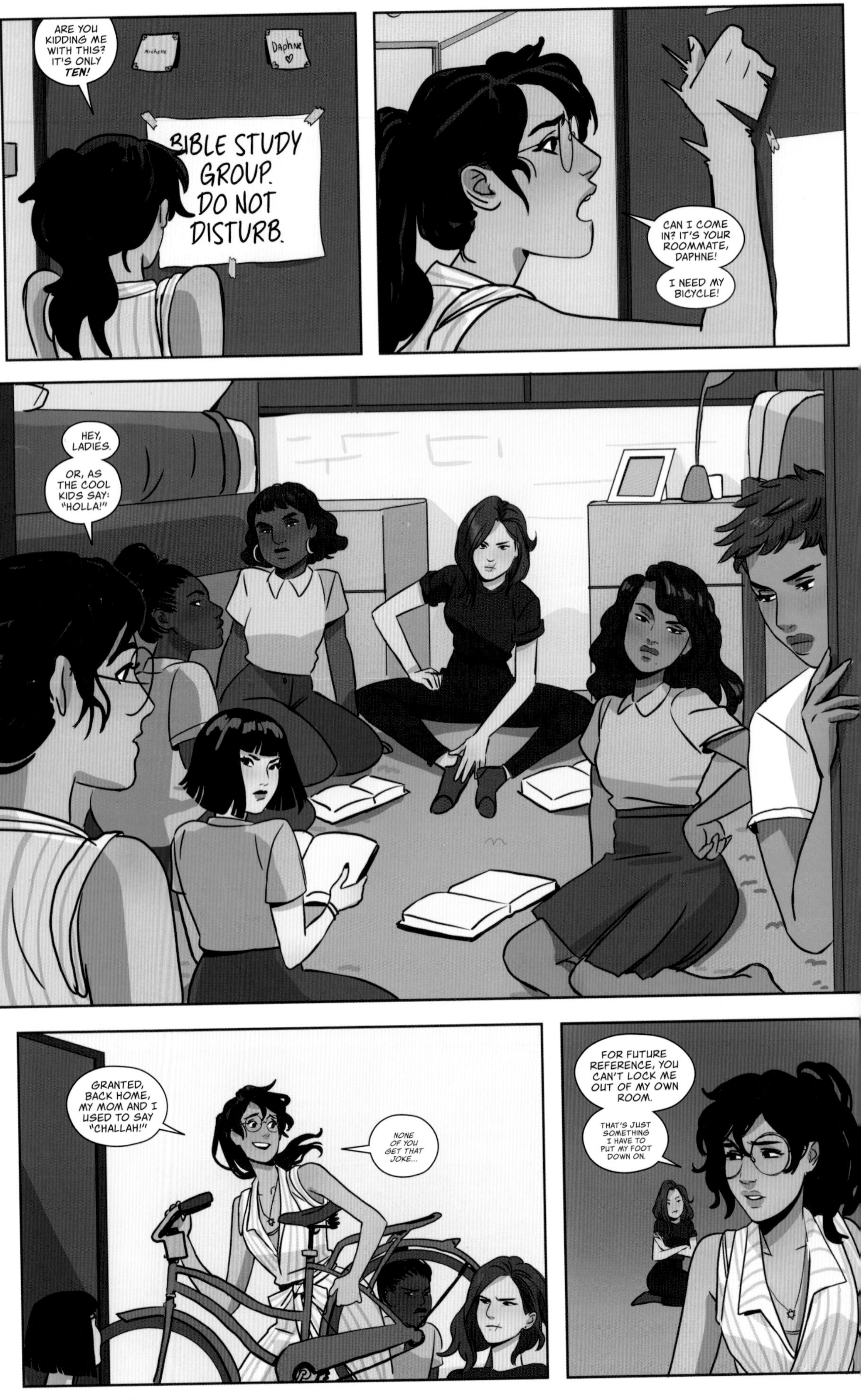
Michelle
Daphne
ARE YOU KIDDING ME WITH THIS? IT'S ONLY TEN!
BIBLE STUDY GROUP. DO NOT DISTURB.
CAN I COME IN? IT'S YOUR ROOMMATE, DAPHNE!
I NEED MY BICYCLE!
HEY, LADIES.
OR, AS THE COOL KIDS SAY: "HOLLA!"
GRANTED, BACK HOME, MY MOM AND I USED TO SAY "CHALLAH!"
NONE OF YOU GET THAT JOKE...
FOR FUTURE REFERENCE, YOU CAN'T LOCK ME OUT OF MY OWN ROOM.
THAT'S JUST SOMETHING I HAVE TO PUT MY FOOT DOWN ON.

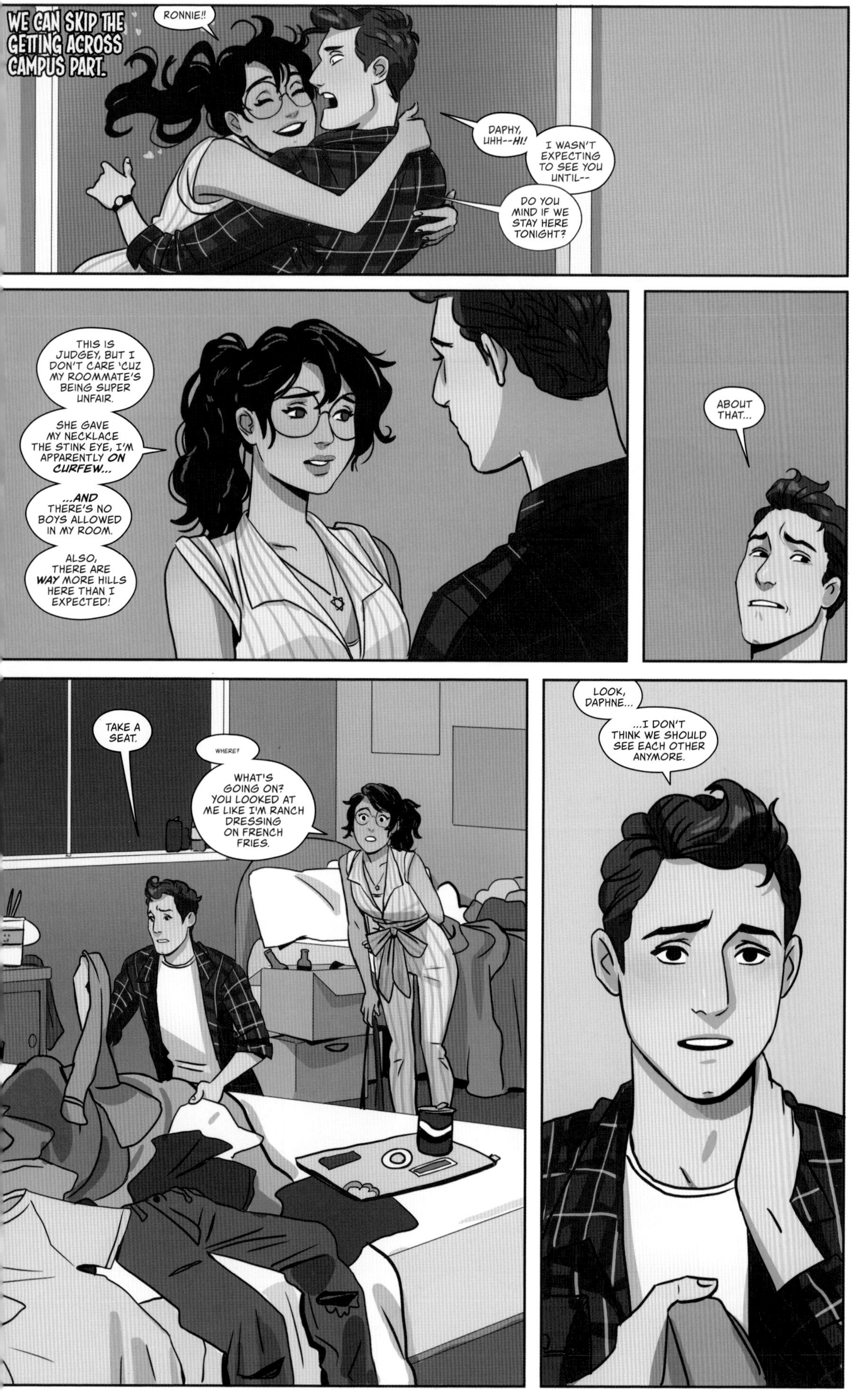
WE CAN SKIP THE GETTING ACROSS CAMPUS PART.
RONNIE!!
DAPHY, UHH--HI!
I WASN'T EXPECTING TO SEE YOU UNTIL--
DO YOU MIND IF WE STAY HERE TONIGHT?
THIS IS JUDGEY, BUT I DON'T CARE 'CUZ MY ROOMMATE'S BEING SUPER UNFAIR.
SHE GAVE MY NECKLACE THE STINK EYE, I'M APPARENTLY ON CURFEW...
...AND THERE'S NO BOYS ALLOWED IN MY ROOM.
ALSO, THERE ARE WAY MORE HILLS HERE THAN I EXPECTED!
ABOUT THAT...
TAKE A SEAT.
WHERE?
WHAT'S GOING ON? YOU LOOKED AT ME LIKE I'M RANCH DRESSING ON FRENCH FRIES.
LOOK, DAPHNE...
...I DON'T THINK WE SHOULD SEE EACH OTHER ANYMORE.

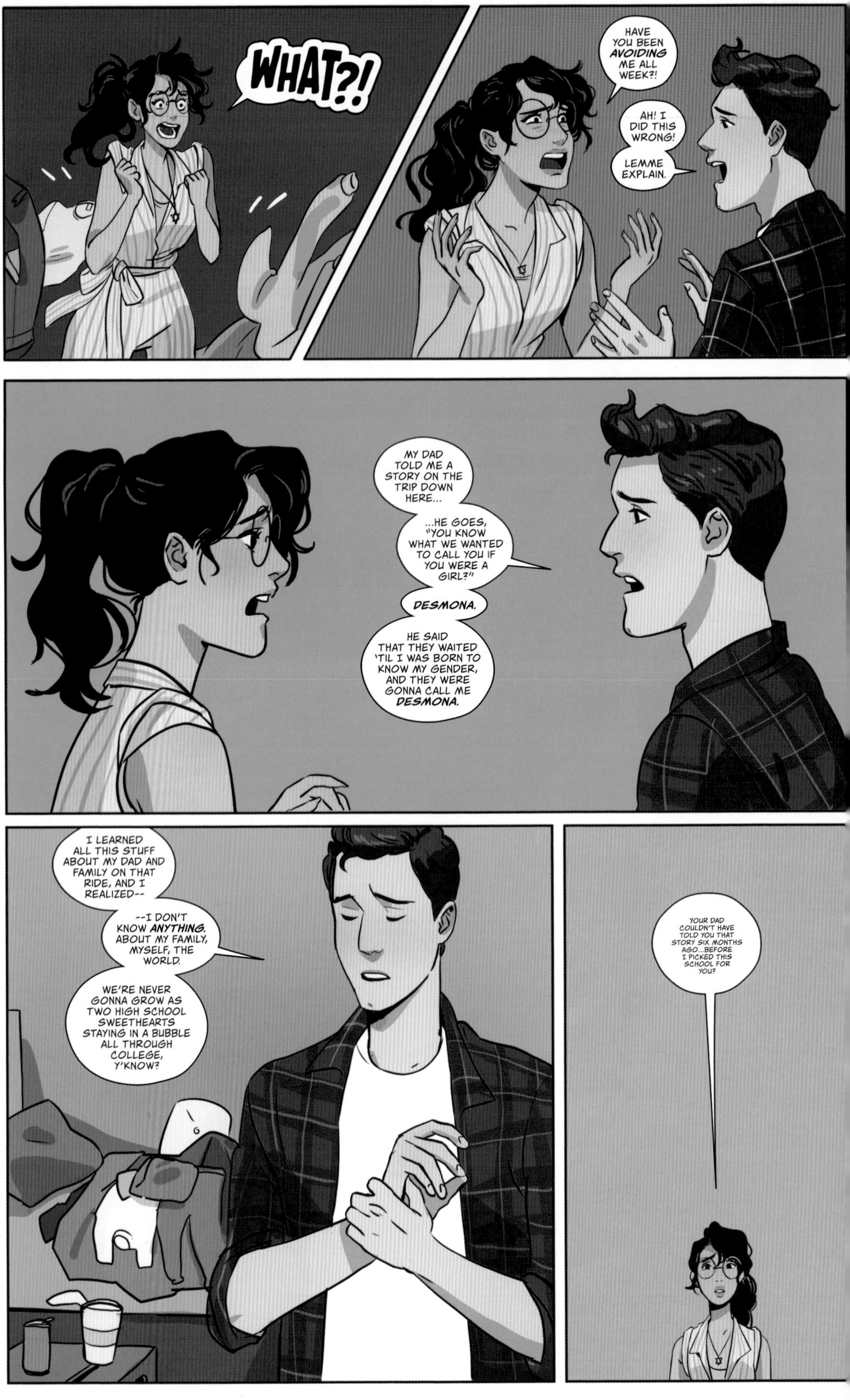
WHAT?!
HAVE YOU BEEN AVOIDING ME ALL WEEK?!
AH! I DID THIS WRONG!
LEMME EXPLAIN.
MY DAD TOLD ME A STORY ON THE TRIP DOWN HERE...
...HE GOES, "YOU KNOW WHAT WE WANTED TO CALL YOU IF YOU WERE A GIRL?"
DESMONA.
HE SAID THAT THEY WAITED 'TIL I WAS BORN TO KNOW MY GENDER, AND THEY WERE GONNA CALL ME DESMONA.
I LEARNED ALL THIS STUFF ABOUT MY DAD AND FAMILY ON THAT RIDE, AND I REALIZED--
--I DON'T KNOW ANYTHING. ABOUT MY FAMILY, MYSELF, THE WORLD.
WE'RE NEVER GONNA GROW AS TWO HIGH SCHOOL SWEETHEARTS STAYING IN A BUBBLE ALL THROUGH COLLEGE, Y'KNOW?
YOUR DAD COULDN'T HAVE TOLD YOU THAT STORY SIX MONTHS AGO...BEFORE I PICKED THIS SCHOOL FOR YOU?

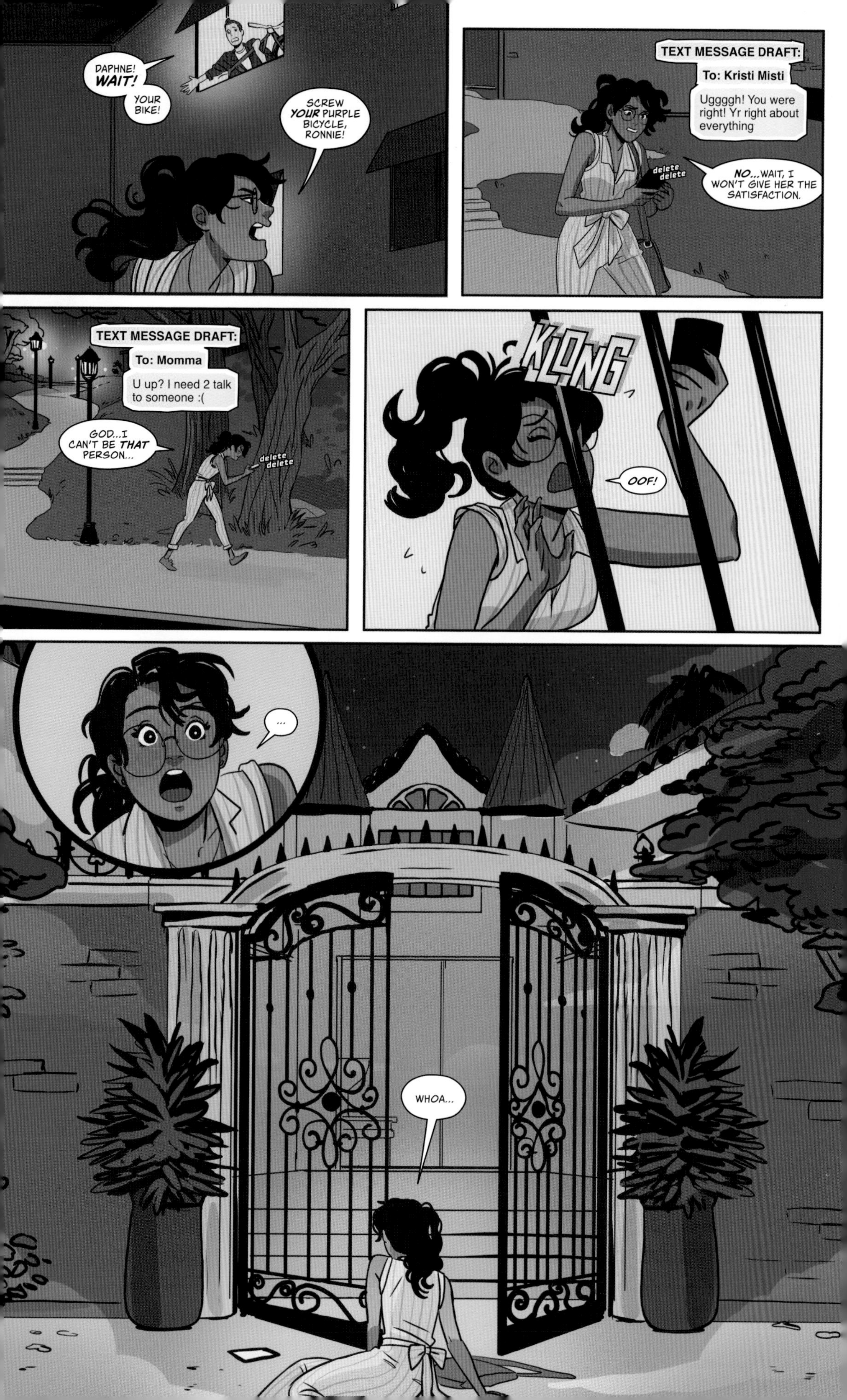
DAPHNE! WAIT!
YOUR BIKE!
SCREW YOUR PURPLE BICYCLE, RONNIE!
TEXT MESSAGE DRAFT:
To: Kristi Misti
Uggggh! You were right! Yr right about everything
delete delete
NO...WAIT, I WON'T GIVE HER THE SATISFACTION.
TEXT MESSAGE DRAFT:
To: Momma
U up? I need 2 talk to someone :(
GOD...I CAN'T BE THAT PERSON...
delete delete
KLONG
OOF!
...
WHOA...

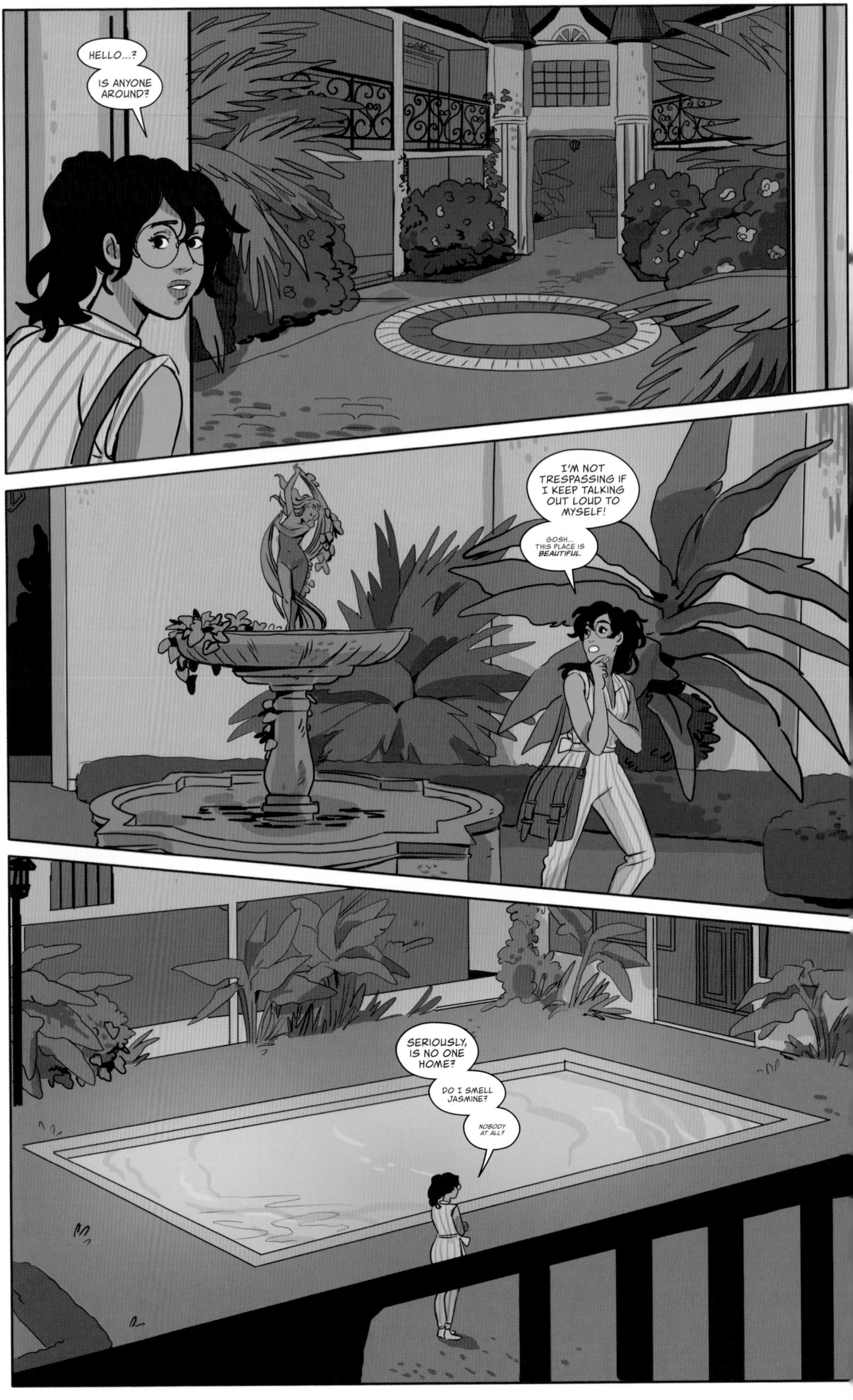
HELLO...?
IS ANYONE AROUND?
I'M NOT TRESPASSING IF I KEEP TALKING OUT LOUD TO MYSELF!
GOSH... THIS PLACE IS BEAUTIFUL.
SERIOUSLY, IS NO ONE HOME?
DO I SMELL JASMINE?
NOBODY AT ALL?

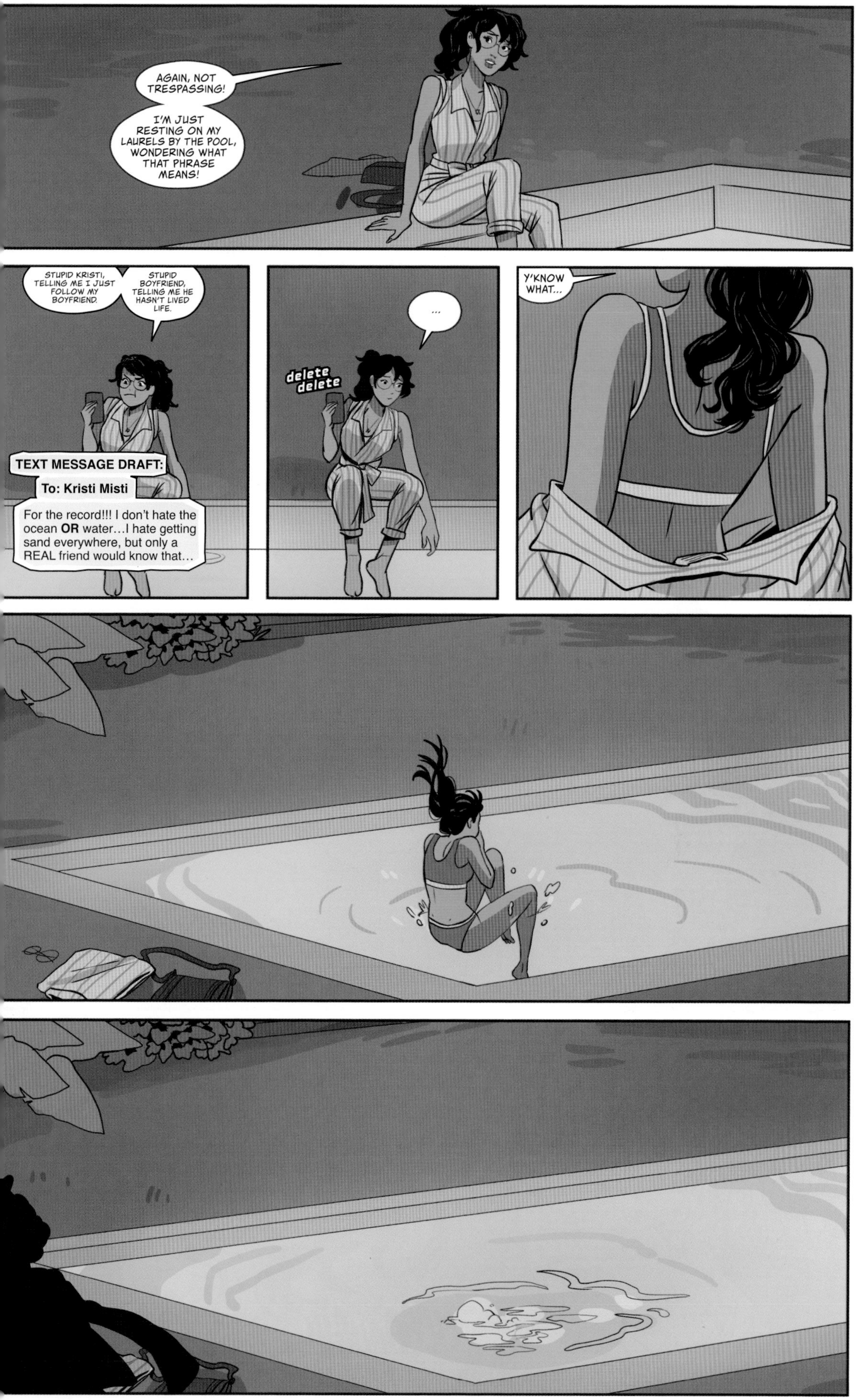

AGAIN, NOT TRESPASSING!
I'M JUST RESTING ON MY LAURELS BY THE POOL, WONDERING WHAT THAT PHRASE MEANS!
STUPID KRISTI, TELLING ME I JUST FOLLOW MY BOYFRIEND.
STUPID BOYFRIEND, TELLING ME HE HASN'T LIVED LIFE.
TEXT MESSAGE DRAFT:
To: Kristi Misti
For the record!!! I don't hate the ocean OR water…I hate getting sand everywhere, but only a REAL friend would know that…
delete delete
...
Y'KNOW WHAT...

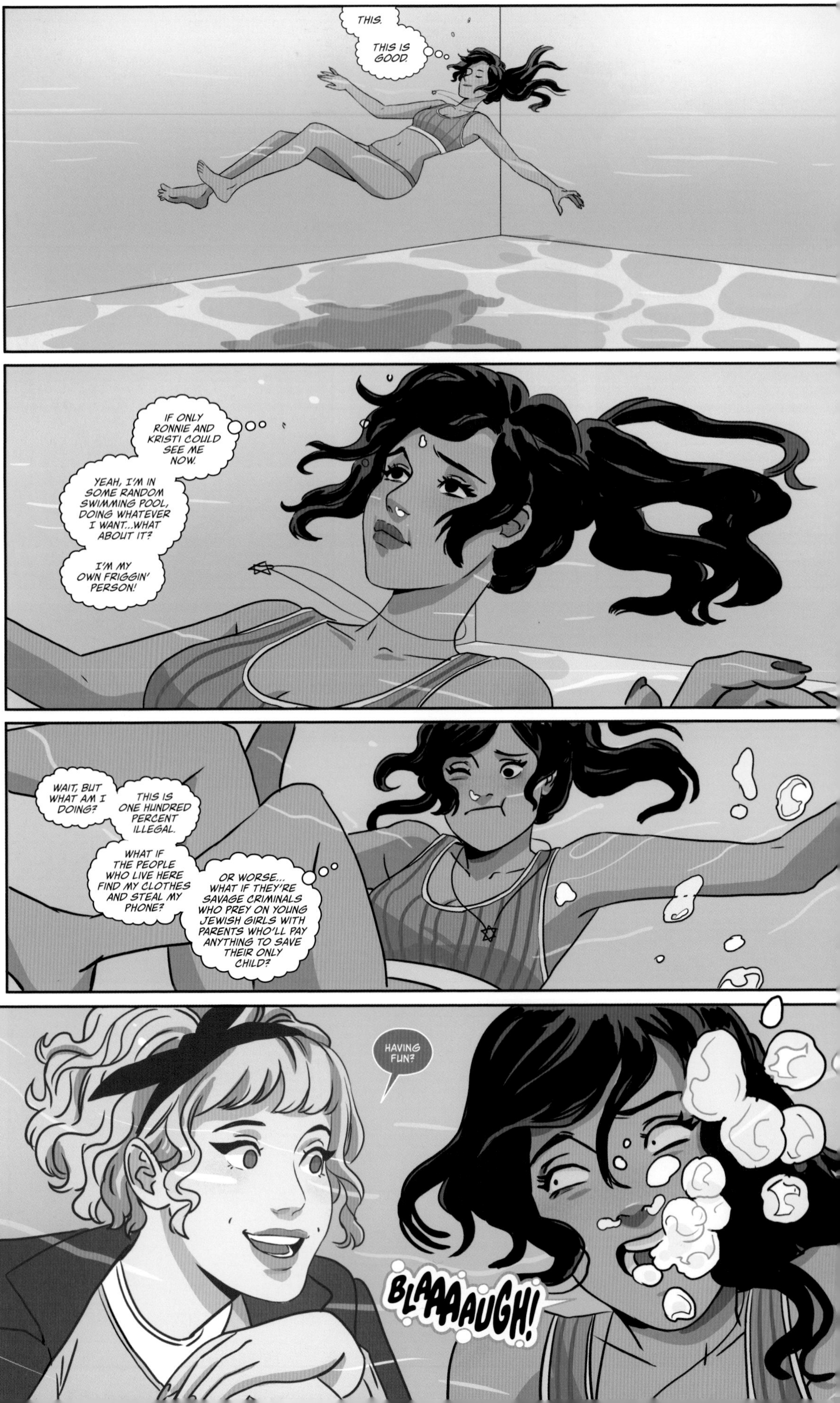
THIS.
THIS IS GOOD.
IF ONLY RONNIE AND KRISTI COULD SEE ME NOW.
YEAH, I'M IN SOME RANDOM SWIMMING POOL, DOING WHATEVER I WANT...WHAT ABOUT IT?
I'M MY OWN FRIGGIN' PERSON!
WAIT, BUT WHAT AM I DOING?
THIS IS ONE HUNDRED PERCENT ILLEGAL.
WHAT IF THE PEOPLE WHO LIVE HERE FIND MY CLOTHES AND STEAL MY PHONE?
OR WORSE... WHAT IF THEY'RE SAVAGE CRIMINALS WHO PREY ON YOUNG JEWISH GIRLS WITH PARENTS WHO'LL PAY ANYTHING TO SAVE THEIR ONLY CHILD?
HAVING FUN?
BLAAAAAUGH!

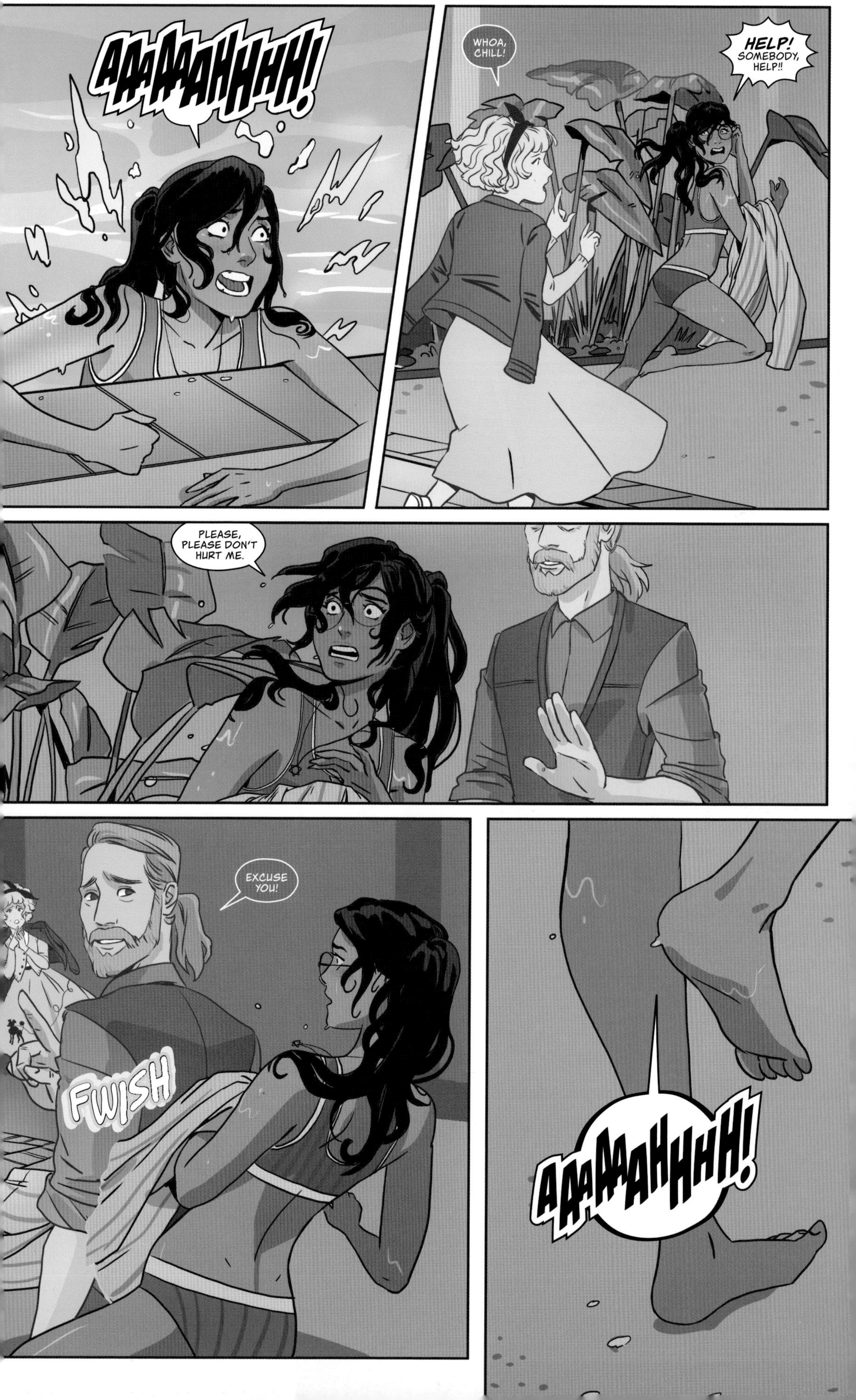
AAAAAAHHHH!
WHOA, CHILL!
HELP! SOMEBODY, HELP!!
PLEASE, PLEASE DON'T HURT ME.
EXCUSE YOU!
FWISH
AAAAAAHHHH!

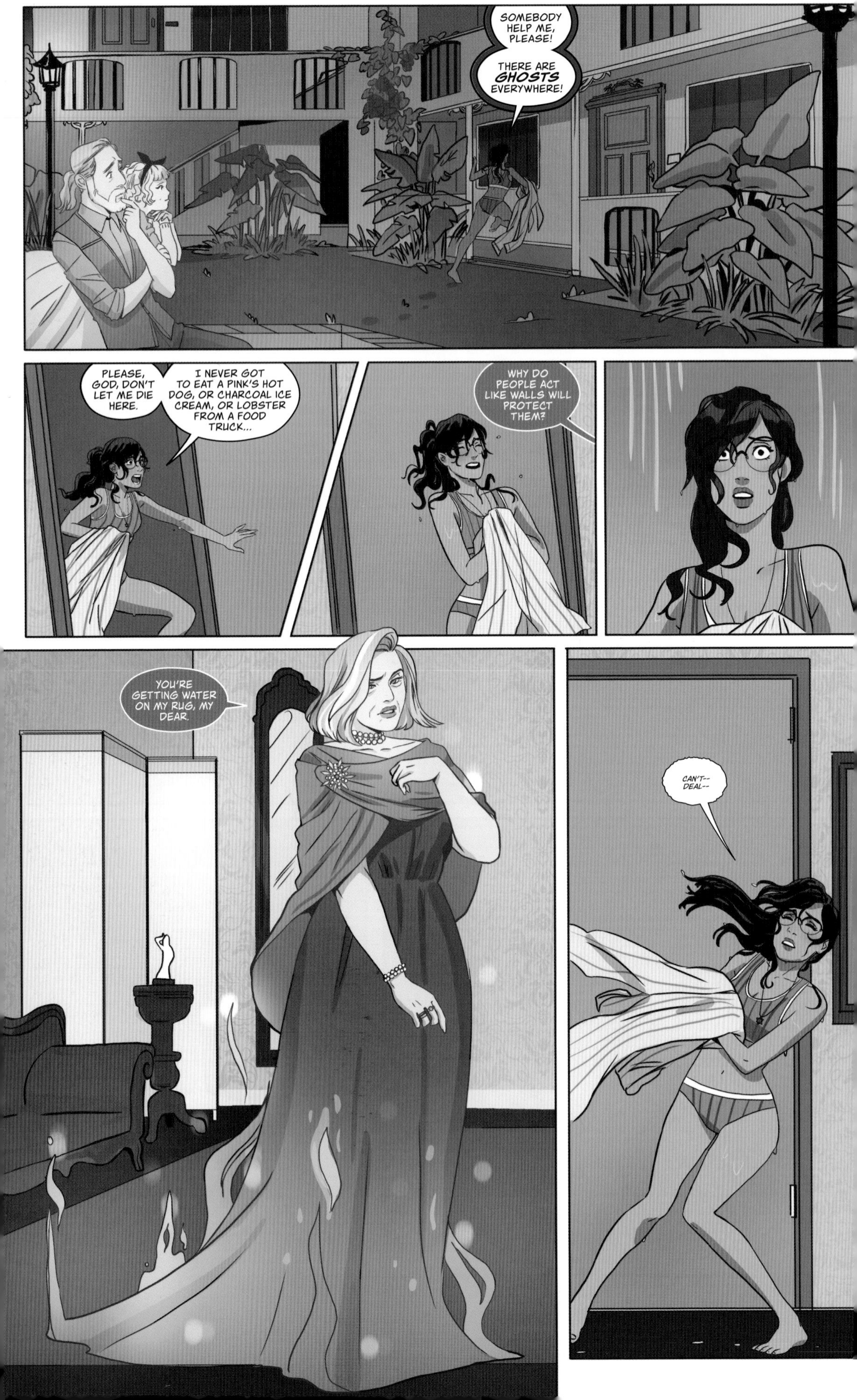
SOMEBODY HELP ME, PLEASE!
THERE ARE GHOSTS EVERYWHERE!
PLEASE, GOD, DON'T LET ME DIE HERE.
I NEVER GOT TO EAT A PINK'S HOT DOG, OR CHARCOAL ICE CREAM, OR LOBSTER FROM A FOOD TRUCK...
WHY DO PEOPLE ACT LIKE WALLS WILL PROTECT THEM?
YOU'RE GETTING WATER ON MY RUG, MY DEAR.
CAN'T-- DEAL--

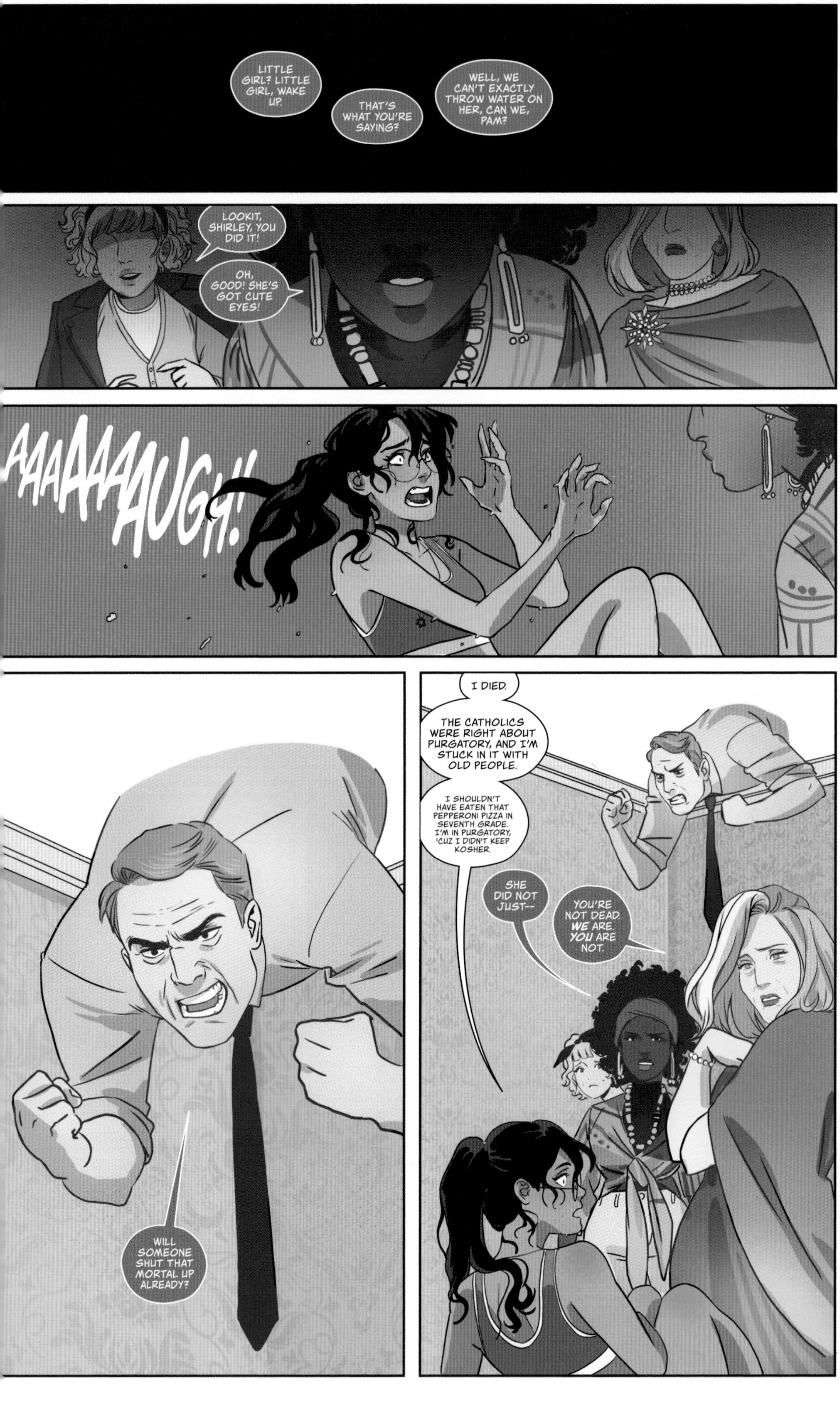
LITTLE GIRL? LITTLE GIRL, WAKE UP.
THAT'S WHAT YOU'RE SAYING?
WELL, WE CAN'T EXACTLY THROW WATER ON HER, CAN WE, PAM?
LOOKIT, SHIRLEY, YOU DID IT!
OH, GOOD! SHE'S GOT CUTE EYES!
AAAAAAAUGH!!
WILL SOMEONE SHUT THAT MORTAL UP ALREADY?
I DIED.
THE CATHOLICS WERE RIGHT ABOUT PURGATORY, AND I'M STUCK IN IT WITH OLD PEOPLE.
I SHOULDN'T HAVE EATEN THAT PEPPERONI PIZZA IN SEVENTH GRADE. I'M IN PURGATORY, 'CUZ I DIDN'T KEEP KOSHER.
SHE DID NOT JUST--
YOU'RE NOT DEAD. WE ARE. YOU ARE NOT.

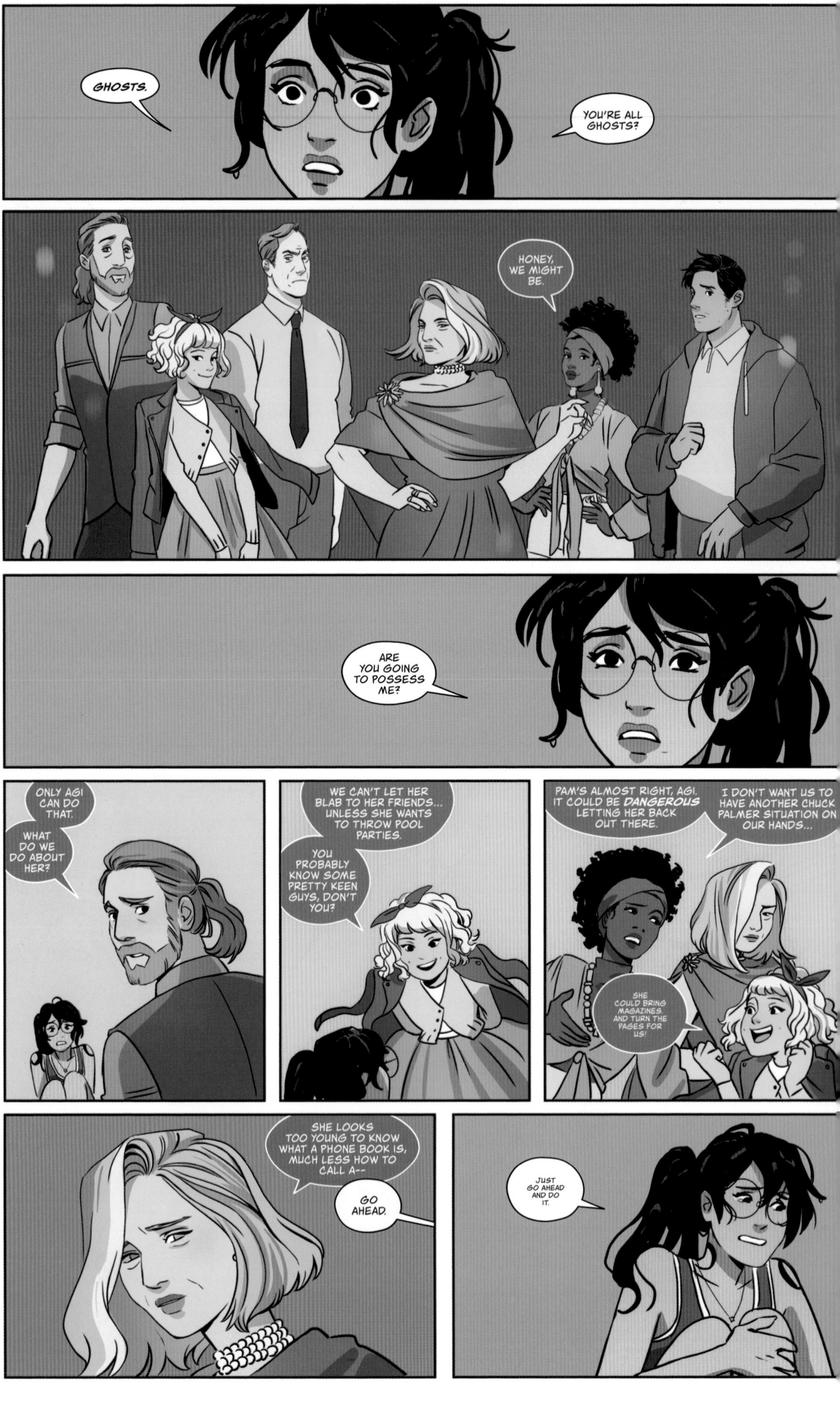
GHOSTS.
YOU'RE ALL GHOSTS?
HONEY, WE MIGHT BE.
ARE YOU GOING TO POSSESS ME?
ONLY AGI CAN DO THAT.
WHAT DO WE DO ABOUT HER?
WE CAN'T LET HER BLAB TO HER FRIENDS... UNLESS SHE WANTS TO THROW POOL PARTIES.
YOU PROBABLY KNOW SOME PRETTY KEEN GUYS, DON'T YOU?
PAM'S ALMOST RIGHT, AGI. IT COULD BE DANGEROUS LETTING HER BACK OUT THERE.
I DON'T WANT US TO HAVE ANOTHER CHUCK PALMER SITUATION ON OUR HANDS...
SHE COULD BRING MAGAZINES. AND TURN THE PAGES FOR US!
SHE LOOKS TOO YOUNG TO KNOW WHAT A PHONE BOOK IS, MUCH LESS HOW TO CALL A--
GO AHEAD.
JUST GO AHEAD AND DO IT.

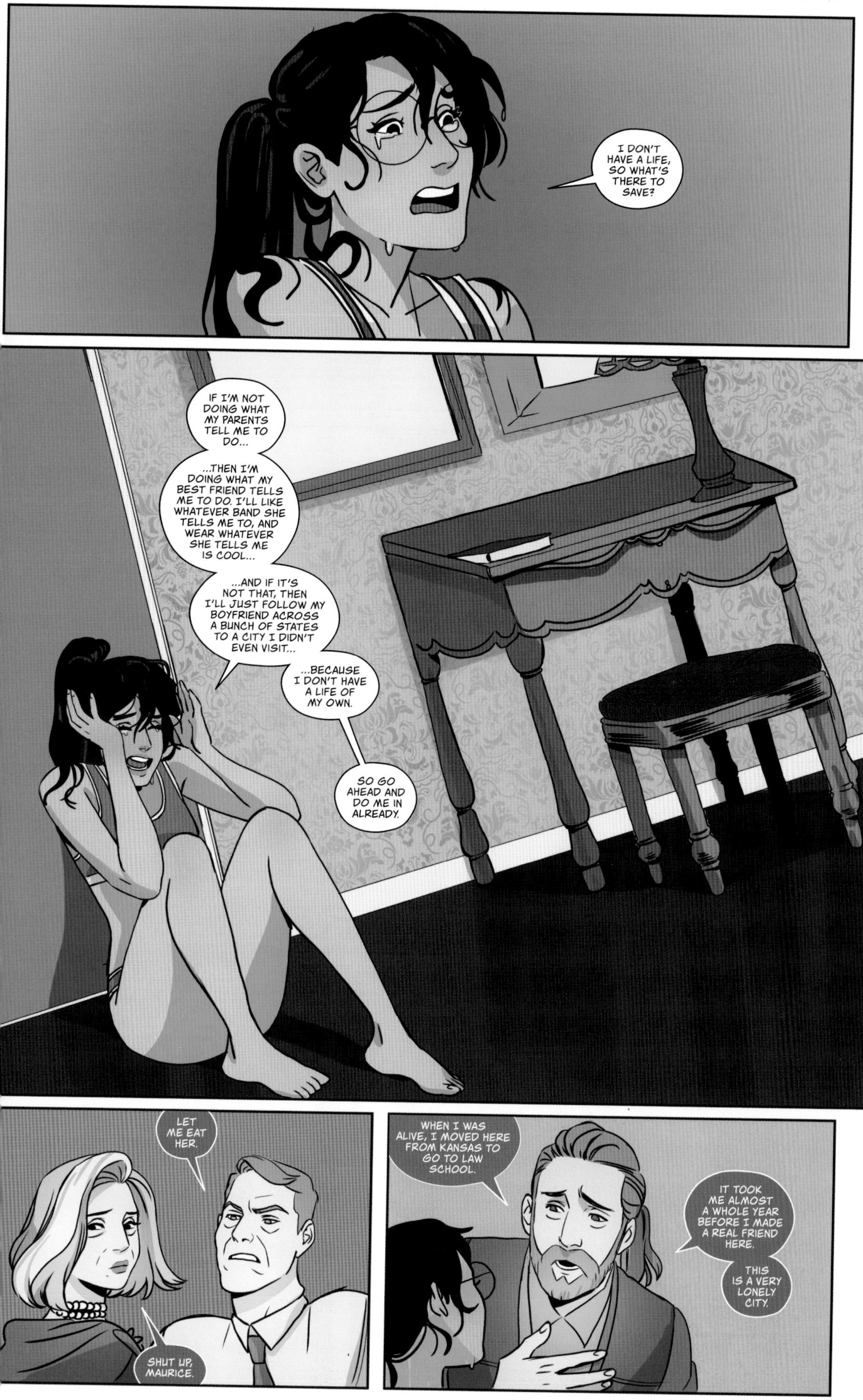
I DON'T HAVE A LIFE, SO WHAT'S THERE TO SAVE?
IF I'M NOT DOING WHAT MY PARENTS TELL ME TO DO...
...THEN I'M DOING WHAT MY BEST FRIEND TELLS ME TO DO. I'LL LIKE WHATEVER BAND SHE TELLS ME TO, AND WEAR WHATEVER SHE TELLS ME IS COOL...
...AND IF IT'S NOT THAT, THEN I'LL JUST FOLLOW MY BOYFRIEND ACROSS A BUNCH OF STATES TO A CITY I DIDN'T EVEN VISIT...
...BECAUSE I DON'T HAVE A LIFE OF MY OWN.
SO GO AHEAD AND DO ME IN ALREADY.
LET ME EAT HER.
SHUT UP, MAURICE.
WHEN I WAS ALIVE, I MOVED HERE FROM KANSAS TO GO TO LAW SCHOOL.
IT TOOK ME ALMOST A WHOLE YEAR BEFORE I MADE A REAL FRIEND HERE.
THIS IS A VERY LONELY CITY.

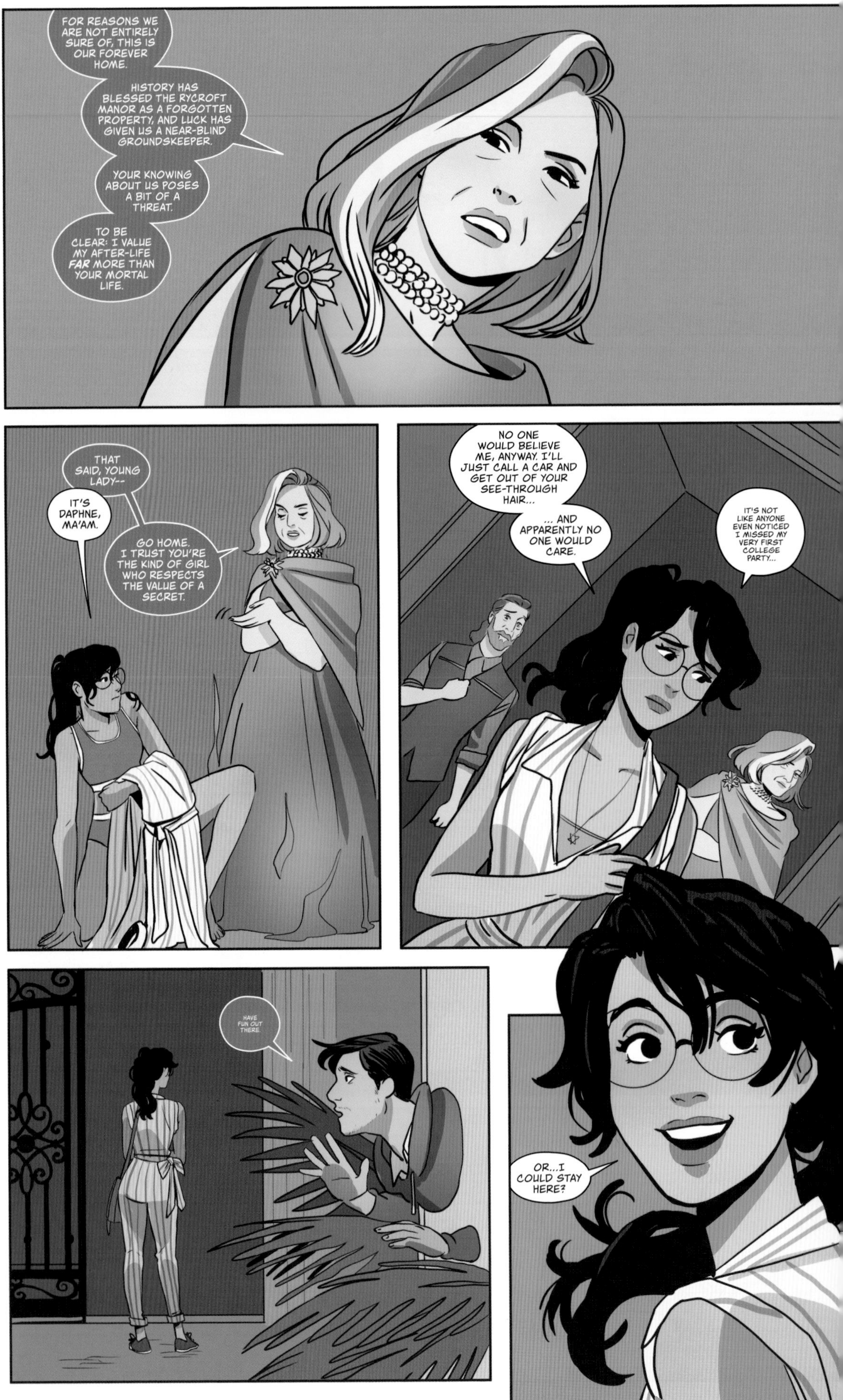
FOR REASONS WE ARE NOT ENTIRELY SURE OF, THIS IS OUR FOREVER HOME.
HISTORY HAS BLESSED THE RYCROFT MANOR AS A FORGOTTEN PROPERTY, AND LUCK HAS GIVEN US A NEAR-BLIND GROUNDSKEEPER.
YOUR KNOWING ABOUT US POSES A BIT OF A THREAT.
TO BE CLEAR: I VALUE MY AFTER-LIFE *FAR* MORE THAN YOUR MORTAL LIFE.
THAT SAID, YOUNG LADY--
IT'S DAPHNE, MA'AM.
GO HOME. I TRUST YOU'RE THE KIND OF GIRL WHO RESPECTS THE VALUE OF A SECRET.
NO ONE WOULD BELIEVE ME, ANYWAY. I'LL JUST CALL A CAR AND GET OUT OF YOUR SEE-THROUGH HAIR...
... AND APPARENTLY NO ONE WOULD CARE.
IT'S NOT LIKE ANYONE EVEN NOTICED I MISSED MY VERY FIRST COLLEGE PARTY...
HAVE FUN OUT THERE.
OR...I COULD STAY HERE?

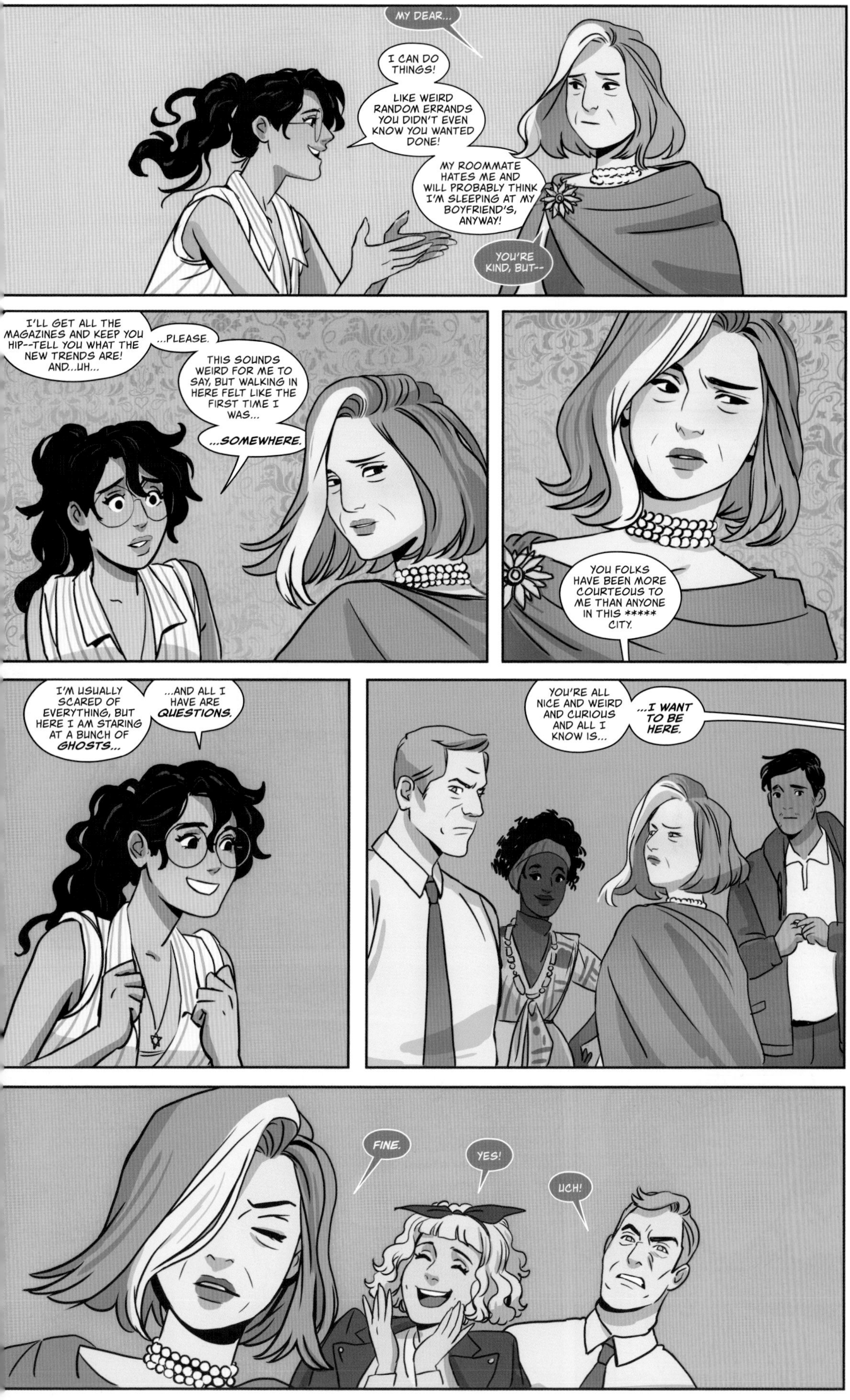
MY DEAR...
I CAN DO THINGS!
LIKE WEIRD RANDOM ERRANDS YOU DIDN'T EVEN KNOW YOU WANTED DONE!
MY ROOMMATE HATES ME AND WILL PROBABLY THINK I'M SLEEPING AT MY BOYFRIEND'S, ANYWAY!
YOU'RE KIND, BUT--
I'LL GET ALL THE MAGAZINES AND KEEP YOU HIP--TELL YOU WHAT THE NEW TRENDS ARE! AND...UH...
...PLEASE.
THIS SOUNDS WEIRD FOR ME TO SAY, BUT WALKING IN HERE FELT LIKE THE FIRST TIME I WAS...
...SOMEWHERE.
YOU FOLKS HAVE BEEN MORE COURTEOUS TO ME THAN ANYONE IN THIS ***** CITY.
I'M USUALLY SCARED OF EVERYTHING, BUT HERE I AM STARING AT A BUNCH OF GHOSTS...
...AND ALL I HAVE ARE QUESTIONS.
YOU'RE ALL NICE AND WEIRD AND CURIOUS AND ALL I KNOW IS...
...I WANT TO BE HERE.
FINE.
YES!
UGH!

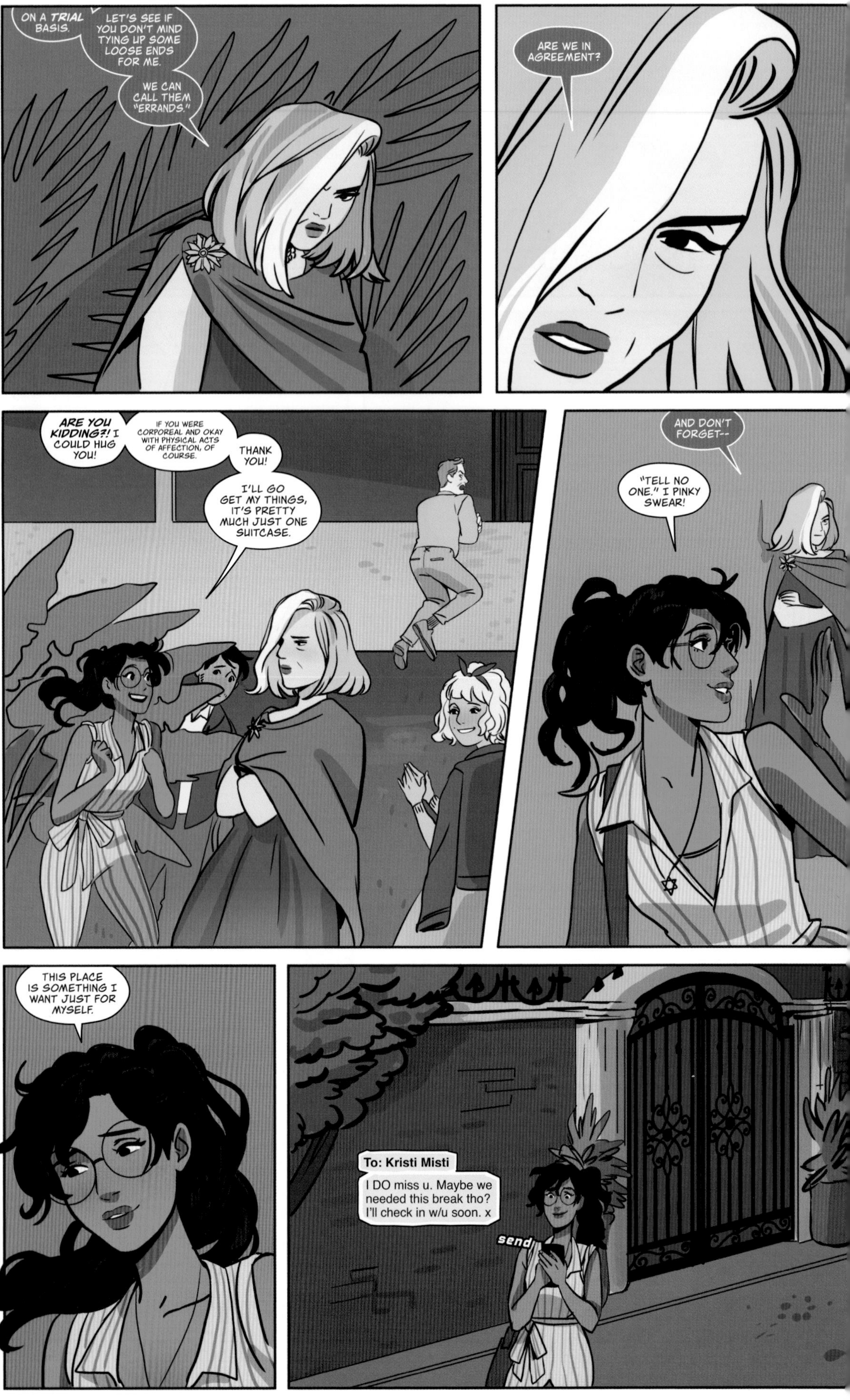
ON A *TRIAL* BASIS.
LET'S SEE IF YOU DON'T MIND TYING UP SOME LOOSE ENDS FOR ME.
WE CAN CALL THEM "ERRANDS."
ARE WE IN AGREEMENT?
ARE YOU KIDDING?! I COULD HUG YOU!
IF YOU WERE CORPOREAL AND OKAY WITH PHYSICAL ACTS OF AFFECTION, OF COURSE.
THANK YOU!
I'LL GO GET MY THINGS, IT'S PRETTY MUCH JUST ONE SUITCASE.
AND DON'T FORGET--
"TELL NO ONE." I PINKY SWEAR!
THIS PLACE IS SOMETHING I WANT JUST FOR MYSELF.
To: Kristi Misti
I DO miss u. Maybe we needed this break tho? I'll check in w/u soon. x
send

Chapter Two

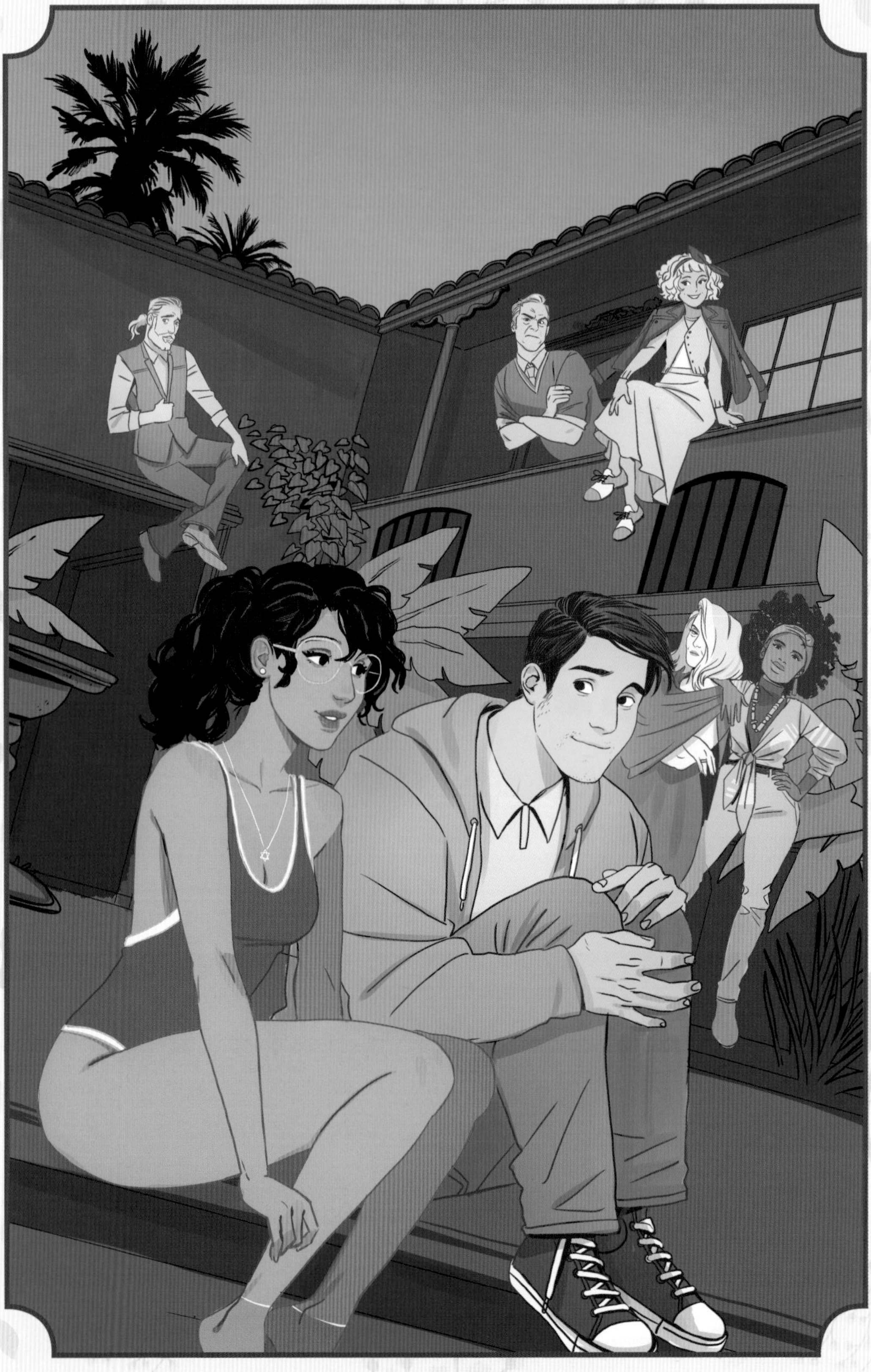

Issue Two Cover by **Siobhan Keenan**

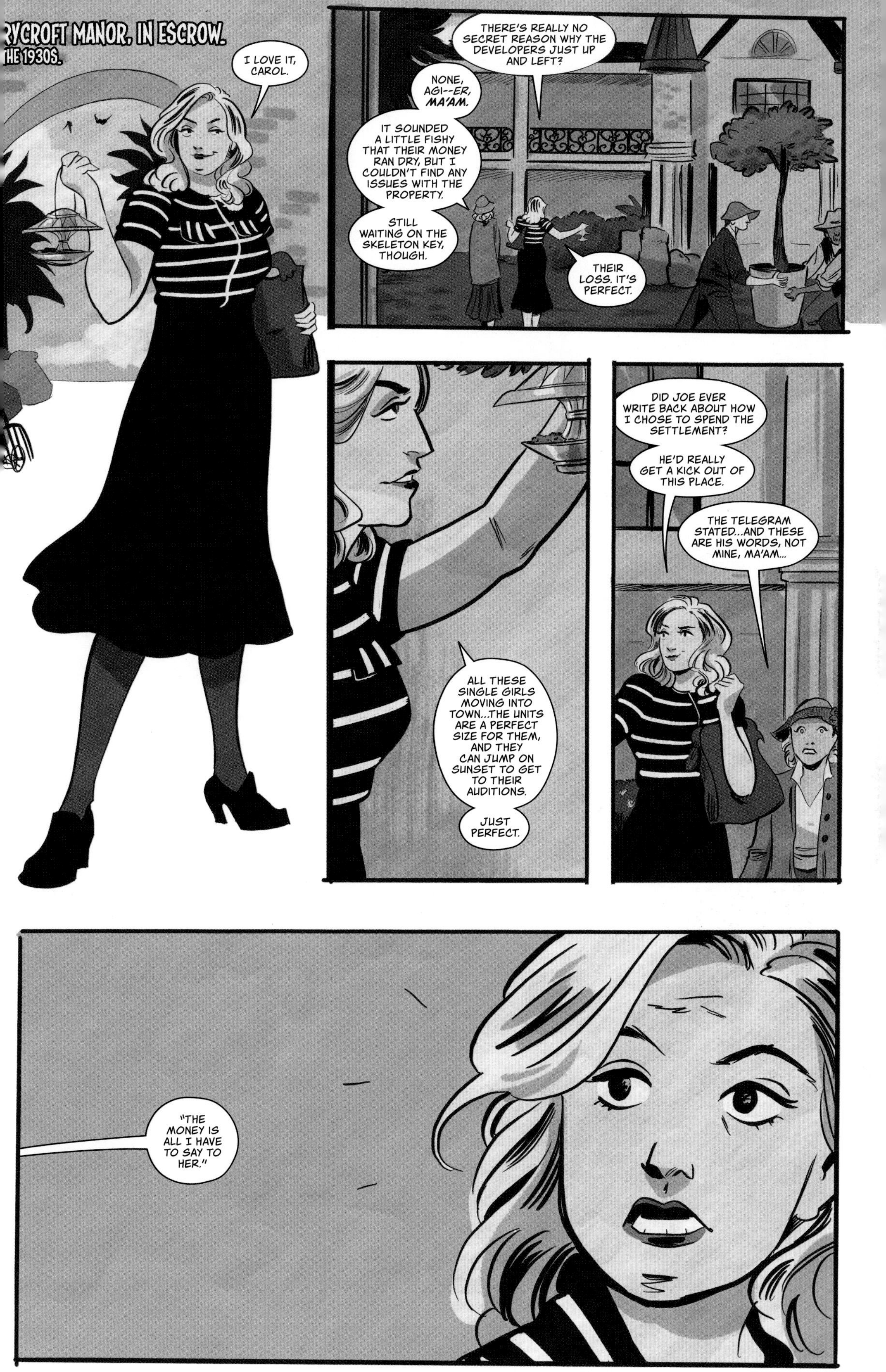

RYCROFT MANOR, IN ESCROW.
THE 1930S.
I LOVE IT, CAROL.
THERE'S REALLY NO SECRET REASON WHY THE DEVELOPERS JUST UP AND LEFT?
NONE, AGI--ER, *MA'AM.*
IT SOUNDED A LITTLE FISHY THAT THEIR MONEY RAN DRY, BUT I COULDN'T FIND ANY ISSUES WITH THE PROPERTY.
STILL WAITING ON THE SKELETON KEY, THOUGH.
THEIR LOSS. IT'S PERFECT.
ALL THESE SINGLE GIRLS MOVING INTO TOWN...THE UNITS ARE A PERFECT SIZE FOR THEM, AND THEY CAN JUMP ON SUNSET TO GET TO THEIR AUDITIONS.
JUST PERFECT.
DID JOE EVER WRITE BACK ABOUT HOW I CHOSE TO SPEND THE SETTLEMENT?
HE'D REALLY GET A KICK OUT OF THIS PLACE.
THE TELEGRAM STATED...AND THESE ARE HIS WORDS, NOT MINE, MA'AM...
"THE MONEY IS ALL I HAVE TO SAY TO HER."

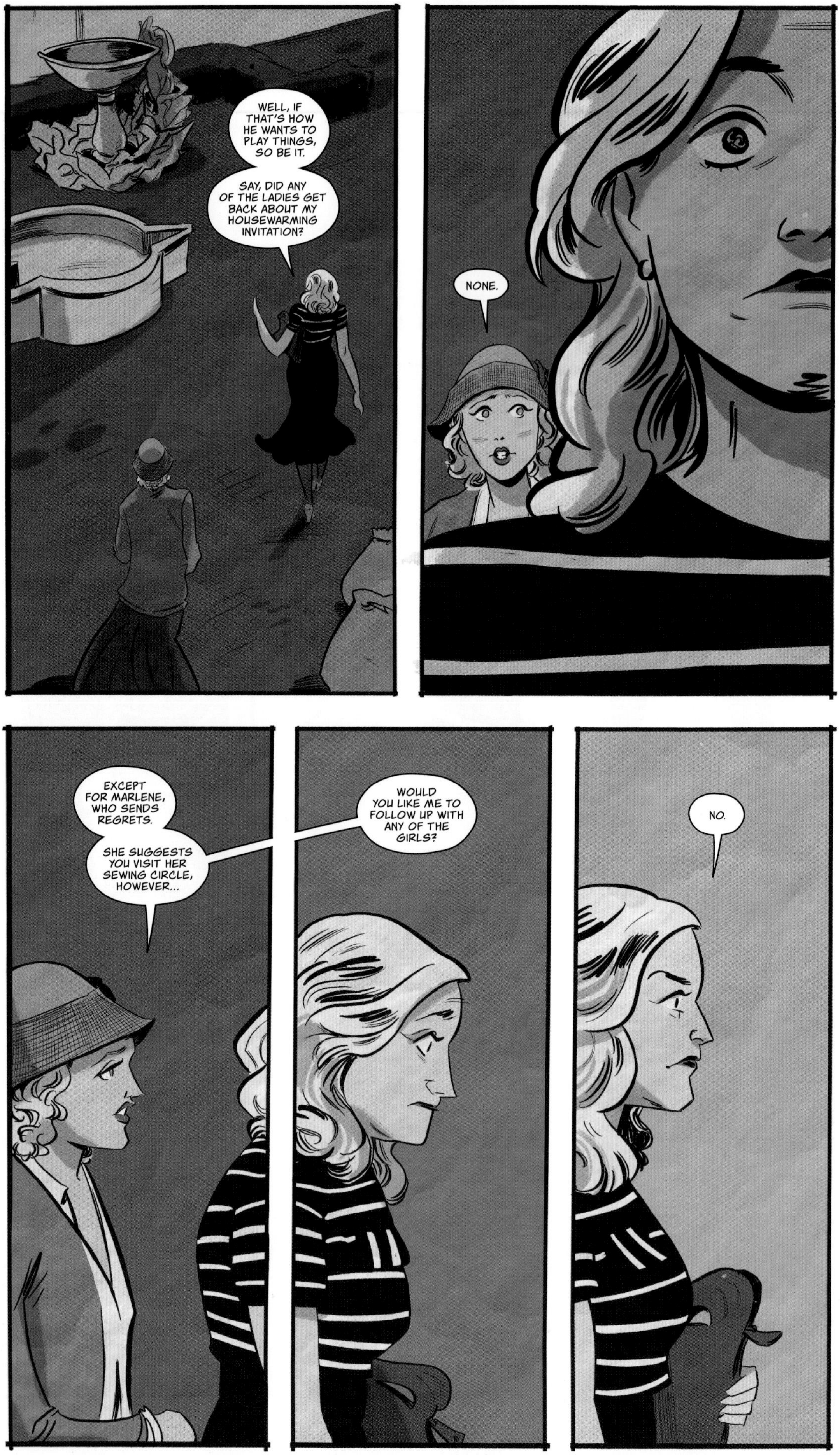

WELL, IF THAT'S HOW HE WANTS TO PLAY THINGS, SO BE IT.
SAY, DID ANY OF THE LADIES GET BACK ABOUT MY HOUSEWARMING INVITATION?
NONE.
EXCEPT FOR MARLENE, WHO SENDS REGRETS.
SHE SUGGESTS YOU VISIT HER SEWING CIRCLE, HOWEVER...
WOULD YOU LIKE ME TO FOLLOW UP WITH ANY OF THE GIRLS?
NO.

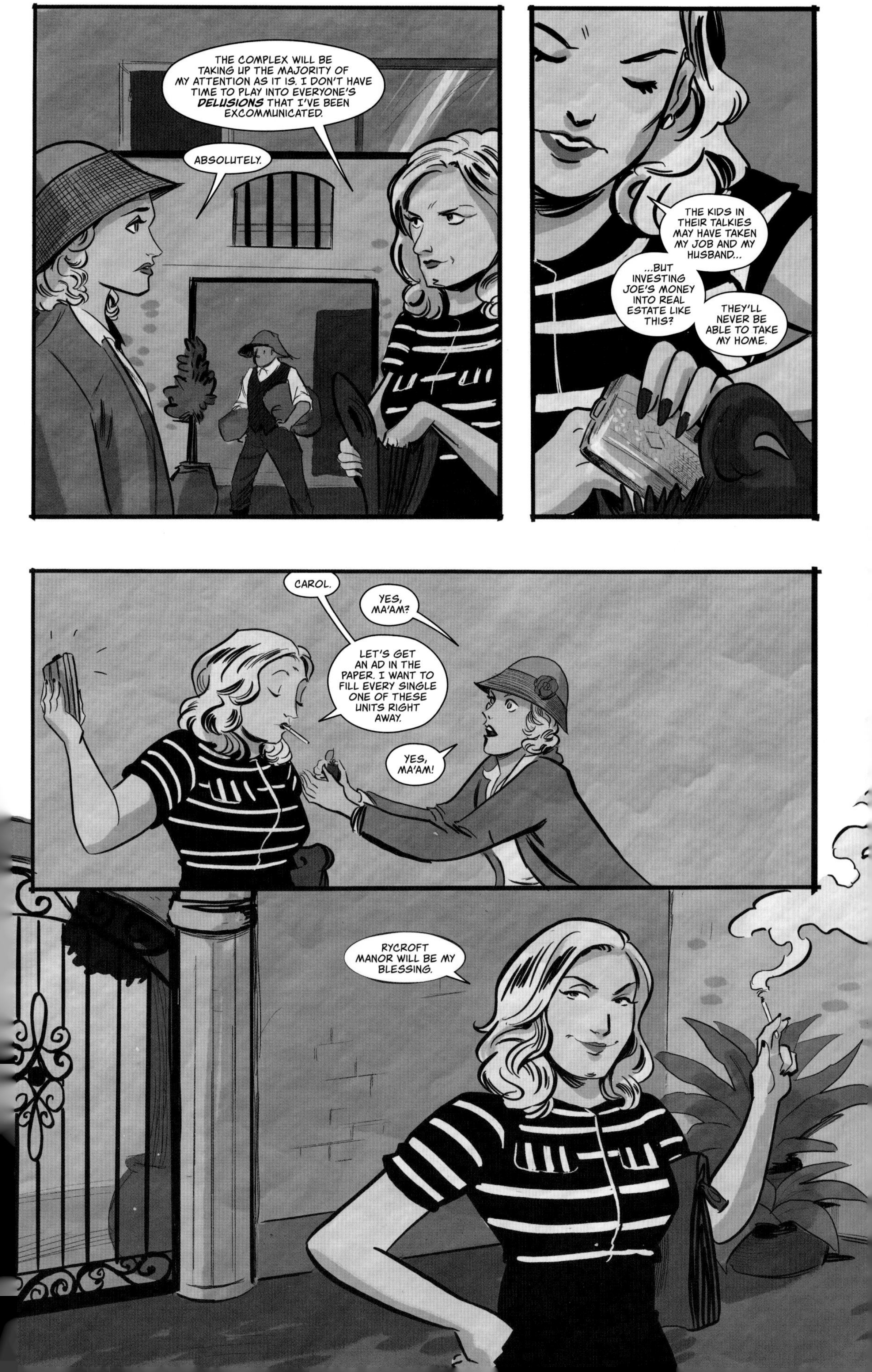
THE COMPLEX WILL BE TAKING UP THE MAJORITY OF MY ATTENTION AS IT IS. I DON'T HAVE TIME TO PLAY INTO EVERYONE'S *DELUSIONS* THAT I'VE BEEN EXCOMMUNICATED.
ABSOLUTELY.
THE KIDS IN THEIR TALKIES MAY HAVE TAKEN MY JOB AND MY HUSBAND...
...BUT INVESTING JOE'S MONEY INTO REAL ESTATE LIKE THIS?
THEY'LL NEVER BE ABLE TO TAKE MY HOME.
CAROL.
YES, MA'AM?
LET'S GET AN AD IN THE PAPER. I WANT TO FILL EVERY SINGLE ONE OF THESE UNITS RIGHT AWAY.
YES, MA'AM!
RYCROFT MANOR WILL BE MY BLESSING.

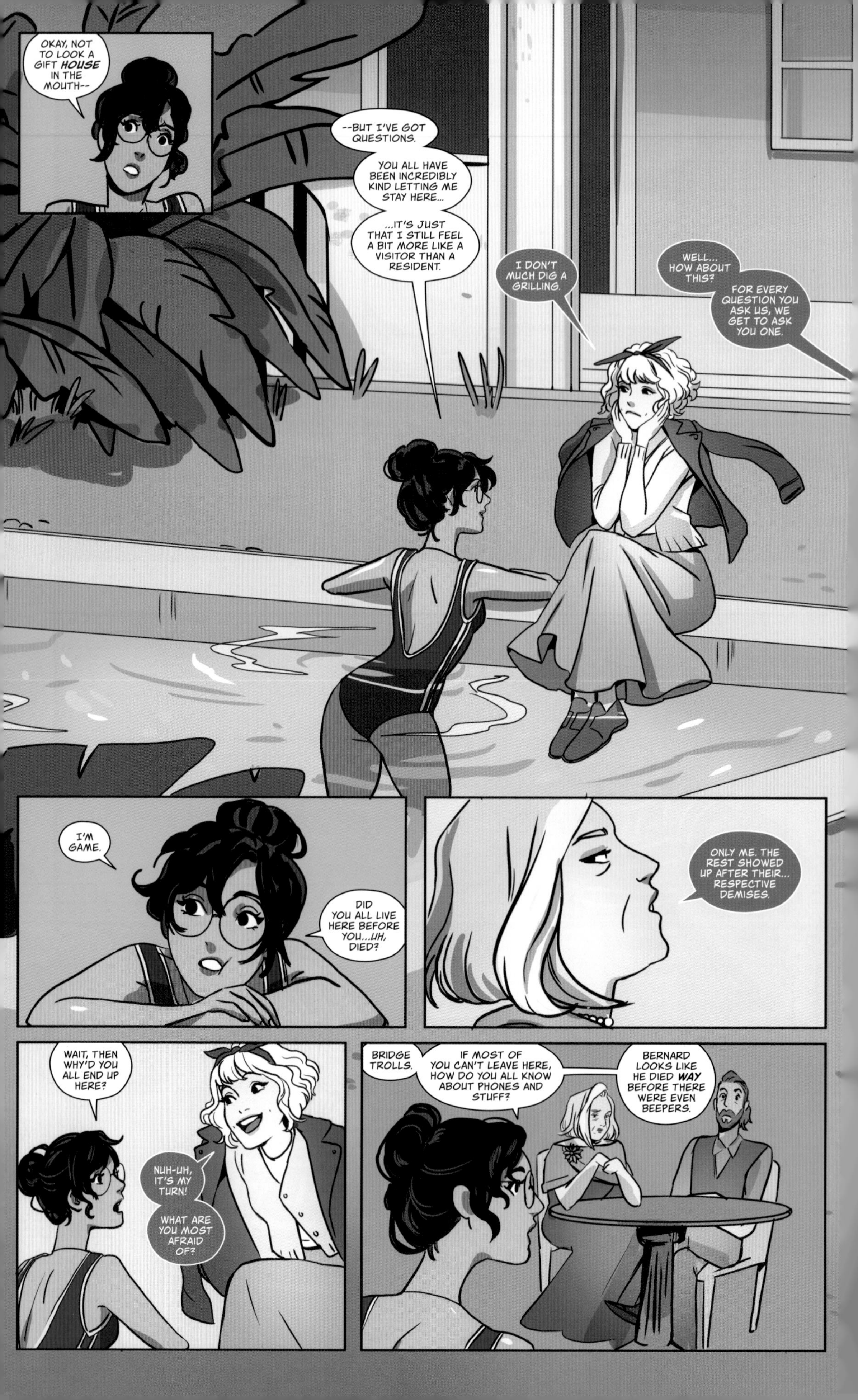

OKAY, NOT TO LOOK A GIFT **HOUSE** IN THE MOUTH--
--BUT I'VE GOT QUESTIONS.
YOU ALL HAVE BEEN INCREDIBLY KIND LETTING ME STAY HERE...
...IT'S JUST THAT I STILL FEEL A BIT MORE LIKE A VISITOR THAN A RESIDENT.
I DON'T MUCH DIG A GRILLING.
WELL... HOW ABOUT THIS?
FOR EVERY QUESTION YOU ASK US, WE GET TO ASK YOU ONE.
I'M GAME.
DID YOU ALL LIVE HERE BEFORE YOU...UH, DIED?
ONLY ME. THE REST SHOWED UP AFTER THEIR... RESPECTIVE DEMISES.
WAIT, THEN WHY'D YOU ALL END UP HERE?
NUH-UH, IT'S MY TURN!
WHAT ARE YOU MOST AFRAID OF?
BRIDGE TROLLS.
IF MOST OF YOU CAN'T LEAVE HERE, HOW DO YOU ALL KNOW ABOUT PHONES AND STUFF?
BERNARD LOOKS LIKE HE DIED **WAY** BEFORE THERE WERE EVEN BEEPERS.

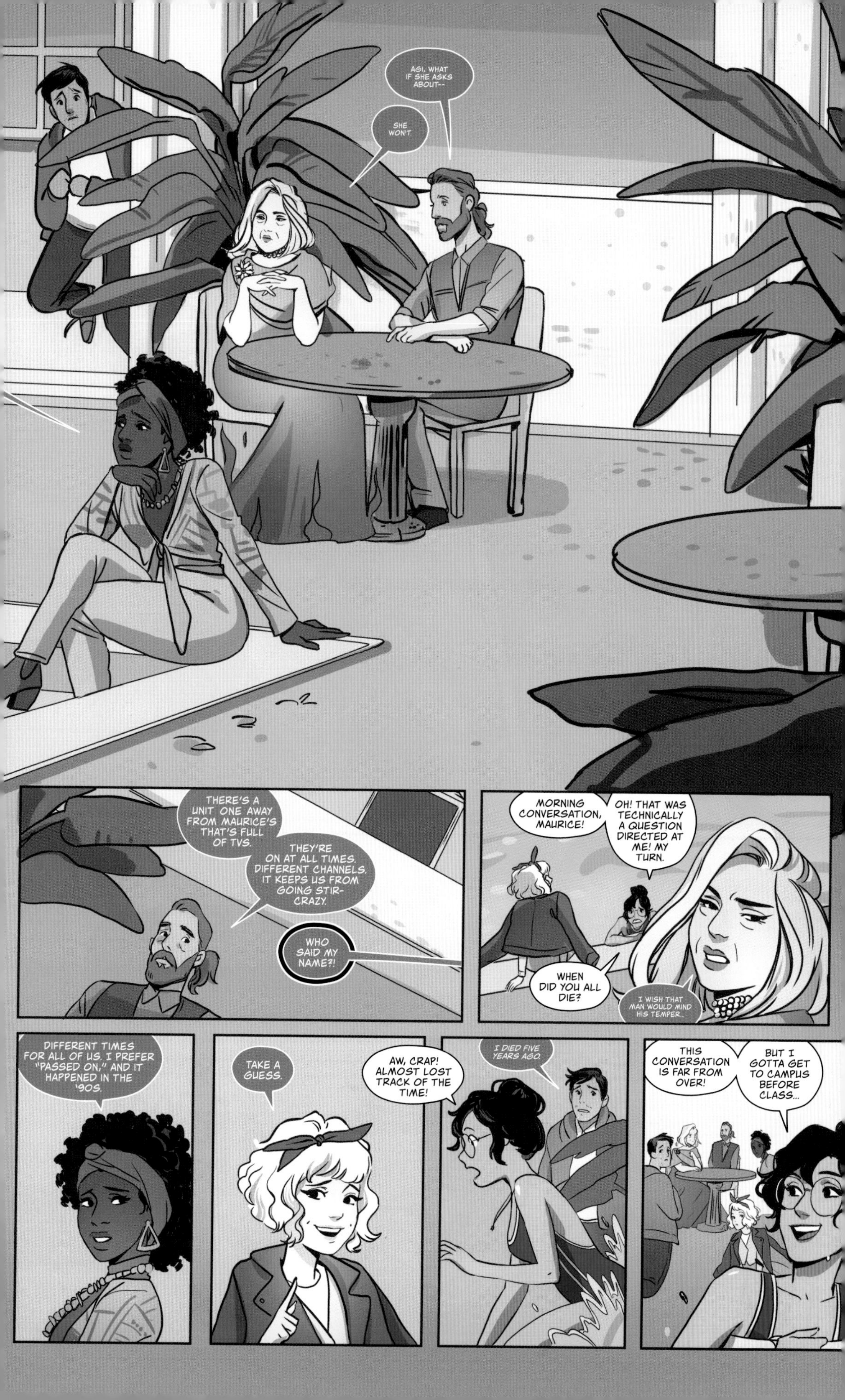
AGI, WHAT IF SHE ASKS ABOUT--
SHE WON'T.
THERE'S A UNIT ONE AWAY FROM MAURICE'S THAT'S FULL OF TVS.
THEY'RE ON AT ALL TIMES. DIFFERENT CHANNELS. IT KEEPS US FROM GOING STIR-CRAZY.
WHO SAID MY NAME?!
MORNING CONVERSATION, MAURICE!
OH! THAT WAS TECHNICALLY A QUESTION DIRECTED AT ME! MY TURN.
WHEN DID YOU ALL DIE?
I WISH THAT MAN WOULD MIND HIS TEMPER...
DIFFERENT TIMES FOR ALL OF US. I PREFER "PASSED ON," AND IT HAPPENED IN THE '90S.
TAKE A GUESS.
AW, CRAP! ALMOST LOST TRACK OF THE TIME!
I DIED FIVE YEARS AGO.
THIS CONVERSATION IS FAR FROM OVER!
BUT I GOTTA GET TO CAMPUS BEFORE CLASS...

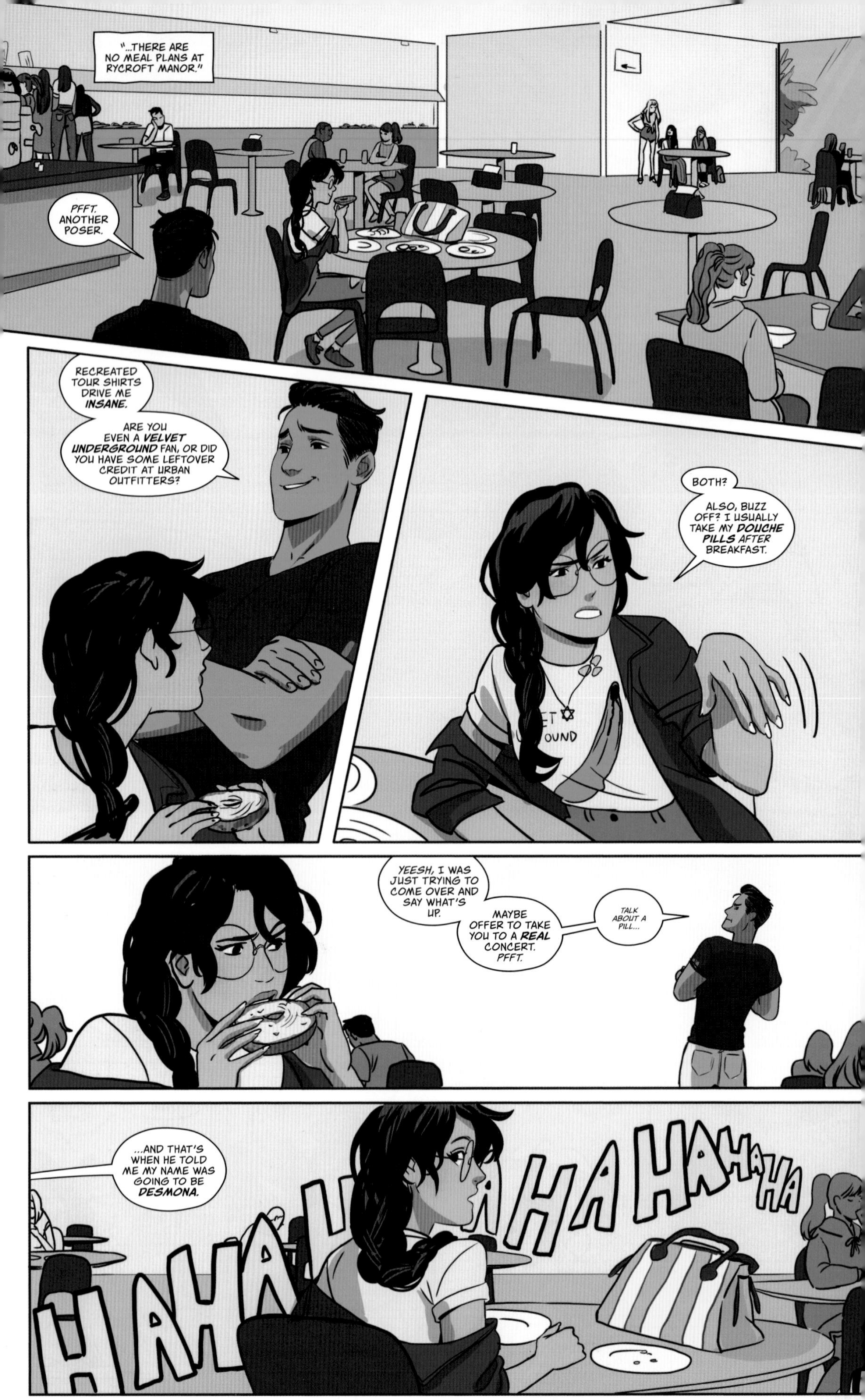
"...THERE ARE NO MEAL PLANS AT RYCROFT MANOR."
PFFT. ANOTHER POSER.
RECREATED TOUR SHIRTS DRIVE ME INSANE.
ARE YOU EVEN A VELVET UNDERGROUND FAN, OR DID YOU HAVE SOME LEFTOVER CREDIT AT URBAN OUTFITTERS?
BOTH?
ALSO, BUZZ OFF? I USUALLY TAKE MY DOUCHE PILLS AFTER BREAKFAST.
YEESH, I WAS JUST TRYING TO COME OVER AND SAY WHAT'S UP.
MAYBE OFFER TO TAKE YOU TO A REAL CONCERT. PFFT.
TALK ABOUT A PILL...
...AND THAT'S WHEN HE TOLD ME MY NAME WAS GOING TO BE DESMONA.
HAHAHAHAHAHAHAHAHA

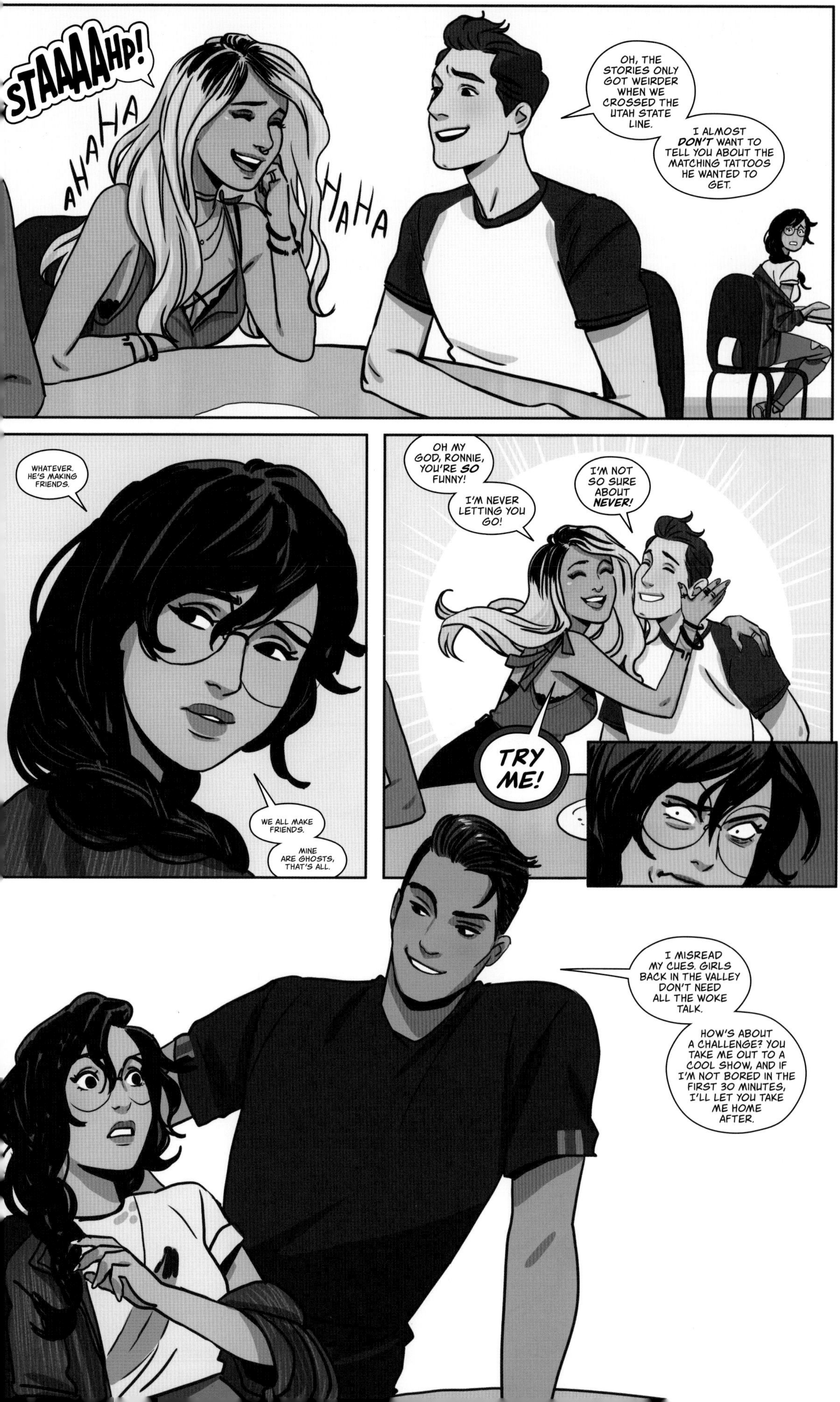
STAAAAHP!
AHAHAHA
HAHA
OH, THE STORIES ONLY GOT WEIRDER WHEN WE CROSSED THE UTAH STATE LINE.
I ALMOST **DON'T** WANT TO TELL YOU ABOUT THE MATCHING TATTOOS HE WANTED TO GET.
WHATEVER. HE'S MAKING FRIENDS.
WE ALL MAKE FRIENDS.
MINE ARE GHOSTS, THAT'S ALL.
OH MY GOD, RONNIE, YOU'RE **SO** FUNNY!
I'M NEVER LETTING YOU GO!
I'M NOT SO SURE ABOUT **NEVER!**
TRY ME!
I MISREAD MY CUES. GIRLS BACK IN THE VALLEY DON'T NEED ALL THE WOKE TALK.
HOW'S ABOUT A CHALLENGE? YOU TAKE ME OUT TO A COOL SHOW, AND IF I'M NOT BORED IN THE FIRST 30 MINUTES, I'LL LET YOU TAKE ME HOME AFTER.

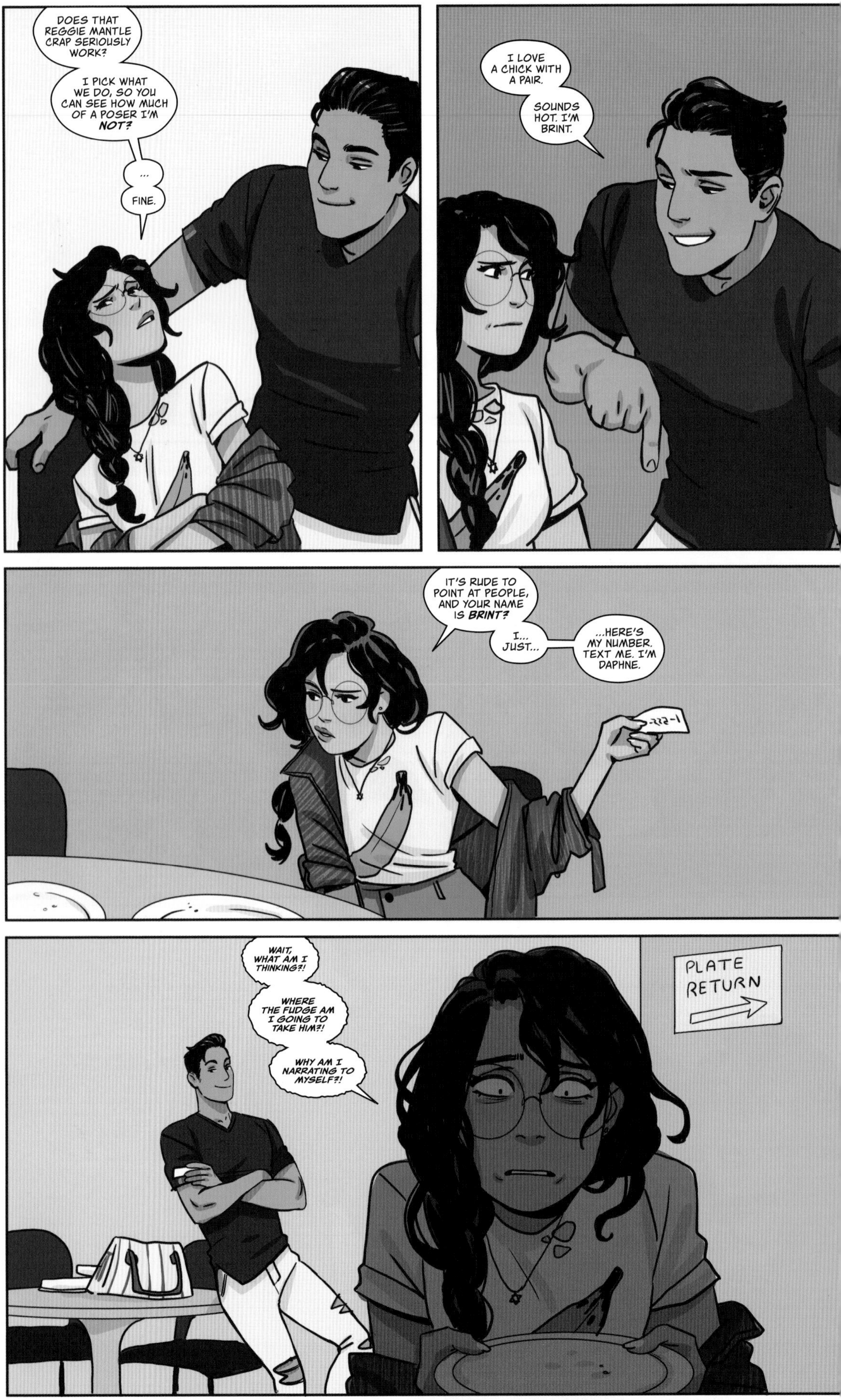
DOES THAT REGGIE MANTLE CRAP SERIOUSLY WORK?
I PICK WHAT WE DO, SO YOU CAN SEE HOW MUCH OF A POSER I'M NOT?
...
FINE.
I LOVE A CHICK WITH A PAIR.
SOUNDS HOT. I'M BRINT.
IT'S RUDE TO POINT AT PEOPLE, AND YOUR NAME IS BRINT?
I... JUST...
...HERE'S MY NUMBER. TEXT ME. I'M DAPHNE.
WAIT, WHAT AM I THINKING?!
WHERE THE FUDGE AM I GOING TO TAKE HIM?!
WHY AM I NARRATING TO MYSELF?!
PLATE RETURN

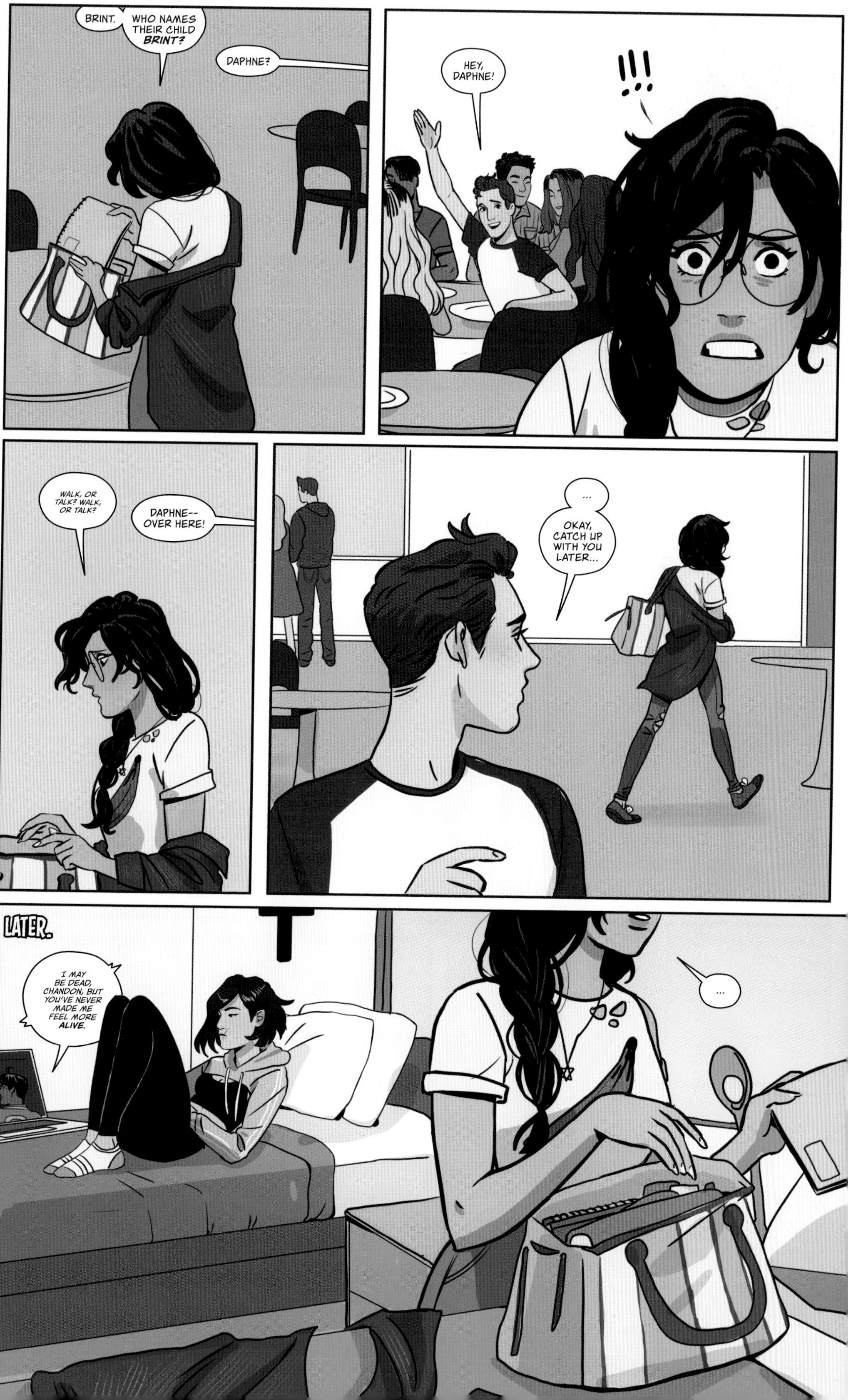
BRINT.
WHO NAMES THEIR CHILD BRINT?
DAPHNE?
HEY, DAPHNE!
!!!
WALK, OR TALK? WALK, OR TALK?
DAPHNE-- OVER HERE!
...
OKAY, CATCH UP WITH YOU LATER...
LATER.
I MAY BE DEAD, CHANDON, BUT YOU'VE NEVER MADE ME FEEL MORE ALIVE.
...

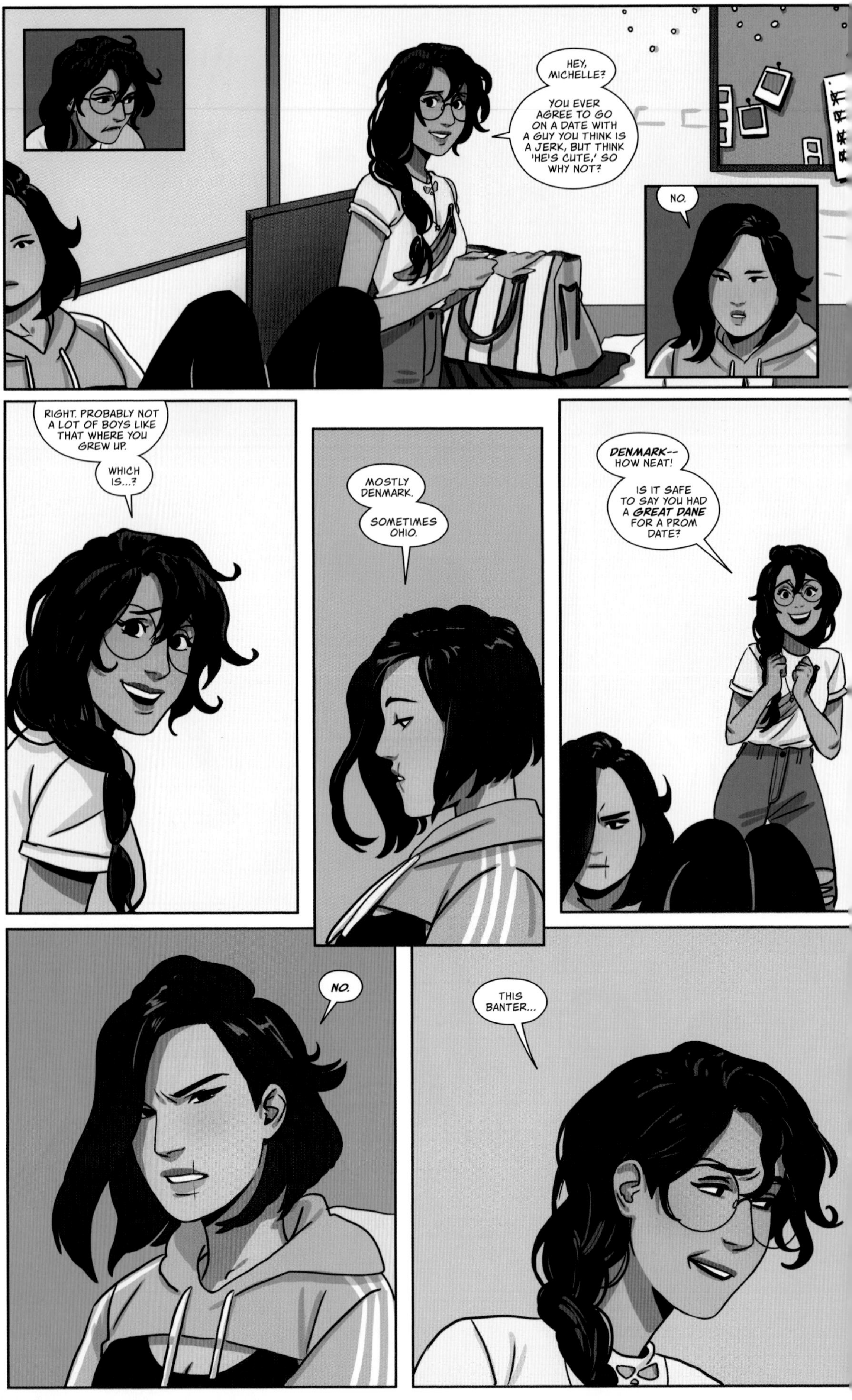
HEY, MICHELLE?
YOU EVER AGREE TO GO ON A DATE WITH A GUY YOU THINK IS A JERK, BUT THINK 'HE'S CUTE,' SO WHY NOT?
NO.
RIGHT. PROBABLY NOT A LOT OF BOYS LIKE THAT WHERE YOU GREW UP.
WHICH IS...?
MOSTLY DENMARK.
SOMETIMES OHIO.
DENMARK-- HOW NEAT!
IS IT SAFE TO SAY YOU HAD A GREAT DANE FOR A PROM DATE?
NO.
THIS BANTER...

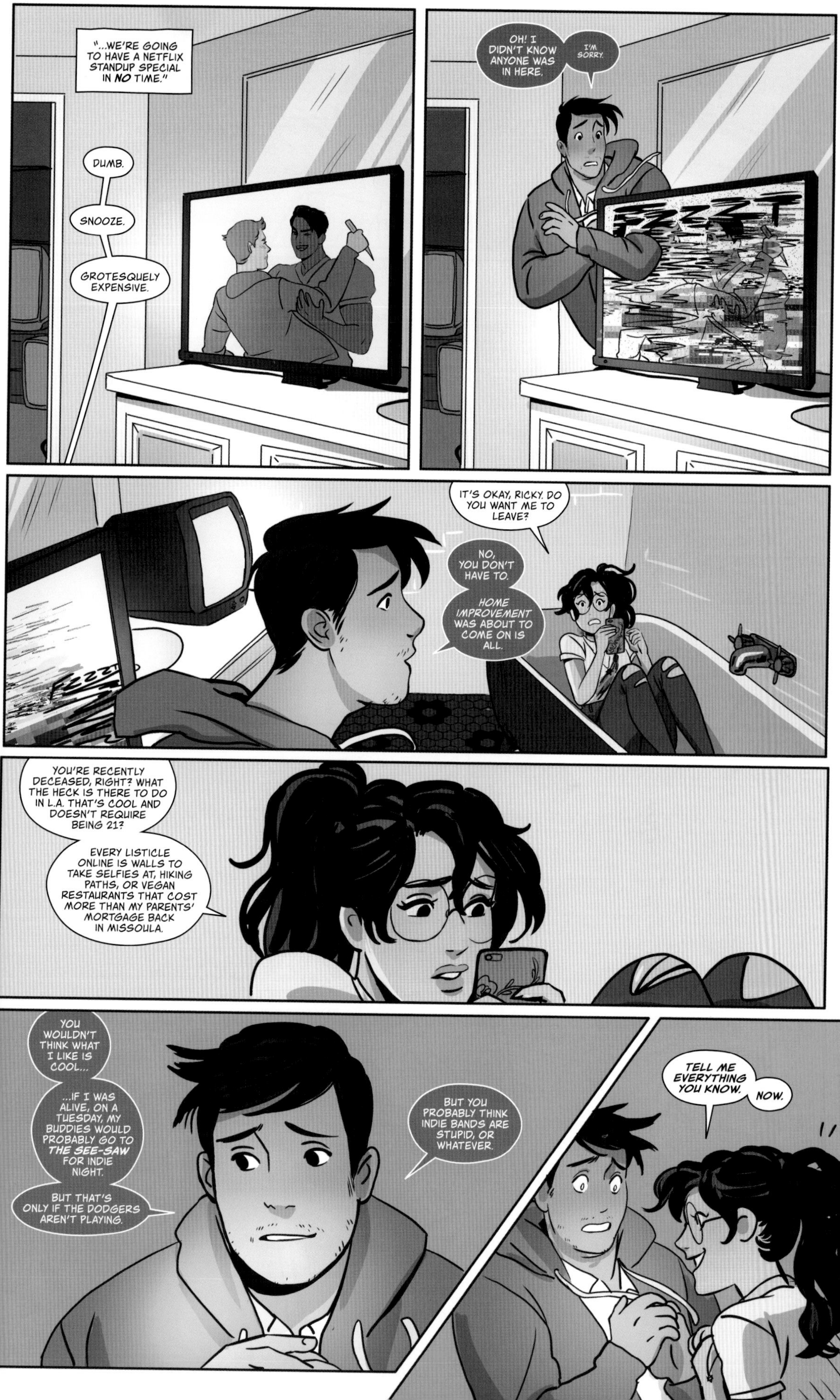

"...WE'RE GOING TO HAVE A NETFLIX STANDUP SPECIAL IN NO TIME."
DUMB.
SNOOZE.
GROTESQUELY EXPENSIVE.
OH! I DIDN'T KNOW ANYONE WAS IN HERE.
I'M SORRY.
FZZZZT
IT'S OKAY, RICKY. DO YOU WANT ME TO LEAVE?
NO, YOU DON'T HAVE TO.
HOME IMPROVEMENT WAS ABOUT TO COME ON IS ALL.
YOU'RE RECENTLY DECEASED, RIGHT? WHAT THE HECK IS THERE TO DO IN L.A. THAT'S COOL AND DOESN'T REQUIRE BEING 21?
EVERY LISTICLE ONLINE IS WALLS TO TAKE SELFIES AT, HIKING PATHS, OR VEGAN RESTAURANTS THAT COST MORE THAN MY PARENTS' MORTGAGE BACK IN MISSOULA.
YOU WOULDN'T THINK WHAT I LIKE IS COOL...
...IF I WAS ALIVE, ON A TUESDAY, MY BUDDIES WOULD PROBABLY GO TO THE SEE-SAW FOR INDIE NIGHT.
BUT THAT'S ONLY IF THE DODGERS AREN'T PLAYING.
BUT YOU PROBABLY THINK INDIE BANDS ARE STUPID, OR WHATEVER.
TELL ME EVERYTHING YOU KNOW.
NOW.

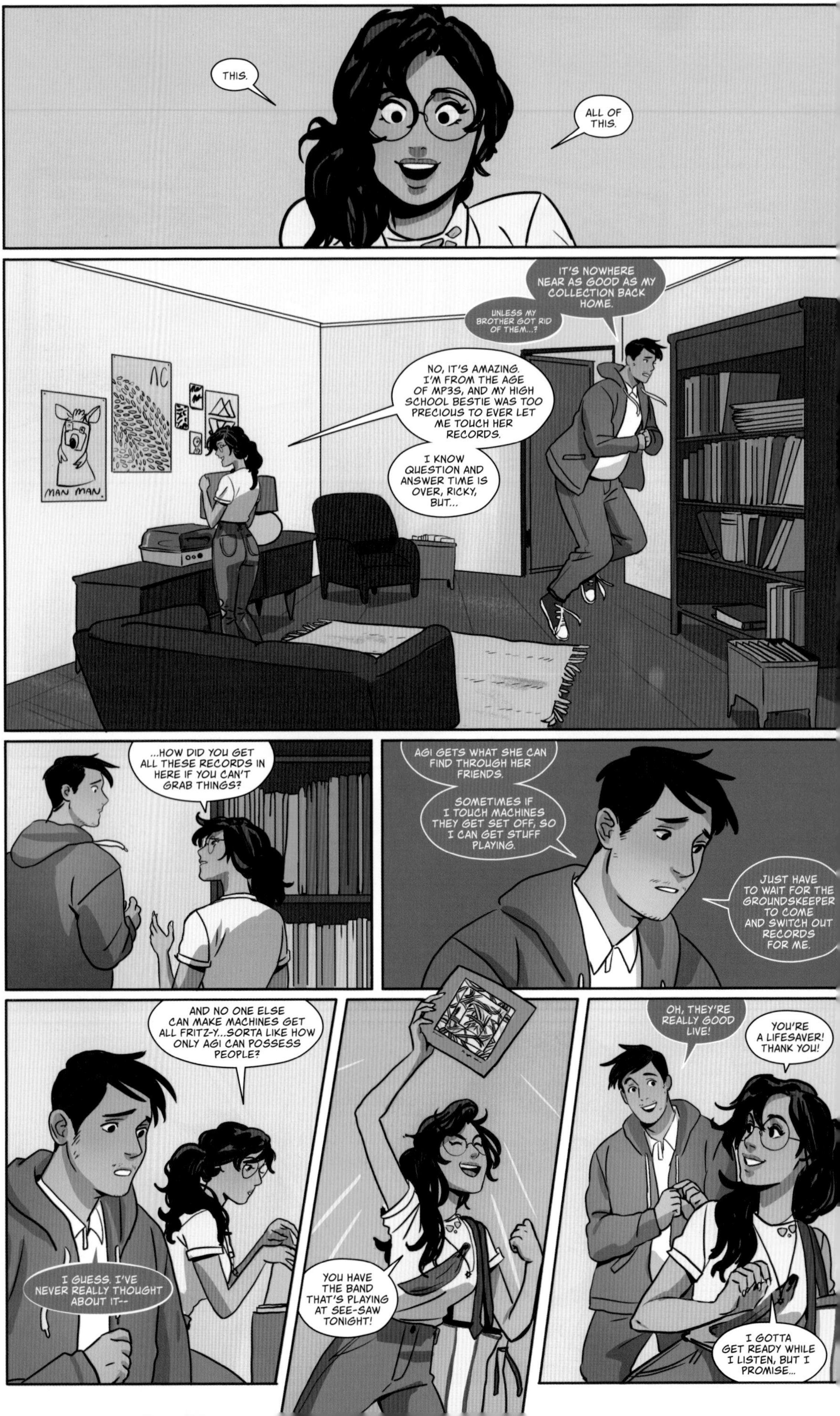
THIS.
ALL OF THIS.
IT'S NOWHERE NEAR AS GOOD AS MY COLLECTION BACK HOME.
UNLESS MY BROTHER GOT RID OF THEM...?
NO, IT'S AMAZING. I'M FROM THE AGE OF MP3S, AND MY HIGH SCHOOL BESTIE WAS TOO PRECIOUS TO EVER LET ME TOUCH HER RECORDS.
I KNOW QUESTION AND ANSWER TIME IS OVER, RICKY, BUT...
MAN MAN.
AC
...HOW DID YOU GET ALL THESE RECORDS IN HERE IF YOU CAN'T GRAB THINGS?
AGI GETS WHAT SHE CAN FIND THROUGH HER FRIENDS.
SOMETIMES IF I TOUCH MACHINES THEY GET SET OFF, SO I CAN GET STUFF PLAYING.
JUST HAVE TO WAIT FOR THE GROUNDSKEEPER TO COME AND SWITCH OUT RECORDS FOR ME.
AND NO ONE ELSE CAN MAKE MACHINES GET ALL FRITZ-Y...SORTA LIKE HOW ONLY AGI CAN POSSESS PEOPLE?
I GUESS. I'VE NEVER REALLY THOUGHT ABOUT IT--
YOU HAVE THE BAND THAT'S PLAYING AT SEE-SAW TONIGHT!
OH, THEY'RE REALLY GOOD LIVE!
YOU'RE A LIFESAVER! THANK YOU!
I GOTTA GET READY WHILE I LISTEN, BUT I PROMISE...

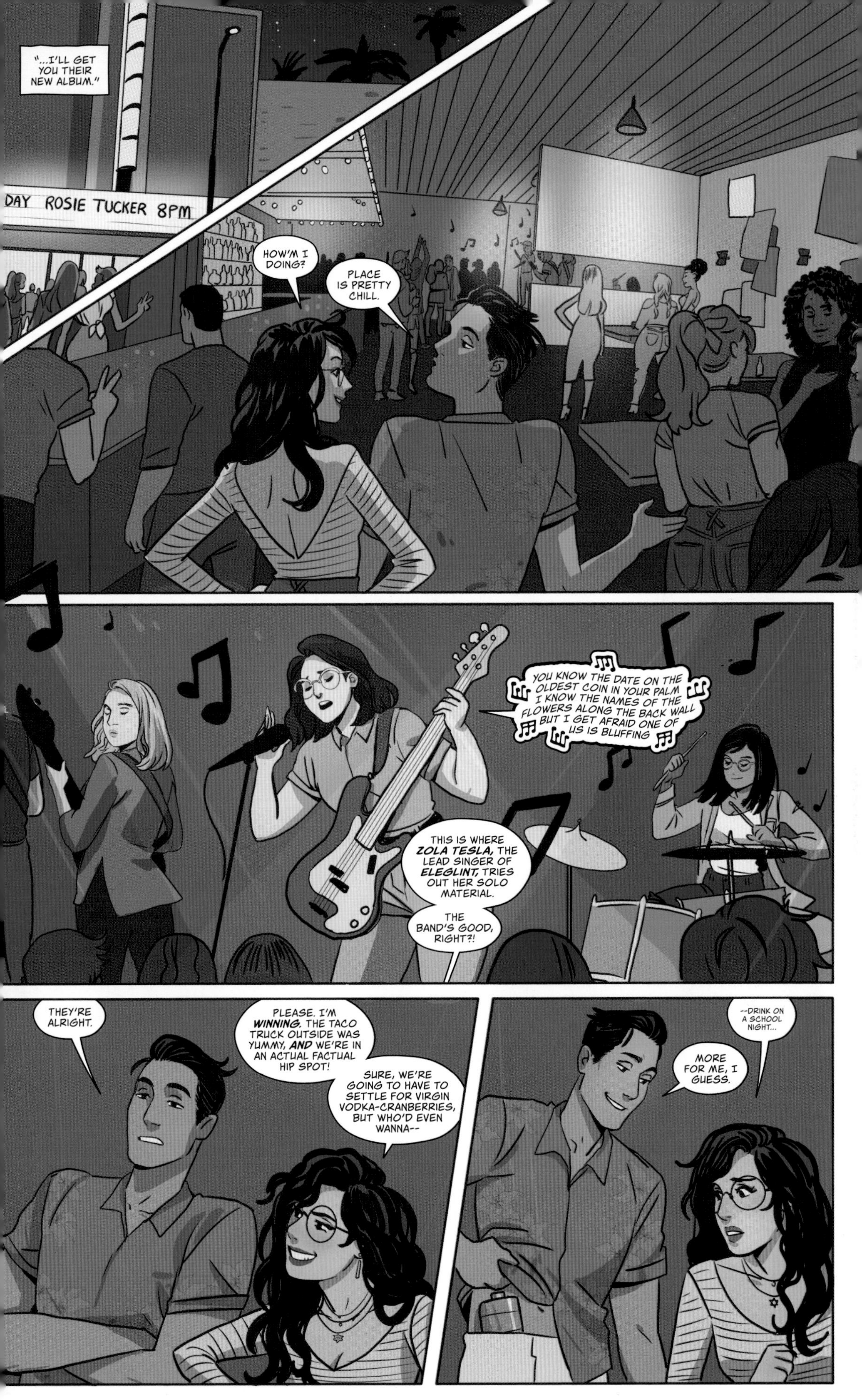
"...I'LL GET YOU THEIR NEW ALBUM."
DAY ROSIE TUCKER 8PM
HOW'M I DOING?
PLACE IS PRETTY CHILL.
YOU KNOW THE DATE ON THE OLDEST COIN IN YOUR PALM I KNOW THE NAMES OF THE FLOWERS ALONG THE BACK WALL BUT I GET AFRAID ONE OF US IS BLUFFING
THIS IS WHERE ZOLA TESLA, THE LEAD SINGER OF ELEGLINT, TRIES OUT HER SOLO MATERIAL.
THE BAND'S GOOD, RIGHT?!
THEY'RE ALRIGHT.
PLEASE. I'M WINNING. THE TACO TRUCK OUTSIDE WAS YUMMY, AND WE'RE IN AN ACTUAL FACTUAL HIP SPOT!
SURE, WE'RE GOING TO HAVE TO SETTLE FOR VIRGIN VODKA-CRANBERRIES, BUT WHO'D EVEN WANNA--
--DRINK ON A SCHOOL NIGHT...
MORE FOR ME, I GUESS.

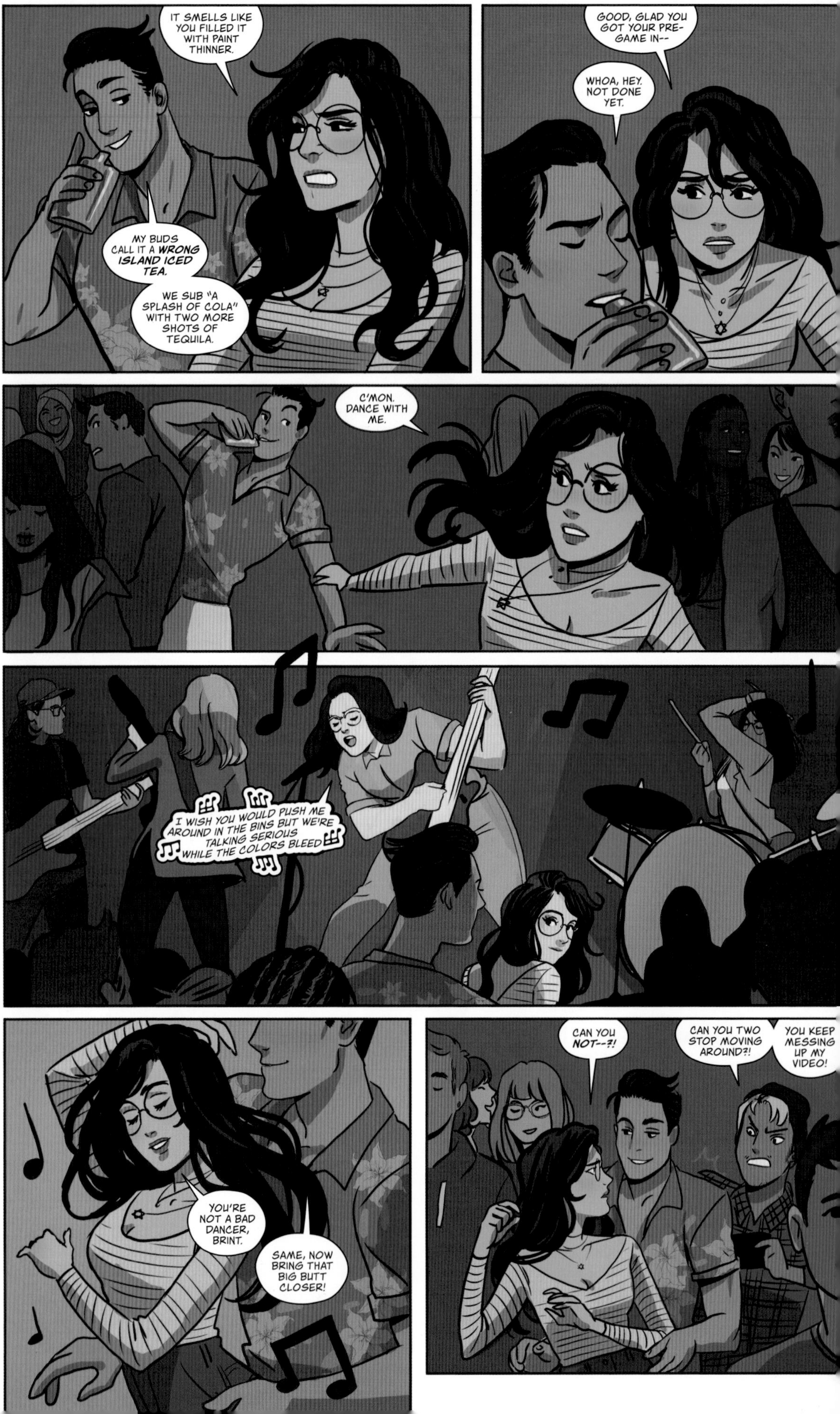
IT SMELLS LIKE YOU FILLED IT WITH PAINT THINNER.
MY BUDS CALL IT A **WRONG ISLAND ICED TEA.**
WE SUB "A SPLASH OF COLA" WITH TWO MORE SHOTS OF TEQUILA.
GOOD, GLAD YOU GOT YOUR PRE-GAME IN--
WHOA, HEY. NOT DONE YET.
C'MON. DANCE WITH ME.
I WISH YOU WOULD PUSH ME AROUND IN THE BINS BUT WE'RE TALKING SERIOUS WHILE THE COLORS BLEED
YOU'RE NOT A BAD DANCER, BRINT.
SAME, NOW BRING THAT BIG BUTT CLOSER!
CAN YOU *NOT--?!*
CAN YOU TWO STOP MOVING AROUND?!
YOU KEEP MESSING UP MY VIDEO!

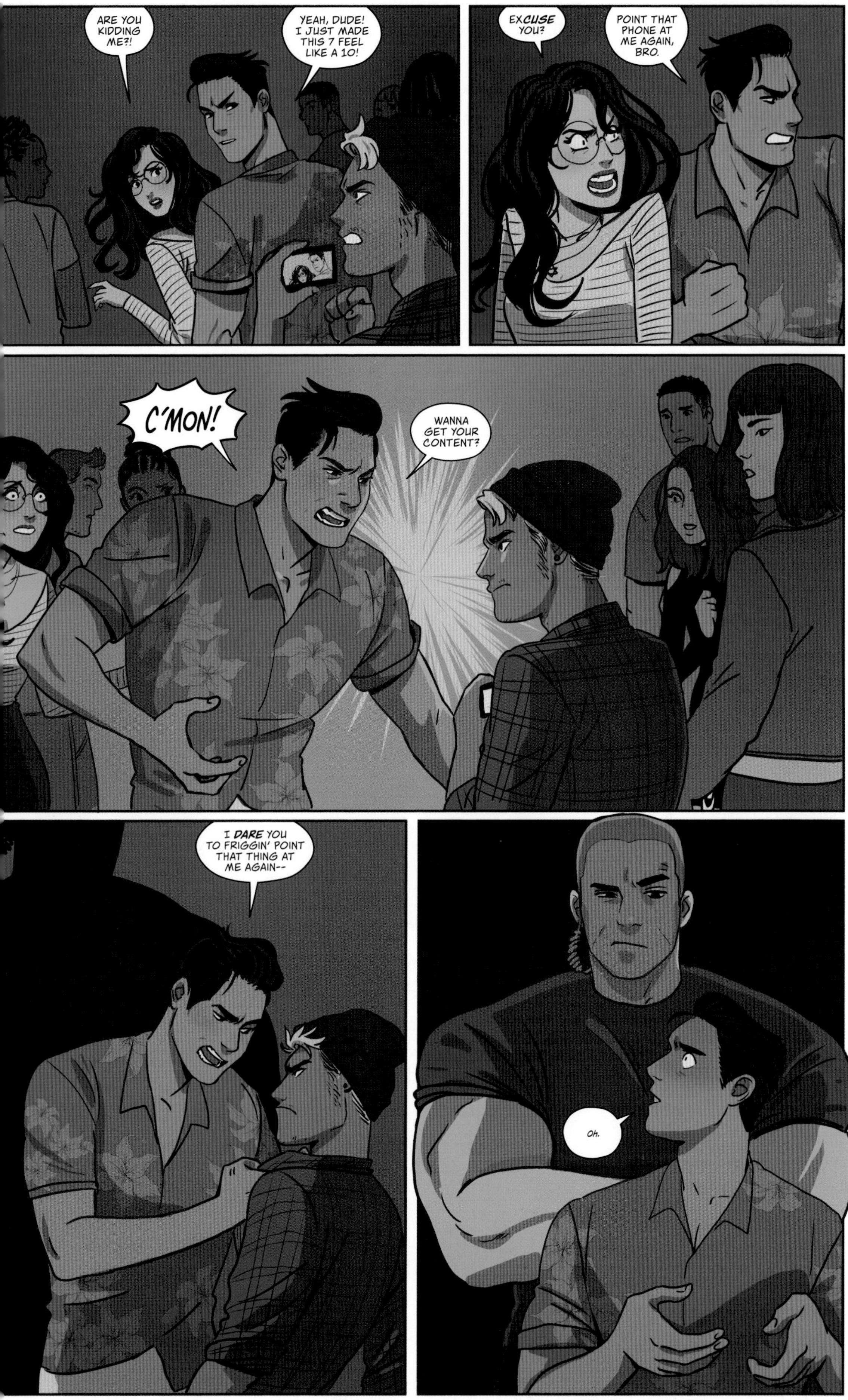
ARE YOU KIDDING ME?!
YEAH, DUDE! I JUST MADE THIS 7 FEEL LIKE A 10!
EXCUSE YOU?
POINT THAT PHONE AT ME AGAIN, BRO.
C'MON!
WANNA GET YOUR CONTENT?
I DARE YOU TO FRIGGIN' POINT THAT THING AT ME AGAIN--
Oh.

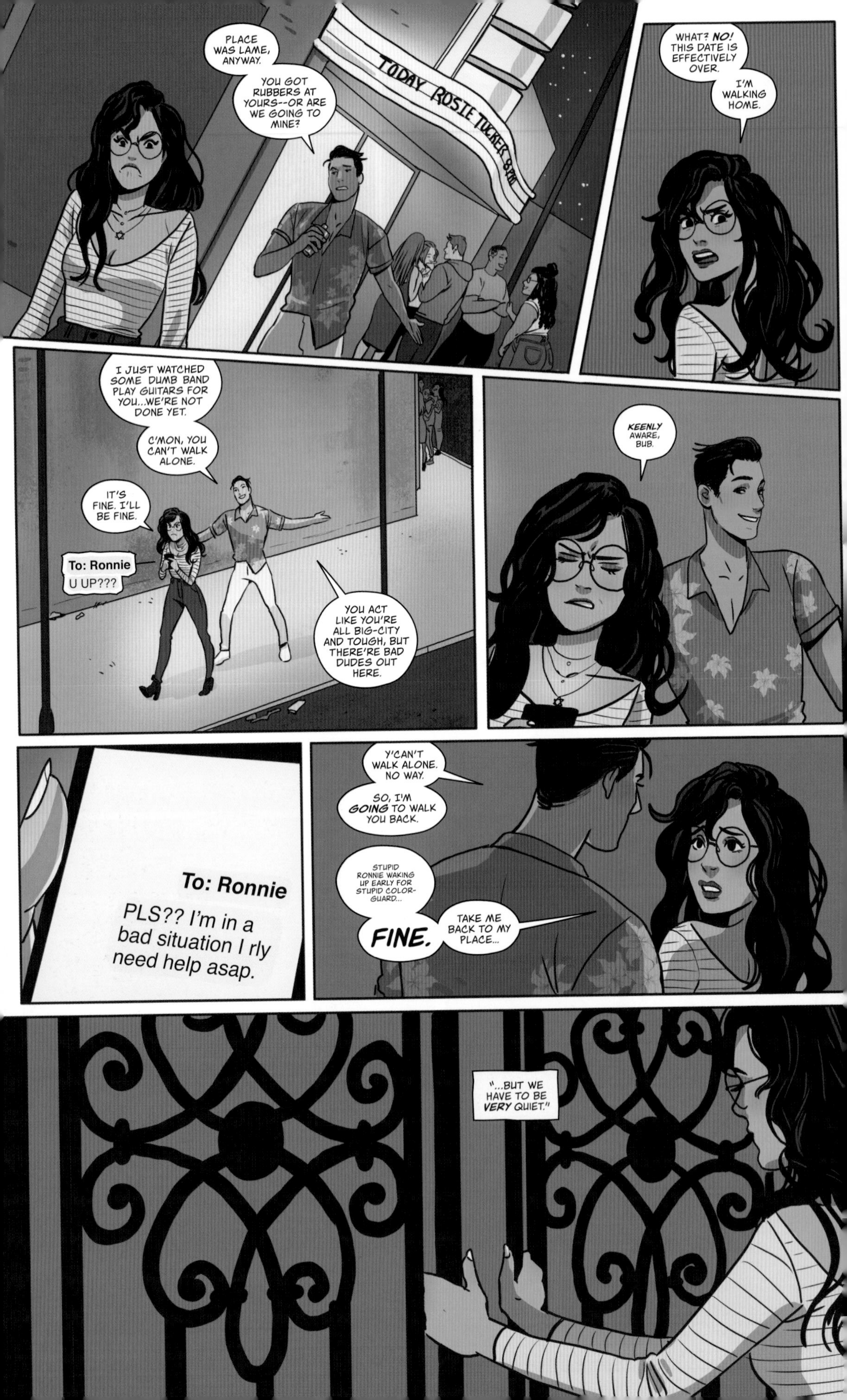
PLACE WAS LAME, ANYWAY.
YOU GOT RUBBERS AT YOURS--OR ARE WE GOING TO MINE?
TODAY ROSIE TUCKER 8PM
WHAT? NO! THIS DATE IS EFFECTIVELY OVER.
I'M WALKING HOME.
I JUST WATCHED SOME DUMB BAND PLAY GUITARS FOR YOU...WE'RE NOT DONE YET.
C'MON, YOU CAN'T WALK ALONE.
IT'S FINE. I'LL BE FINE.
To: Ronnie
U UP???
YOU ACT LIKE YOU'RE ALL BIG-CITY AND TOUGH, BUT THERE'RE BAD DUDES OUT HERE.
KEENLY AWARE, BUB.
To: Ronnie
PLS?? I'm in a bad situation I rly need help asap.
Y'CAN'T WALK ALONE. NO WAY.
SO, I'M GOING TO WALK YOU BACK.
STUPID RONNIE WAKING UP EARLY FOR STUPID COLOR-GUARD...
FINE.
TAKE ME BACK TO MY PLACE...
"...BUT WE HAVE TO BE VERY QUIET."

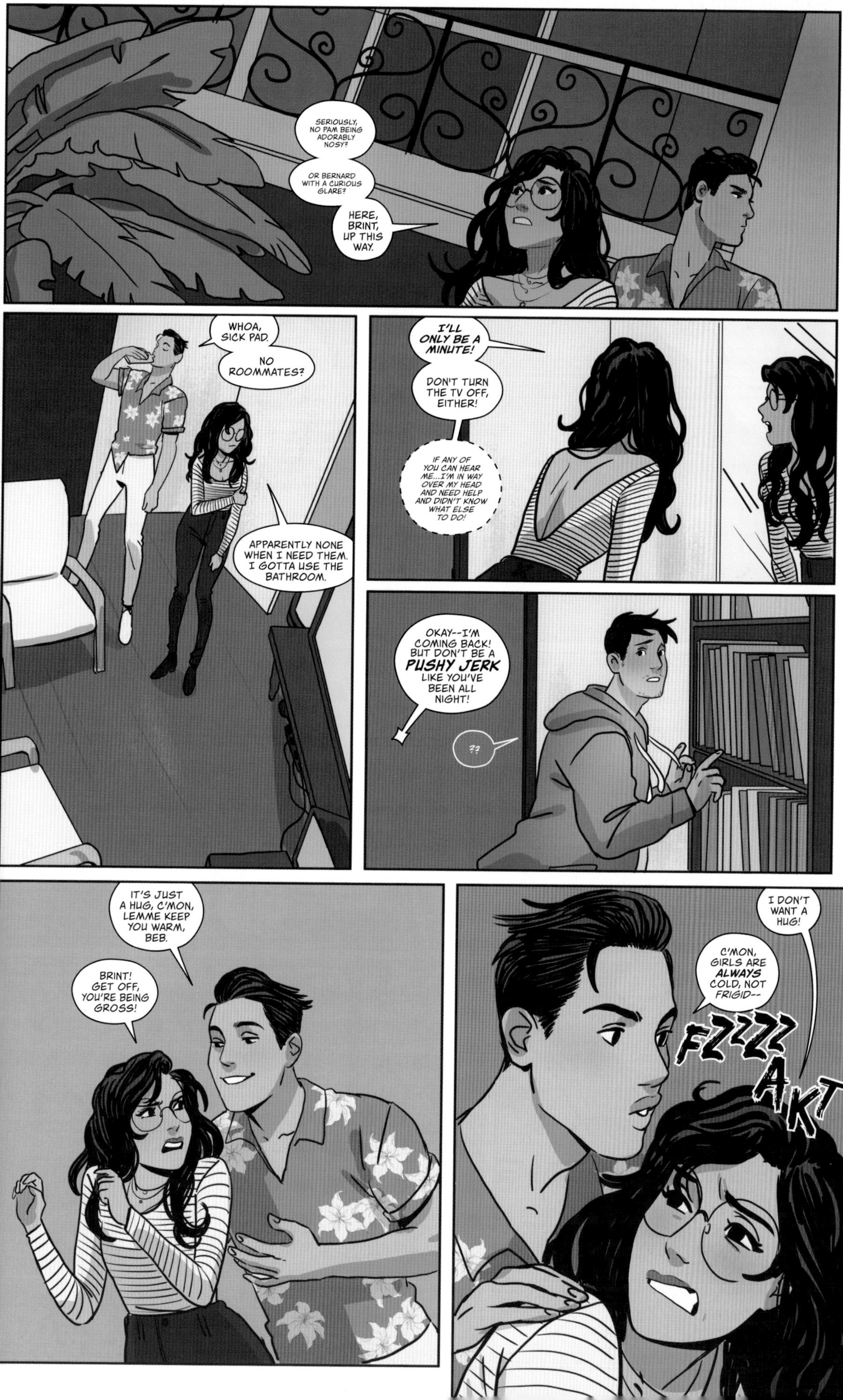

SERIOUSLY, NO PAM BEING ADORABLY NOSY?
OR BERNARD WITH A CURIOUS GLARE?
HERE, BRINT, UP THIS WAY.
WHOA, SICK PAD.
NO ROOMMATES?
APPARENTLY NONE WHEN I NEED THEM. I GOTTA USE THE BATHROOM.
I'LL ONLY BE A MINUTE!
DON'T TURN THE TV OFF, EITHER!
IF ANY OF YOU CAN HEAR ME...I'M IN WAY OVER MY HEAD AND NEED HELP AND DIDN'T KNOW WHAT ELSE TO DO!
OKAY--I'M COMING BACK! BUT DON'T BE A PUSHY JERK LIKE YOU'VE BEEN ALL NIGHT!
??
IT'S JUST A HUG, C'MON, LEMME KEEP YOU WARM, BEB.
BRINT! GET OFF, YOU'RE BEING GROSS!
I DON'T WANT A HUG!
C'MON, GIRLS ARE ALWAYS COLD, NOT FRIGID--
FZZZZAKT

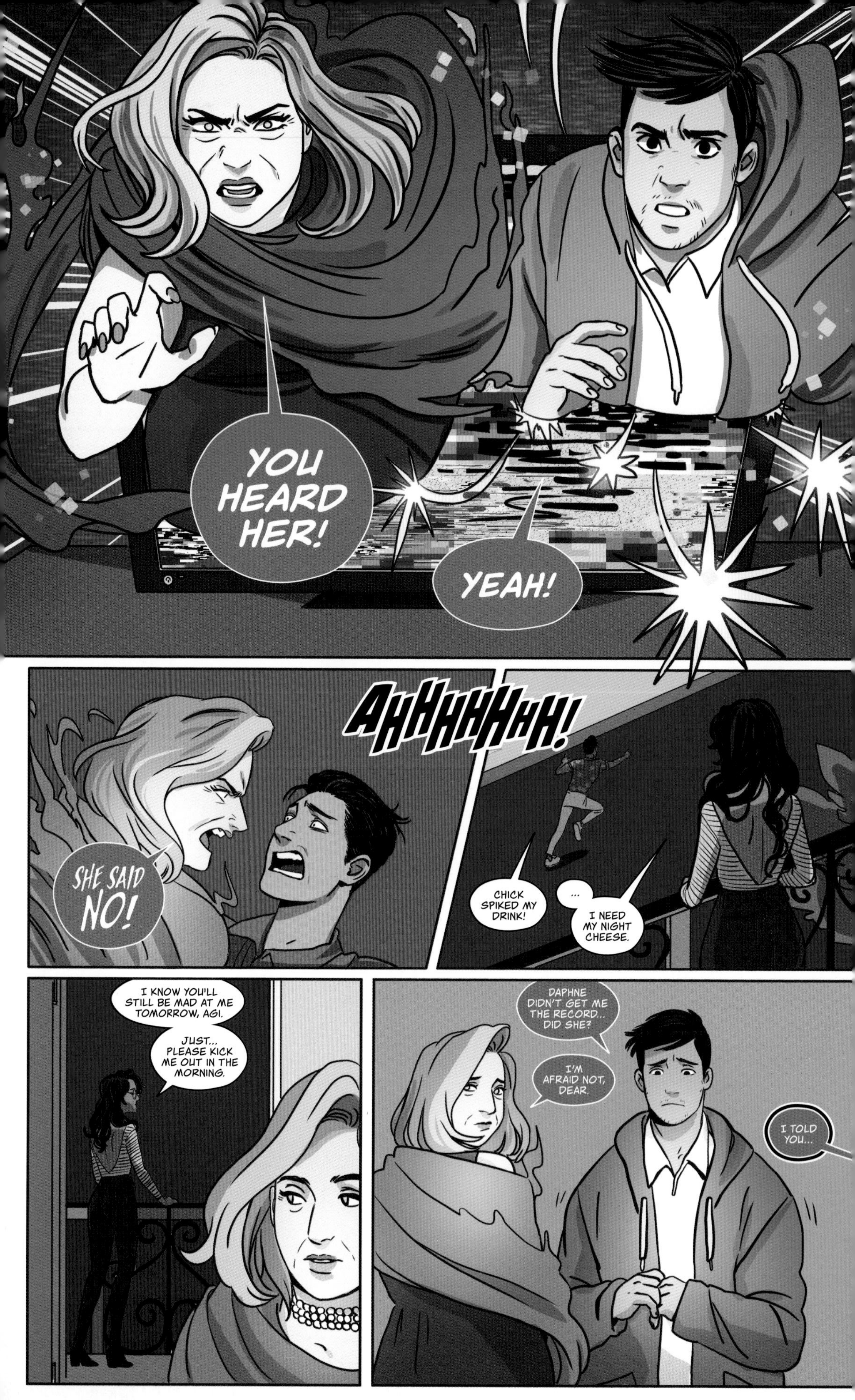
YOU HEARD HER!
YEAH!
AHHHHHHH!
SHE SAID NO!
CHICK SPIKED MY DRINK!
...
I NEED MY NIGHT CHEESE.
I KNOW YOU'LL STILL BE MAD AT ME TOMORROW, AGI.
JUST... PLEASE KICK ME OUT IN THE MORNING.
DAPHNE DIDN'T GET ME THE RECORD... DID SHE?
I'M AFRAID NOT, DEAR.
I TOLD YOU...

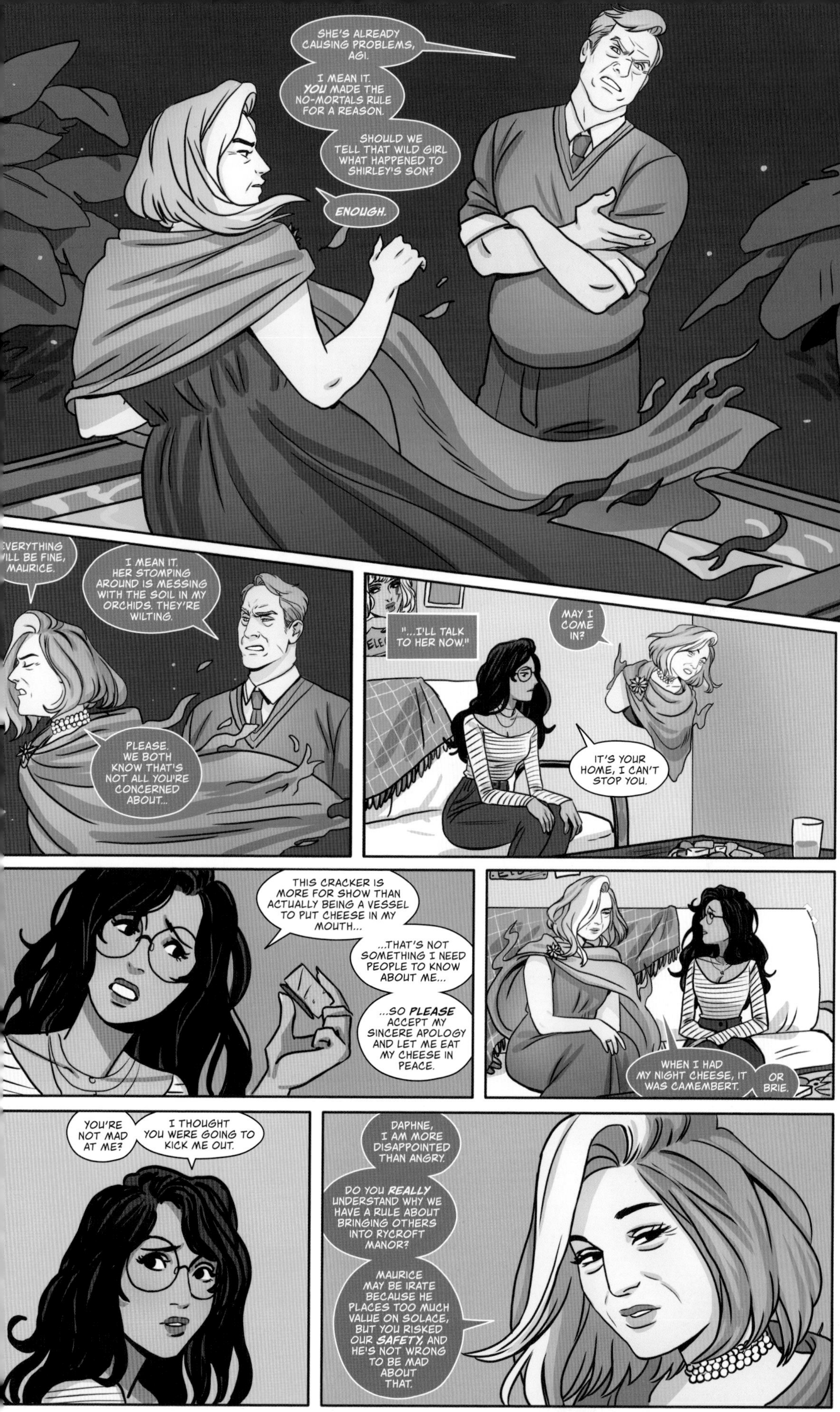
SHE'S ALREADY CAUSING PROBLEMS, AGI.
I MEAN IT. YOU MADE THE NO-MORTALS RULE FOR A REASON.
SHOULD WE TELL THAT WILD GIRL WHAT HAPPENED TO SHIRLEY'S SON?
ENOUGH.
EVERYTHING WILL BE FINE, MAURICE.
I MEAN IT. HER STOMPING AROUND IS MESSING WITH THE SOIL IN MY ORCHIDS. THEY'RE WILTING.
PLEASE. WE BOTH KNOW THAT'S NOT ALL YOU'RE CONCERNED ABOUT...
"...I'LL TALK TO HER NOW."
MAY I COME IN?
IT'S YOUR HOME, I CAN'T STOP YOU.
THIS CRACKER IS MORE FOR SHOW THAN ACTUALLY BEING A VESSEL TO PUT CHEESE IN MY MOUTH...
...THAT'S NOT SOMETHING I NEED PEOPLE TO KNOW ABOUT ME...
...SO PLEASE ACCEPT MY SINCERE APOLOGY AND LET ME EAT MY CHEESE IN PEACE.
WHEN I HAD MY NIGHT CHEESE, IT WAS CAMEMBERT.
OR BRIE.
YOU'RE NOT MAD AT ME?
I THOUGHT YOU WERE GOING TO KICK ME OUT.
DAPHNE, I AM MORE DISAPPOINTED THAN ANGRY.
DO YOU REALLY UNDERSTAND WHY WE HAVE A RULE ABOUT BRINGING OTHERS INTO RYCROFT MANOR?
MAURICE MAY BE IRATE BECAUSE HE PLACES TOO MUCH VALUE ON SOLACE, BUT YOU RISKED OUR SAFETY, AND HE'S NOT WRONG TO BE MAD ABOUT THAT.

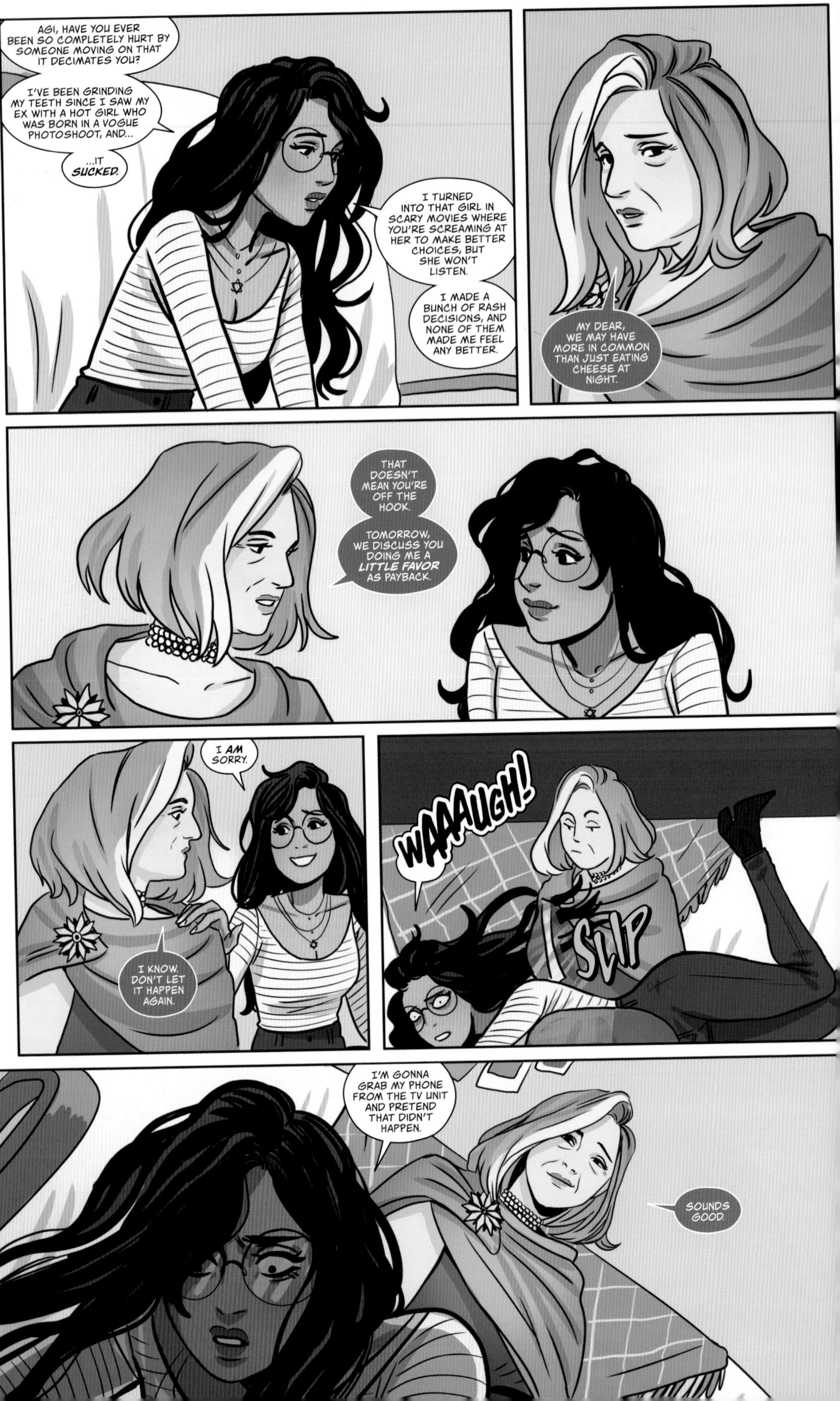
AGI, HAVE YOU EVER BEEN SO COMPLETELY HURT BY SOMEONE MOVING ON THAT IT DECIMATES YOU?
I'VE BEEN GRINDING MY TEETH SINCE I SAW MY EX WITH A HOT GIRL WHO WAS BORN IN A VOGUE PHOTOSHOOT, AND...
...IT SUCKED.
I TURNED INTO THAT GIRL IN SCARY MOVIES WHERE YOU'RE SCREAMING AT HER TO MAKE BETTER CHOICES, BUT SHE WON'T LISTEN.
I MADE A BUNCH OF RASH DECISIONS, AND NONE OF THEM MADE ME FEEL ANY BETTER.
MY DEAR, WE MAY HAVE MORE IN COMMON THAN JUST EATING CHEESE AT NIGHT.
THAT DOESN'T MEAN YOU'RE OFF THE HOOK.
TOMORROW, WE DISCUSS YOU DOING ME A LITTLE FAVOR AS PAYBACK.
I AM SORRY.
I KNOW. DON'T LET IT HAPPEN AGAIN.
WAAAUGH!
SLIP
I'M GONNA GRAB MY PHONE FROM THE TV UNIT AND PRETEND THAT DIDN'T HAPPEN.
SOUNDS GOOD.

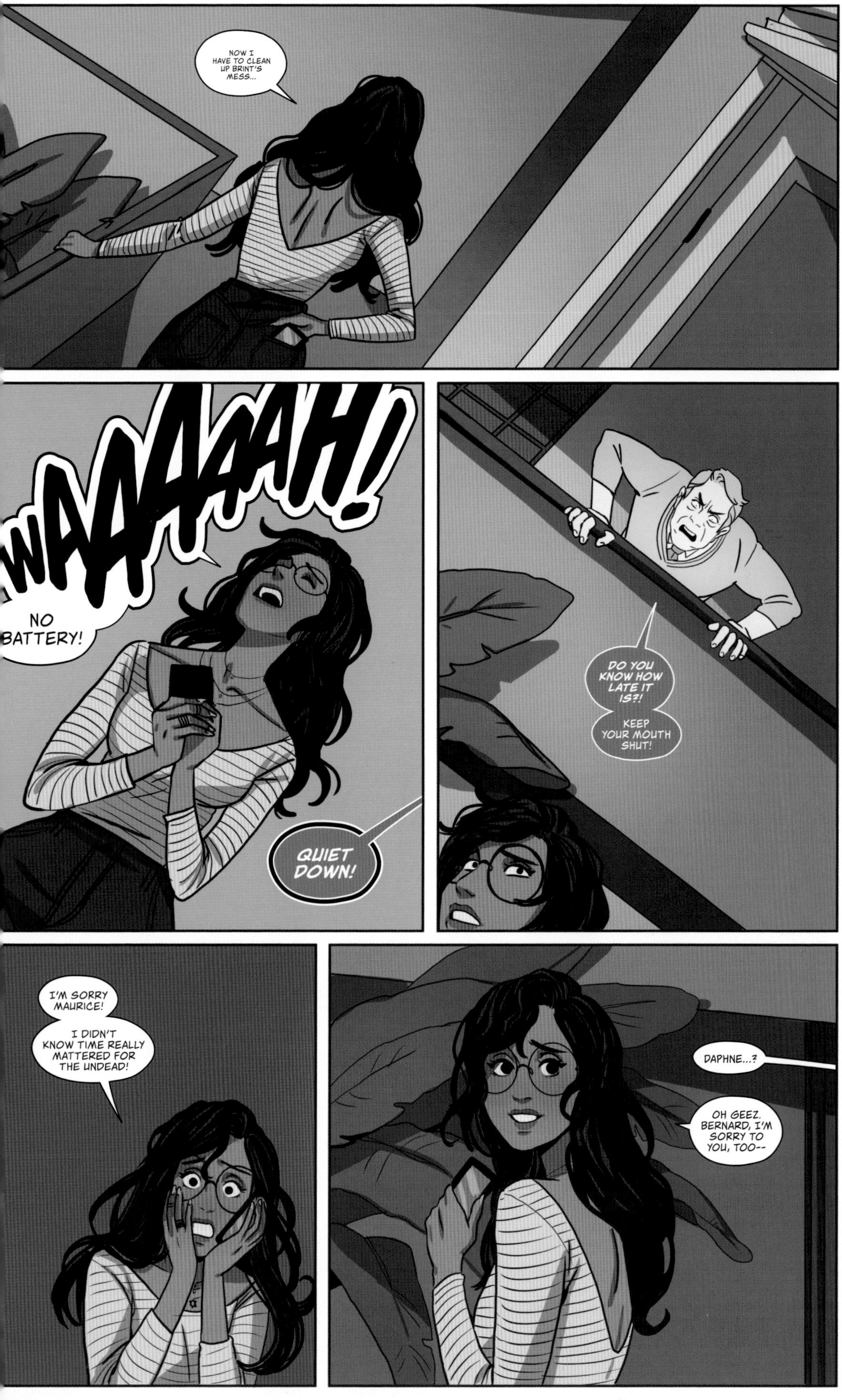
NOW I HAVE TO CLEAN UP BRINT'S MESS...
WAAAAAH!
NO BATTERY!
QUIET DOWN!
DO YOU KNOW HOW LATE IT IS?!
KEEP YOUR MOUTH SHUT!
I'M SORRY MAURICE!
I DIDN'T KNOW TIME REALLY MATTERED FOR THE UNDEAD!
DAPHNE...?
OH GEEZ. BERNARD, I'M SORRY TO YOU, TOO--

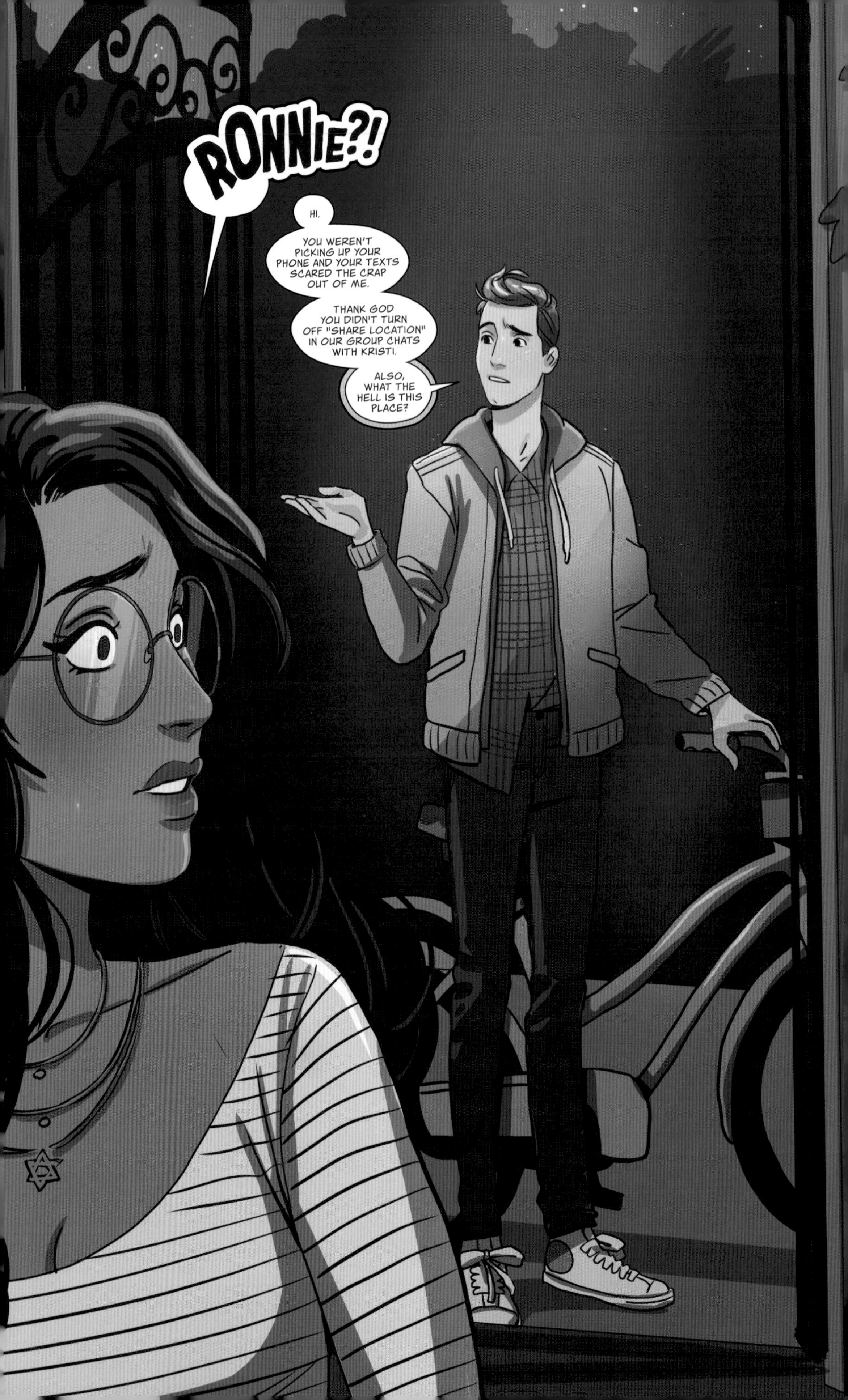
RONNIE?!
HI.
YOU WEREN'T PICKING UP YOUR PHONE AND YOUR TEXTS SCARED THE CRAP OUT OF ME.
THANK GOD YOU DIDN'T TURN OFF "SHARE LOCATION" IN OUR GROUP CHATS WITH KRISTI.
ALSO, WHAT THE HELL IS THIS PLACE?

Chapter Three

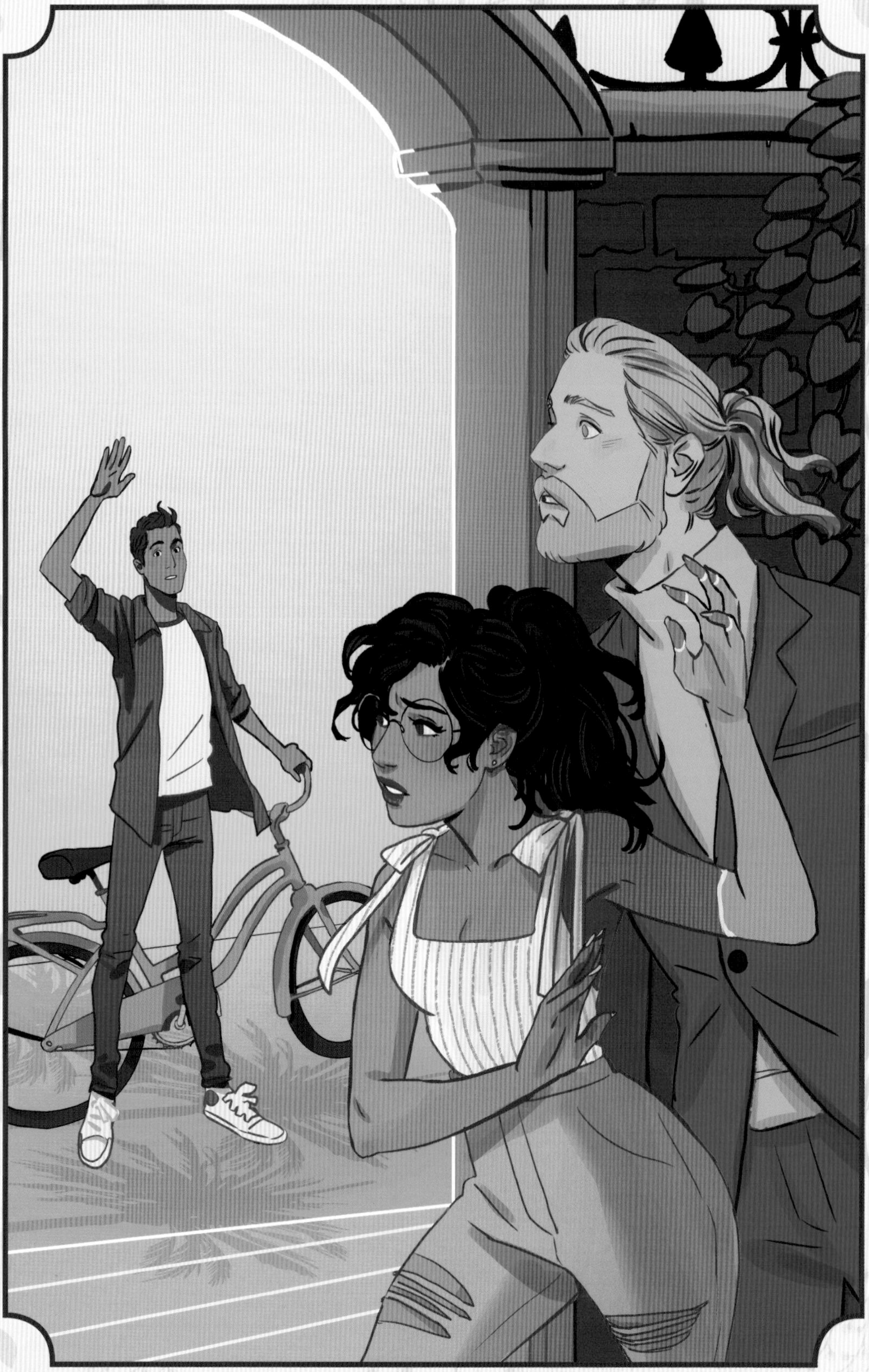

Issue Three Cover by **Siobhan Keenan**

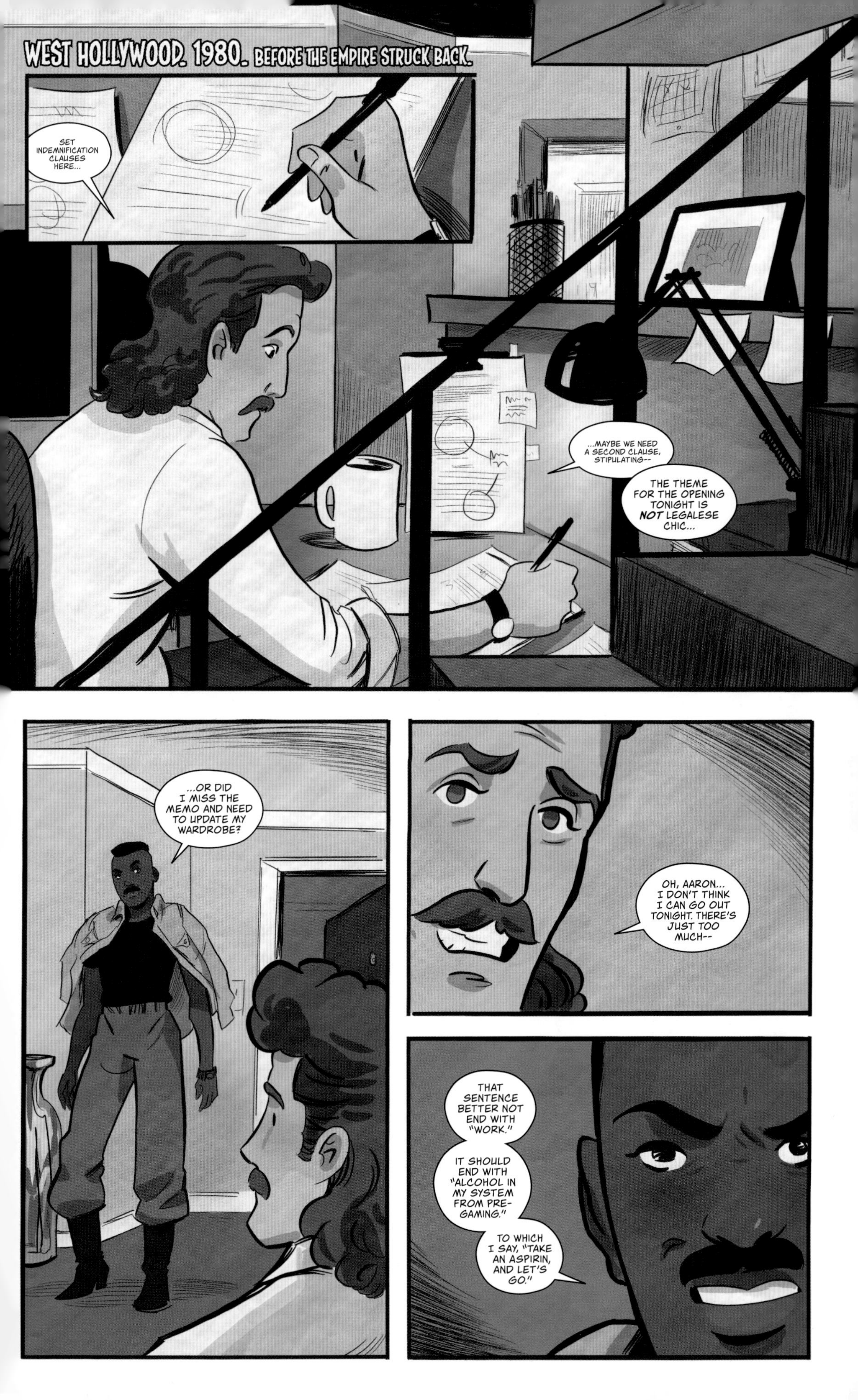
WEST HOLLYWOOD. 1980. BEFORE THE EMPIRE STRUCK BACK.
SET INDEMNIFICATION CLAUSES HERE...
...MAYBE WE NEED A SECOND CLAUSE, STIPULATING--
THE THEME FOR THE OPENING TONIGHT IS NOT LEGALESE CHIC...
...OR DID I MISS THE MEMO AND NEED TO UPDATE MY WARDROBE?
OH, AARON... I DON'T THINK I CAN GO OUT TONIGHT. THERE'S JUST TOO MUCH--
THAT SENTENCE BETTER NOT END WITH "WORK."
IT SHOULD END WITH "ALCOHOL IN MY SYSTEM FROM PRE-GAMING."
TO WHICH I SAY, "TAKE AN ASPIRIN, AND LET'S GO."

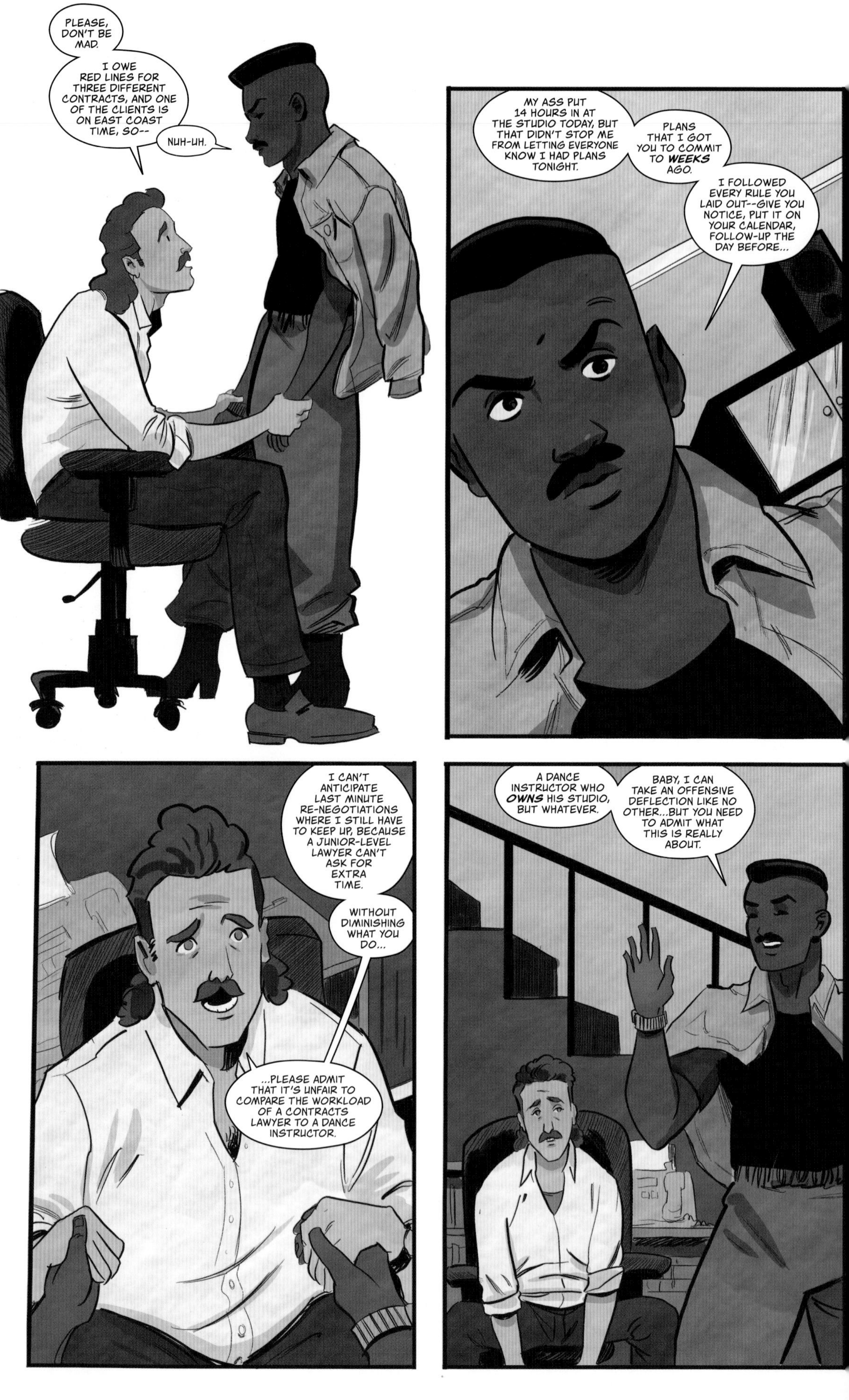
PLEASE, DON'T BE MAD.
I OWE RED LINES FOR THREE DIFFERENT CONTRACTS, AND ONE OF THE CLIENTS IS ON EAST COAST TIME, SO--
NUH-UH.
MY ASS PUT 14 HOURS IN AT THE STUDIO TODAY, BUT THAT DIDN'T STOP ME FROM LETTING EVERYONE KNOW I HAD PLANS TONIGHT.
PLANS THAT I GOT YOU TO COMMIT TO WEEKS AGO.
I FOLLOWED EVERY RULE YOU LAID OUT--GIVE YOU NOTICE, PUT IT ON YOUR CALENDAR, FOLLOW-UP THE DAY BEFORE...
I CAN'T ANTICIPATE LAST MINUTE RE-NEGOTIATIONS WHERE I STILL HAVE TO KEEP UP, BECAUSE A JUNIOR-LEVEL LAWYER CAN'T ASK FOR EXTRA TIME.
WITHOUT DIMINISHING WHAT YOU DO...
...PLEASE ADMIT THAT IT'S UNFAIR TO COMPARE THE WORKLOAD OF A CONTRACTS LAWYER TO A DANCE INSTRUCTOR.
A DANCE INSTRUCTOR WHO OWNS HIS STUDIO, BUT WHATEVER.
BABY, I CAN TAKE AN OFFENSIVE DEFLECTION LIKE NO OTHER...BUT YOU NEED TO ADMIT WHAT THIS IS REALLY ABOUT.

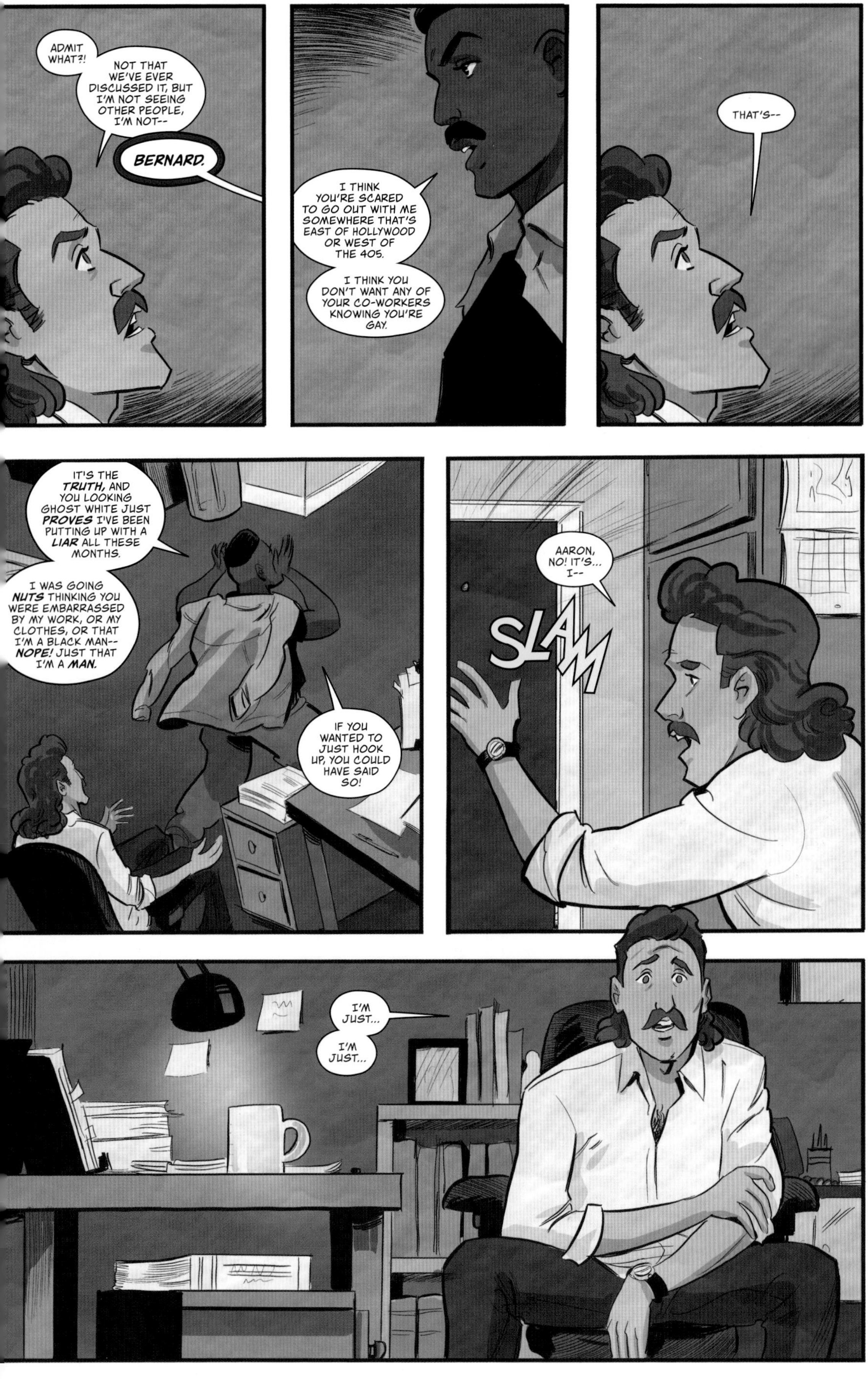
ADMIT WHAT?!
NOT THAT WE'VE EVER DISCUSSED IT, BUT I'M NOT SEEING OTHER PEOPLE, I'M NOT--
BERNARD.
I THINK YOU'RE SCARED TO GO OUT WITH ME SOMEWHERE THAT'S EAST OF HOLLYWOOD OR WEST OF THE 405.
I THINK YOU DON'T WANT ANY OF YOUR CO-WORKERS KNOWING YOU'RE GAY.
THAT'S--
IT'S THE TRUTH, AND YOU LOOKING GHOST WHITE JUST PROVES I'VE BEEN PUTTING UP WITH A LIAR ALL THESE MONTHS.
I WAS GOING NUTS THINKING YOU WERE EMBARRASSED BY MY WORK, OR MY CLOTHES, OR THAT I'M A BLACK MAN-- NOPE! JUST THAT I'M A MAN.
IF YOU WANTED TO JUST HOOK UP, YOU COULD HAVE SAID SO!
AARON, NO! IT'S... I--
SLAM
I'M JUST...
I'M JUST...

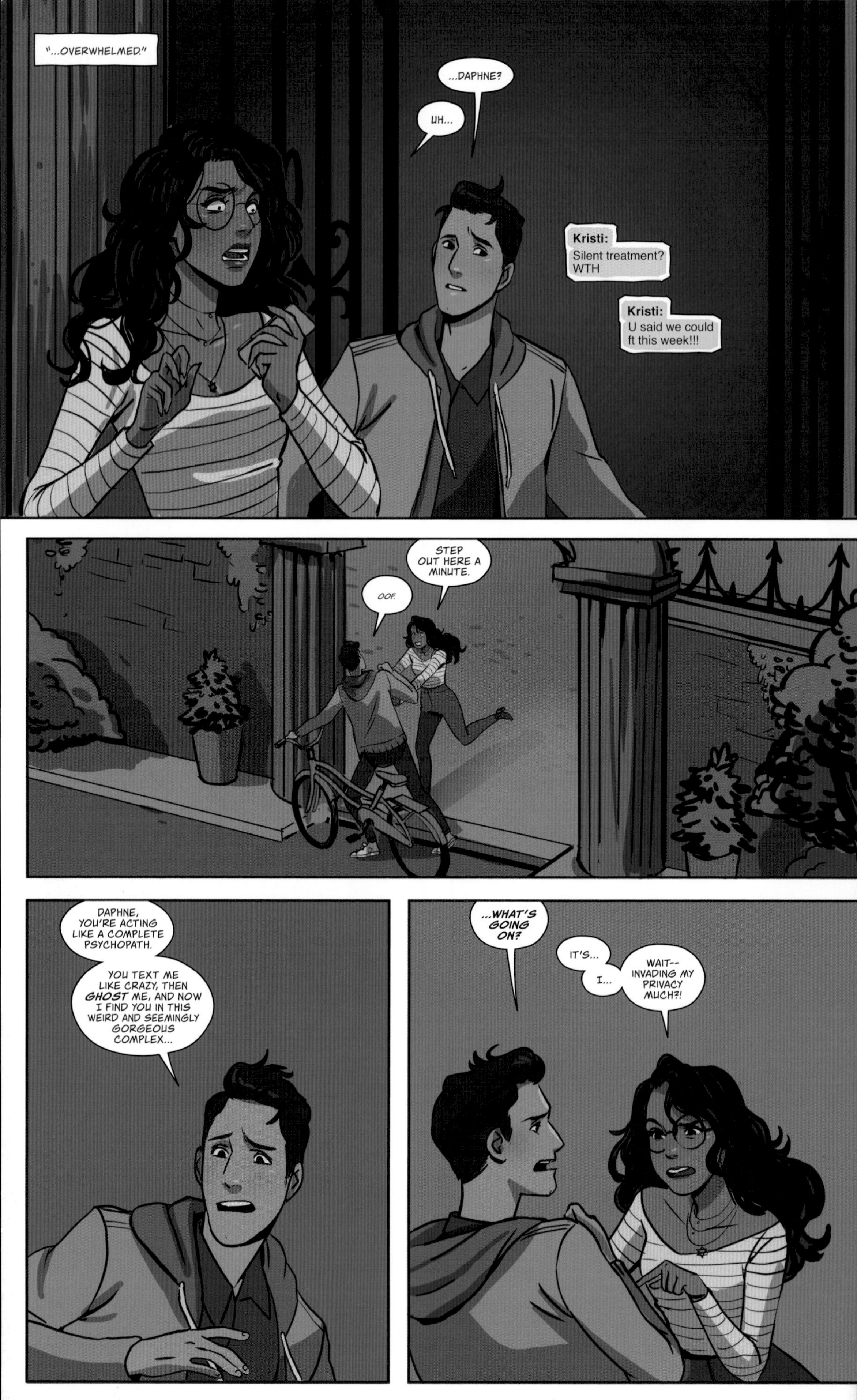
"...OVERWHELMED."
UH...
...DAPHNE?
Kristi:
Silent treatment? WTH
Kristi:
U said we could ft this week!!!
STEP OUT HERE A MINUTE.
OOF.
DAPHNE, YOU'RE ACTING LIKE A COMPLETE PSYCHOPATH.
YOU TEXT ME LIKE CRAZY, THEN GHOST ME, AND NOW I FIND YOU IN THIS WEIRD AND SEEMINGLY GORGEOUS COMPLEX...
...WHAT'S GOING ON?
IT'S...
I...
WAIT-- INVADING MY PRIVACY MUCH?!

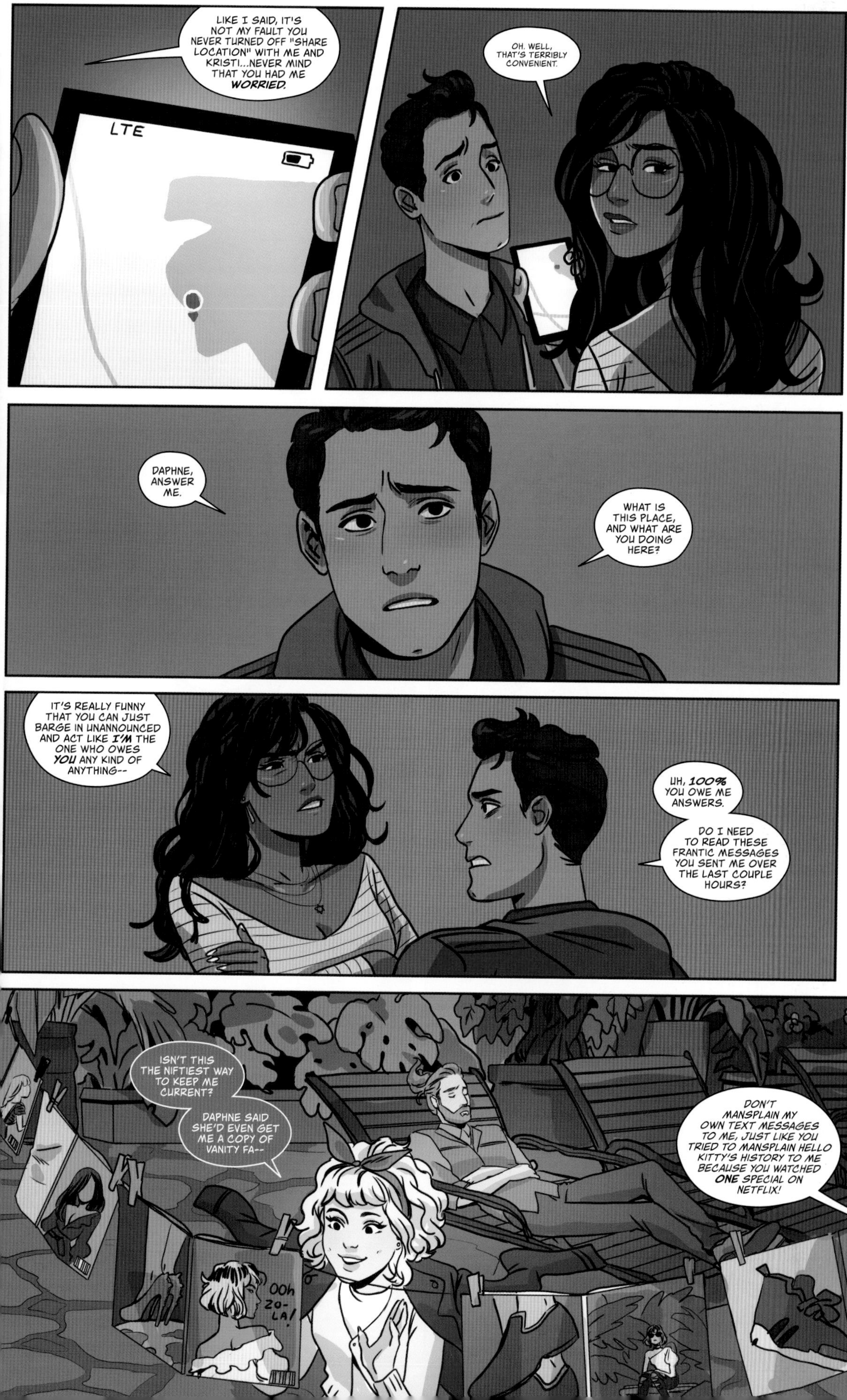
LIKE I SAID, IT'S NOT MY FAULT YOU NEVER TURNED OFF "SHARE LOCATION" WITH ME AND KRISTI...NEVER MIND THAT YOU HAD ME WORRIED.
LTE
OH. WELL, THAT'S TERRIBLY CONVENIENT.
DAPHNE, ANSWER ME.
WHAT IS THIS PLACE, AND WHAT ARE YOU DOING HERE?
IT'S REALLY FUNNY THAT YOU CAN JUST BARGE IN UNANNOUNCED AND ACT LIKE I'M THE ONE WHO OWES YOU ANY KIND OF ANYTHING--
UH, 100% YOU OWE ME ANSWERS.
DO I NEED TO READ THESE FRANTIC MESSAGES YOU SENT ME OVER THE LAST COUPLE HOURS?
ISN'T THIS THE NIFTIEST WAY TO KEEP ME CURRENT?
DAPHNE SAID SHE'D EVEN GET ME A COPY OF VANITY FA--
OOH ZO-LA!
DON'T MANSPLAIN MY OWN TEXT MESSAGES TO ME, JUST LIKE YOU TRIED TO MANSPLAIN HELLO KITTY'S HISTORY TO ME BECAUSE YOU WATCHED ONE SPECIAL ON NETFLIX!

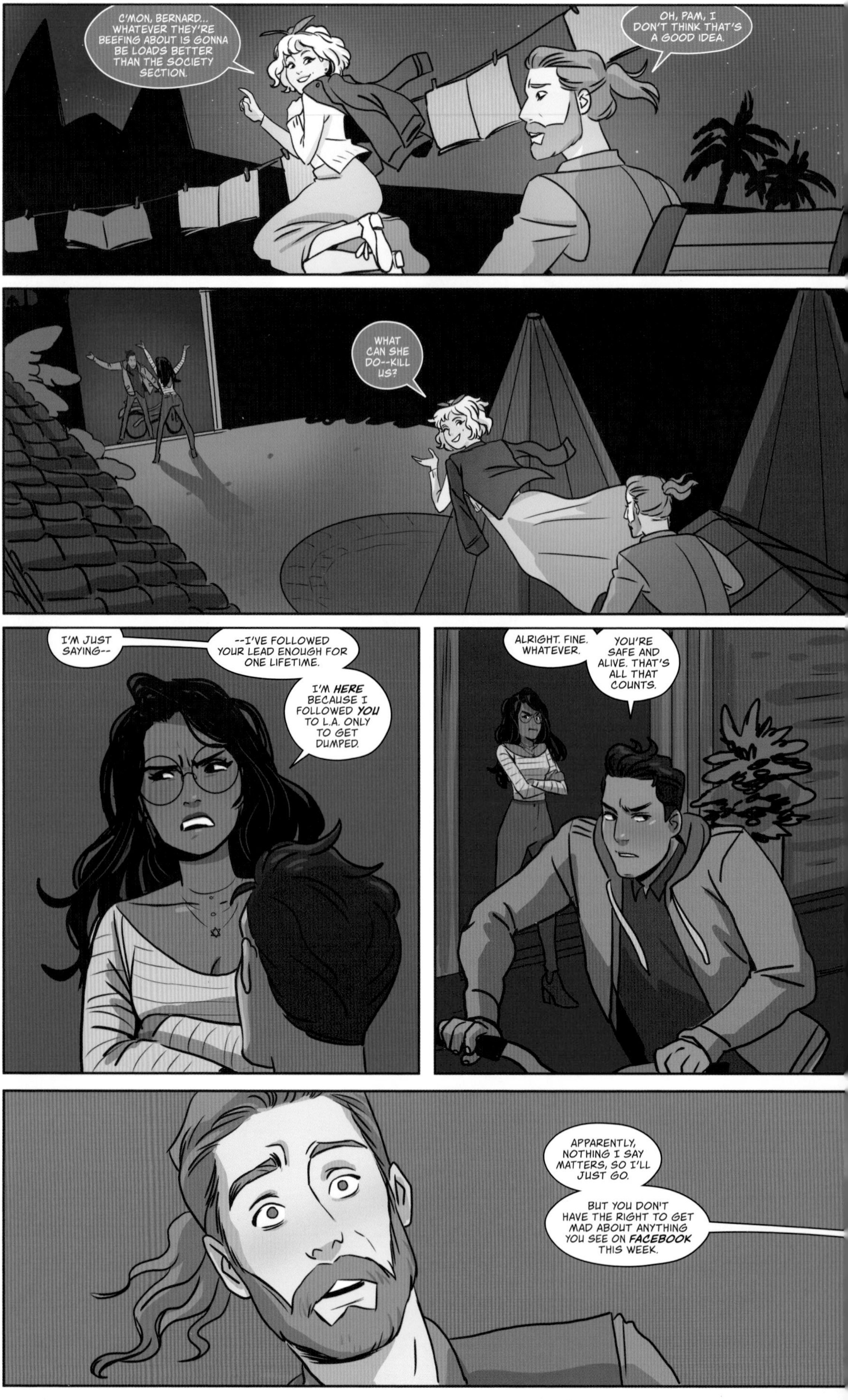

C'MON, BERNARD... WHATEVER THEY'RE BEEFING ABOUT IS GONNA BE LOADS BETTER THAN THE SOCIETY SECTION.
OH, PAM, I DON'T THINK THAT'S A GOOD IDEA.
WHAT CAN SHE DO--KILL US?
I'M JUST SAYING--
--I'VE FOLLOWED YOUR LEAD ENOUGH FOR ONE LIFETIME.
I'M HERE BECAUSE I FOLLOWED YOU TO L.A. ONLY TO GET DUMPED.
ALRIGHT. FINE. WHATEVER.
YOU'RE SAFE AND ALIVE. THAT'S ALL THAT COUNTS.
APPARENTLY, NOTHING I SAY MATTERS, SO I'LL JUST GO.
BUT YOU DON'T HAVE THE RIGHT TO GET MAD ABOUT ANYTHING YOU SEE ON FACEBOOK THIS WEEK.

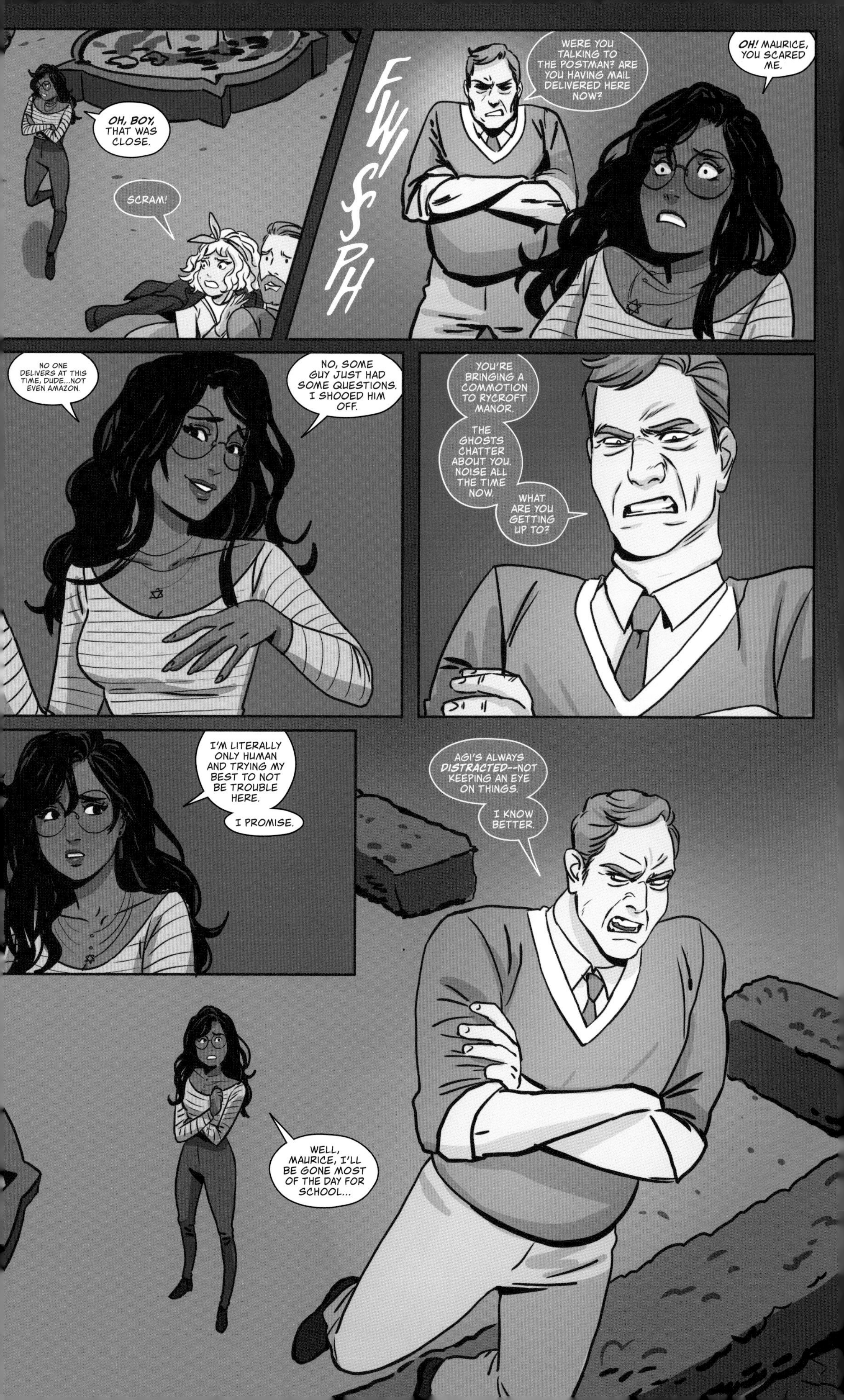

OH, BOY, THAT WAS CLOSE.
SCRAM!
FWISSPH
WERE YOU TALKING TO THE POSTMAN? ARE YOU HAVING MAIL DELIVERED HERE NOW?
OH! MAURICE, YOU SCARED ME.
NO ONE DELIVERS AT THIS TIME, DUDE...NOT EVEN AMAZON.
NO, SOME GUY JUST HAD SOME QUESTIONS. I SHOOED HIM OFF.
YOU'RE BRINGING A COMMOTION TO RYCROFT MANOR.
THE GHOSTS CHATTER ABOUT YOU. NOISE ALL THE TIME NOW.
WHAT ARE YOU GETTING UP TO?
I'M LITERALLY ONLY HUMAN AND TRYING MY BEST TO NOT BE TROUBLE HERE.
I PROMISE.
AGI'S ALWAYS DISTRACTED--NOT KEEPING AN EYE ON THINGS.
I KNOW BETTER.
WELL, MAURICE, I'LL BE GONE MOST OF THE DAY FOR SCHOOL...

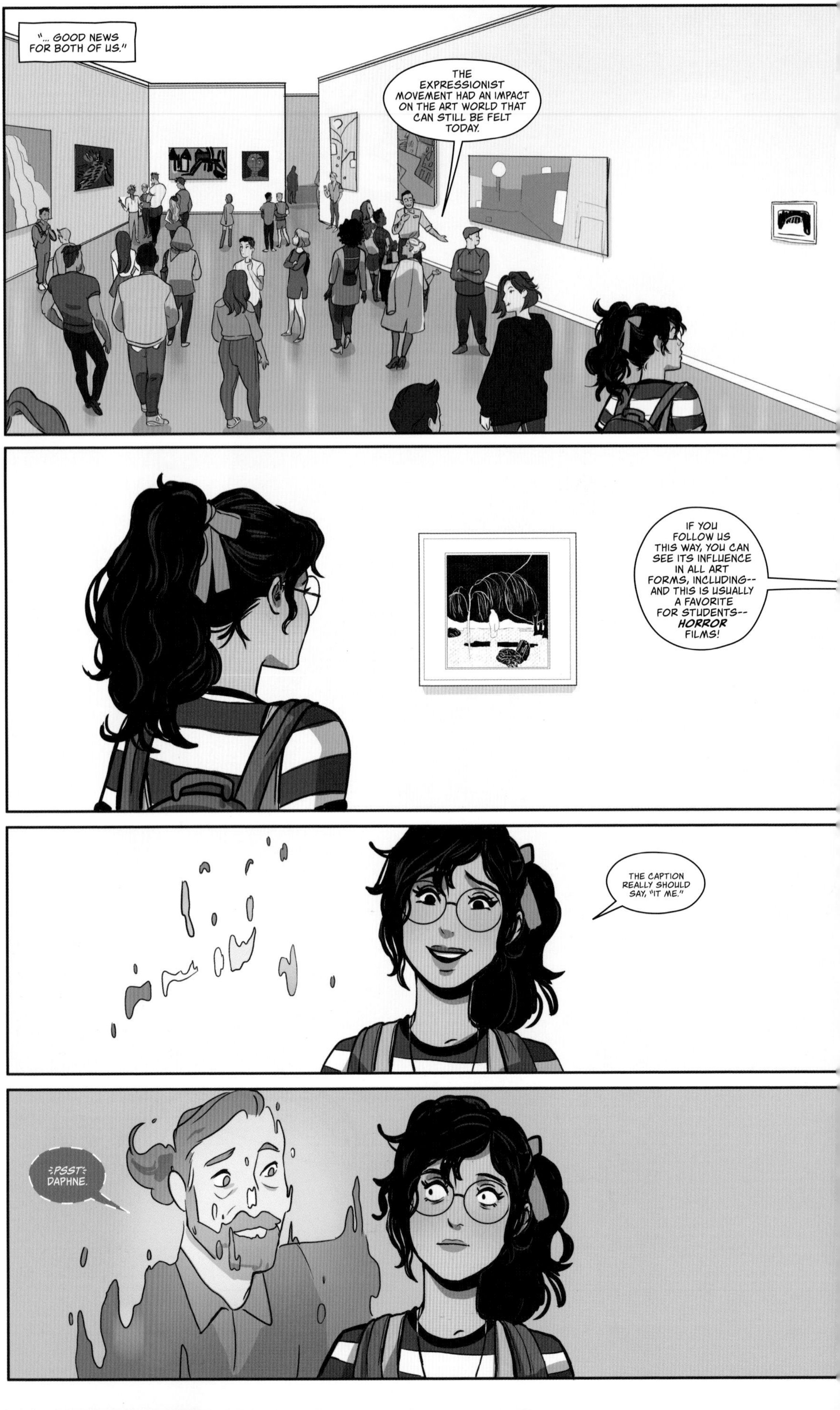
"... GOOD NEWS FOR BOTH OF US."
THE EXPRESSIONIST MOVEMENT HAD AN IMPACT ON THE ART WORLD THAT CAN STILL BE FELT TODAY.
IF YOU FOLLOW US THIS WAY, YOU CAN SEE ITS INFLUENCE IN ALL ART FORMS, INCLUDING-- AND THIS IS USUALLY A FAVORITE FOR STUDENTS-- **HORROR** FILMS!
THE CAPTION REALLY SHOULD SAY, "IT ME."
PSST DAPHNE.

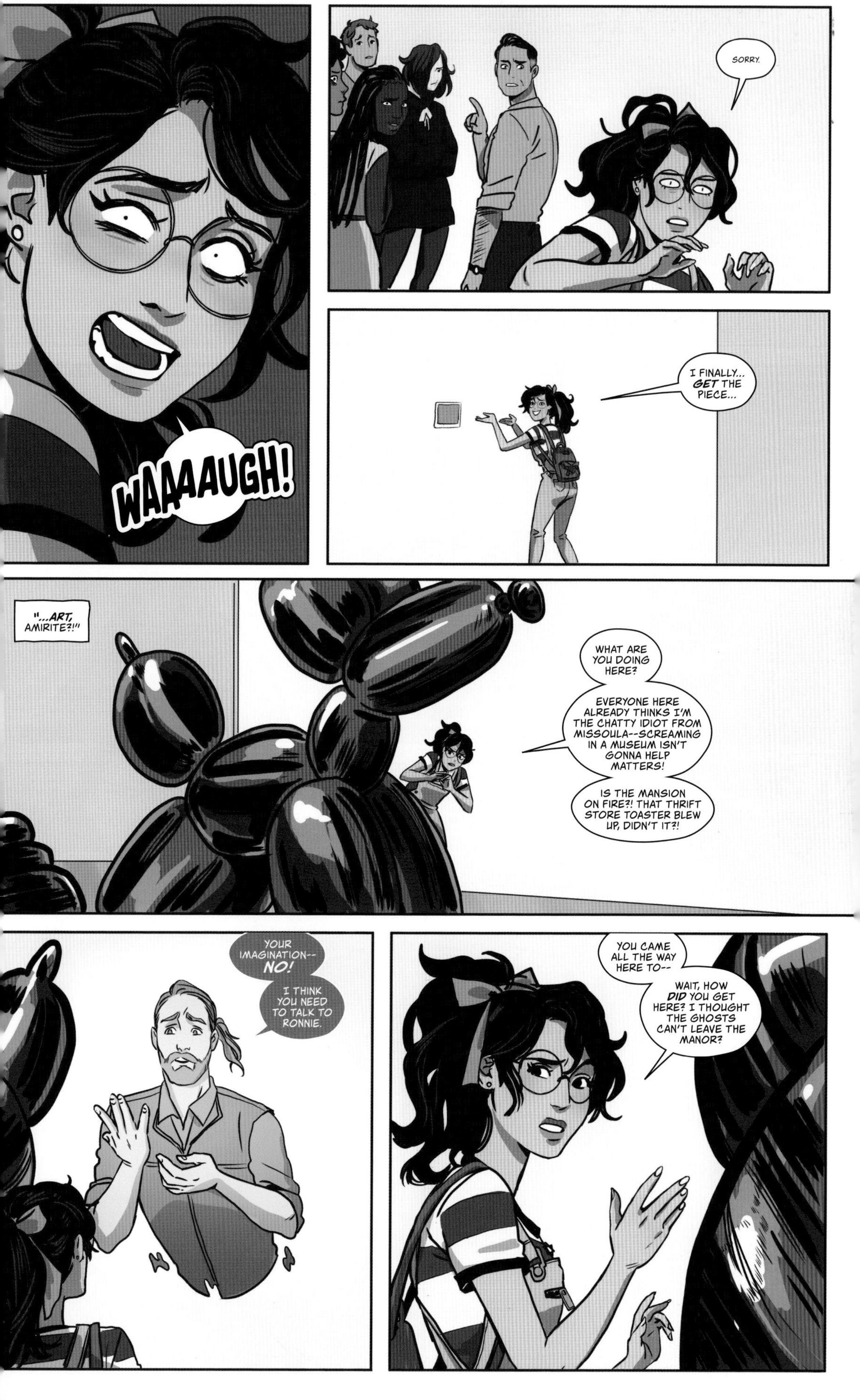
WAAAAUGH!
SORRY.
I FINALLY... GET THE PIECE...
"...ART, AMIRITE?!"
WHAT ARE YOU DOING HERE?
EVERYONE HERE ALREADY THINKS I'M THE CHATTY IDIOT FROM MISSOULA--SCREAMING IN A MUSEUM ISN'T GONNA HELP MATTERS!
IS THE MANSION ON FIRE?! THAT THRIFT STORE TOASTER BLEW UP, DIDN'T IT?!
YOUR IMAGINATION-- NO!
I THINK YOU NEED TO TALK TO RONNIE.
YOU CAME ALL THE WAY HERE TO--
WAIT, HOW DID YOU GET HERE? I THOUGHT THE GHOSTS CAN'T LEAVE THE MANOR?

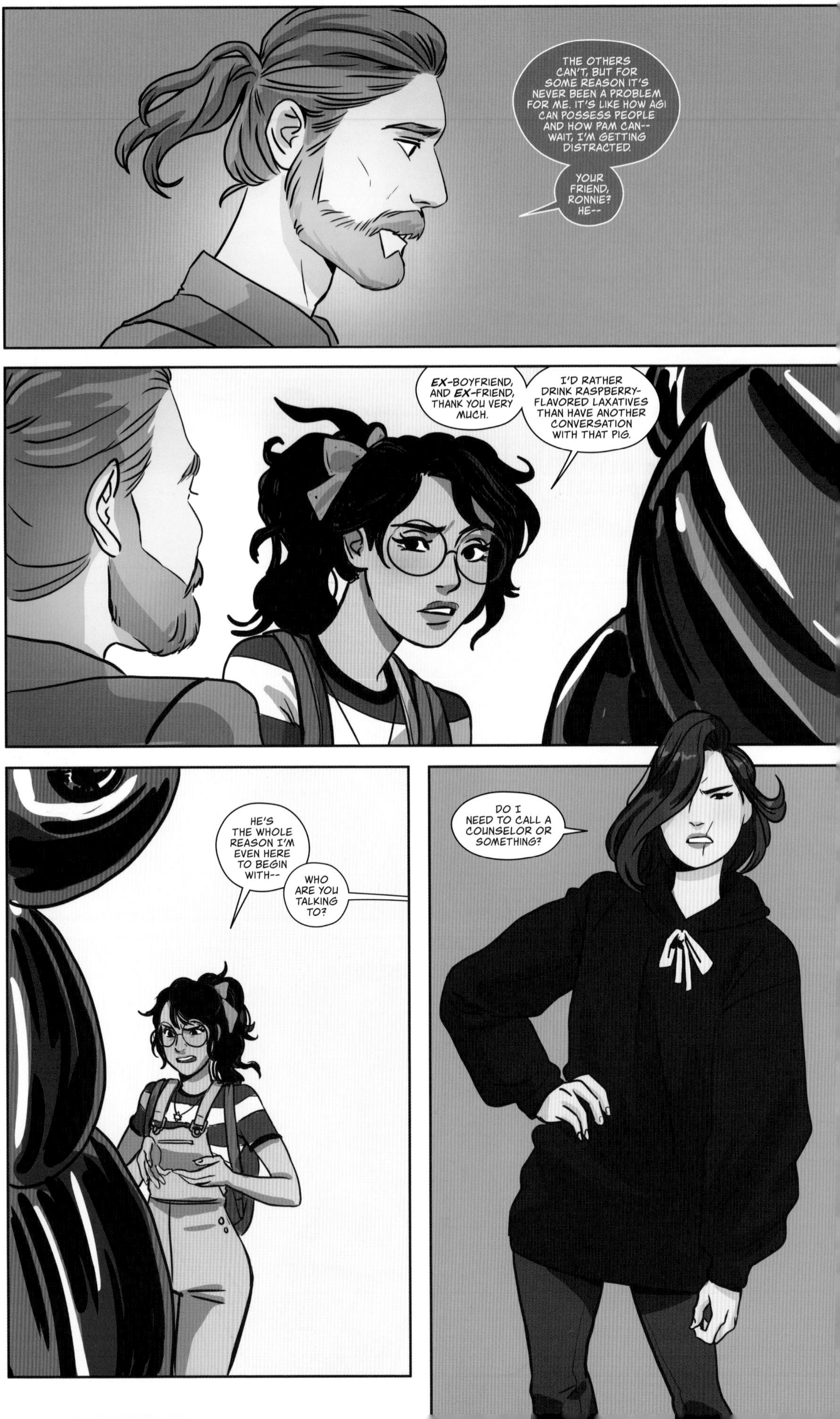
THE OTHERS CAN'T, BUT FOR SOME REASON IT'S NEVER BEEN A PROBLEM FOR ME. IT'S LIKE HOW AGI CAN POSSESS PEOPLE AND HOW PAM CAN-- WAIT, I'M GETTING DISTRACTED.
YOUR FRIEND, RONNIE? HE--
EX-BOYFRIEND, AND EX-FRIEND, THANK YOU VERY MUCH.
I'D RATHER DRINK RASPBERRY-FLAVORED LAXATIVES THAN HAVE ANOTHER CONVERSATION WITH THAT PIG.
HE'S THE WHOLE REASON I'M EVEN HERE TO BEGIN WITH--
WHO ARE YOU TALKING TO?
DO I NEED TO CALL A COUNSELOR OR SOMETHING?

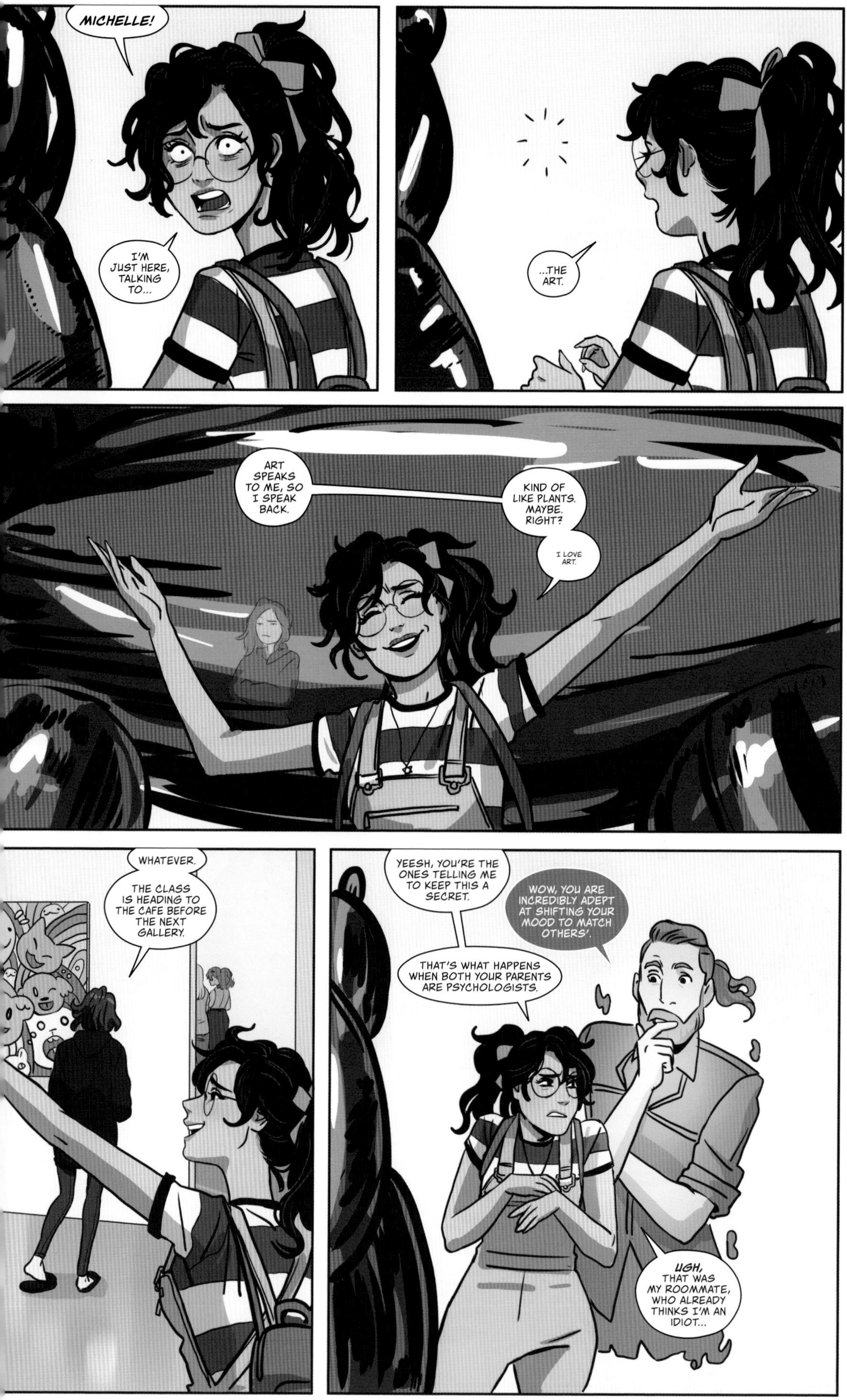
MICHELLE!
I'M JUST HERE, TALKING TO...
...THE ART.
ART SPEAKS TO ME, SO I SPEAK BACK.
KIND OF LIKE PLANTS. MAYBE. RIGHT?
I LOVE ART.
WHATEVER.
THE CLASS IS HEADING TO THE CAFE BEFORE THE NEXT GALLERY.
YEESH, YOU'RE THE ONES TELLING ME TO KEEP THIS A SECRET.
WOW, YOU ARE INCREDIBLY ADEPT AT SHIFTING YOUR MOOD TO MATCH OTHERS'.
THAT'S WHAT HAPPENS WHEN BOTH YOUR PARENTS ARE PSYCHOLOGISTS.
UGH, THAT WAS MY ROOMMATE, WHO ALREADY THINKS I'M AN IDIOT...

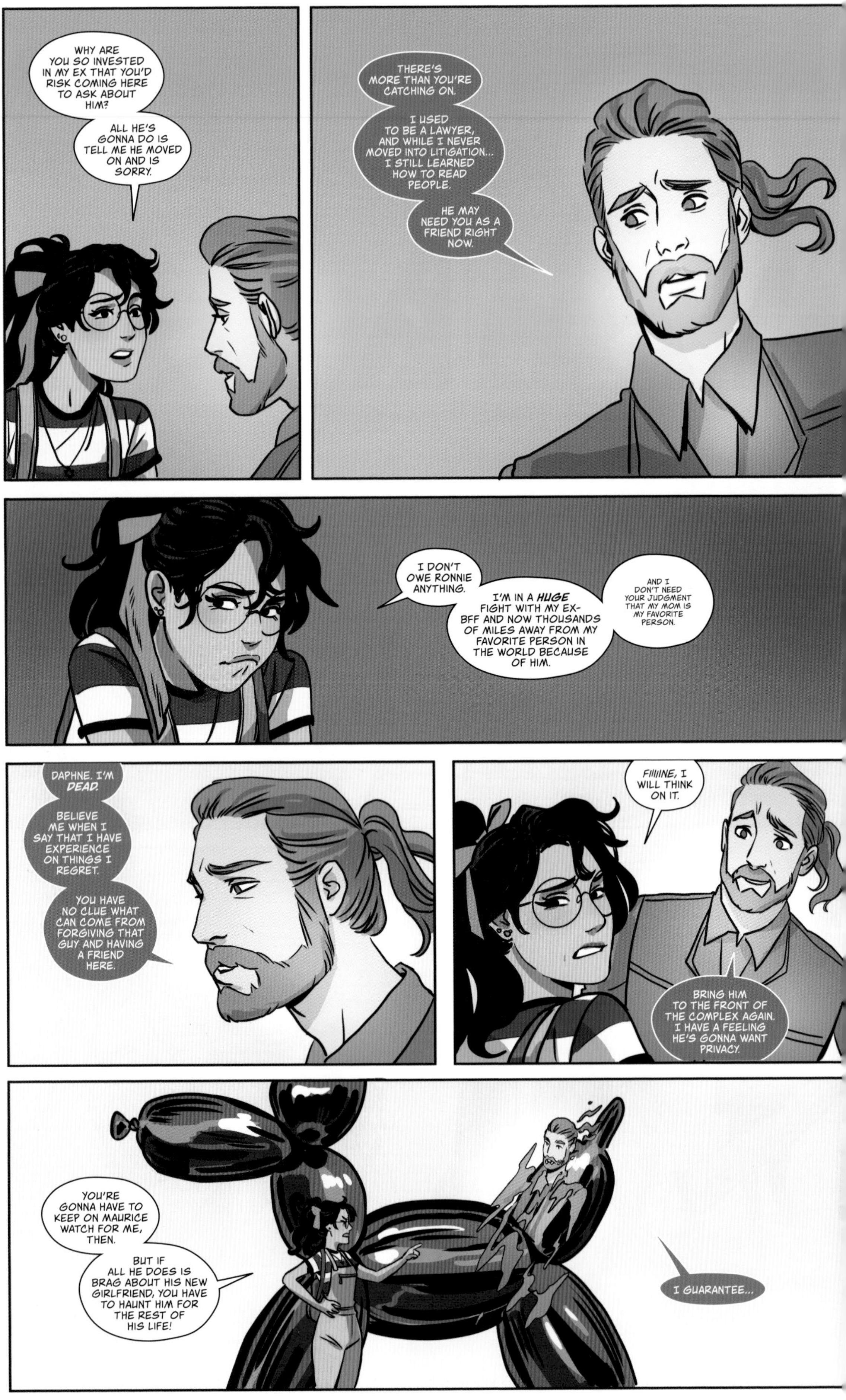

WHY ARE YOU SO INVESTED IN MY EX THAT YOU'D RISK COMING HERE TO ASK ABOUT HIM?
ALL HE'S GONNA DO IS TELL ME HE MOVED ON AND IS SORRY.
THERE'S MORE THAN YOU'RE CATCHING ON.
I USED TO BE A LAWYER, AND WHILE I NEVER MOVED INTO LITIGATION... I STILL LEARNED HOW TO READ PEOPLE.
HE MAY NEED YOU AS A FRIEND RIGHT NOW.
I DON'T OWE RONNIE ANYTHING.
I'M IN A HUGE FIGHT WITH MY EX-BFF AND NOW THOUSANDS OF MILES AWAY FROM MY FAVORITE PERSON IN THE WORLD BECAUSE OF HIM.
AND I DON'T NEED YOUR JUDGMENT THAT MY MOM IS MY FAVORITE PERSON.
DAPHNE. I'M DEAD.
BELIEVE ME WHEN I SAY THAT I HAVE EXPERIENCE ON THINGS I REGRET.
YOU HAVE NO CLUE WHAT CAN COME FROM FORGIVING THAT GUY AND HAVING A FRIEND HERE.
FIIIIINE, I WILL THINK ON IT.
BRING HIM TO THE FRONT OF THE COMPLEX AGAIN. I HAVE A FEELING HE'S GONNA WANT PRIVACY.
YOU'RE GONNA HAVE TO KEEP ON MAURICE WATCH FOR ME, THEN.
BUT IF ALL HE DOES IS BRAG ABOUT HIS NEW GIRLFRIEND, YOU HAVE TO HAUNT HIM FOR THE REST OF HIS LIFE!
I GUARANTEE...

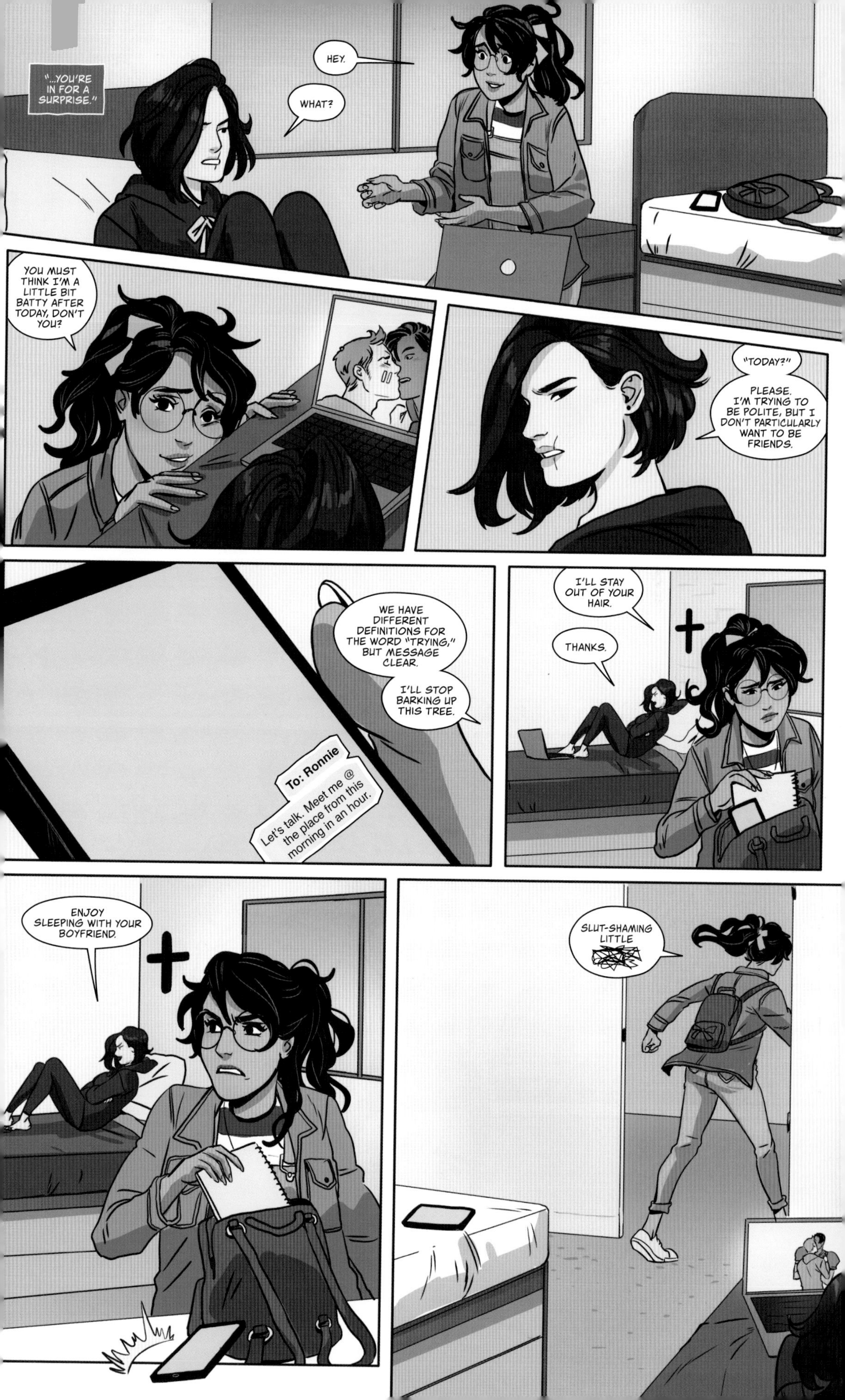
"...YOU'RE IN FOR A SURPRISE."
HEY.
WHAT?
YOU MUST THINK I'M A LITTLE BIT BATTY AFTER TODAY, DON'T YOU?
"TODAY?"
PLEASE. I'M TRYING TO BE POLITE, BUT I DON'T PARTICULARLY WANT TO BE FRIENDS.
WE HAVE DIFFERENT DEFINITIONS FOR THE WORD "TRYING," BUT MESSAGE CLEAR.
I'LL STOP BARKING UP THIS TREE.
To: Ronnie
Let's talk. Meet me @ the place from this morning in an hour.
I'LL STAY OUT OF YOUR HAIR.
THANKS.
ENJOY SLEEPING WITH YOUR BOYFRIEND.
SLUT-SHAMING LITTLE

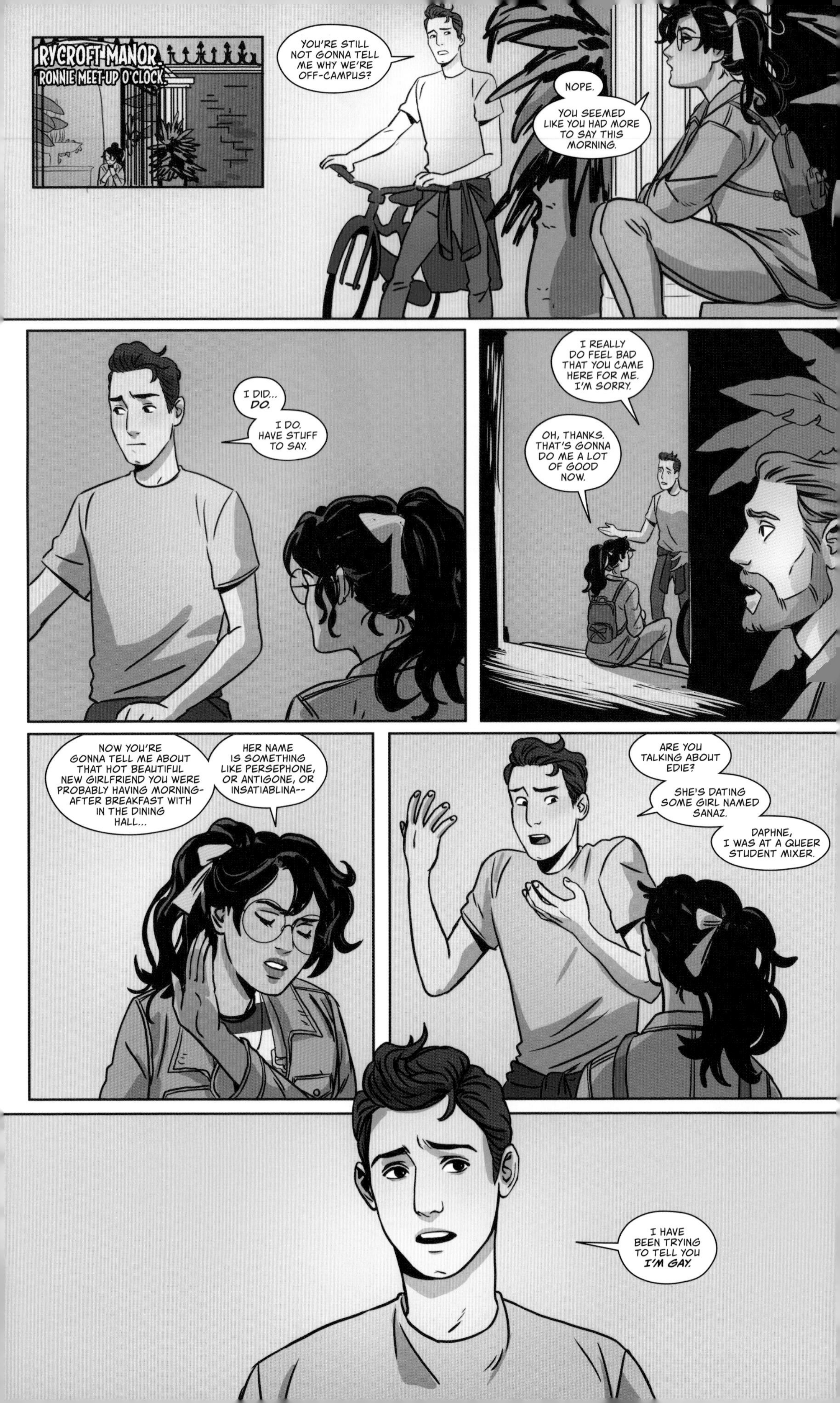
RYCROFT MANOR.
RONNIE MEET-UP O'CLOCK.
YOU'RE STILL NOT GONNA TELL ME WHY WE'RE OFF-CAMPUS?
NOPE.
YOU SEEMED LIKE YOU HAD MORE TO SAY THIS MORNING.
I DID... DO.
I DO. HAVE STUFF TO SAY.
I REALLY DO FEEL BAD THAT YOU CAME HERE FOR ME. I'M SORRY.
OH, THANKS. THAT'S GONNA DO ME A LOT OF GOOD NOW.
NOW YOU'RE GONNA TELL ME ABOUT THAT HOT BEAUTIFUL NEW GIRLFRIEND YOU WERE PROBABLY HAVING MORNING-AFTER BREAKFAST WITH IN THE DINING HALL...
HER NAME IS SOMETHING LIKE PERSEPHONE, OR ANTIGONE, OR INSATIABLINA--
ARE YOU TALKING ABOUT EDIE?
SHE'S DATING SOME GIRL NAMED SANAZ.
DAPHNE, I WAS AT A QUEER STUDENT MIXER.
I HAVE BEEN TRYING TO TELL YOU I'M GAY.

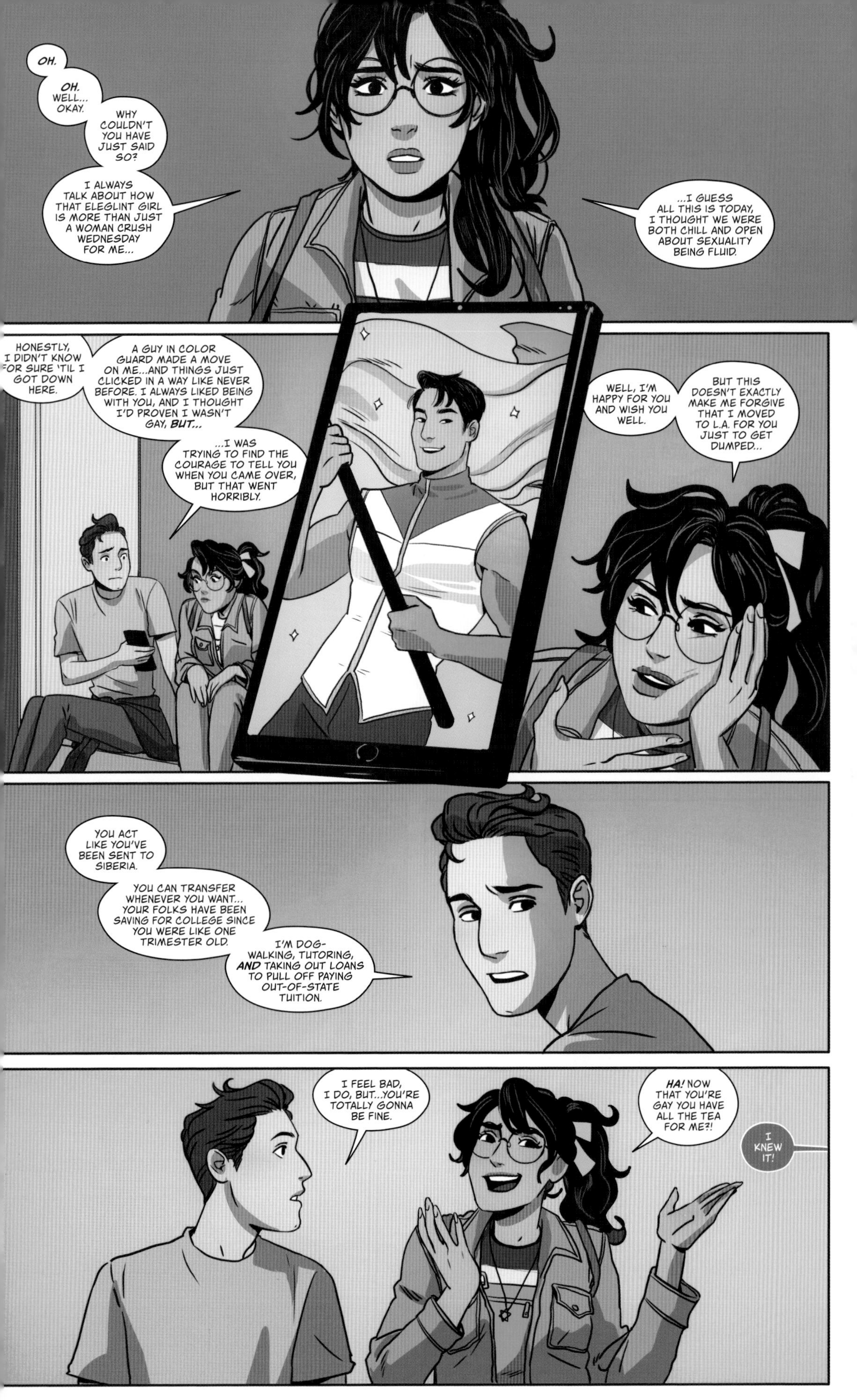
OH.
OH. WELL... OKAY.
WHY COULDN'T YOU HAVE JUST SAID SO?
I ALWAYS TALK ABOUT HOW THAT ELEGLINT GIRL IS MORE THAN JUST A WOMAN CRUSH WEDNESDAY FOR ME...
...I GUESS ALL THIS IS TODAY, I THOUGHT WE WERE BOTH CHILL AND OPEN ABOUT SEXUALITY BEING FLUID.
HONESTLY, I DIDN'T KNOW FOR SURE 'TIL I GOT DOWN HERE.
A GUY IN COLOR GUARD MADE A MOVE ON ME...AND THINGS JUST CLICKED IN A WAY LIKE NEVER BEFORE. I ALWAYS LIKED BEING WITH YOU, AND I THOUGHT I'D PROVEN I WASN'T GAY, BUT...
...I WAS TRYING TO FIND THE COURAGE TO TELL YOU WHEN YOU CAME OVER, BUT THAT WENT HORRIBLY.
WELL, I'M HAPPY FOR YOU AND WISH YOU WELL.
BUT THIS DOESN'T EXACTLY MAKE ME FORGIVE THAT I MOVED TO L.A. FOR YOU JUST TO GET DUMPED...
YOU ACT LIKE YOU'VE BEEN SENT TO SIBERIA.
YOU CAN TRANSFER WHENEVER YOU WANT... YOUR FOLKS HAVE BEEN SAVING FOR COLLEGE SINCE YOU WERE LIKE ONE TRIMESTER OLD.
I'M DOG-WALKING, TUTORING, AND TAKING OUT LOANS TO PULL OFF PAYING OUT-OF-STATE TUITION.
I FEEL BAD, I DO, BUT...YOU'RE TOTALLY GONNA BE FINE.
HA! NOW THAT YOU'RE GAY YOU HAVE ALL THE TEA FOR ME?!
I KNEW IT!

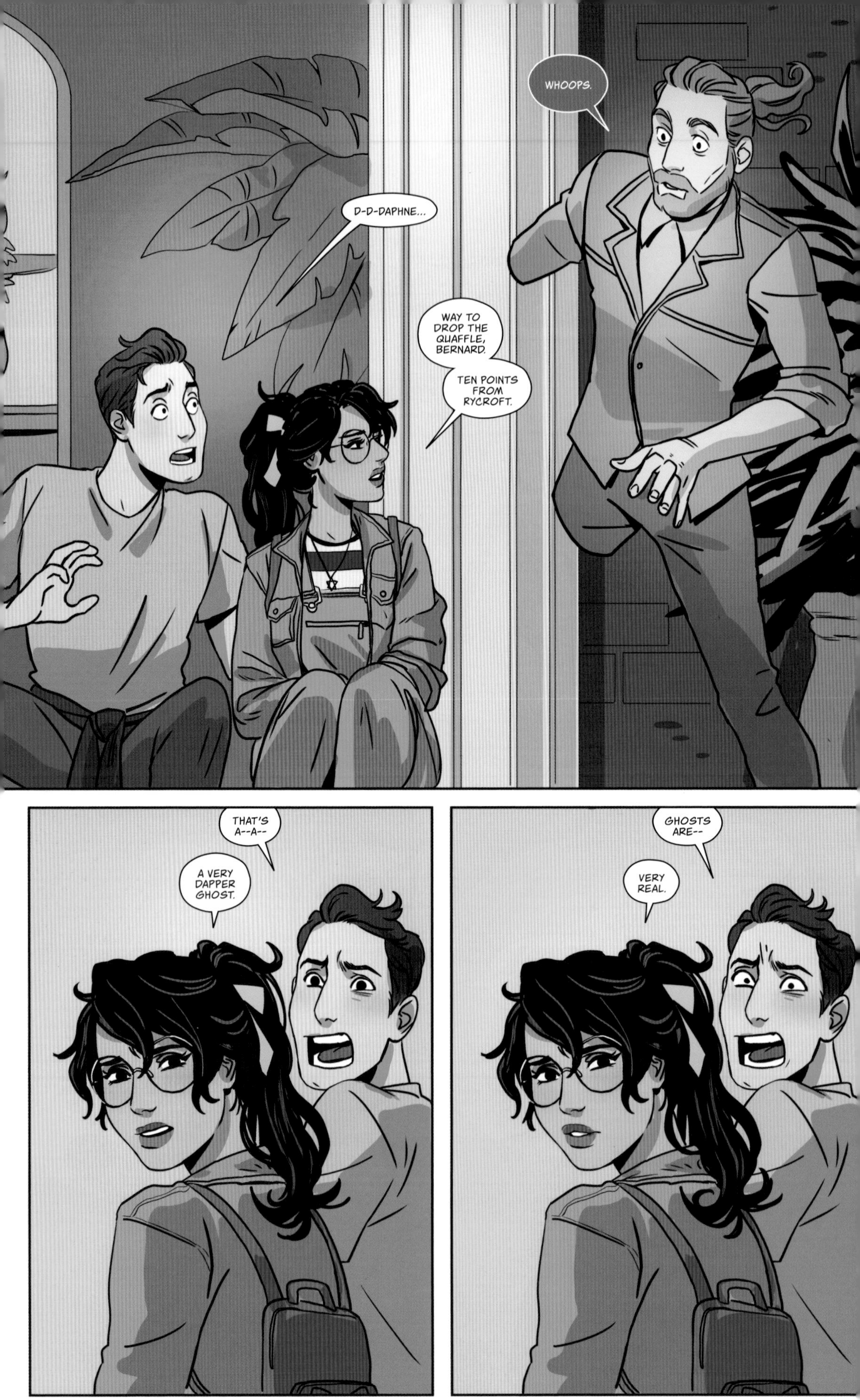
WHOOPS.
D-D-DAPHNE...
WAY TO DROP THE QUAFFLE, BERNARD.
TEN POINTS FROM RYCROFT.
THAT'S A--A--
A VERY DAPPER GHOST.
GHOSTS ARE--
VERY REAL.

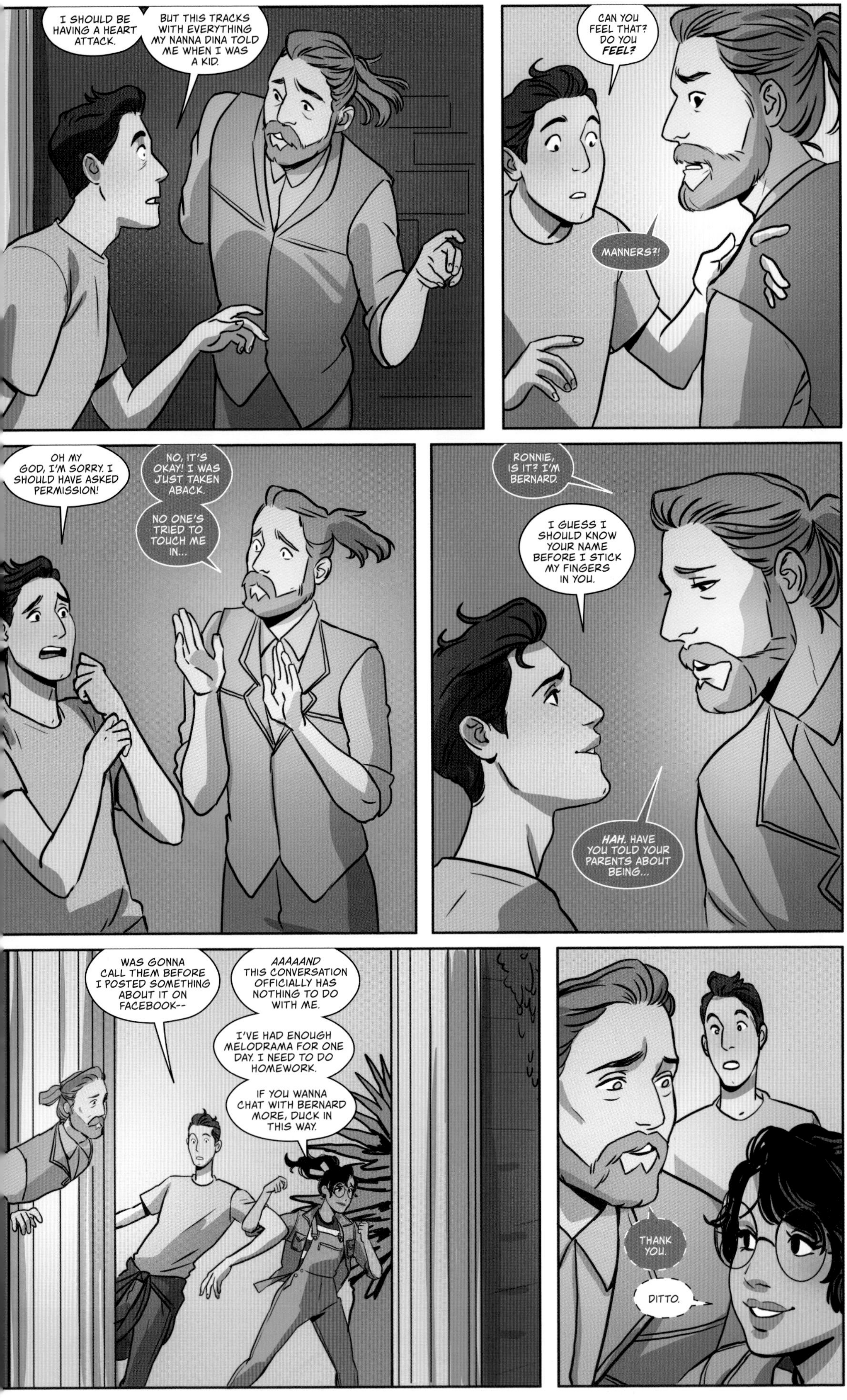
I SHOULD BE HAVING A HEART ATTACK.
BUT THIS TRACKS WITH EVERYTHING MY NANNA DINA TOLD ME WHEN I WAS A KID.
CAN YOU FEEL THAT? DO YOU *FEEL?*
MANNERS?!
OH MY GOD, I'M SORRY. I SHOULD HAVE ASKED PERMISSION!
NO, IT'S OKAY! I WAS JUST TAKEN ABACK.
NO ONE'S TRIED TO TOUCH ME IN...
RONNIE, IS IT? I'M BERNARD.
I GUESS I SHOULD KNOW YOUR NAME BEFORE I STICK MY FINGERS IN YOU.
HAH. HAVE YOU TOLD YOUR PARENTS ABOUT BEING...
WAS GONNA CALL THEM BEFORE I POSTED SOMETHING ABOUT IT ON FACEBOOK--
AAAAAND THIS CONVERSATION OFFICIALLY HAS NOTHING TO DO WITH ME.
I'VE HAD ENOUGH MELODRAMA FOR ONE DAY. I NEED TO DO HOMEWORK.
IF YOU WANNA CHAT WITH BERNARD MORE, DUCK IN THIS WAY.
THANK YOU.
DITTO.

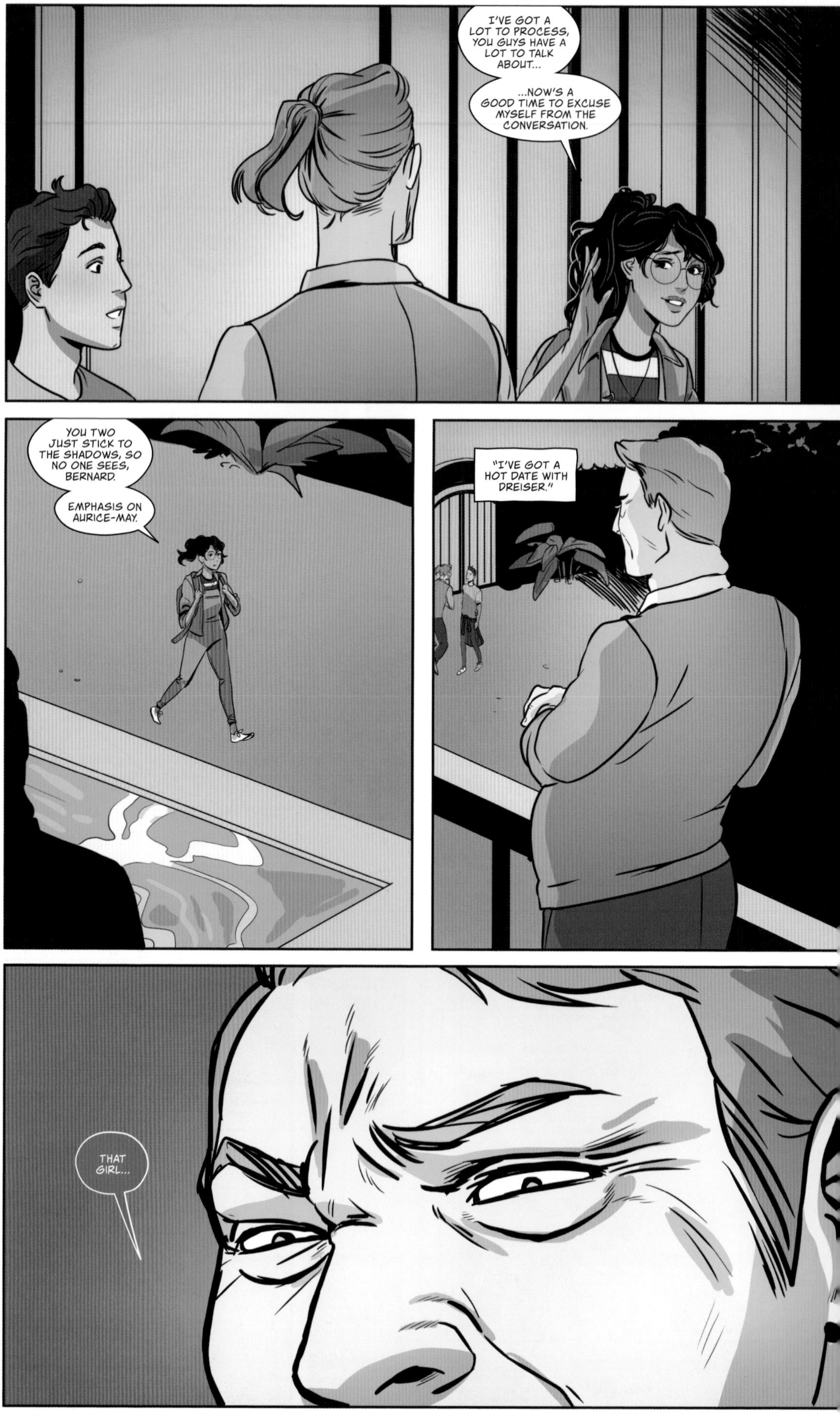
I'VE GOT A LOT TO PROCESS, YOU GUYS HAVE A LOT TO TALK ABOUT...
...NOW'S A GOOD TIME TO EXCUSE MYSELF FROM THE CONVERSATION.
YOU TWO JUST STICK TO THE SHADOWS, SO NO ONE SEES, BERNARD.
EMPHASIS ON AURICE-MAY.
"I'VE GOT A HOT DATE WITH DREISER."
THAT GIRL...

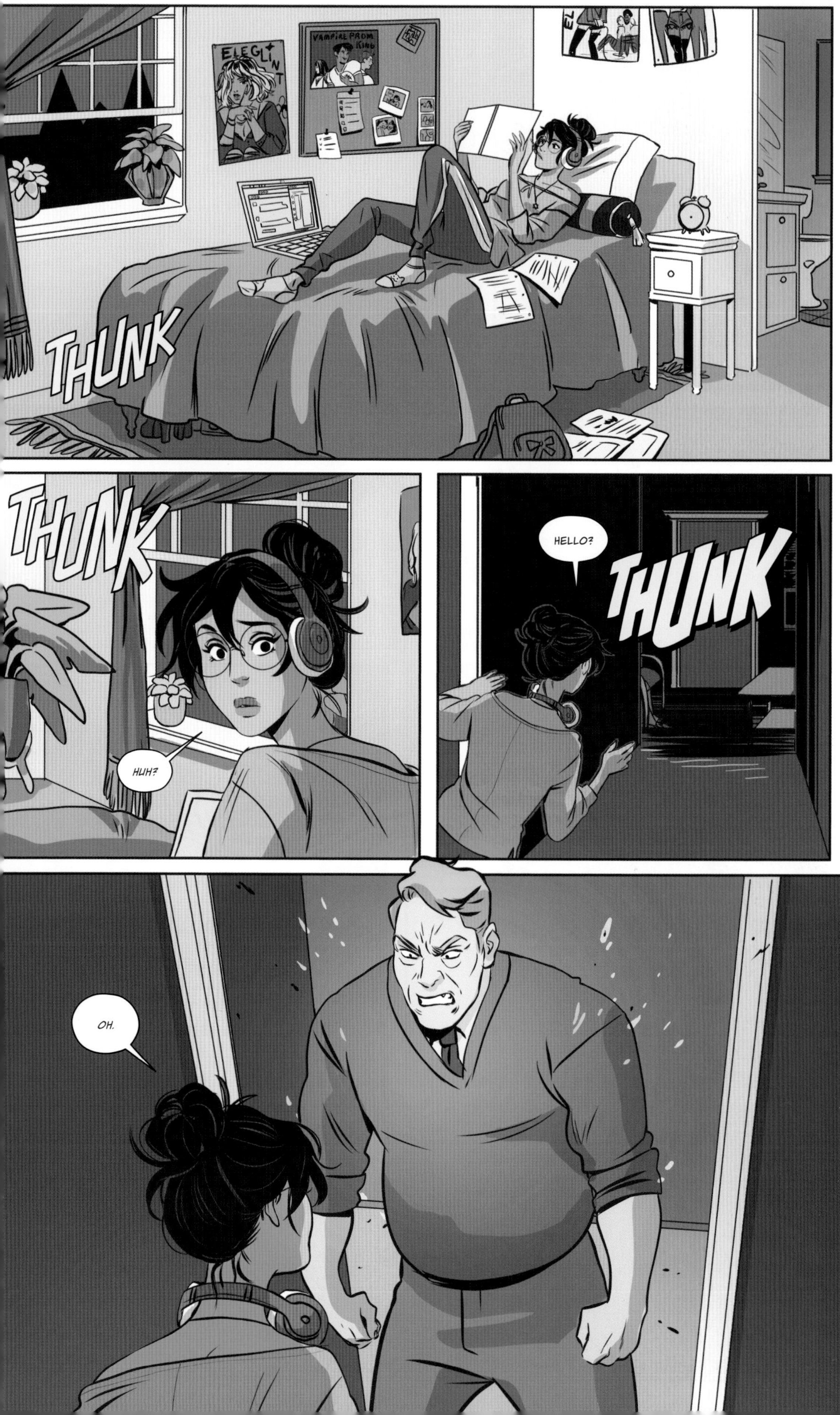

ELEGLINT
VAMPIRE PROM KING
THUNK
THUNK
HUH?
HELLO?
THUNK
OH.

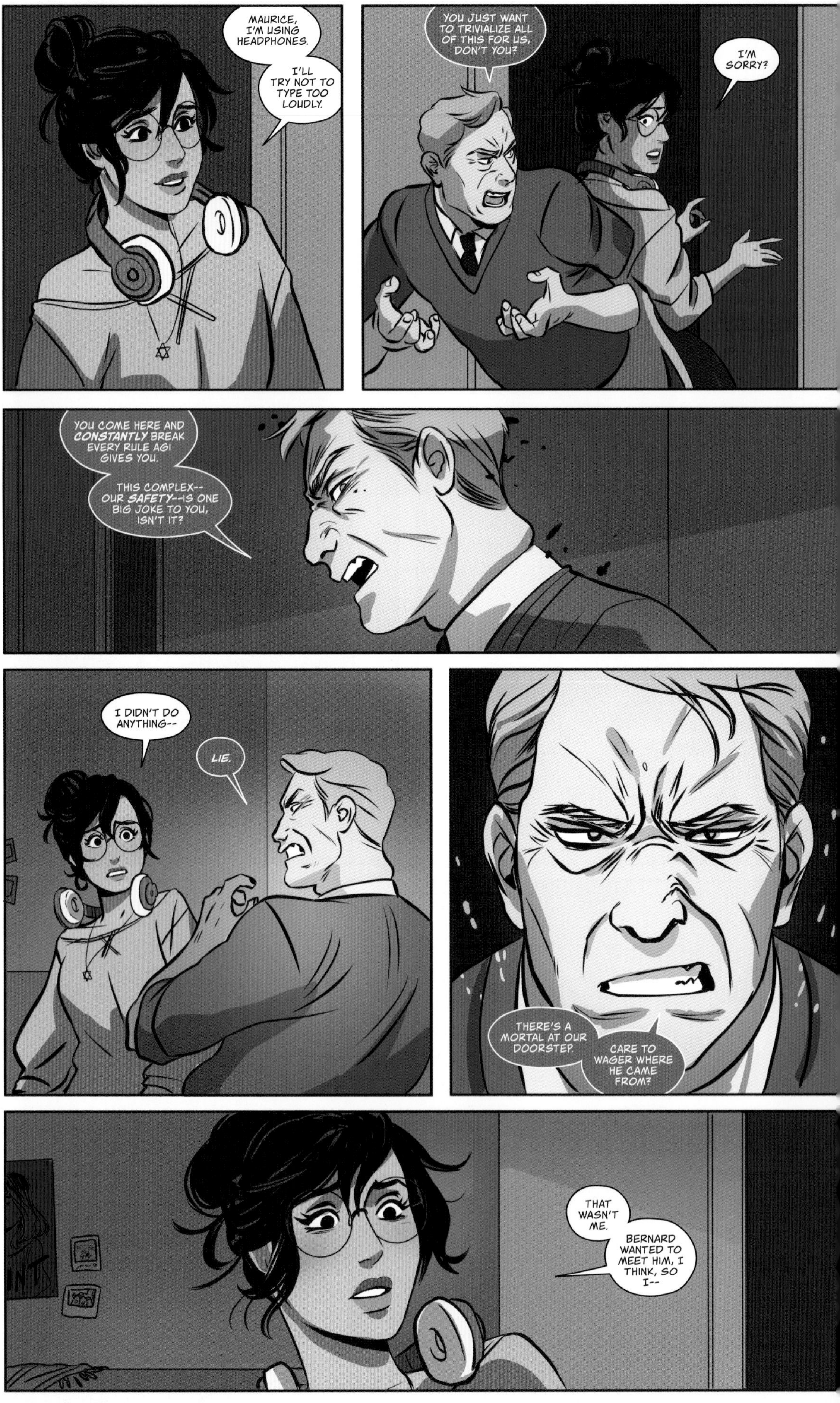

MAURICE, I'M USING HEADPHONES.
I'LL TRY NOT TO TYPE TOO LOUDLY.
YOU JUST WANT TO TRIVIALIZE ALL OF THIS FOR US, DON'T YOU?
I'M SORRY?
YOU COME HERE AND CONSTANTLY BREAK EVERY RULE AGI GIVES YOU.
THIS COMPLEX--OUR SAFETY--IS ONE BIG JOKE TO YOU, ISN'T IT?
I DIDN'T DO ANYTHING--
LIE.
THERE'S A MORTAL AT OUR DOORSTEP.
CARE TO WAGER WHERE HE CAME FROM?
THAT WASN'T ME.
BERNARD WANTED TO MEET HIM, I THINK, SO I--

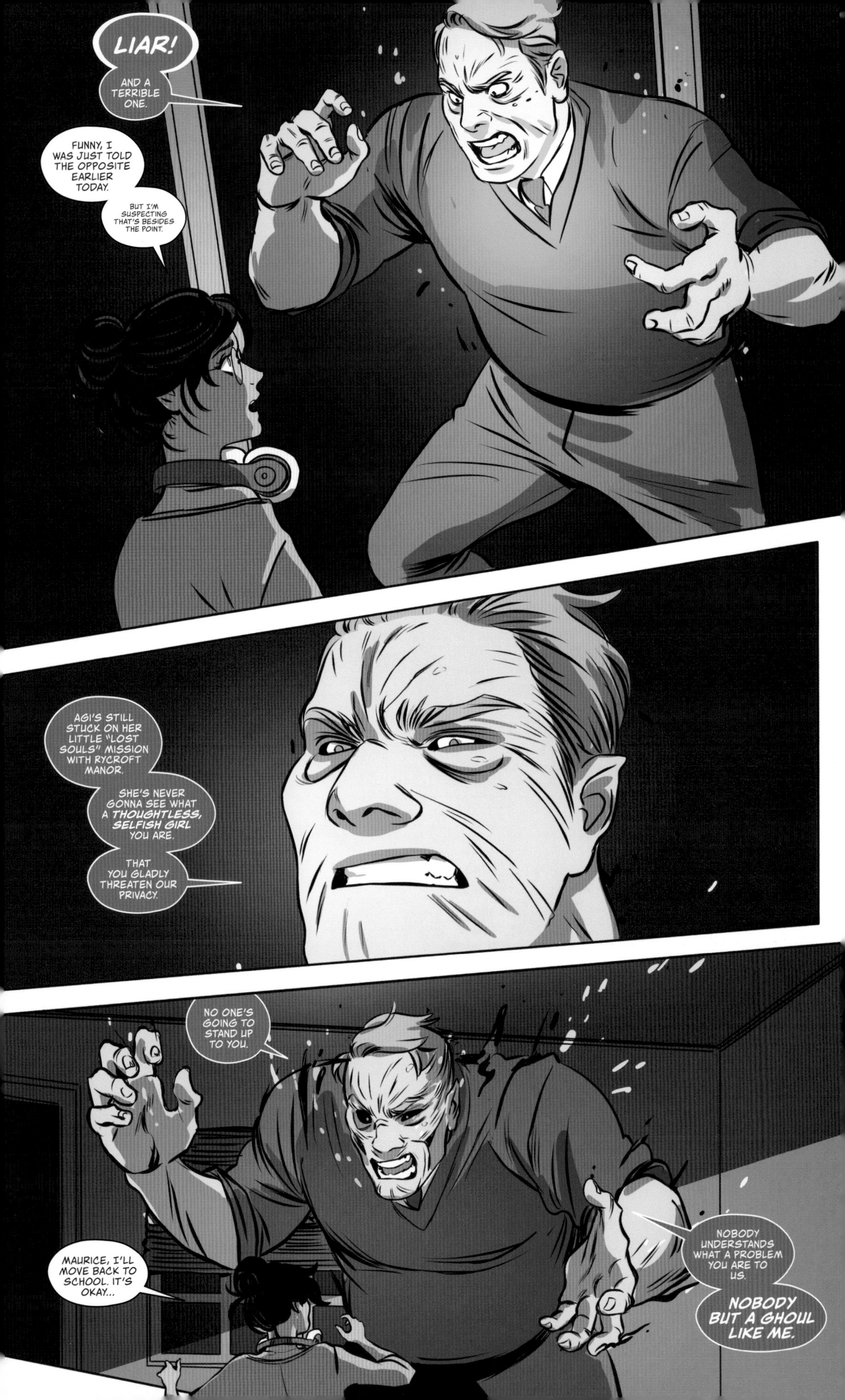
LIAR!
AND A TERRIBLE ONE.
FUNNY, I WAS JUST TOLD THE OPPOSITE EARLIER TODAY.
BUT I'M SUSPECTING THAT'S BESIDES THE POINT.
AGI'S STILL STUCK ON HER LITTLE "LOST SOULS" MISSION WITH RYCROFT MANOR.
SHE'S NEVER GONNA SEE WHAT A THOUGHTLESS, SELFISH GIRL YOU ARE.
THAT YOU GLADLY THREATEN OUR PRIVACY.
NO ONE'S GOING TO STAND UP TO YOU.
MAURICE, I'LL MOVE BACK TO SCHOOL. IT'S OKAY...
NOBODY UNDERSTANDS WHAT A PROBLEM YOU ARE TO US.
NOBODY BUT A GHOUL LIKE ME.

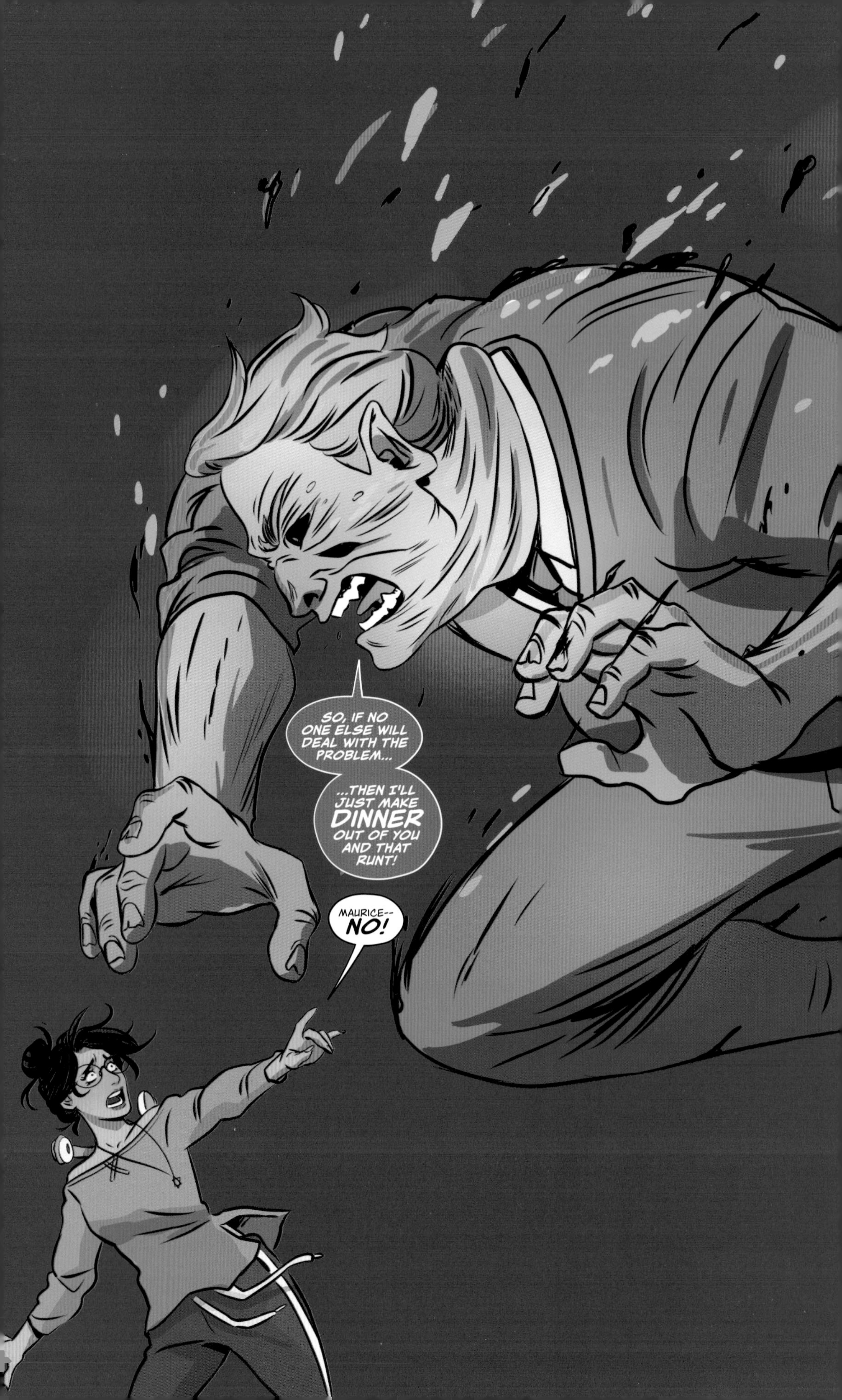
SO, IF NO ONE ELSE WILL DEAL WITH THE PROBLEM...
...THEN I'LL JUST MAKE DINNER OUT OF YOU AND THAT RUNT!
MAURICE-- NO!

Chapter Four

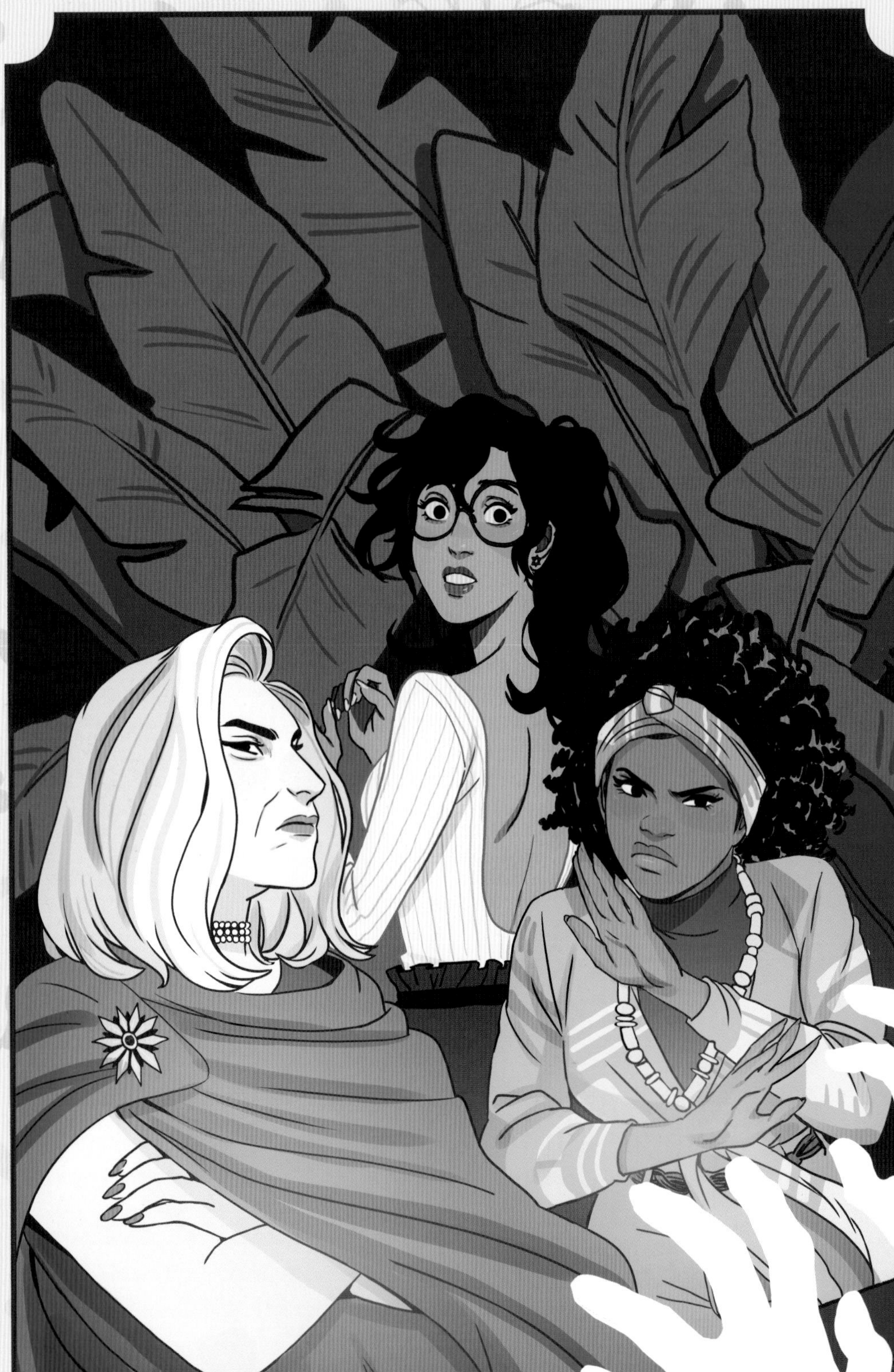

Issue Four Cover by **Siobhan Keenan**

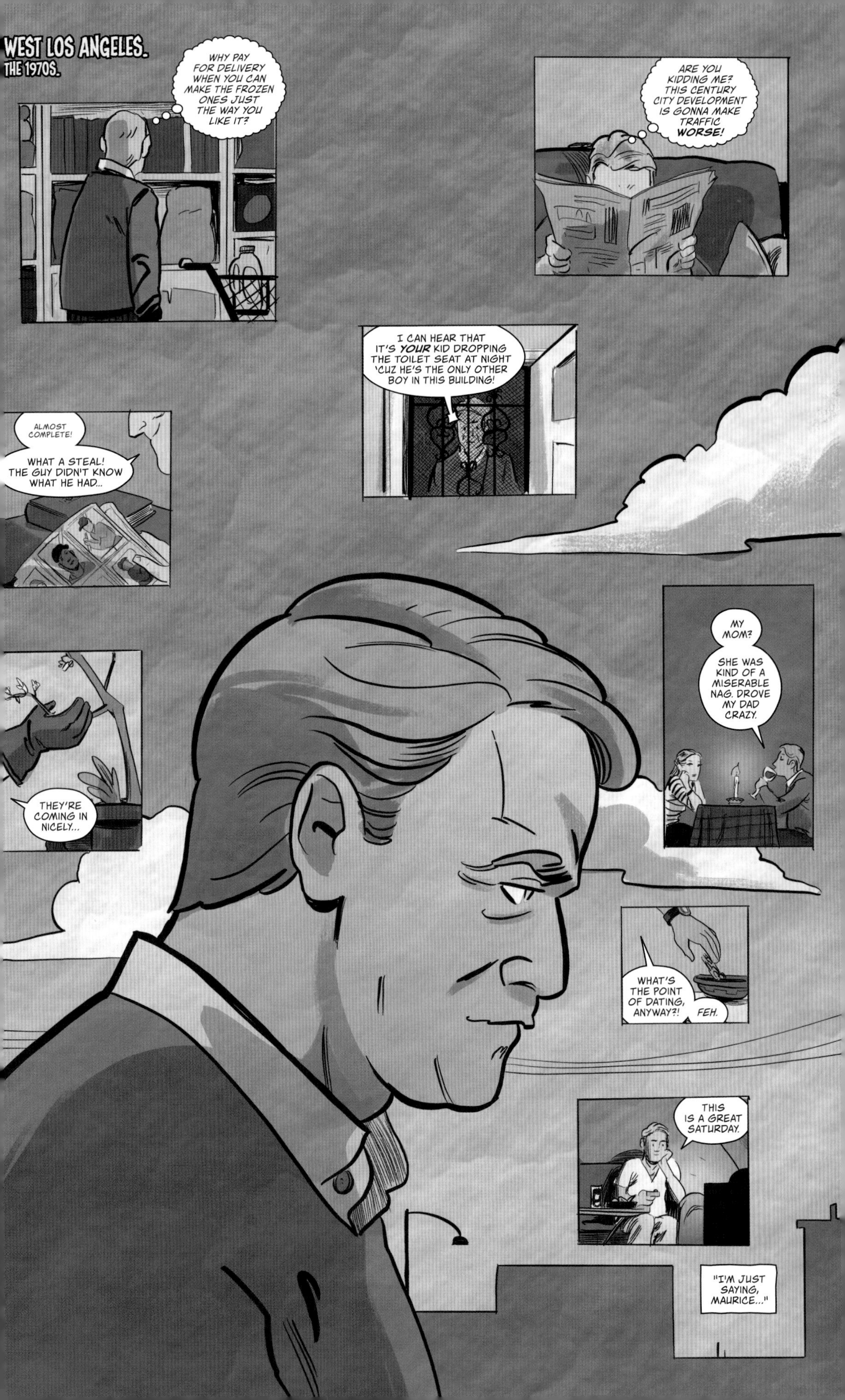
WEST LOS ANGELES.
THE 1970S.
WHY PAY FOR DELIVERY WHEN YOU CAN MAKE THE FROZEN ONES JUST THE WAY YOU LIKE IT?
ARE YOU KIDDING ME? THIS CENTURY CITY DEVELOPMENT IS GONNA MAKE TRAFFIC **WORSE!**
I CAN HEAR THAT IT'S ***YOUR*** KID DROPPING THE TOILET SEAT AT NIGHT 'CUZ HE'S THE ONLY OTHER BOY IN THIS BUILDING!
ALMOST COMPLETE!
WHAT A STEAL! THE GUY DIDN'T KNOW WHAT HE HAD...
MY MOM?
SHE WAS KIND OF A MISERABLE NAG. DROVE MY DAD CRAZY.
THEY'RE COMING IN NICELY...
WHAT'S THE POINT OF DATING, ANYWAY?!
FEH.
THIS IS A GREAT SATURDAY.
"I'M JUST SAYING, MAURICE..."

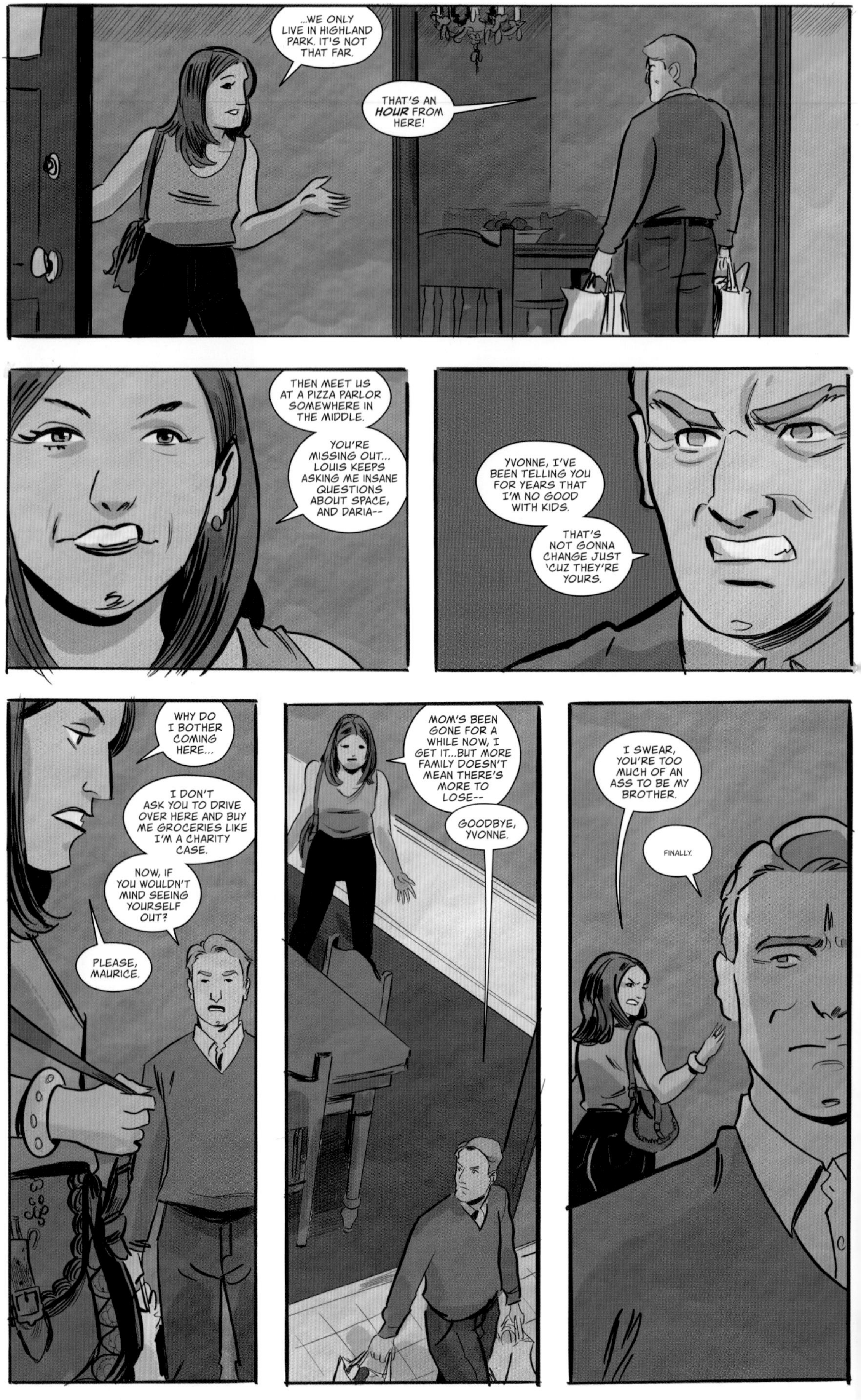
...WE ONLY LIVE IN HIGHLAND PARK. IT'S NOT THAT FAR.
THAT'S AN HOUR FROM HERE!
THEN MEET US AT A PIZZA PARLOR SOMEWHERE IN THE MIDDLE.
YOU'RE MISSING OUT... LOUIS KEEPS ASKING ME INSANE QUESTIONS ABOUT SPACE, AND DARIA--
YVONNE, I'VE BEEN TELLING YOU FOR YEARS THAT I'M NO GOOD WITH KIDS.
THAT'S NOT GONNA CHANGE JUST 'CUZ THEY'RE YOURS.
WHY DO I BOTHER COMING HERE...
I DON'T ASK YOU TO DRIVE OVER HERE AND BUY ME GROCERIES LIKE I'M A CHARITY CASE.
NOW, IF YOU WOULDN'T MIND SEEING YOURSELF OUT?
PLEASE, MAURICE.
MOM'S BEEN GONE FOR A WHILE NOW, I GET IT...BUT MORE FAMILY DOESN'T MEAN THERE'S MORE TO LOSE--
GOODBYE, YVONNE.
I SWEAR, YOU'RE TOO MUCH OF AN ASS TO BE MY BROTHER.
FINALLY.

A LITTLE WARMER, C'MON.

OH! ALMOST FORGOT...

...THE PAPER--

KNK

THREE DAYS LATER.

HELLO? ANYONE HOME? JUST DOING A WELFARE CHECK-IN.

NEIGHBOR SAID THE PAPERS WERE STACKING UP.

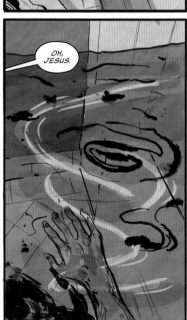

OH, JESUS.

"THEN WHAT HAPPENED?"

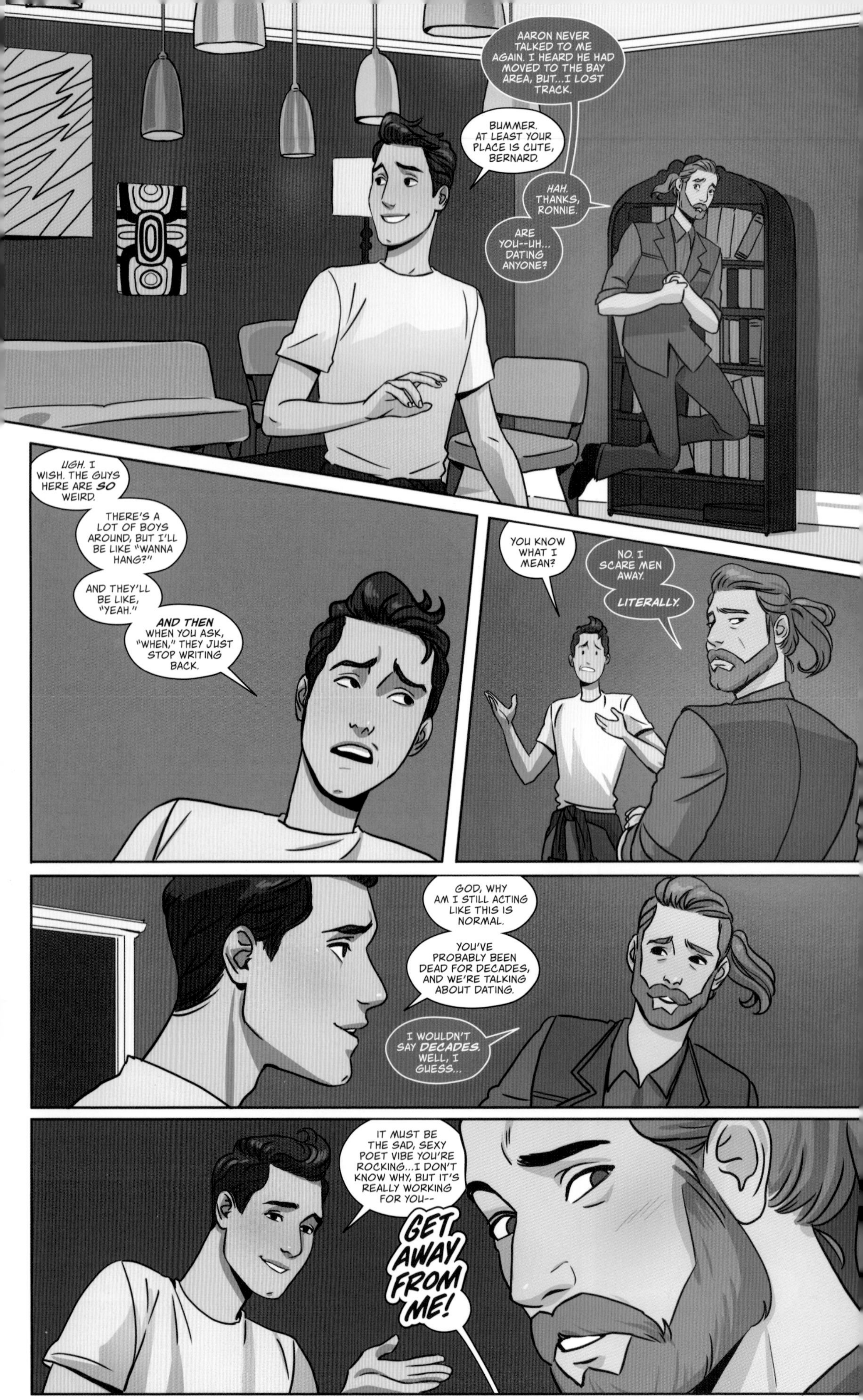
AARON NEVER TALKED TO ME AGAIN. I HEARD HE HAD MOVED TO THE BAY AREA, BUT...I LOST TRACK.
BUMMER. AT LEAST YOUR PLACE IS CUTE, BERNARD.
HAH. THANKS, RONNIE.
ARE YOU--UH... DATING ANYONE?
UGH. I WISH. THE GUYS HERE ARE SO WEIRD.
THERE'S A LOT OF BOYS AROUND, BUT I'LL BE LIKE "WANNA HANG?"
AND THEY'LL BE LIKE, "YEAH."
AND THEN WHEN YOU ASK, "WHEN," THEY JUST STOP WRITING BACK.
YOU KNOW WHAT I MEAN?
NO. I SCARE MEN AWAY.
LITERALLY.
GOD, WHY AM I STILL ACTING LIKE THIS IS NORMAL.
YOU'VE PROBABLY BEEN DEAD FOR DECADES, AND WE'RE TALKING ABOUT DATING.
I WOULDN'T SAY DECADES. WELL, I GUESS...
IT MUST BE THE SAD, SEXY POET VIBE YOU'RE ROCKING...I DON'T KNOW WHY, BUT IT'S REALLY WORKING FOR YOU--
GET AWAY FROM ME!

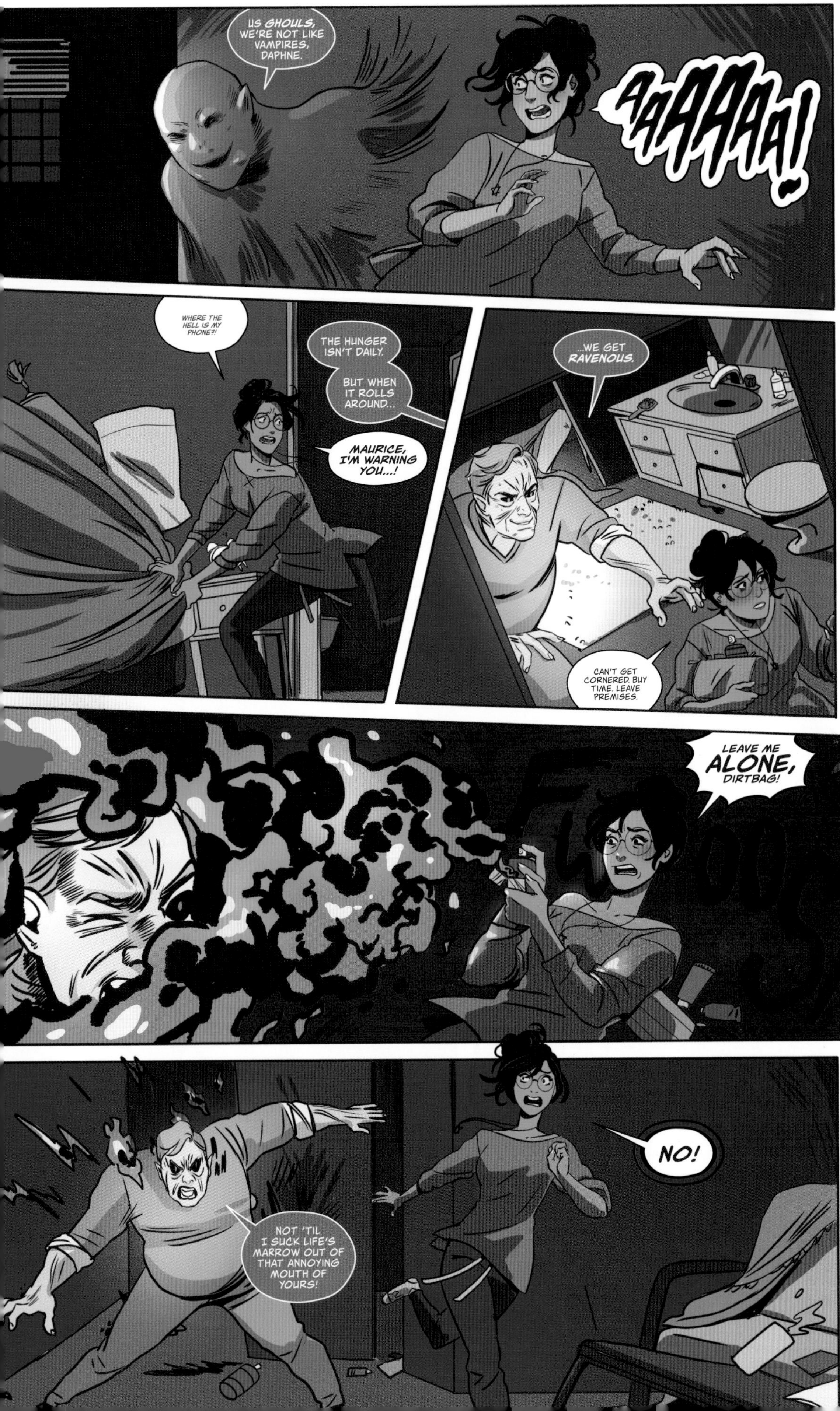
US GHOULS, WE'RE NOT LIKE VAMPIRES, DAPHNE.
AAAAAAA!
WHERE THE HELL IS MY PHONE?!
THE HUNGER ISN'T DAILY.
BUT WHEN IT ROLLS AROUND...
MAURICE, I'M WARNING YOU...!
...WE GET RAVENOUS.
CAN'T GET CORNERED. BUY TIME. LEAVE PREMISES.
LEAVE ME ALONE, DIRTBAG!
FWOOSH
NO!
NOT 'TIL I SUCK LIFE'S MARROW OUT OF THAT ANNOYING MOUTH OF YOURS!

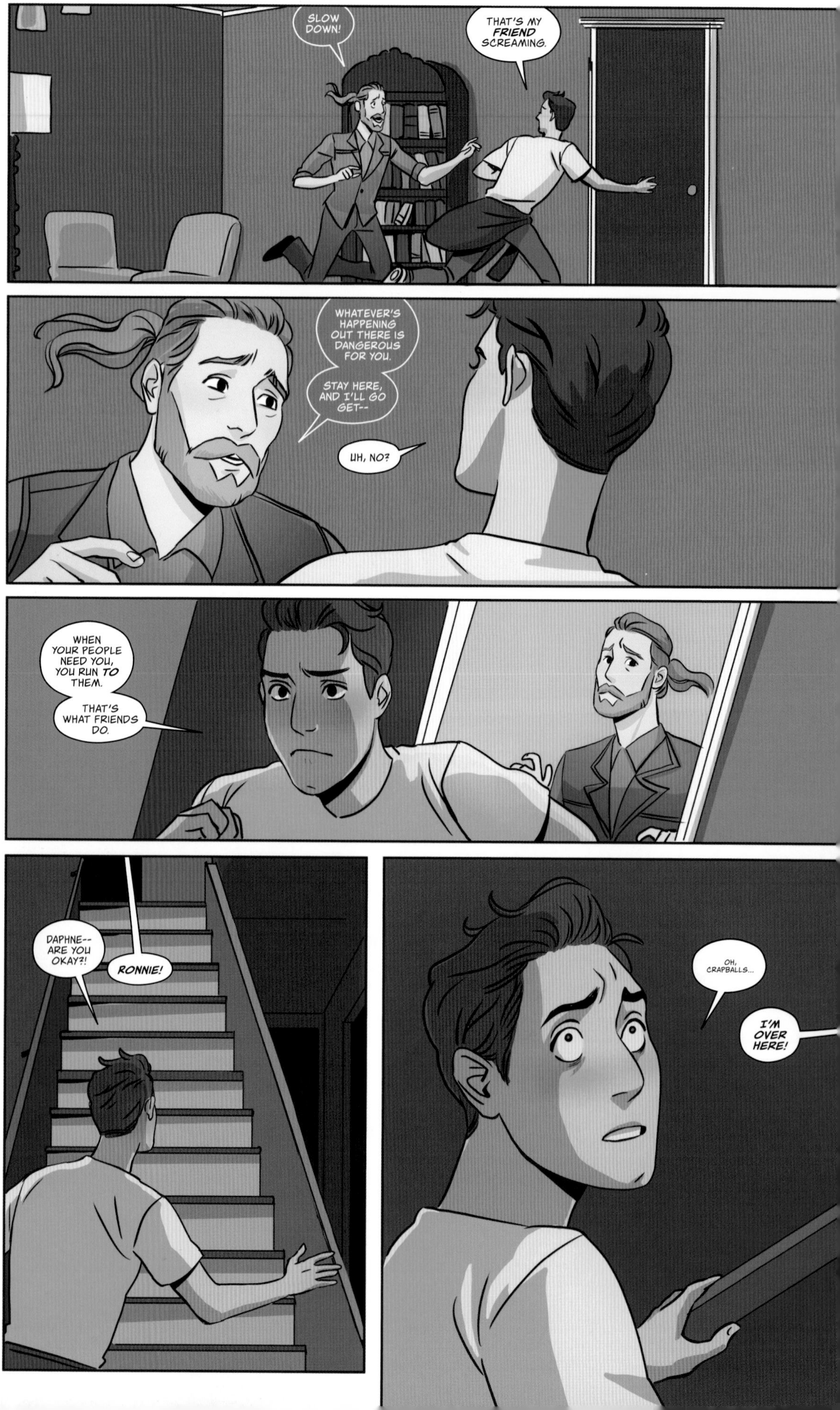
SLOW DOWN!
THAT'S MY FRIEND SCREAMING.
WHATEVER'S HAPPENING OUT THERE IS DANGEROUS FOR YOU.
STAY HERE, AND I'LL GO GET--
UH, NO?
WHEN YOUR PEOPLE NEED YOU, YOU RUN TO THEM.
THAT'S WHAT FRIENDS DO.
DAPHNE-- ARE YOU OKAY?!
RONNIE!
OH, CRAPBALLS...
I'M OVER HERE!

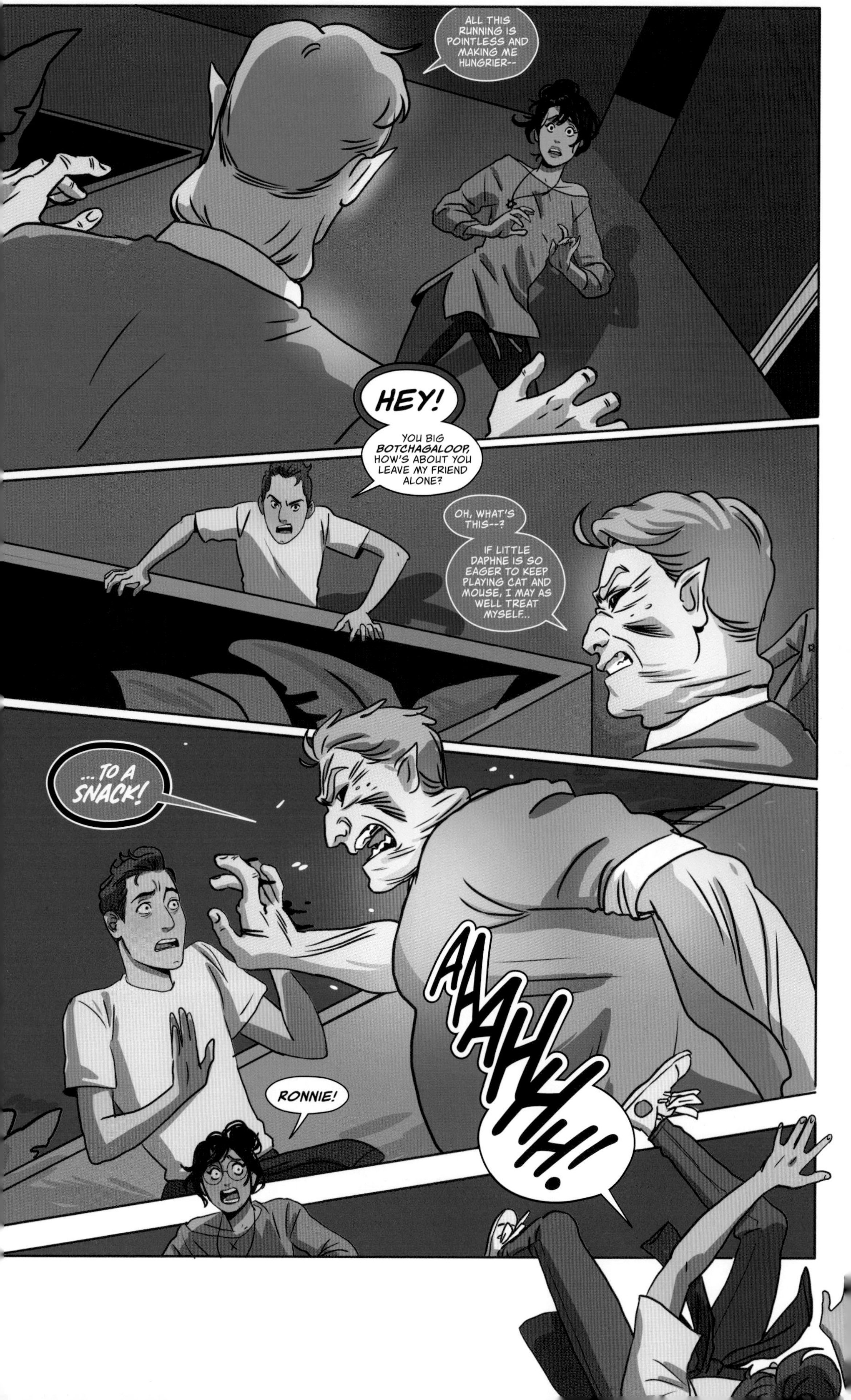
ALL THIS RUNNING IS POINTLESS AND MAKING ME HUNGRIER--
HEY!
YOU BIG BOTCHAGALOOP, HOW'S ABOUT YOU LEAVE MY FRIEND ALONE?
OH, WHAT'S THIS--?
IF LITTLE DAPHNE IS SO EAGER TO KEEP PLAYING CAT AND MOUSE, I MAY AS WELL TREAT MYSELF...
...TO A SNACK!
RONNIE!
AAAHHH!

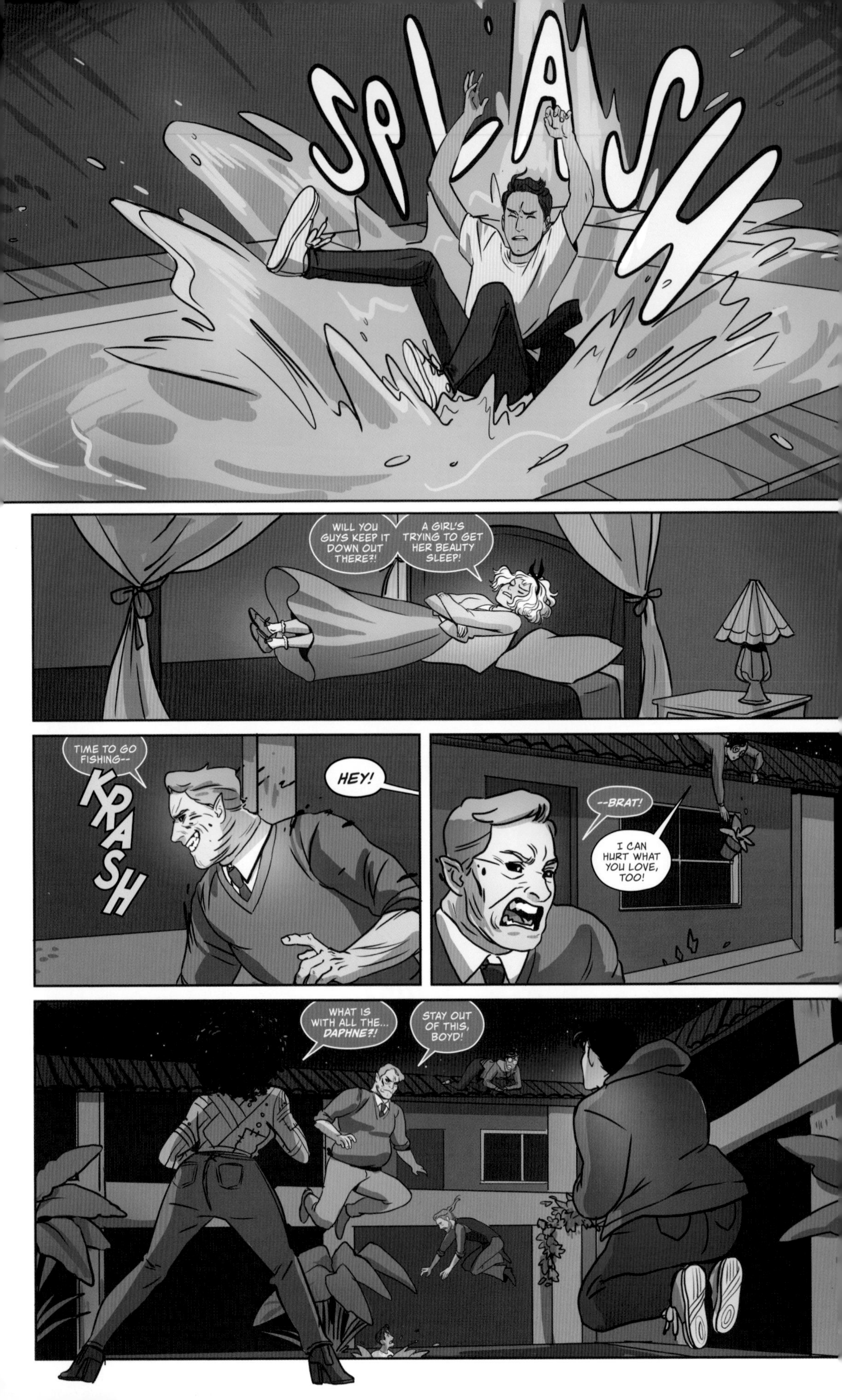
SPLASH
WILL YOU GUYS KEEP IT DOWN OUT THERE?!
A GIRL'S TRYING TO GET HER BEAUTY SLEEP!
TIME TO GO FISHING--
KRASH
HEY!
--BRAT!
I CAN HURT WHAT YOU LOVE, TOO!
WHAT IS WITH ALL THE... DAPHNE?!
STAY OUT OF THIS, BOYD!

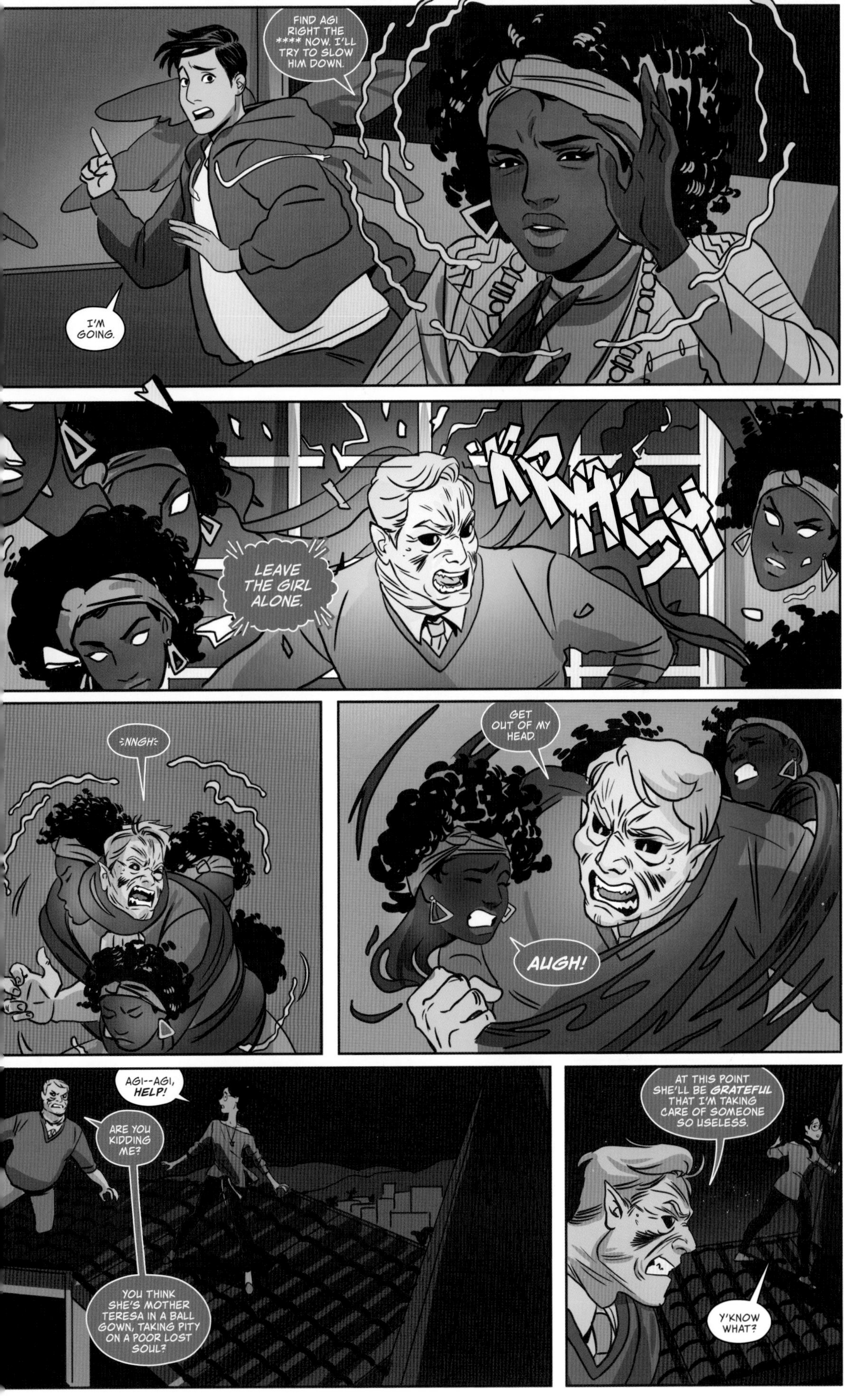
FIND AGI RIGHT THE **** NOW. I'LL TRY TO SLOW HIM DOWN.
I'M GOING.
KRASH
LEAVE THE GIRL ALONE.
NNGH
GET OUT OF MY HEAD.
AUGH!
AGI--AGI, HELP!
ARE YOU KIDDING ME?
YOU THINK SHE'S MOTHER TERESA IN A BALL GOWN, TAKING PITY ON A POOR LOST SOUL?
AT THIS POINT SHE'LL BE GRATEFUL THAT I'M TAKING CARE OF SOMEONE SO USELESS.
Y'KNOW WHAT?

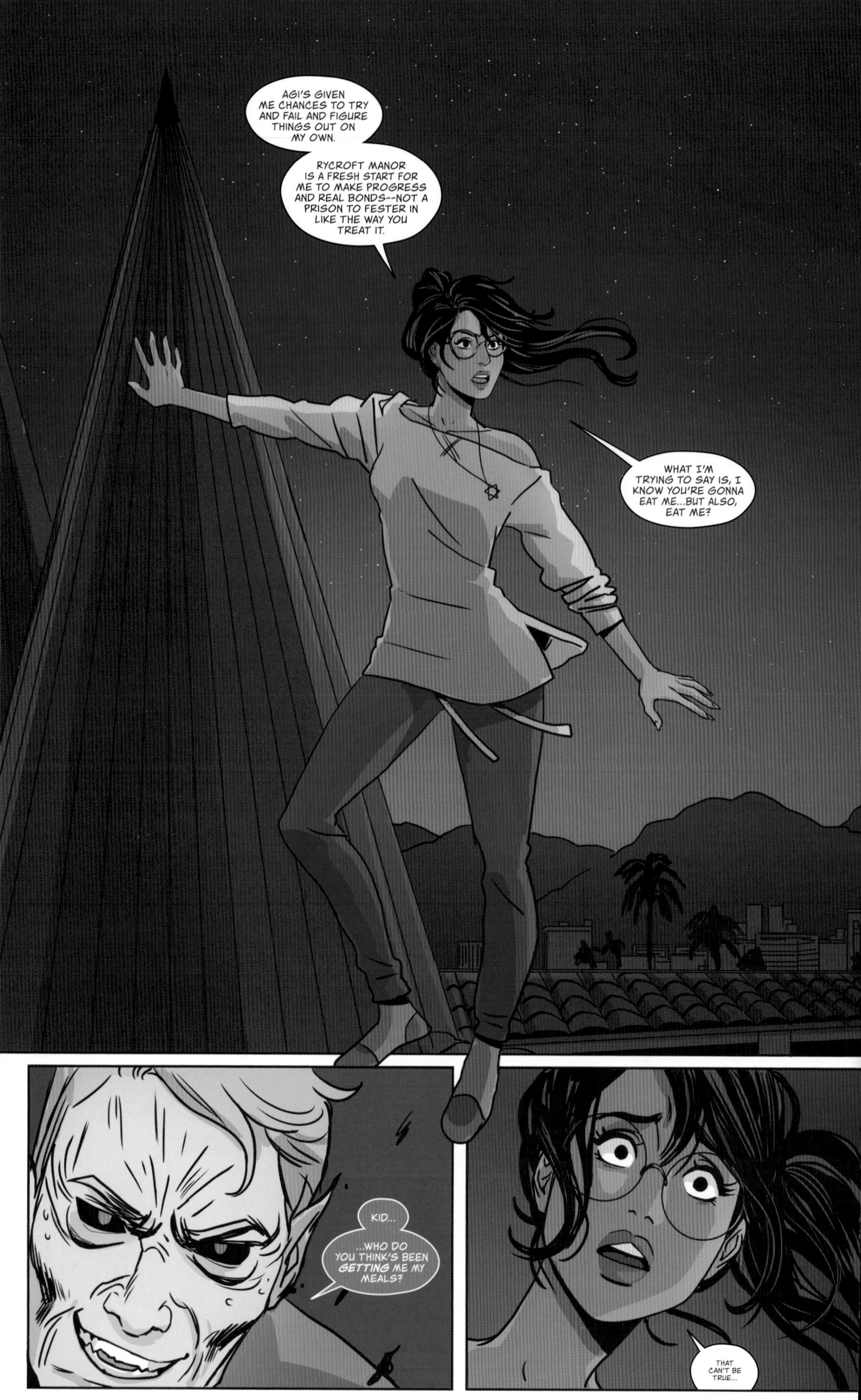
AGI'S GIVEN ME CHANCES TO TRY AND FAIL AND FIGURE THINGS OUT ON MY OWN.
RYCROFT MANOR IS A FRESH START FOR ME TO MAKE PROGRESS AND REAL BONDS--NOT A PRISON TO FESTER IN LIKE THE WAY YOU TREAT IT.
WHAT I'M TRYING TO SAY IS, I KNOW YOU'RE GONNA EAT ME...BUT ALSO, EAT ME?
KID...
...WHO DO YOU THINK'S BEEN *GETTING* ME MY MEALS?
THAT CAN'T BE TRUE...

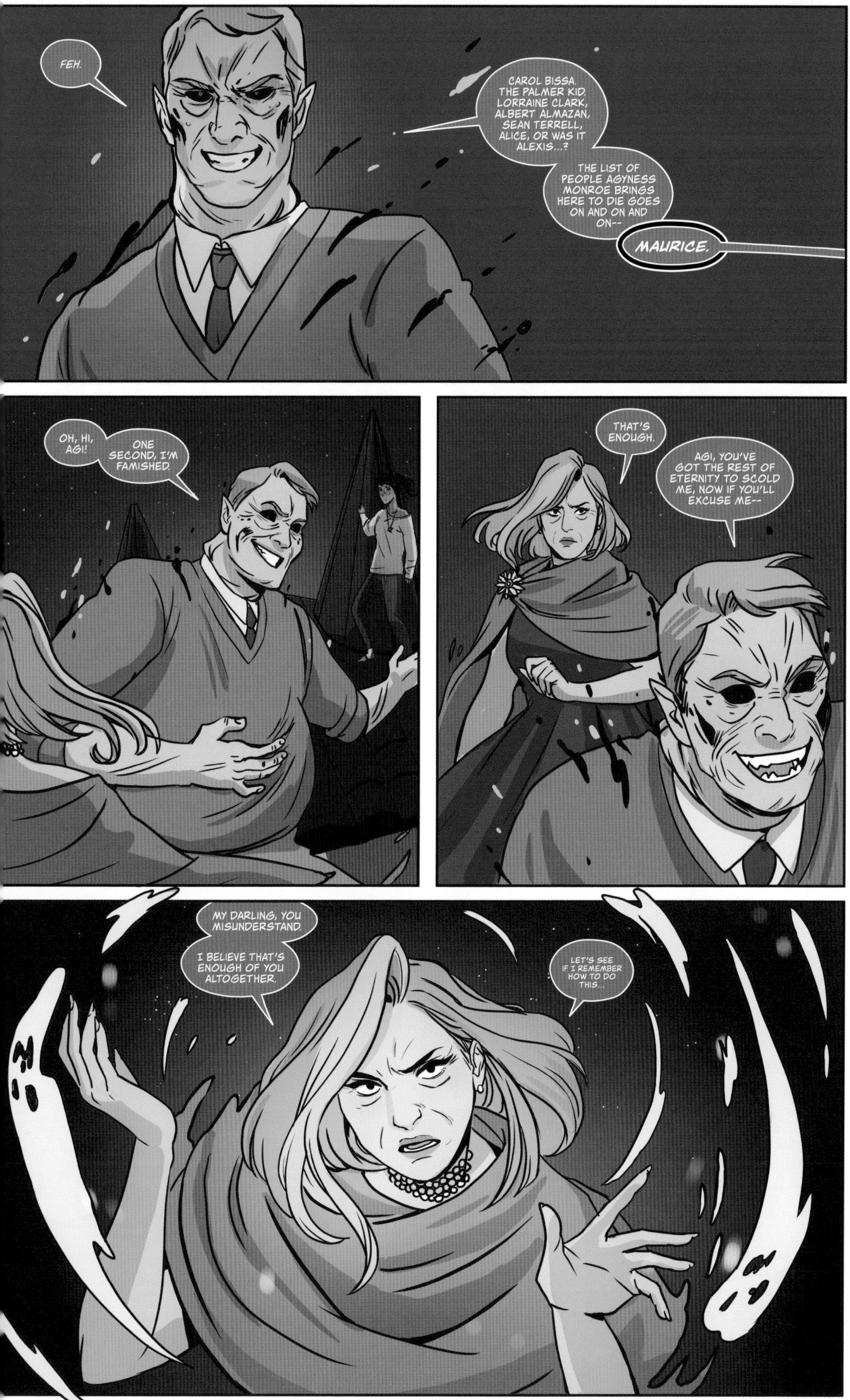
FEH.
CAROL BISSA. THE PALMER KID. LORRAINE CLARK, ALBERT ALMAZAN, SEAN TERRELL, ALICE, OR WAS IT ALEXIS...?
THE LIST OF PEOPLE AGYNESS MONROE BRINGS HERE TO DIE GOES ON AND ON AND ON--
MAURICE.
OH, HI, AGI!
ONE SECOND, I'M FAMISHED.
THAT'S ENOUGH.
AGI, YOU'VE GOT THE REST OF ETERNITY TO SCOLD ME, NOW IF YOU'LL EXCUSE ME--
MY DARLING, YOU MISUNDERSTAND.
I BELIEVE THAT'S ENOUGH OF YOU ALTOGETHER.
LET'S SEE IF I REMEMBER HOW TO DO THIS...

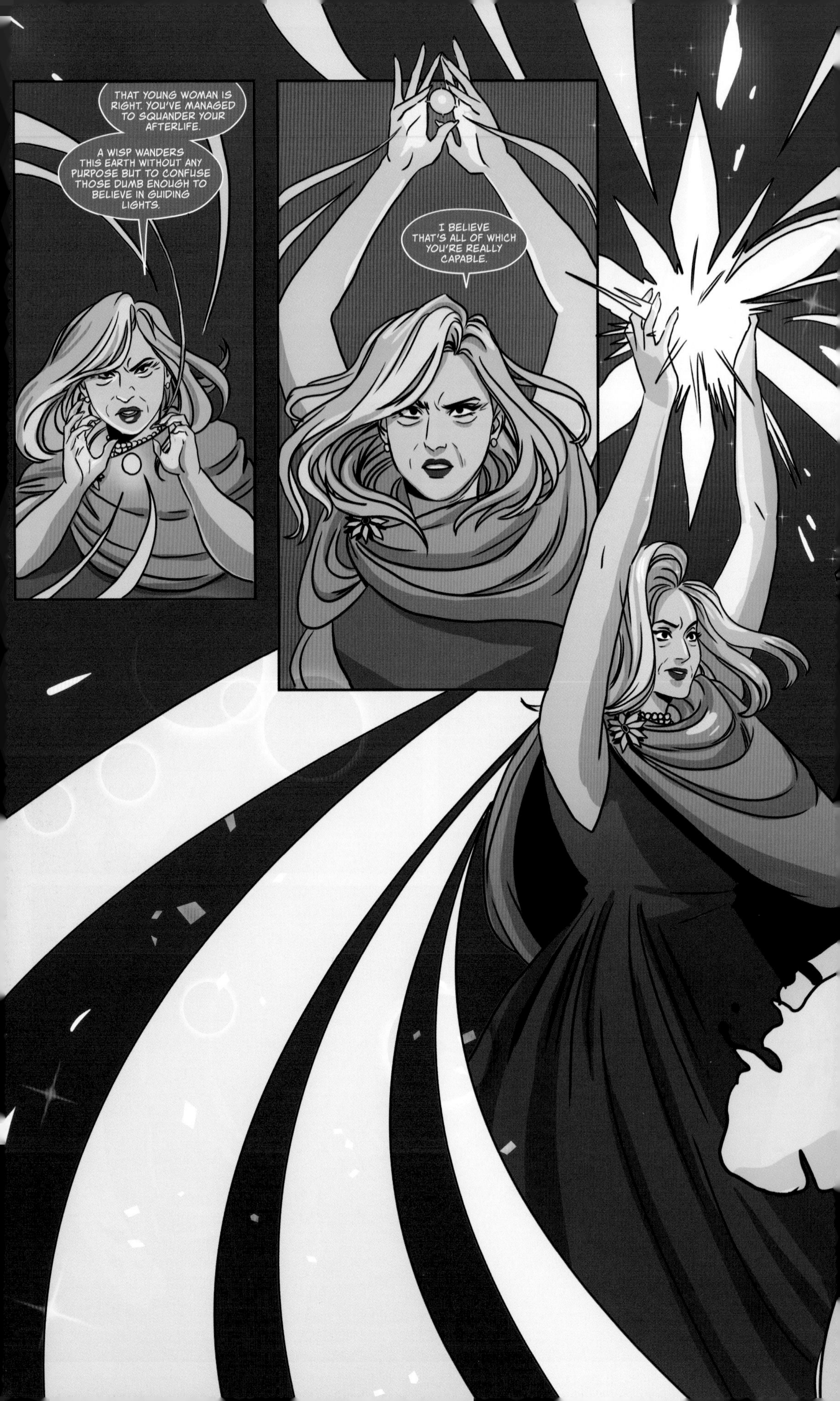

THAT YOUNG WOMAN IS RIGHT. YOU'VE MANAGED TO SQUANDER YOUR AFTERLIFE.
A WISP WANDERS THIS EARTH WITHOUT ANY PURPOSE BUT TO CONFUSE THOSE DUMB ENOUGH TO BELIEVE IN GUIDING LIGHTS.
I BELIEVE THAT'S ALL OF WHICH YOU'RE REALLY CAPABLE.

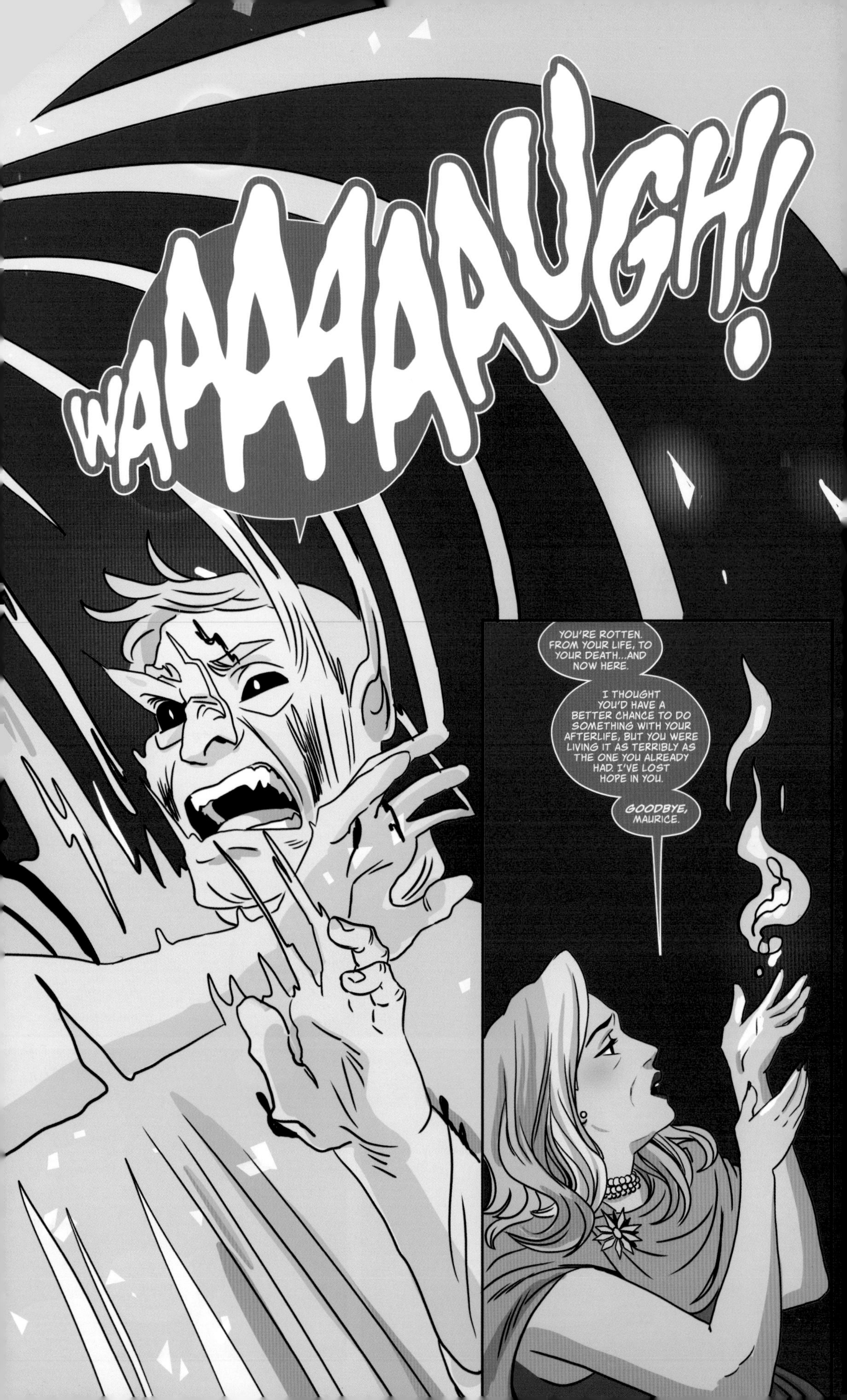
WAAAAAUGH!
YOU'RE ROTTEN. FROM YOUR LIFE, TO YOUR DEATH...AND NOW HERE.
I THOUGHT YOU'D HAVE A BETTER CHANCE TO DO SOMETHING WITH YOUR AFTERLIFE, BUT YOU WERE LIVING IT AS TERRIBLY AS THE ONE YOU ALREADY HAD. I'VE LOST HOPE IN YOU.
GOODBYE, MAURICE.

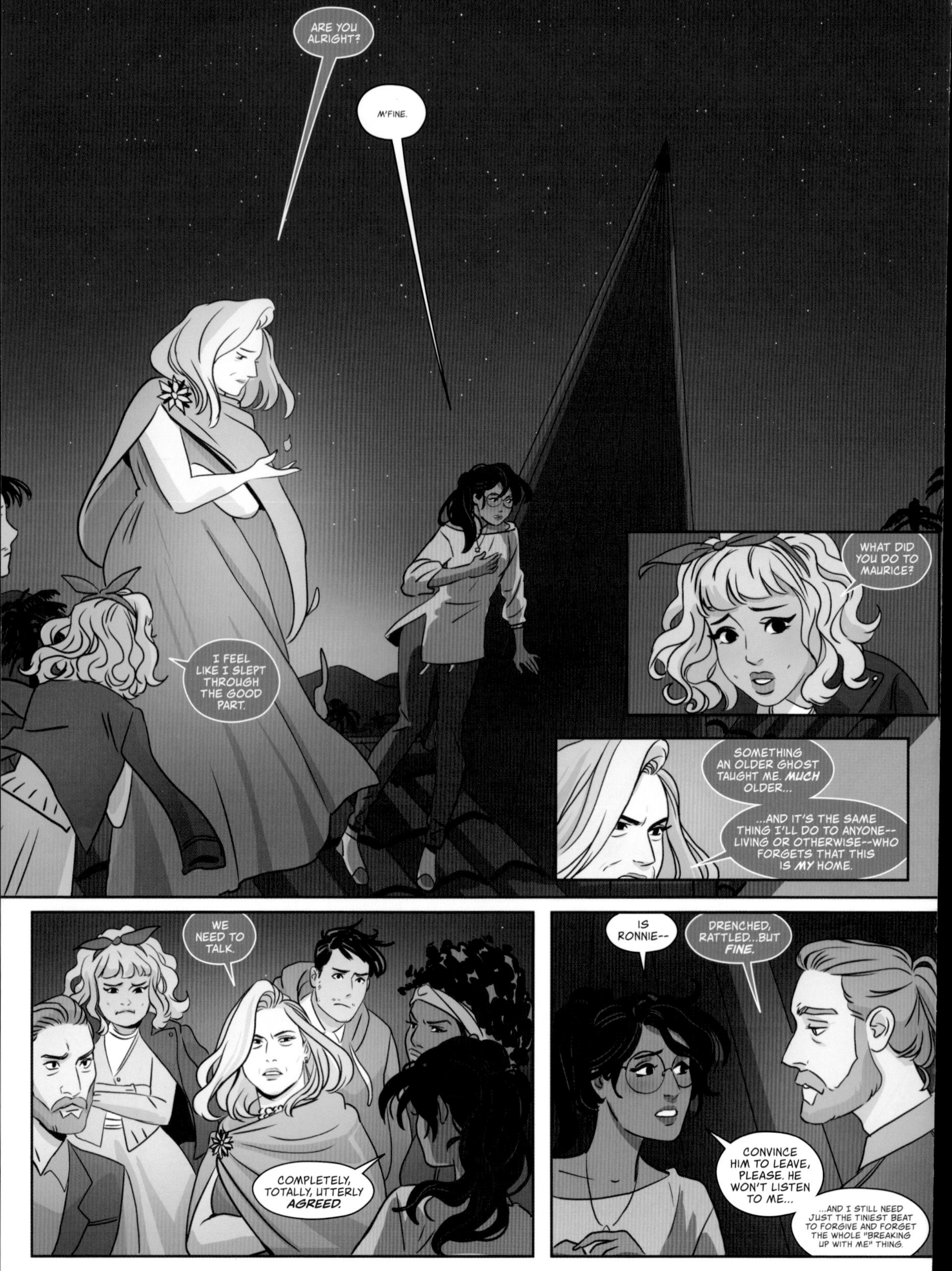
ARE YOU ALRIGHT?
M'FINE.
I FEEL LIKE I SLEPT THROUGH THE GOOD PART.
WHAT DID YOU DO TO MAURICE?
SOMETHING AN OLDER GHOST TAUGHT ME. MUCH OLDER...
...AND IT'S THE SAME THING I'LL DO TO ANYONE--LIVING OR OTHERWISE--WHO FORGETS THAT THIS IS MY HOME.
WE NEED TO TALK.
COMPLETELY, TOTALLY, UTTERLY AGREED.
IS RONNIE--
DRENCHED, RATTLED...BUT FINE.
CONVINCE HIM TO LEAVE, PLEASE. HE WON'T LISTEN TO ME...
...AND I STILL NEED JUST THE TINIEST BEAT TO FORGIVE AND FORGET THE WHOLE "BREAKING UP WITH ME" THING.

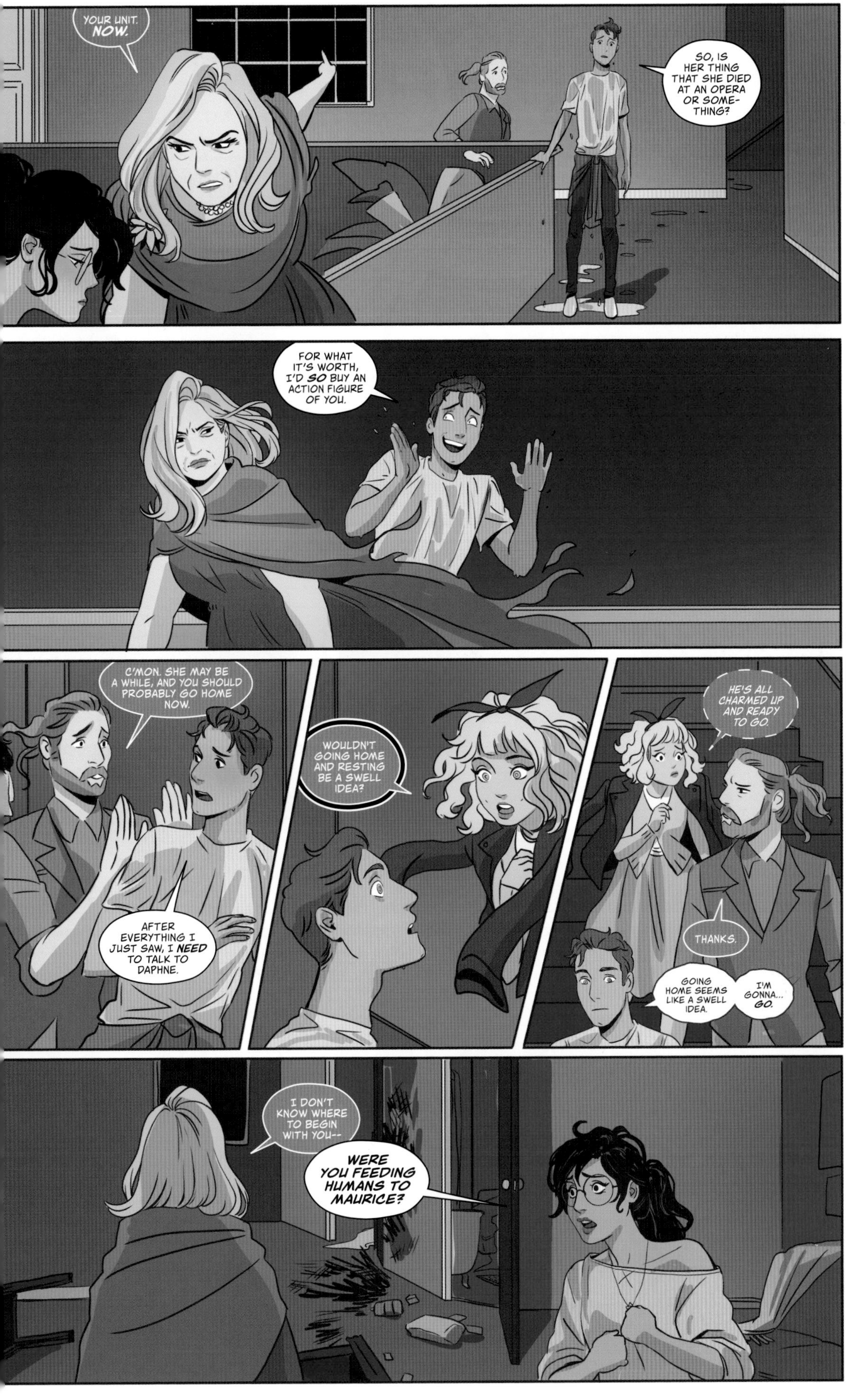
YOUR UNIT. NOW.
SO, IS HER THING THAT SHE DIED AT AN OPERA OR SOME-THING?
FOR WHAT IT'S WORTH, I'D SO BUY AN ACTION FIGURE OF YOU.
C'MON. SHE MAY BE A WHILE, AND YOU SHOULD PROBABLY GO HOME NOW.
AFTER EVERYTHING I JUST SAW, I NEED TO TALK TO DAPHNE.
WOULDN'T GOING HOME AND RESTING BE A SWELL IDEA?
HE'S ALL CHARMED UP AND READY TO GO.
THANKS.
GOING HOME SEEMS LIKE A SWELL IDEA.
I'M GONNA... GO.
I DON'T KNOW WHERE TO BEGIN WITH YOU--
WERE YOU FEEDING HUMANS TO MAURICE?

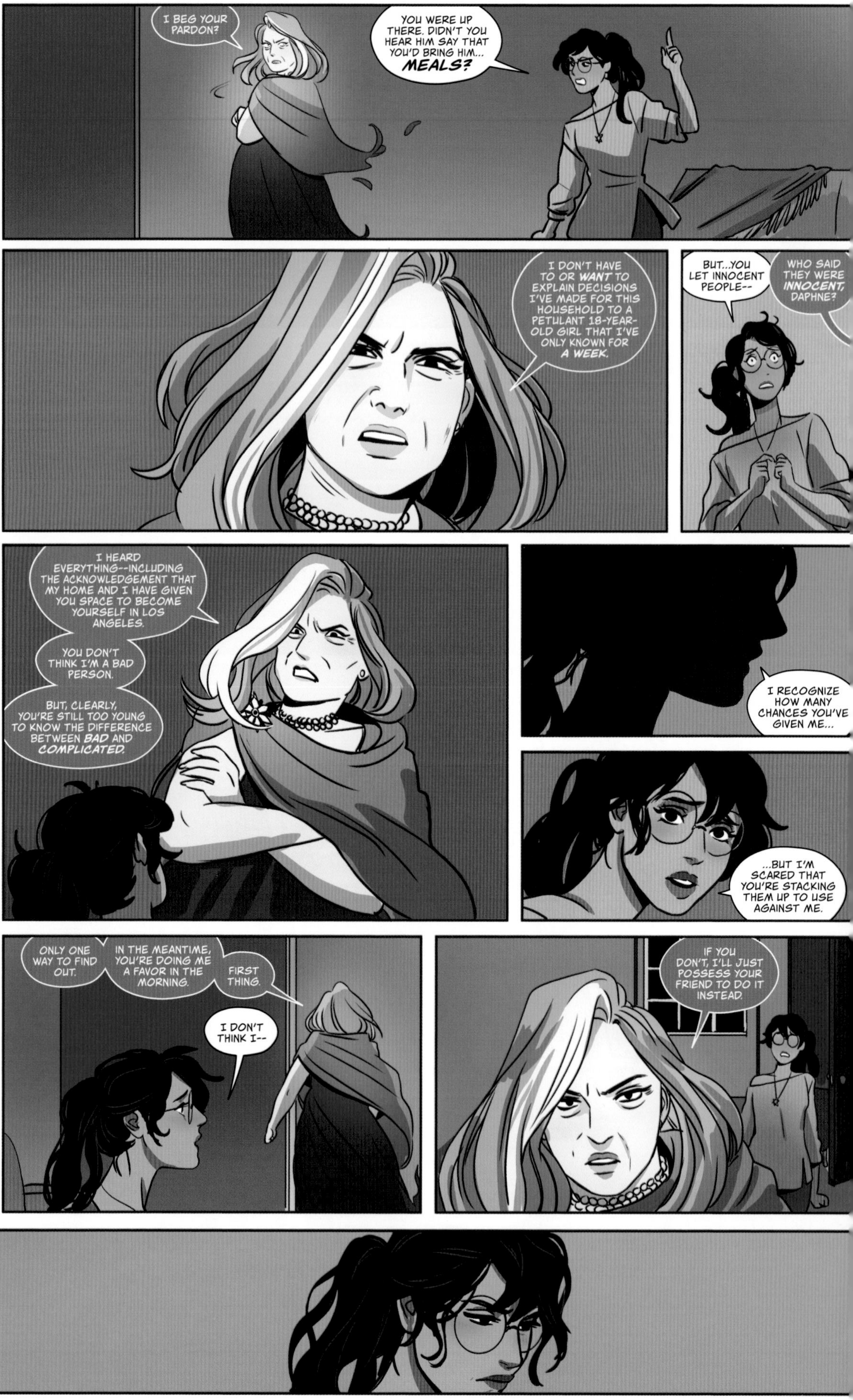
I BEG YOUR PARDON?
YOU WERE UP THERE. DIDN'T YOU HEAR HIM SAY THAT YOU'D BRING HIM... MEALS?
I DON'T HAVE TO OR WANT TO EXPLAIN DECISIONS I'VE MADE FOR THIS HOUSEHOLD TO A PETULANT 18-YEAR-OLD GIRL THAT I'VE ONLY KNOWN FOR A WEEK.
BUT...YOU LET INNOCENT PEOPLE--
WHO SAID THEY WERE INNOCENT, DAPHNE?
I HEARD EVERYTHING--INCLUDING THE ACKNOWLEDGEMENT THAT MY HOME AND I HAVE GIVEN YOU SPACE TO BECOME YOURSELF IN LOS ANGELES.
YOU DON'T THINK I'M A BAD PERSON.
BUT, CLEARLY, YOU'RE STILL TOO YOUNG TO KNOW THE DIFFERENCE BETWEEN BAD AND COMPLICATED.
I RECOGNIZE HOW MANY CHANCES YOU'VE GIVEN ME...
...BUT I'M SCARED THAT YOU'RE STACKING THEM UP TO USE AGAINST ME.
ONLY ONE WAY TO FIND OUT.
IN THE MEANTIME, YOU'RE DOING ME A FAVOR IN THE MORNING.
FIRST THING.
I DON'T THINK I--
IF YOU DON'T, I'LL JUST POSSESS YOUR FRIEND TO DO IT INSTEAD.

"I NEED YOU TO VISIT SOMEONE FOR ME.

"HE'S A BIT OUT OF THE WAY, SO LEAVE EARLY BEFORE TRAFFIC SETS IN.

"BRING FLOWERS. ONLY PEONIES, DAISIES, AND CARNATIONS. ANY CARNATIONS WILL DO...

"...EXCEPT RED ONES."

OOH!

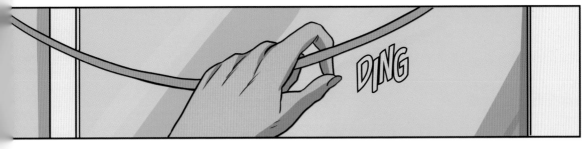

DING

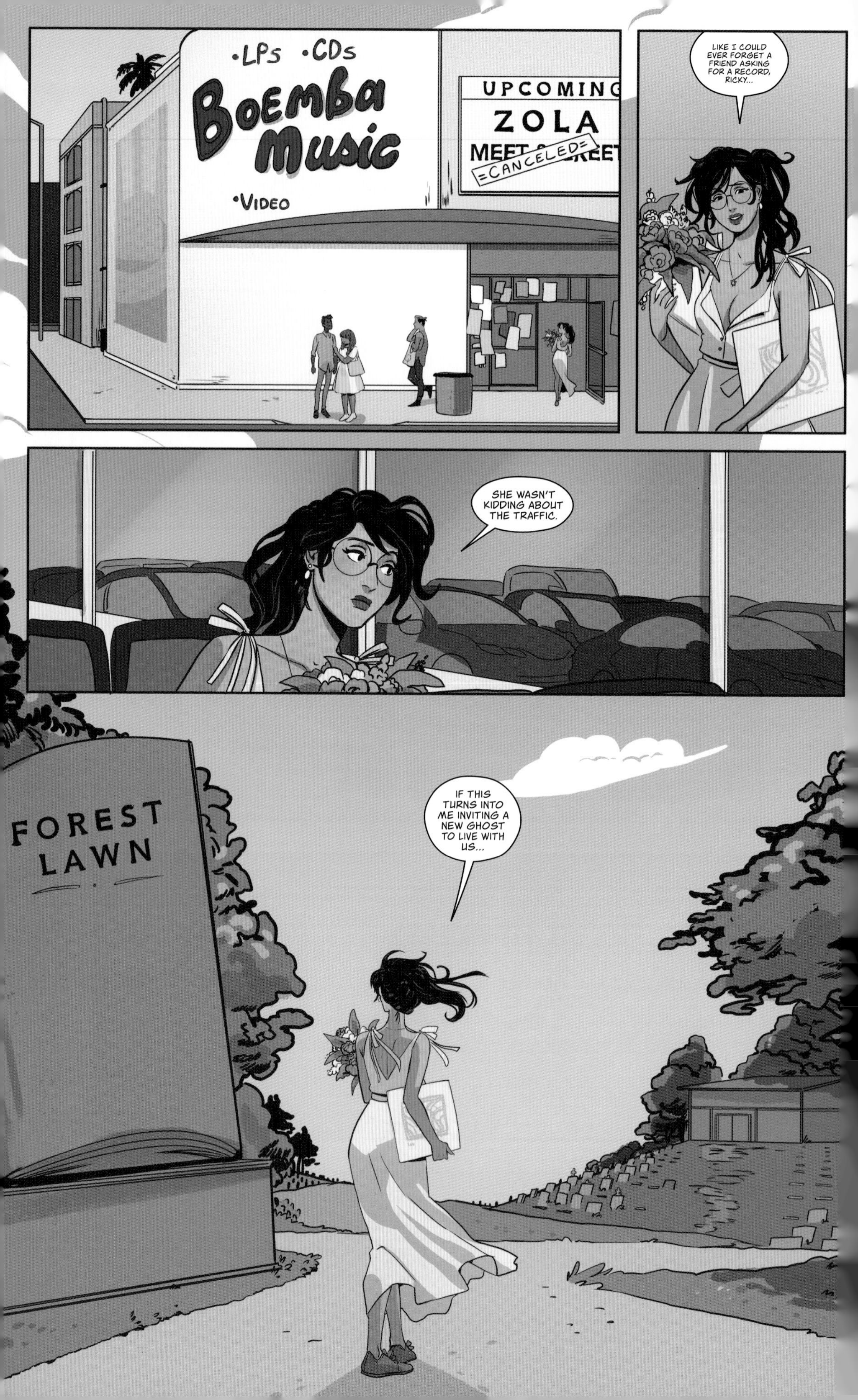
• LPs • CDs
Boemba Music
• Video
UPCOMING
ZOLA
=CANCELED=
LIKE I COULD EVER FORGET A FRIEND ASKING FOR A RECORD, RICKY...
SHE WASN'T KIDDING ABOUT THE TRAFFIC.
FOREST LAWN
IF THIS TURNS INTO ME INVITING A NEW GHOST TO LIVE WITH US...

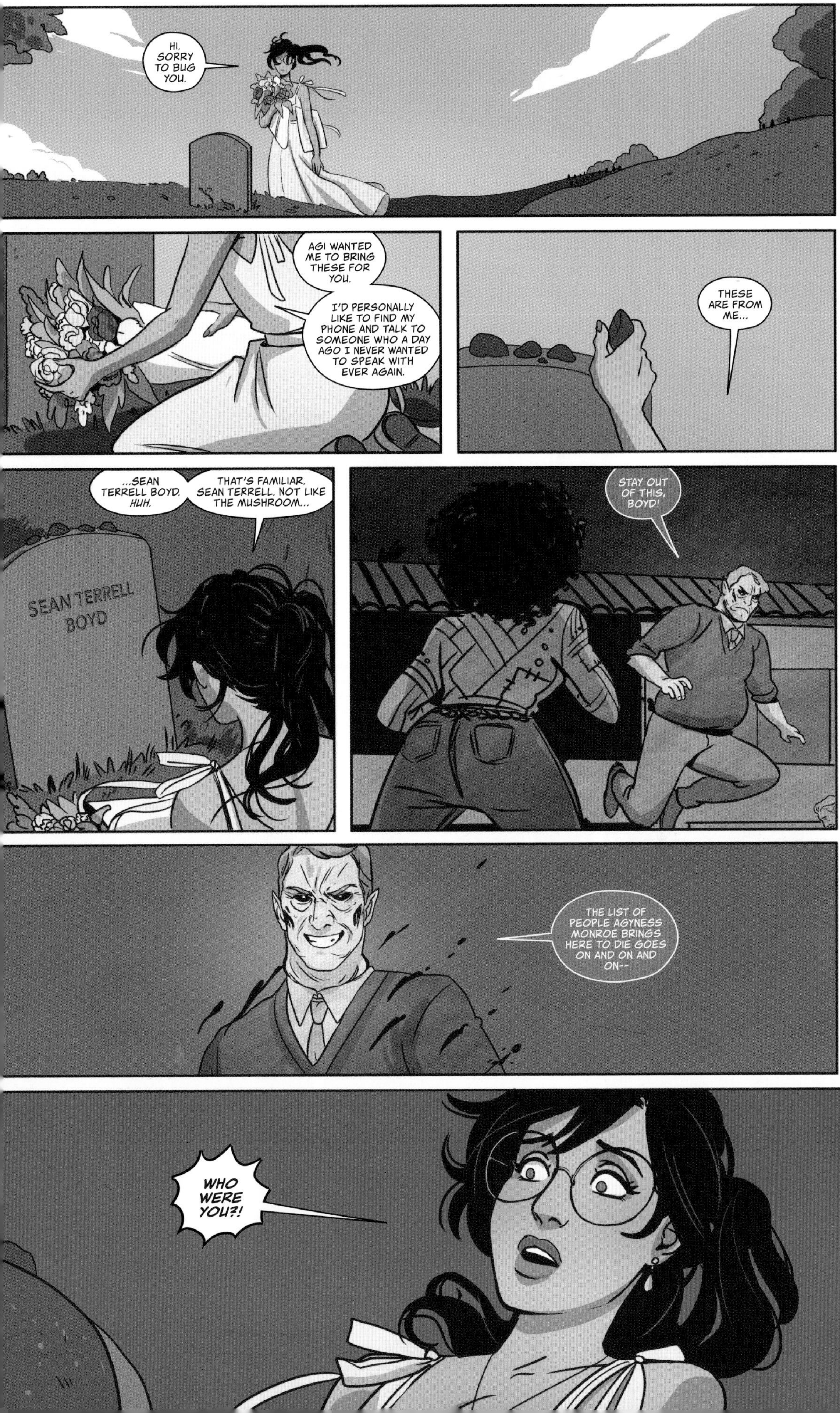
HI. SORRY TO BUG YOU.
AGI WANTED ME TO BRING THESE FOR YOU.
I'D PERSONALLY LIKE TO FIND MY PHONE AND TALK TO SOMEONE WHO A DAY AGO I NEVER WANTED TO SPEAK WITH EVER AGAIN.
THESE ARE FROM ME...
...SEAN TERRELL BOYD. HUH.
THAT'S FAMILIAR. SEAN TERRELL. NOT LIKE THE MUSHROOM...
SEAN TERRELL BOYD
STAY OUT OF THIS, BOYD!
THE LIST OF PEOPLE AGYNESS MONROE BRINGS HERE TO DIE GOES ON AND ON AND ON--
WHO WERE YOU?!

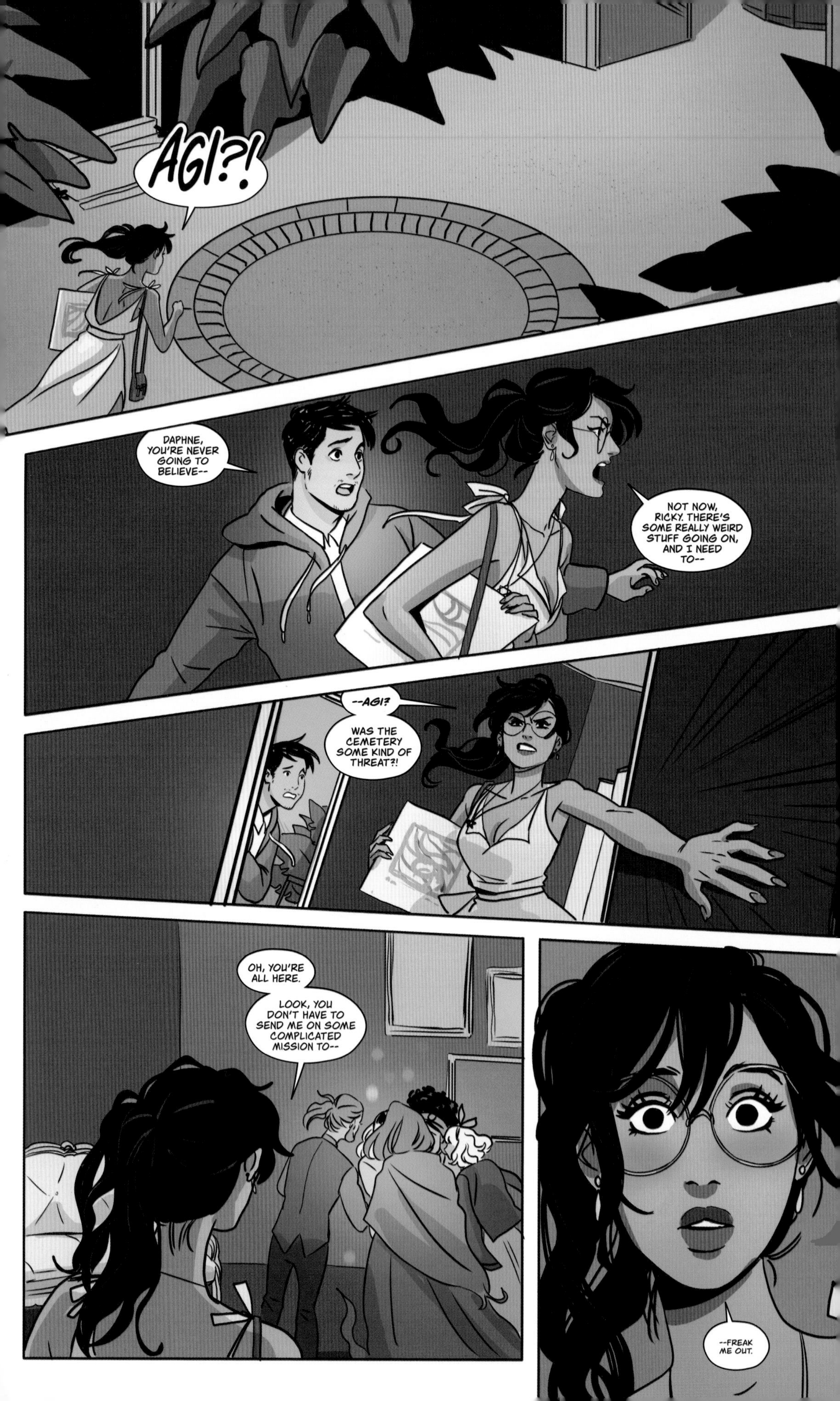

AGI?!
DAPHNE, YOU'RE NEVER GOING TO BELIEVE--
NOT NOW, RICKY. THERE'S SOME REALLY WEIRD STUFF GOING ON, AND I NEED TO--
--AGI?
WAS THE CEMETERY SOME KIND OF THREAT?!
OH, YOU'RE ALL HERE.
LOOK, YOU DON'T HAVE TO SEND ME ON SOME COMPLICATED MISSION TO--
--FREAK ME OUT.

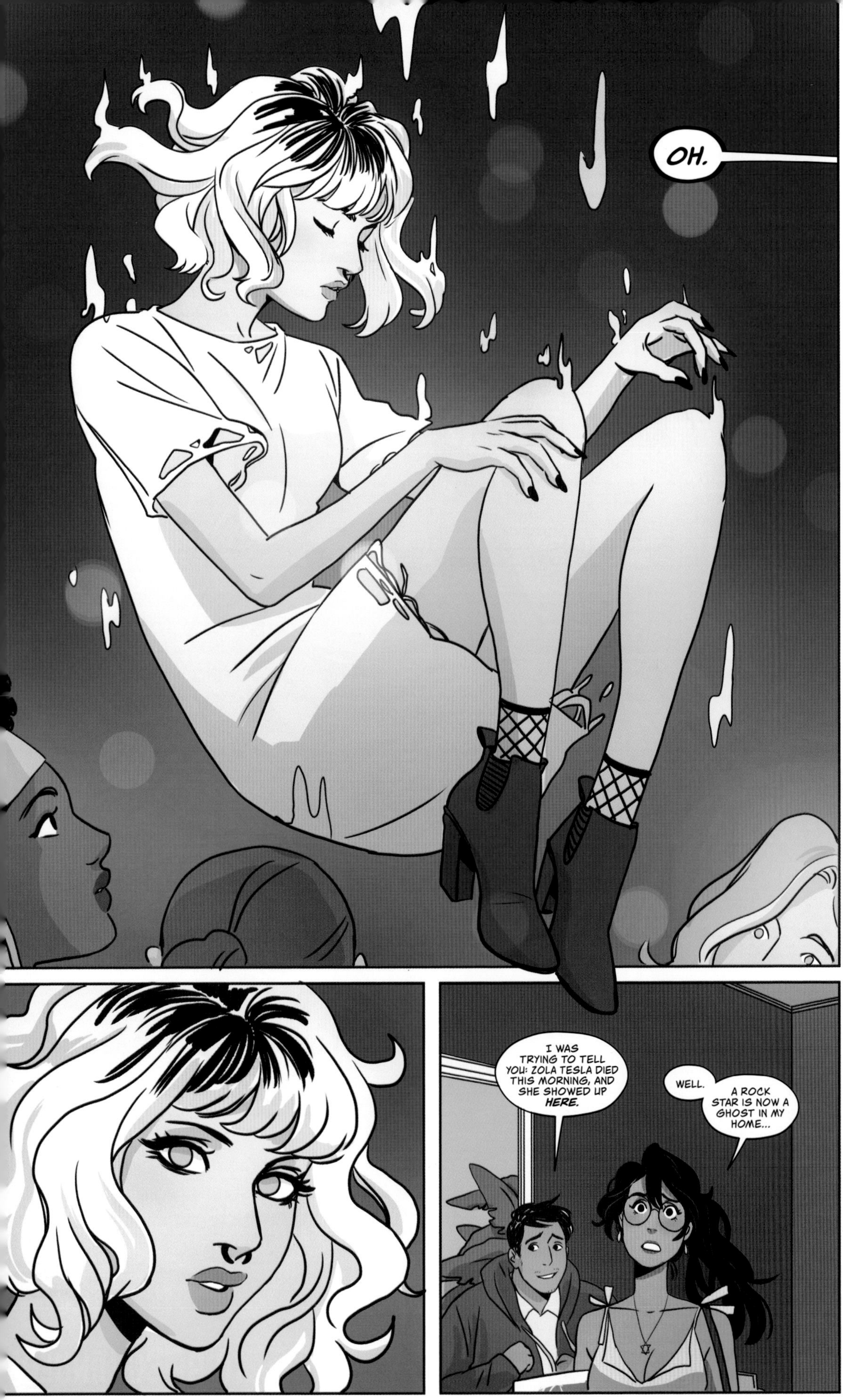
OH.
I WAS TRYING TO TELL YOU: ZOLA TESLA DIED THIS MORNING, AND SHE SHOWED UP HERE.
WELL.
A ROCK STAR IS NOW A GHOST IN MY HOME...

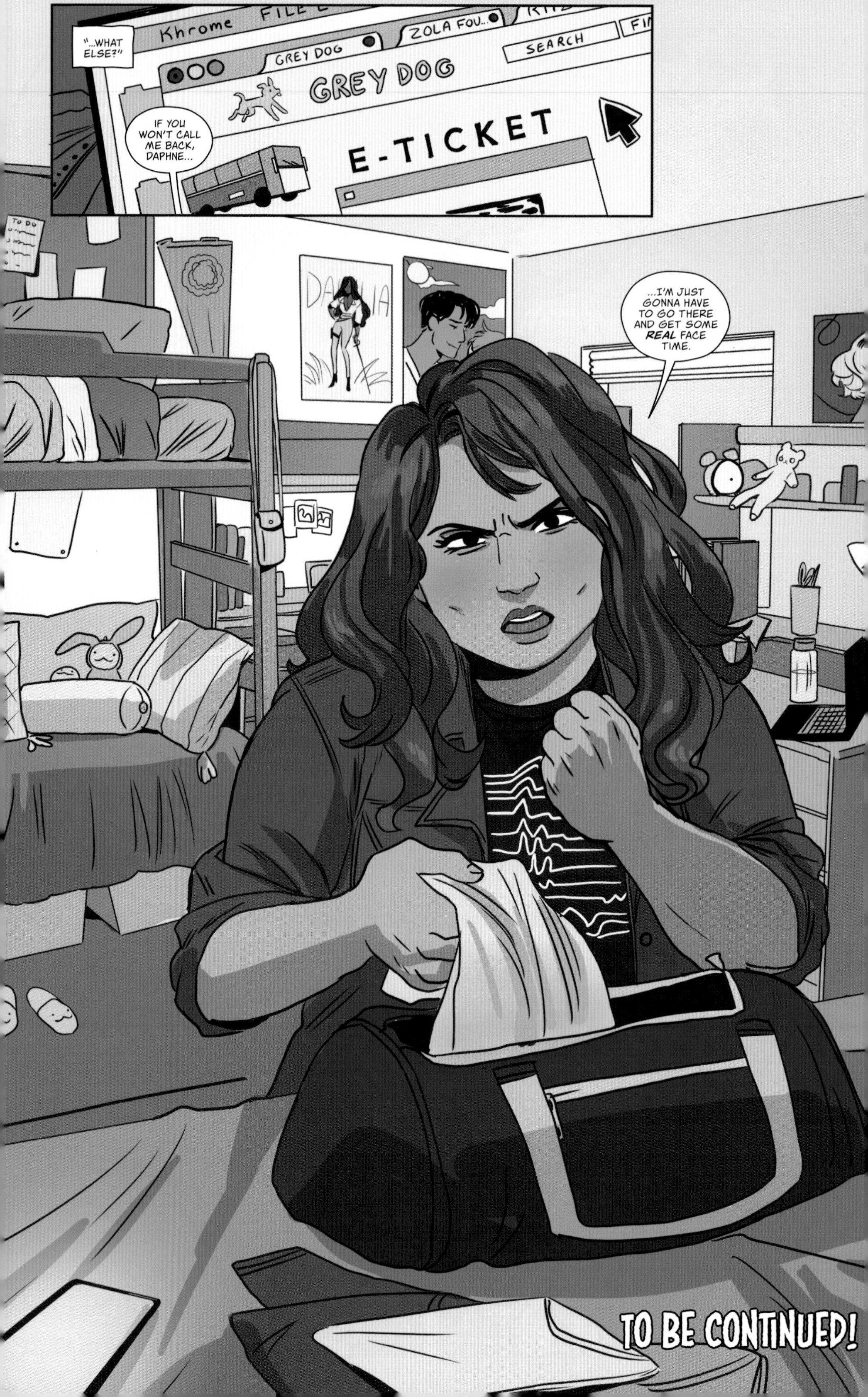

"...WHAT ELSE?"
IF YOU WON'T CALL ME BACK, DAPHNE...
Khrome
ZOLA FOU...
GREY DOG
SEARCH
GREY DOG
E-TICKET
...I'M JUST GONNA HAVE TO GO THERE AND GET SOME **REAL** FACE TIME.
TO BE CONTINUED!

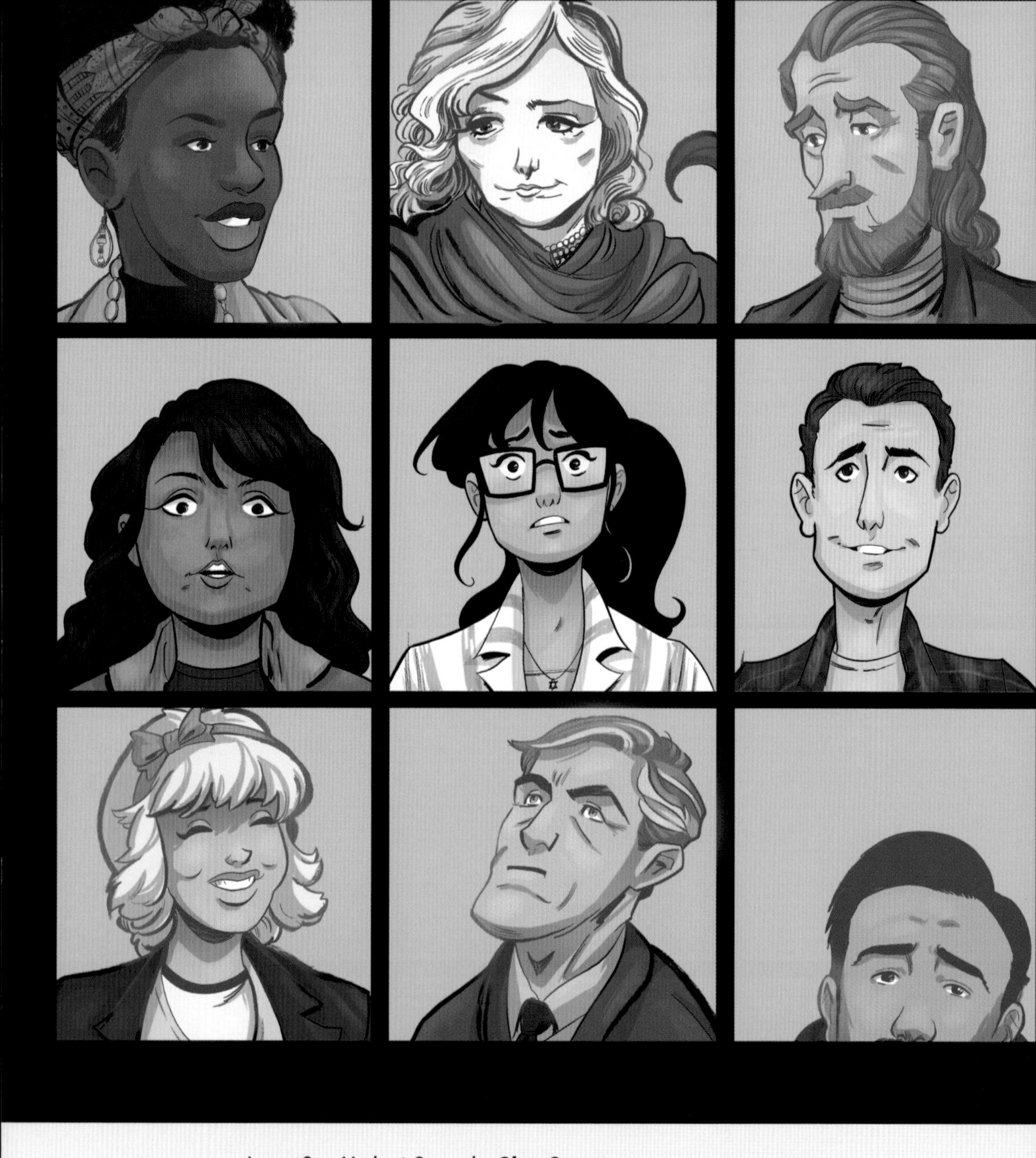

Issue One Variant Cover by **Sina Grace** with Colors by **Jamie Loughran**

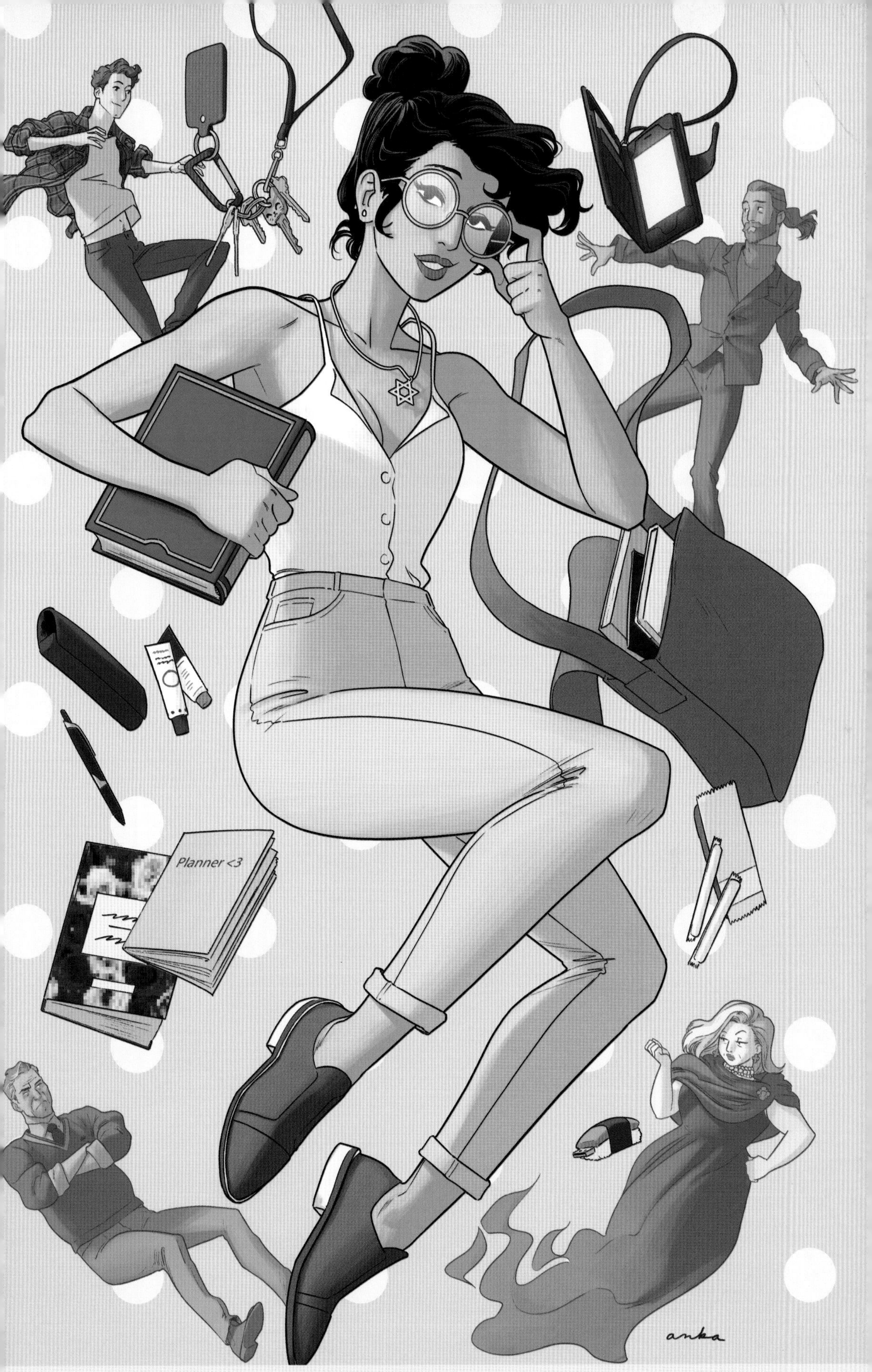
Planner <3
anka

Issue One Unlocked Retailer Variant Cover by **Kris Anka**

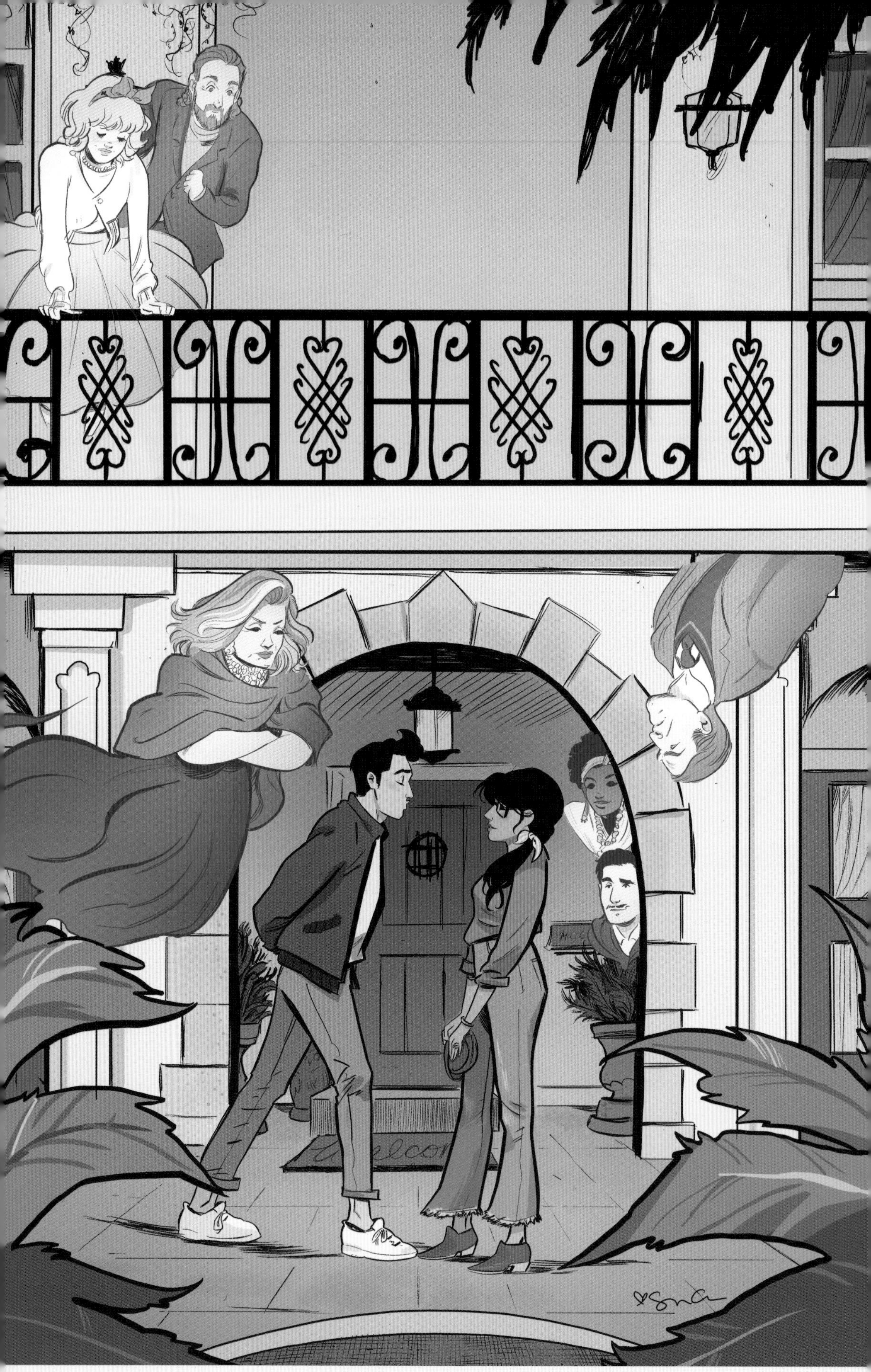

Issue Two Variant Cover by **Sina Grace** with Colors by **Cathy Le**

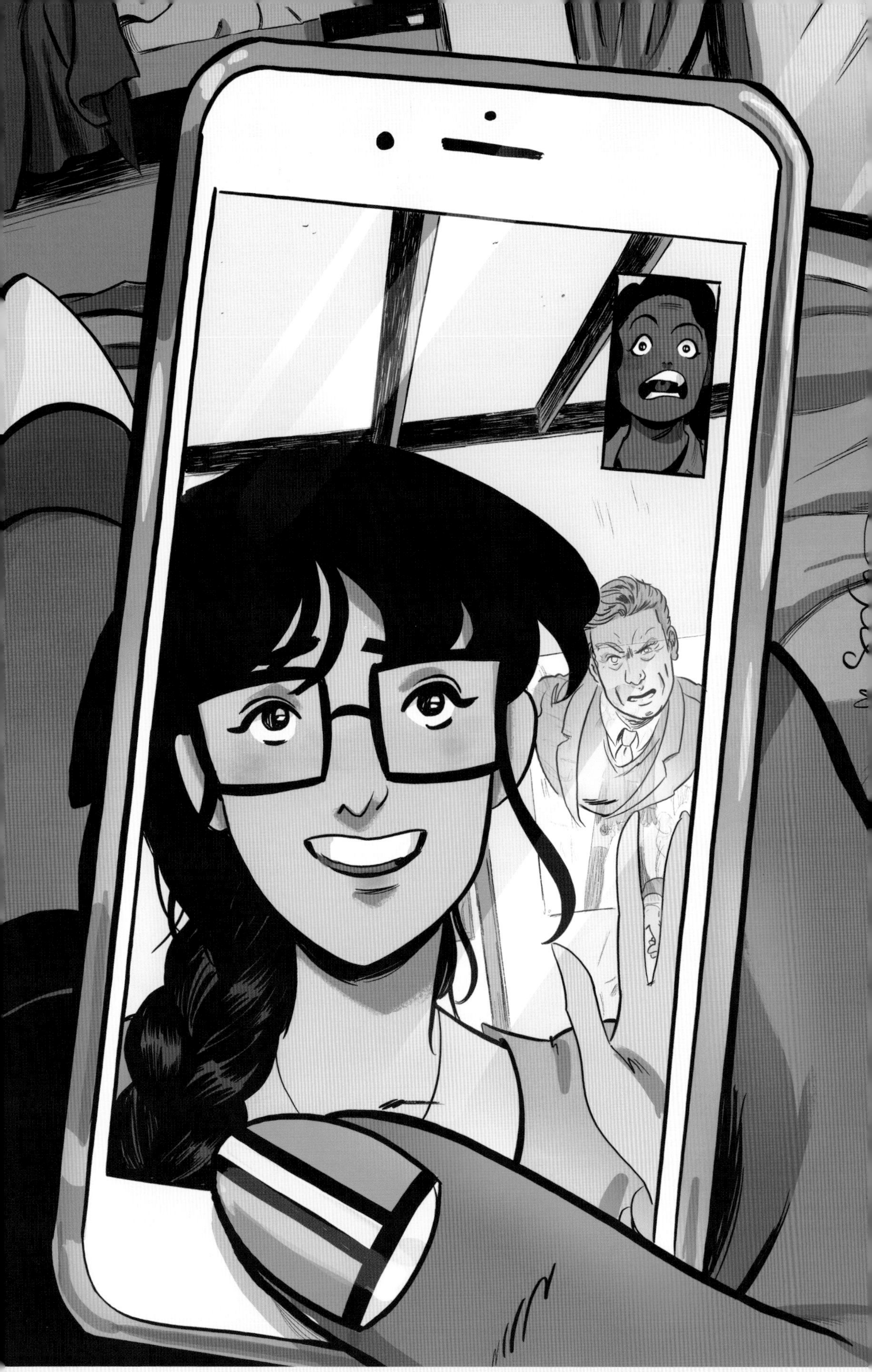

Issue Three Variant Cover by **Sina Grace** with Colors by **Cathy Le**

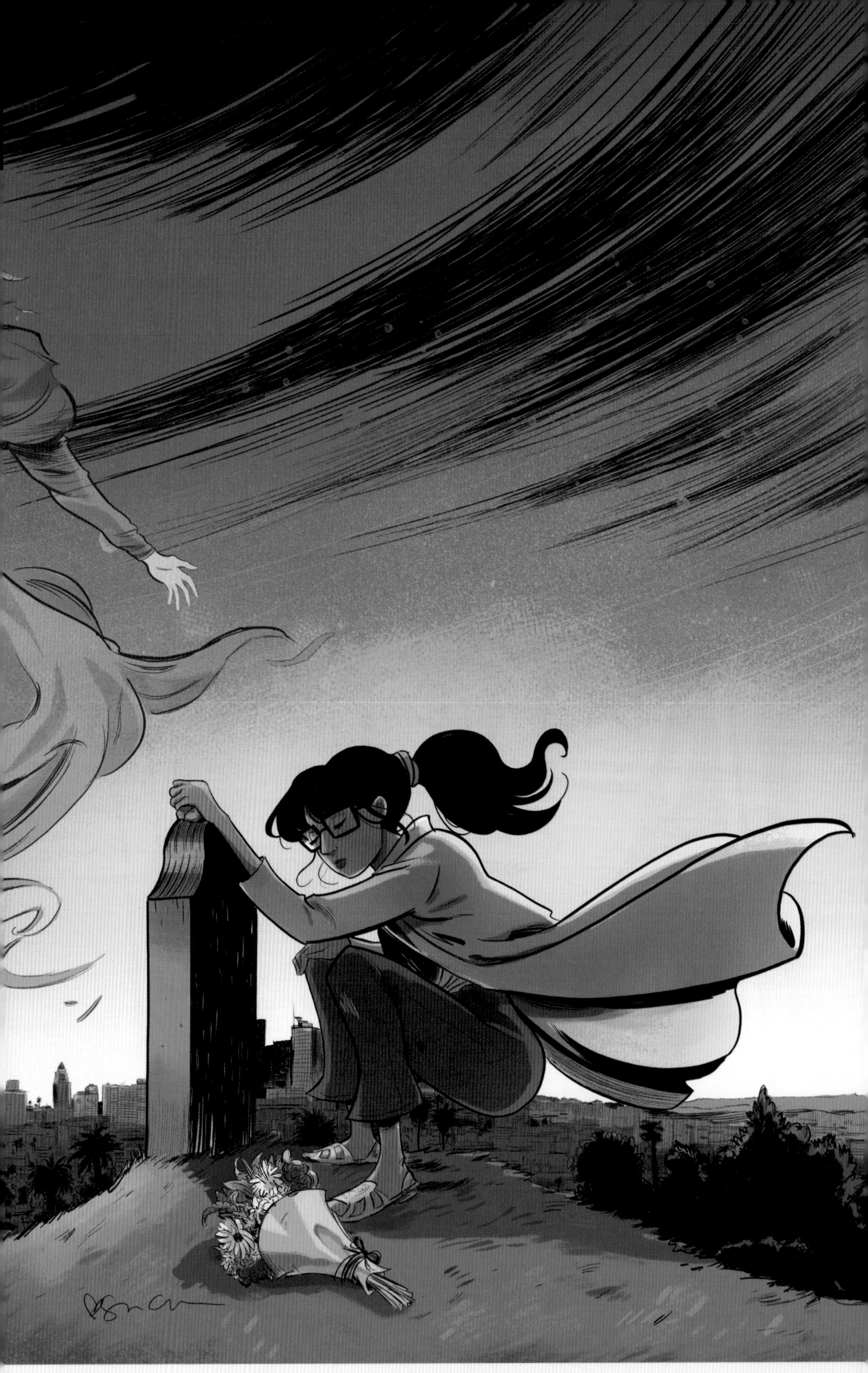

Issue Four Variant Cover by **Sina Grace** with Colors by **Cathy Le**

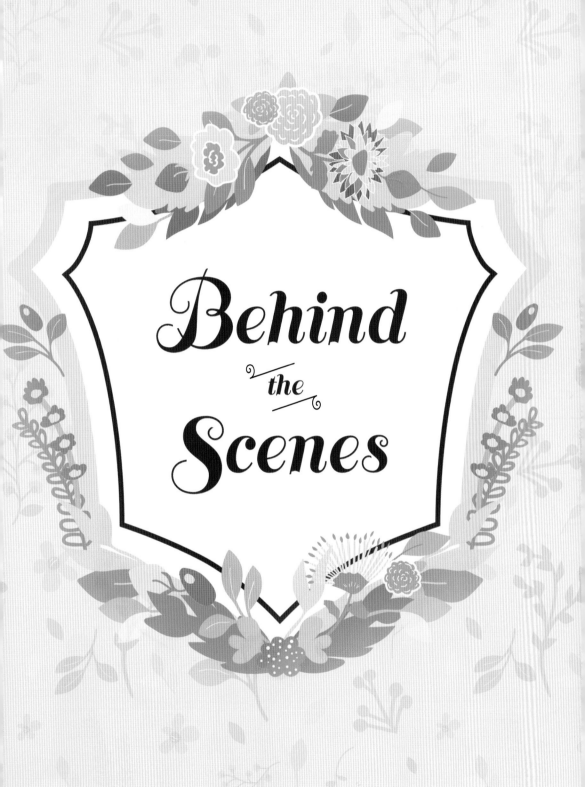

Behind
the
Scenes

One of the most exciting parts of creating comics is designing a cast of characters from the ground up! Take a look at the original sketches that Sina Grace and Siobhan Keenan made to land on a final look for the folks inhabiting Rycroft Manor!

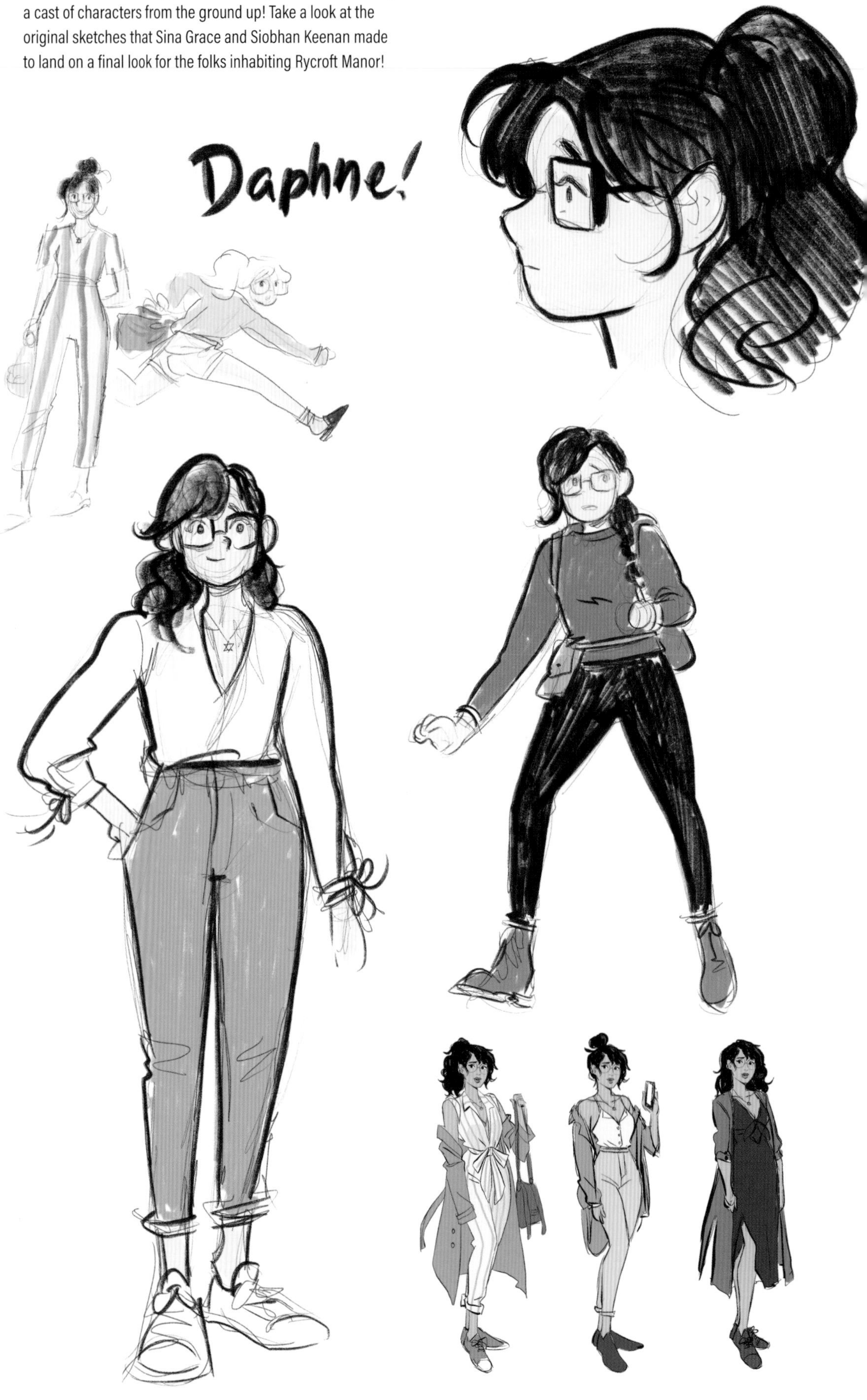
Daphne!

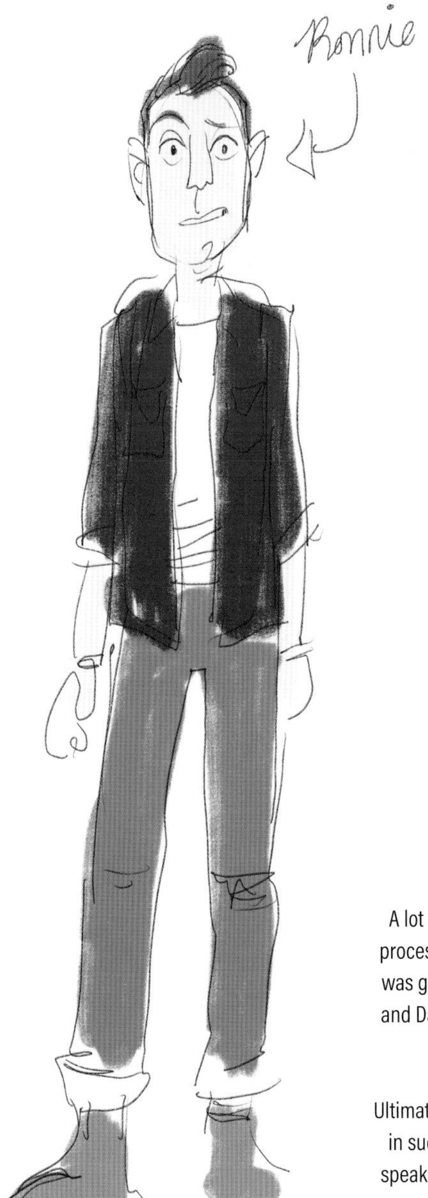
Ronnie

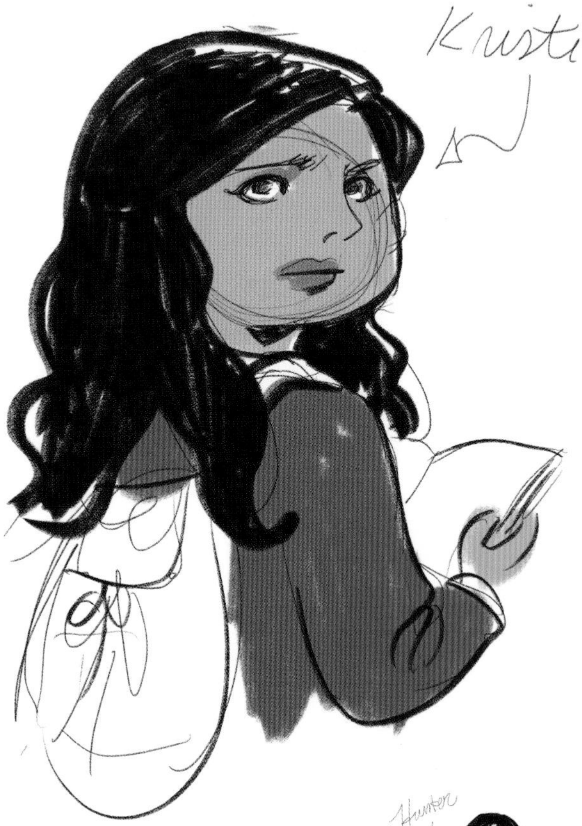
Kristi

A lot of changes can happen in the design process. There was a minute where Michelle was going to play less of a role in the series, and Daphne would come upon a mysterious zealot named **Hunter**!

Ultimately, Sina's plans for Michelle developed in such a way that her character ended up speaking more to what the Hunter character would have been in the series.

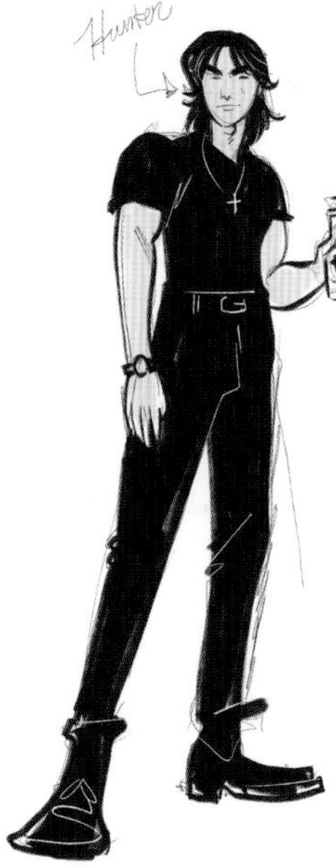
Hunter

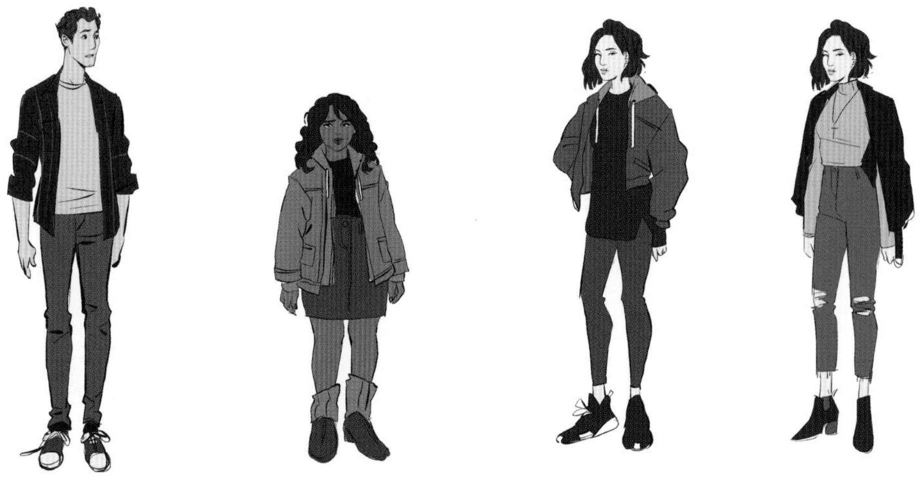

Each of the ghosts inhabiting Rycroft Manor needed to evoke the era in which they lived. Fashion played a major role in the designs, and Siobhan's final sketches nail it!

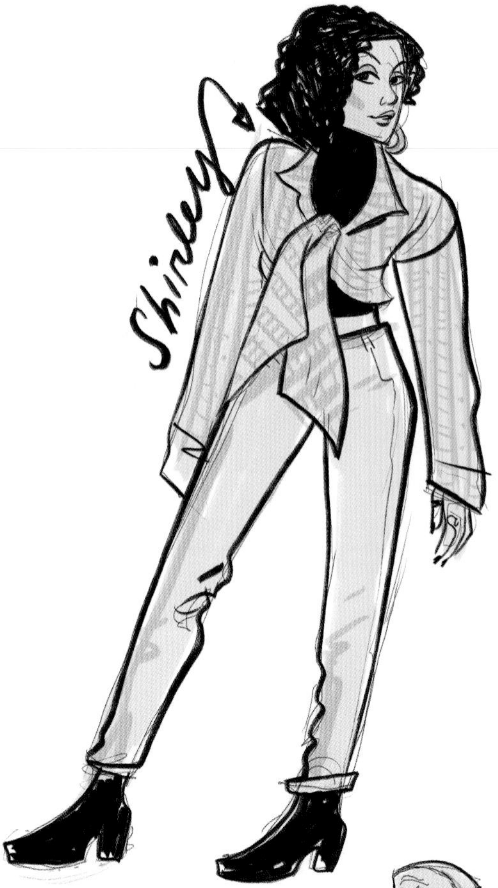
Shirley

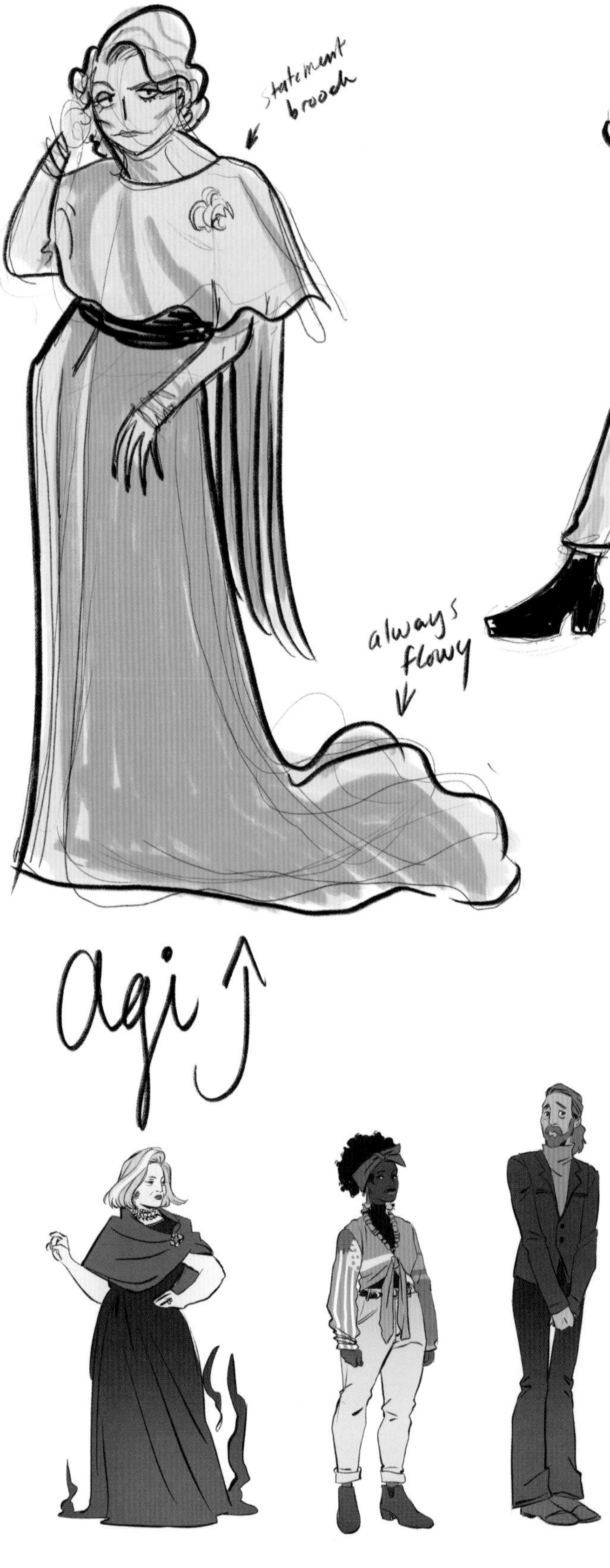
statement brooch
always flowy
agi

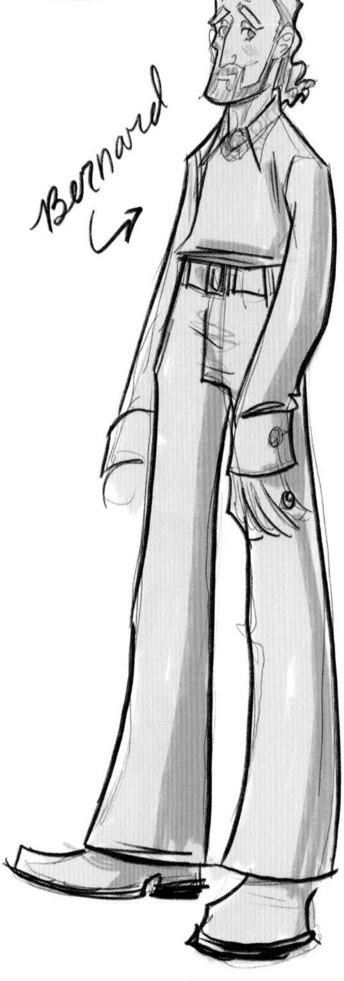
Bernard

Of the cast of ghosts, Maurice got the biggest makeover, as everyone decided his character would be a much more interesting presence as an uptight ghoul than a lazy curmudgeon!

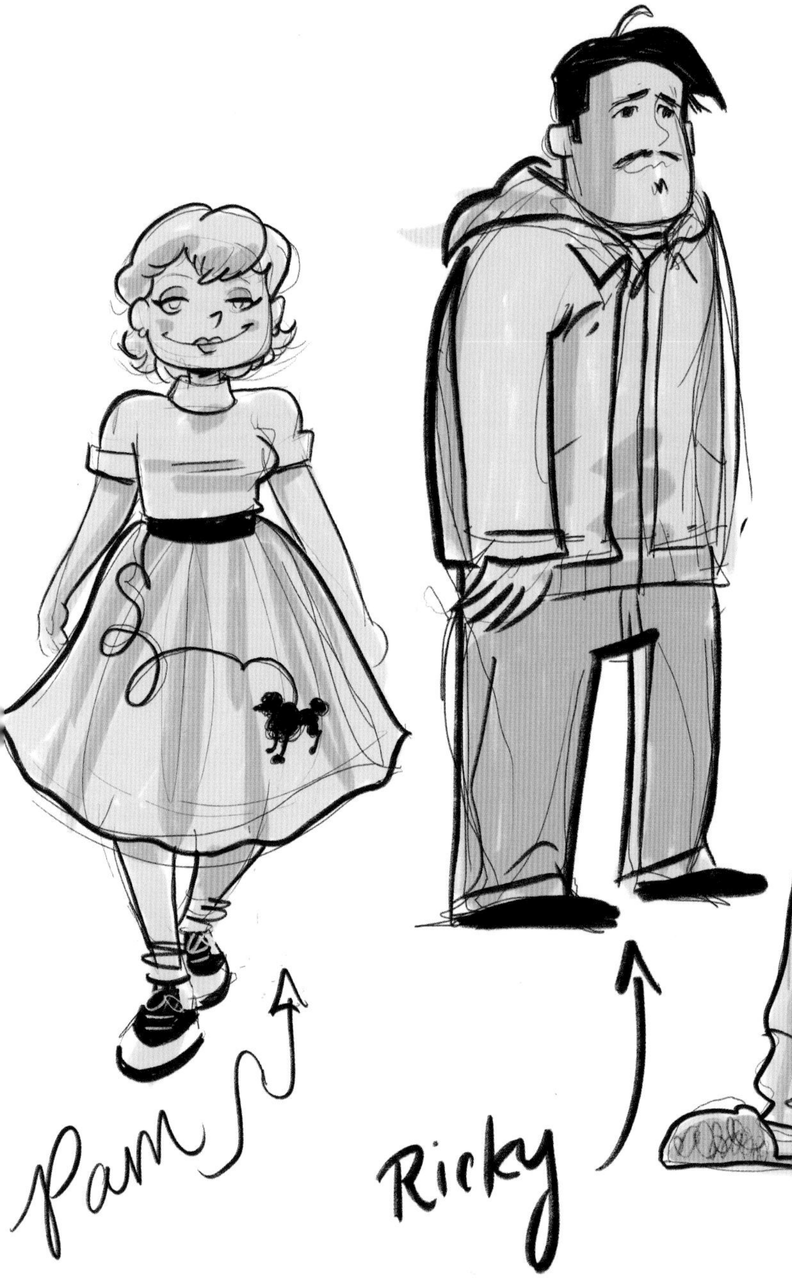
Pam
Ricky

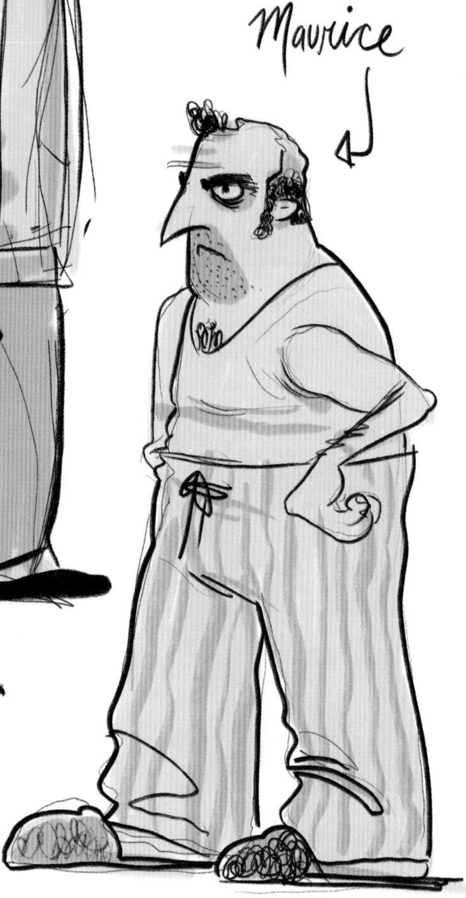
Maurice

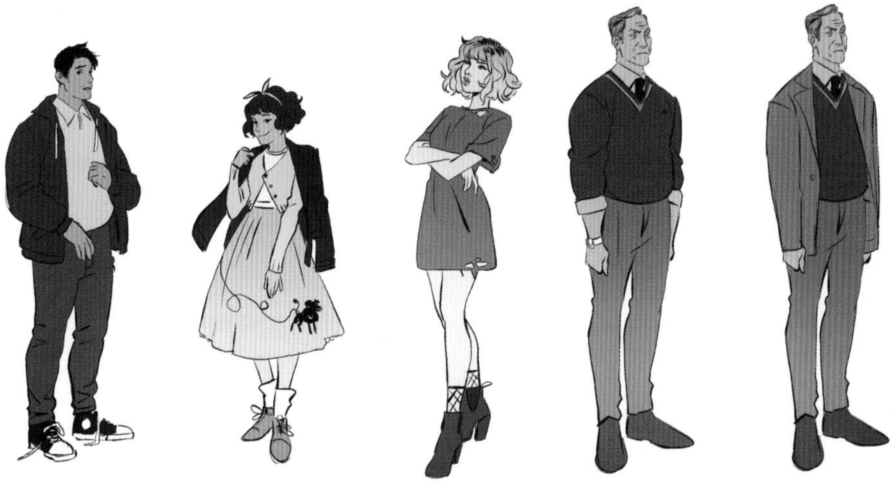

DISCOVER
ALL THE HITS

STEVENSON • ELLIS • WATTERS • ALLEN
LUMBERJANES
BEWARE THE KITTEN HOLY
NEW YORK TIMES BESTSELLING SERIES

Allison + Treiman + Cogar
GIANT DAYS
VOLUME ONE

From a writer of Disney's Moana
RIBON • FISH • PEER
SLAM!
VOLUME ONE

Hope Larson • Brittney Williams • Sarah Stern
GOLDIE VANCE
"Scoot over Nancy Drew..."
—Los Angeles Times
Volume One

JAMES TYNION IV • RIAN SYGH • WALTER BAIAMONTE
THE BACKSTAGERS

TYSON HESSE'S
DIESEL
IGNITION

Lumberjanes
Noelle Stevenson, Shannon Watters, Grace Ellis, Brooklyn Allen, and Others
Volume 1: Beware the Kitten Holy
ISBN: 978-1-60886-687-8 | $14.99 US
Volume 2: Friendship to the Max
ISBN: 978-1-60886-737-0 | $14.99 US
Volume 3: A Terrible Plan
ISBN: 978-1-60886-803-2 | $14.99 US
Volume 4: Out of Time
ISBN: 978-1-60886-860-5 | $14.99 US
Volume 5: Band Together
ISBN: 978-1-60886-919-0 | $14.99 US

Giant Days
John Allison, Lissa Treiman, Max Sarin
Volume 1
ISBN: 978-1-60886-789-9 | $9.99 US
Volume 2
ISBN: 978-1-60886-804-9 | $14.99 US
Volume 3
ISBN: 978-1-60886-851-3 | $14.99 US

Jonesy
Sam Humphries, Caitlin Rose Boyle
Volume 1
ISBN: 978-1-60886-883-4 | $9.99 US
Volume 2
ISBN: 978-1-60886-999-2 | $14.99 US

Slam!
Pamela Ribon, Veronica Fish, Brittany Peer
Volume 1
ISBN: 978-1-68415-004-5 | $14.99 US

Goldie Vance
Hope Larson, Brittney Williams
Volume 1
ISBN: 978-1-60886-898-8 | $9.99 US
Volume 2
ISBN: 978-1-60886-974-9 | $14.99 US

The Backstagers
James Tynion IV, Rian Sygh
Volume 1
ISBN: 978-1-60886-993-0 | $14.99 US

Tyson Hesse's Diesel: Ignition
Tyson Hesse
ISBN: 978-1-60886-907-7 | $14.99 US

Coady & The Creepies
Liz Prince, Amanda Kirk, Hannah Fisher
ISBN: 978-1-68415-029-8 | $14.99 US

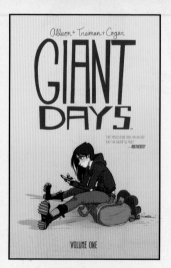

BOOM! BOX

AVAILABLE AT YOUR LOCAL COMICS SHOP AND BOOKSTORE
To find a comics shop in your area, visit www.comicshoplocator.com
WWW.**BOOM-STUDIOS**.COM